PRAVDA

BOOKS BY EDWARD DOCX

THE CALLIGRAPHER

PRAVDA

PRAVDA

Edward Docx

HOUGHTON MIFFLIN COMPANY
Boston / New York / 2008

For my mother, Lila,
who taught me what matters
and what does not

For information about permission to reproduce
selections from this book, write to Permissions,
Houghton Mifflin Company, 215 Park Avenue South,
New York, New York 10003.

www.houghtonmifflinbooks.com

Library of Congress Cataloging-in-Publication Data
Docx, Edward.
  Pravda / Edward Docx.
    p. cm.
  ISBN-13: 978-0-618-53440-1
  ISBN-10: 0-618-53440-7
  1. Family secrets—Fiction. I. Title.
  PR6104.O28P73 2007
  823'.92 — dc22   2007008523

Book design by Melissa Lotfy

Printed in the United States of America

MP 10 9 8 7 6 5 4 3 2 1

Part I

OCTOBER

The truth was obscure, too profound and too pure,
to live it you have to explode.

—BOB DYLAN, "Where Are You Tonight?
(Journey Through Dark Heat)"

LOVE AND CHAOS

1

Gabriel Glover

H E WAS RELIEVED to be again among the Russians. Nothing to do with his head, or even his heart, but in his soul: some kind of internal alignment or tessellation. He looked up at the clock on the wall above the brown lift doors. He'd lost two hours with the delays. But the London panic had given way to cool urgency, a calculating haste. There would be the visa and passport queues. There would be the usual wrangle with the taxi driver — unless he agreed up front to pay the tourist price. And then there would be traffic on Moskovsky . . . An hour and a quarter and he should be there.

The doors opened. The other Europeans and the Americans hesitated. He pushed his way inside with the Russians and a Finnish businessman with a tatty attaché. Everyone was already smoking. He squashed up and breathed it in: the flavor of the tobacco — more aromatic, *smokier*. An old woman swathed in a heavy black shawl with her hair tied up in a scalp-tightening white bun began shouldering her myriad straps, grasping numberless bags, grimly determined to be the first out.

But he was quicker. He walked swiftly across the vast immigration hall — the high two-tone walls, light Soviet tan at the base and dark Soviet mahogany at the top. There were only two queues for nonresidents. He had hoped for three or four. The first was shorter but comprised disorderly families and excited tourists; the second was mainly businessmen, money people. Follow the money. Money, after all, had won.

He put down his bag. These last few miles always seemed such an incremental agony, especially when the previous thousand he had scorched across the curve of the Earth. And now the candor that he had been evading for the past thirty-six hours finally ambushed him: okay, yes, it was true, this call *had* been different. Much worse. Something was really wrong. Something serious. Otherwise why would he have gone straight to the airport this morning and taken the first flight via Hel-bloody-sinki?

The slab-faced man in the booth looked up from the pages of the passport and met his eyes through the bulletproof glass.

"Your name?"

"Gabriel Glover."

"How old are you?"

"Thirty-two."

There was a long scrutinizing pause, as if the official were formulating a difficult third question, something beginning with "why." Gabriel straightened up, consciously pulling his shoulders back, as both Lina and Connie reminded him to do—one thing at least they had in common—and stood with proper posture at his full five-eleven. He was dressed half scruffily, in cheap jeans and scuffed boots, and half elegantly, in a dark tailored pure wool suit jacket and fine white shirt—as though he had not been able to make up his mind about who he really was or which side he was on when he set out. He had the figure of someone thin through restlessness, through exercise of the mind rather than of the body; he had liquid dark eyes and his hair was near-black and kicked and kinked at the ends, not so much a style as a lack of one, stylishly passing itself off. Immigration officials usually had him down as Mediterranean before they opened up his passport: *Her Britannic Majesty requests and requires . . .*

The official's silence was becoming a test of stamina. He felt the urge to say something—anything—whatever confession was most required. But at last the Russian gave a grotesque smile followed by a parody of that long-suffering American imperative: "Enjoy."

"Thank you."

And his passport was returned to him slowly beneath the glass, as if it documented nothing but the transit excuses of a notorious pimp turned pederast turned priest turned politician. (Truly these people were the masters of contempt.) Now he had to wait for his luggage. They had forced him to check it in: too heavy.

For five minutes he fidgeted by the jaws of the empty carousel like an actor misguidedly aping madness. Then he could stand it no longer. He struck yet another deal with himself — no smoking in London, but okay, fine abroad — and set off to buy some cigarettes from the kiosk with the rubles he had left over from the last trip. When was that? Six weeks ago? No, less . . . Four weeks ago. This had to stop.

There was no relief at first — just acridity and watering eyes — but by midway through the second he was tempered, smoking greedily and watching the Russians. If ever there was a nation that understood waiting . . . And it occurred to him all over again why she had wanted to come back: because there was something that appealed to her particular vanity here, something fierce and irreducible, some semi-nihilistic condition of character.

He remembered her speaking about just this quality when he was a child. She too must have been quite young then, at one of the London parties, perhaps — he and Isabella, his twin sister, had been allowed to stay up, listening carefully for their cues in the adult conversation. She had been talking to Grandpa Max: "The difference between the Russian character and the Western is that we Russians have learned to live our days in the full knowledge that whatever transpires in the interim, the sun will eventually expand and humanity will be incinerated. It's a way of life precisely opposite to the American Dream. Call it Russian fatalism if you like. But it gives us a sense of perspective, a sense of humor, and perhaps a certain dignity."

He exhaled smoke through his nose. Her declarations and her pronunciations — was ever a person so convinced of the absolute truth of her latest opinion? She must have been unbearable when she was younger. Her voice was in his head too much these days, especially since the calls had started in earnest; indeed, there were moments when he found himself unable to distinguish his thoughts from hers. His luggage.

"You're just like your father."

"I'm not listening to this. That's not even true. I've got to go to bed now."

"You are still with Lina?"

(Lina's voice through the open bedroom door: "Gabriel? Are you off the phone? Can you bring me some water? And put the lettuce back in the fridge.")

"Since we spoke yesterday?" It was Sunday night. He tried to keep the anger out of his voice. "Am I still with Lina since this time yesterday? Yeah. Since yesterday, I'm still with Lina. The same as the last four years. Nothing has changed. Listen, I am —"

"And Connie?"

The line clicked irregularly, all the way across Europe.

"Nothing has changed in the last twenty-four hours." He almost hissed the words. That was unusually devious and unnecessary, even by her standards. "But you know I can't speak . . ."

"You can always speak to me."

He had started whispering. "Lina is awake. It's . . . it's midnight. I have to go to bed."

"Going sideways, going sideways, going sideways. Can't go forward. Can't go back. So you go sideways."

"I'll call tomorrow from work."

"Like your father."

"No. Stop. That's it. I'll call you tom —"

"Don't go."

Her voice contained a new note of . . . of what? Desperation?

"I promise I will call you tomorrow."

"*Gabriel.*"

He felt her reaching in for his heart. And he felt his heart uncoil. "Okay. But I *do* have to go soon. And — and you should be in bed too. It's what? Christ, it's past three with you. It's the middle of the night."

"It's difficult for you. I know."

"What is? You're not sounding great. You're rasping. Seriously, is everything okay?"

"To inhabit yourself fully. Very few people do this anymore. But you and I, we try — correct? We try to hold the line . . . Even though this will cost us almost everything we have — this great indignity, this great antagonism, this great protest." She coughed. "Which is itself pointless."

He was unnerved now. More riddles. His attention wholly focused.

"But — listen to me." She spoke more steadily. "You have to be fierce in the face of all the cowardice you see around you. And you have to say, 'No. For me, no. I will not. I will not lie down and I will not give up. I will not do or be or become anything that you wish me to. However you disguise it, however you describe it — politics, religion, economics — I will continue to stand here and tell you that what you believe in is a lie and what you have become is a falsehood.'"

"Why — *why* — are you talking to me like this?"

Another cough and suddenly she became urgent. "Will you come tomorrow?"

"To Petersburg?"

"Yes."

"I can't. I'm at work tomorrow."

"Your work is a joke. Come tomorrow."

"I can't just . . . Why are you laughing? Jesus — you're *coughing*." He continued to speak, but he knew that she could not hear. "Oh God . . . It's getting worse."

For nearly a minute he stood there listening to her hacking. But it was unendurable. So he started up again, shouting into the phone, regardless of waking Lina. "Can you hear me? Are you there? Hold the phone up." A few seconds of quiet, her breathing like wind through rusted barbed wire. "Oh God . . . You're crying."

And then this: "Do you love me, Gabriel?"

She had never asked him such a thing. Not once.

"Yes. Of course. You know I do."

"Say it in Russian."

"*Ya tyebya lyublyu.*"

"Come tomorrow. Promise me."

"You've got to move back to London. And you don't have to live in the old house." He would have set out that instant if he could have made it there any faster by doing so.

"Petersburg is my home. You must be here tomorrow. I will give you the money. I want to see you. I *will* talk. There are so many things I have to tell you."

"I need a visa."

"Come the day after, then. Get an express visa. I'll pay."

"Are you crying?"

"Promise me."

"Okay. Okay. I promise."

It was one thirty-five U.K. time when he finally hung up. Three and a half hours later, he was standing at the front of the already lengthening queue outside the Russian embassy on Kensington Palace Gardens, watching a grout-gray dawn seep slowly through the cracks in the east.

The driver was crazier than he had dared hope. He clasped the handrail above the passenger door, the muscles tensing in his upper arm as the taxi veered left onto Moskovsky. Wide and straight, the road into town was as Stalin-soaked in the monochrome of tyranny as the center of the city was bright and colorful with the light of eighteenth-century autocracy.

"Democracy is difficult for us, Gabriel," she often said. "In Russia we are required to live within the pathologies of the strongest man — whatever he titles himself. That way we all know where we are and what we are doing. However bad it gets."

The cars were moving freely — the battered Czech wrecks and tattered Russian rust crates, the sleek German saloons and the tinted American SUVs, overtaking, undertaking, switching lanes in a fat salsa of metal and gasoline. Still no phone network; it didn't usually take this long. He shifted in the back seat, lit his fourth cigarette, and wound down the window as the cab slowed for the lights. A mortally decrepit bus bullied its way across the intersection, discharging plumes of what looked like . . . like coal dust. The pollution was worsening: particles seemed to hang heavy and brazen as nails in the lower air, a blunt parody of the fine mists that must have once come dancing up the Neva from the sea to greet great Peter himself as he rode out across the marshes to meet his enemies.

He would stay with the cab: twenty minutes and he'd be there. No need to jump out and take the underground. Gorolov-Geroev Park was just ahead now — he could see the scrub trees behind the tarnished railings, and there was the crooked-nosed old man with that same heavily lapeled sports jacket still selling books and magazines on the corner. Not really selling. More like minding them for someone or something never to come. Jesus, it was as if he had not been away. How many times was he going to have to do this?

He bent to look up. The sky was low and lowering. The plane had been in rainclouds for much of the descent. The wind must be carrying them inland from the west. He tried to listen to the music from the ill-tuned station on the car radio; it sounded like Kino. Something off *Gruppa Krovi* maybe — he couldn't be sure — beauty and despair bound in razor wire and thrown overboard together, white-lipped now beneath the ice, thrashing it out, life and death. His sister would have known the exact song, the exact version. A current of anger joined the stream of his thinking. Isabella hadn't been over for nearly a year. Longer, in fact — twenty-one months: Christmas — the Mariinsky — that vicious wind on the walk home, which froze the nose and iced the eyeballs, three atheists on their knees at Kazan Cathedral early the next morning.

The truth was that he wished he had managed to get hold of Isabella last night instead of leaving a message. The truth was that he was no longer sure of the truth. And he trusted his sister to apprehend things precisely — to seek out the quiddity of things and, once grasped, never let go, to insist, to assert, to confirm. Whereas for him . . . for him the truth seemed to be slipping away with each passing year, losing distinctiveness, losing clarity, losing weight. Duplicity, hypocrisy, and cant, the primary colors he once would have scorned, he now saw in softer shades. Perhaps this was the aging process: bit by bit truth grows faint until she vanishes completely, leaving you stranded on the path, required to choose a replacement guide from those few stragglers left among your party — Surly Prejudice, Grinning Bewilderment, Purblind Grievance.

The thin beep of his phone locating a network. He sat up smartly, let the cigarette fall outside the window, and pressed the last dial button. A child's unmediated eagerness ran through him. With every second he expected her voice . . . But the ringing continued as if to spite him. And he began to picture the phone shrilling on the side table by the bay window — the dusty light, the red-cushioned casement seats, the chess set forever ready for action. He imagined her climbing from the bath, or hurrying from the shower, or fumbling with keys and bags at the door.

Eventually the line went dead.

He hit redial. They were coming toward Moskovskaya — he could see the statue of Lenin a little farther on, the right arm aloft — one of the few still standing. This time he listened intently to the exact pitch and interval of the ring tone. No answer. No bloody answer.

The line went dead again. She must be out. Maybe she was tired of waiting and he'd get there to find one of her notes on the table: "At café such and such with so and so, come and join" — as if he should know the café or the friend. Or maybe she was just refusing to pick up the phone for reasons she would soon be telling him — something dark and colossally unlikely involving organized crime, her time in the Secretariat. Redial. The fact was that he was utterly at a loss as to what she was really trying to communicate to him. The direct accusations, sly allusions, subject swerves, sudden changes of register that served (and were meant to serve) only to draw further attention to the preceding hints. Redial. Individual exchanges made sense, and yet when he got off the phone he could not discern what lay behind her pointed choice of subject, her denouncements, her fabrications. He gave up as the line went dead the fourth time. *Why wasn't she answering the bloody phone?* And suddenly all his anger passed away. And he knew that he would do this forever if necessary.

His mobile had heated his ear and he put it down on the seat away from him as the driver slowed for the traffic again. And here they were crawling beneath mighty Lenin's arm. "That failure," she always said, "is our failure, Gabriel, is the failure of all of us. Such dreams expired. More dreams than we can imagine—all extinguished by that failure. Not just in the past but in the future too: and that's the real sadness, the real tragedy. We have—all of us, the whole world—we have all lost our belief in our better selves. And the great told-you-so of capitalism will roll out across the earth until there is no hiding place. And every day that passes, Marx will be proved more emphatically right. And all the men and women waking in the winter to the slavery of their wages will know it in their heart."

He stood for an anxious moment by the iron railings of the canal embankment, putting away his wallet and glancing up at the second-floor balcony. The tall windows were closed. But the curtains were not drawn. The driver struggled with the lock of the buckled trunk, the gusting wind causing his jacket to billow. Rain was coming. Gabriel could smell the dampness in the air. He took his bag and hurried across the street.

He reached the gates that blocked his way to the courtyard—like most in the old part of town, the flats were accessed from the various staircases within. And only now he remembered the need to punch in the security code. What was the number? He couldn't recall. He pressed the buzzer and waited. Maybe she had been in the bath when he rang. Or maybe her phone wasn't working. He simply hadn't thought about this. He'd assumed she would be home. And if by some strange chance not, then he had all the keys to let himself in . . . but the security code? No. He'd forgotten all about the bloody security code.

He tried a few combinations at random. He jabbed at her buzzer repeatedly. Nothing happened. And there was no voice from the intercom. The first twist of rain came and he leaned against the gate to get beneath the shallow arch. Water began to drip onto his bag. Maybe he could try one of the other buzzers and explain . . . But even if they spoke English—unlikely—there was no way on earth they'd let him in; crime had seen to that. He pressed her buzzer again. He did not know what else to do.

No answer.

Abruptly the full force of his panic returned — a tightening in his throat, a clamping of his teeth at the back of his jaw, the sound of his own blood coursing in his ears. (The fear — yes, that was what it was — the fear in her voice on the telephone.) He looked around, face taut now, hoping for a car or another resident approaching. Someone to open the gate. Where *was* everybody? The whole of the city had vanished. This was insane. Over on the other side of the canal, two men were sprinting for shelter. They ducked down the stairs into the café opposite.

Yana. Of course. Yana would know the code. Yana's mother was in and out all the time — cleaning, officially, though mainly consuming expensive tea and gossiping. Oh please Christ Yana's working today. He picked up his bag and dashed across the bridge. *The Kokushkin Bridge on which poor Rodya stared into the murky water to contemplate his crime — Gabriel, can you imagine it?*

He was across. He dived down the café stairs, slipped on the wet stone and nearly fell, reached out for the door to stop himself, and somehow bloodied his knuckle as he crashed inside. But he cared nothing for the eyes that were on him as he walked over to the bar cursing under his breath.

"Is Yana here? Do you speak English?"

"Yes, I do." The girl at the bar had a staff T-shirt: "CCCP Café: The Party People."

"Is Yana here? Yana."

"Yes. She is. What —"

"Can you get her?" He had not seen this girl before; he tried to ameliorate his manner, but to little effect. "Sorry. I'm sorry. Can you tell her Gabriel is here? It's about Maria — she'll know."

"Okay." The girl had registered his urgency and locked the till as quickly as she could. "Please. Wait here."

"Yes. I'll wait." He glanced at the walls, which were pasted with lacquered old editions of *Pravda:* Khrushchev kissing a dead astronaut's son, Andropov, Old Joe himself — always a shock to see that, yes, he was a person of flesh and blood and conversation — leaning forward to say something to the woman seated beside his driver as the state car processed down Nevsky Prospekt. How many times had he and Isabella tried to read these walls and recreate in their minds what it must have been —

"Gabe. Hi. Hello. How are you? I did not know you were coming back. Katja says you are a man who lost it."

"Sorry. Yana, I'm just — I can't get in." He raised his thumb to indicate behind himself. "What's the combination? The security gate. Do you know it?"

"Yes, of course." She told him the number, becoming conscious of the alarm in his eyes. "Is everything okay? How long you here? I didn't know you were coming back. It's lucky you came today, though — I am going to Kiev tomorrow. I have to —"

"It's a flying visit." He interrupted her. "I just got in. But I'll be back later. Promise." He was already turning for the door. "We'll go out. Definitely. You can tell me about what is really happening — the news isn't clear."

The rain had soused the cobbles but this time he crossed the bridge at a flat sprint, all the while keeping his eyes on the window above the balcony. Nobody paid him any attention — the random autumn flurries of wet weather that came squalling in off the Gulf of Finland often caused old and young alike to scurry and dash. A woman holding a magazine above her head left the shelter of the hairdresser's canopy and scuttled to her car door.

He was back at the security gate. He pressed in the numbers. The metal doors began to swing open jerkily: a moment to marvel at how the simple fact of knowing the right combination was all the difference and then he was through, into the courtyard.

The rain was slicking his hair onto his forehead and causing him to blink. The cars within looked more numerous than the last time. He was unashamedly thinking with her voice now: *There you go — capitalism's pubescent little triumphs on every hand, see how they vaunt it.* Water was gushing down the side of the building where the guttering was broken. His mind would not focus. But his heart was pestling itself mad against the mortar of the present, suffering now from some inarticulate dread — a terrifying feeling that came at him as he reached the staircase in the corner of the quadrangle, grinding his very quick to powder.

The stench of cat urine assailed him, slowed him, as he hit the stairs. She was a little demented, perhaps. Admit it. That's why he couldn't get at what she meant, what she was really saying to him. She contradicted herself twelve times a day, twelve times an hour, and who can believe someone who . . . Distraction, though, distraction, he breathed: back to now, back. Up we go. Up we go. Why wasn't he running anymore? Maybe she was refusing to answer the entryphone on purpose. And the telephone. In two minutes she would be taking her perverse Petersburg pleasure in telling him how the criminal gangs were now calling door to door in the afternoons in the hope of being admitted without the need for time-consuming breaking-and-entering procedures. *It's not as bad as Moscow, but it's very dangerous sometimes here, Gabriel. And there was another murder just over in Sennaya . . .*

He turned to take the third flight. The seconds were stalling. He noticed details he had never noticed before. The filth and the smell, the colors, the lack of colors, the chipped and broken sad stone stairs, the million cigarette butts underfoot, the unconcealed pipes all caked thick with dust and grime forever wheezing and choking up and down and back and across the stairwell, the metal-slabbed apartment doors riveted with legions of bolts and locks and tarnished somehow—despite the steel—by nameless cats or poisonous leaks or dogs or rats . . . Her thick exterior padlock was undone.

So she must be in.

She must be in—because there was no possibility that she'd leave that padlock undone if she had gone out. She must be in. But he turned his key and entered the apartment in silence because he could not bring himself to call her name.

The light was dim. The wooden floor smelled of polish. He stepped onto the narrow carpet that ran down the center of the hall. And now he stopped moving altogether. The familiar pictures—his father in Paris in 1968, Isabella in New York, the Highgate house, his father on the telephone with a cigarette, Nicholas II and his family, he and his sister as babies in a pram, some famous clown white-faced in Red Square, the map of Europe stained with the brown ring mark of a wineglass over the Balkans, the icons, especially the bloody icons . . . These familiar pictures seemed suddenly remote, alien, unconnected with him, as though he had wandered into the flat of a vanished stranger whose life he must untangle.

Someone dropped something in the apartment above. He let his bag fall and ran, left, toward her bedroom. The door was open. The heavy curtains drawn. Her books piled untidily on the floor by her fallen lamp. Flowers thirsty in the vase. Her favorite shawl spread across the floor by the chest. A full mug of black tea by the bed. Pills. The upright piano. The bed itself empty. He ran back down the corridor, pushing doors as he went—bathroom, kitchen, study . . . But he slowed on the threshold of the last, the drawing room, as she called it—high ceilings, grand, *with my tall windows for the White*

Nights, Gabriel, for the cool air in the summer, for the best view in all of Petersburg, where our history is made.

His mother was lying on the floor by the desk. He was on his knees and by her side in an instant. Her eyes were open but shrouded somehow in a shimmering film of reflected light. And when he called her name out loud at last and raised her up, her body was cold and slight. And she seemed to have shrunk, to be falling down — down into herself, down into the floor, seeking the earth. And there was neither voice nor breath from her lips.

2

Isabella Glover

HER DREAMS CAME just before dawn, stealing past the watch of the New York City night, slipping past the sentries of the heart.

And this was a bad one. More of a nightmare, if truth be told. She flopped back down and closed her eyes and let old respiration soothe her modern nerves, concentrating on the out breaths, waiting for the chemical, physical, and emotional residue to drain away. And how real, she thought, this response of the body to the counterfeiting of dreams.

Isabella Glover stretched out to her full five-seven. Her hair, which reached almost to the shoulder, was so black that by some lights it looked almost blue. But her eyes were not quite as dark as her brother's, nor so undefended, moving quickly beneath a protective sheen of silent laughter. She was thin, but no longer painfully so; light on her feet, gamine; the reluctant possessor of that rare quality, the precise opposite of blond, which seems to grow more intense the longer its presence remains in a room. And she had one of those not-immediately-beautiful-but-on-reflection-actually-*very*-beautiful faces that you see in Renaissance paintings of young Italian noblewomen carrying bowls of fruit.

She stared at the fault lines cracked across her ceiling. It was the letters that were causing all the trouble, of course.

Oh, shitting hell. Might as well get up.

She kicked back the sheet and sat on the side of the bed. She felt hot. She lifted her hair from the back of her neck. Yes, these winter pajamas, she now admitted to herself, were a totally unnecessary choice — more a statement than anything else: Don't touch me,

Sasha; the secret codes of our relationship have all been changed; I am not touchable by you—to touch me is now a violation punishable by outrage and complete withdrawal. (Men and women with their constant signals-intelligence chatter back and forth and all of it so *unreliable*.) She stood up and moved toward their little dresser to take a swig of the mineral water, which, she was pleased to discover, had lost its irritating sparkle overnight.

Unnecessary because of course Sasha never would touch her after an argument—his side of the bed was empty. He would be splayed out on the couch on the other side of the door. After an argument, he hadn't got the nerve even to sleep in the same room as she, never mind anything else. So why bother with the pajamas? Just in case he suddenly transformed his entire personality and popped his head in to say sorry for shouting and being so rude and then promised never to be such a selfish, self-centered, self-*obsessed* two-year-old again? She took another, deeper swig. Or because she wanted to walk past him thus armored in the morning? To make visual the rupture? Intimacy and its withdrawal as a weapon . . . Not very subtle, Is, not very subtle.

She bit her lip.

So no, she would not go parading past in her bloody silly pajamas; she would not go banging into the bathroom; she would not make a sound. Lights would stay off. The kettle would not be boiled. There would be no statement, deliberate or otherwise, of her going to work—as I do every morning, by the way, Sasha, every single morning.

She looked across at the alarm clock again—a self-satisfied digital with lurid red numbers calling itself "The Executive." His clock. It was only quarter past six—normally too early to call on Molly, her downstairs neighbor, except that three days ago Molly badly twisted her ankle and so was not sleeping and there was every chance she would be awake, the same as on Sunday, when the emergency text had come in: "In agony and bored. R U Awake?" This time, Isabella thought, she would text Molly—on the way to Veselka's, just to check. Fetch the tea and whatever else Molly fancied and bring it back for her. A civilized breakfast before work, some lies about their boiler being broken, and then a bath (oh God, yes, a *bath* instead of that dribble of a shower) in Molly's glorious tub. And, oh shit, she'd better remember to call her mother from the office this morning, before Petersburg went to sleep.

Her eyes went back to the latest communiqué, set down askew on top of the books on her bedside table and energetically inhabiting the envelope on which her mother's calligraphic hand had rendered her own name in crimson ink. With deepening confusion, she had read it for a second time last night directly before going to sleep—a good way of distracting herself after the row with Sasha and his subsequent (rather protracted) storming out.

The new letter was a single page only, but far stranger than the previous one. Isabella crossed back to the bed and took it from the envelope. A Finnish stamp—like everyone else, her mother used one of the hotel mail services via Helsinki. Some stuff about the president, a disparaging mention of her brother's so-called career in contract publishing, news of a bomb in Moscow and ten more people "ripped limb from limb" by the "bastards" in Chechnya, and then this: "So, dear Is, be sure to visit me first, before you visit your father. It is better that you understand from me. Oh, you know how scheming he is, and he'll be sure to distort everything. He will want to be certain that you love him, especially now he is getting older."

Leaving aside the lingering oddness of her mother's writing style — "I am a Russian never forget, Is, forced to slum it in second class with this fat little ruffian English, so full of himself and yet so empty and vague"—this new letter was seriously weird because Isabella had absolutely no intention of visiting her father, nor indeed of finding out where he was. Neither she nor her brother had spoken a single word to Nicholas Glover for more than ten years. Not since the death of Grandpa Max (when her father had turned up only to make sure he got all the money). And Isabella was certain that her mother knew this. So what the hell was she going on about? Seriously weird too because what was there to understand? What was there to distort? It was extremely difficult to tell what was real and what was fantasy, given the background level of histrionics and exaggeration that her mother liked to live with, and she was certainly not above coming on all portentous in order to secure a visit or whatever obscure point she had set herself to make.

For Christ's sake—Isabella collapsed onto her back again, holding the letter aloft—the very act of writing on paper, in crimson ink, and using the mail was theatrical these days. There were times when she marveled (as if she herself were not involved) at her mother's ability to target her sense of . . . sense of what? Shame? Guilt? Loyalty? Indebtedness? Conspiracy? *Daughterliness?* It was as if her own genes were coded to recognize and instantly respond to the parental call regardless of her private will as a separate thirty-two-year-old individual. All the same . . .

All the same, maybe this time it *was* something serious. And given that she had not written back after the two previous letters, she really had better call today. As soon as she got in.

She puffed out her cheeks, kicked herself up again, crossed the room, and locked the letter in her private drawer with the others. Then, without opening the blinds, though conscious that the light was already sharpening against the skyline, she slipped on her sweat pants and sneakers and an old top. Amazing, really, that the New York birds still bothered with a dawn chorus.

Now the task was to get out without waking Sasha.

She opened their little closet — too shallow to hang anything in — and unhooked her charcoal suit. She felt relieved that the day was under way. She could be honest about her motives, too. She was leaving without waking him not because she feared further fighting, nor reconciliation, nor a silent standoff. It was less personal than that. She was leaving surreptitiously because she did not want to have to respond to, or negotiate with, another consciousness. No; what she wanted, above all else, was to start this day without his hijacking her psyche and making her cross or remorseful or resentful or mawkish or forgiving or having any other response she didn't want to have to experience. For now, she wished only to be by herself in her own mind — a reasonable thing for a woman to wish for every so often. And when she was clear, when she was centered, then she would talk to Sasha. Really, it was just silly anyway.

She approached the door of the bedroom and inched it open. His head (at the end of the couch) would be just the other side. She stopped a millimeter before the point where she knew the creak would begin. And then she slipped through.

But all the long and narrow way past the sofa, taking care not to tread on the plate or the glass or knock over the bottle of armagnac that he had so affectedly taken to drinking, she knew that he was awake, pretending to be asleep. And after four years together, he knew that she knew. And she knew that he knew that she knew and so on and so on and so on and so *why the bloody sham?* And why, a second later, was she frowning with concentration as she tried to judge the exact force required to pull the front door of their apartment shut while making as little sound as possible?

Abruptly, and with a sickening feeling, she realized that her heart had a false floor and had been concealing its contraband throughout: she had been aware all along that he would be wide awake, and she had been aware that she would pretend he wasn't. Jesus, was there no subject on which heart and mind might be candid with each other?

She slammed the door.

And then none of it mattered because she was hurrying down the tight stairwell, down the narrow corridor, down the steep stoop, and onto the freedom and anonymity and endless possibility of the sidewalk. New York's forgiving embrace — inclusion in the shared idea of a city, however true or untrue. A union of states. The infinite context of America.

But just the same, she dared not allow her mind to look up, for she sensed that the tattered images of her dreams were still hung high on the masts of her consciousness like the ragged remainders of sails flapping after a storm.

Molly Weeks let her paper fall onto her lap, transferred her steaming takeout tea from left to right hand, and sucked her sensitive teeth, which, she occasionally reflected, were seven or so years younger than the rest of her and therefore still in their thirties. A conventional English girl from an actual convent school, Molly had married the American singer in a New Romantic band twenty-five years ago — the first of two feckless husbands — and she had since acquired that quick-switching manner wherein raw-hearted sensitivity vied with the don't-mess attitude of the serial survivor. She wore thick-framed wedge-shaped glasses, her hair was a perpetually self-contending frizz of red and blond, and these days she was sole owner, chief executive, and chairman of the ever more successful MagicalMusic.com.

She spoke now with mock exasperation: "The world is going to all kinds of hell and nobody seems to be able to do anything about it." She adjusted her leg, the ankle of which was propped up on a pillow. "How's the career, Is?"

The subject of Isabella's job was one of their private jokes. Though, like most private jokes, it was also a way of dealing with a private seriousness: an abiding desire to encourage (and to liberate) on the part of the older woman; an abiding desire to evade for the time being on the part of her younger neighbor.

"Heading the same way." Isabella, who was sitting on a dining chair that she had dragged in from the other room, abandoned the lifestyle article she was (hating) reading. "My own fault, though." Isabella drew her finger quickly across her throat. "Last night."

"Bad?"

"Uh-hmm. Definitely should not have told them that I drink a bottle of vodka every morning before I come into work."

Molly chuckled and had to hold out her tea at arm's length to prevent herself from spilling it. "This was the client party you told me about, right? The chairman and all the cheeses present?"

"Yep." Isabella nodded. "All of them — Jerk, Snicker, Robe, and even the Smooth." Isabella's colleagues were well known by their various epithets.

"After everything we said about building mutually affirmative relationships in the workplace." Molly approximated the disappointed face of the daytime-TV life coach.

Isabella played along. "I feel as though I've let my whole family down."

Molly grinned. "I can't believe they took you seriously."

"They took me more than seriously. They looked at me like I'd just beheaded the secretary of state live on CBS." Without flinching, Isabella sipped her tea, which was still ferociously hot, and suddenly remembered what she had been meaning to tell her friend. "Hey, you know there's a new Russian restaurant opening up? Right around the corner from Veselka's."

"Another one? No way. You serious?" Molly was a champion of all things neighborhood.

"Really." Isabella nodded.

"How do you know?" Molly shifted her ankle again.

"The waitress told me."

"The waitress in Veselka's? Which one?"

"Don't know her name. The one with the suspicious expression that makes you think you must definitely be dining with terrorists or whatever."

Molly expressed puzzlement and shook her head, the highest outreaches of her crazed hair seeming to follow a moment behind, as if uncertain whether to go their own way or not.

"You know, Mol — heavy floral-pattern dresses." Isabella laid her hand delicately over her chest. "Ruched."

"Oh, you mean Dora." Molly smiled her recognition.

"Yeah — Dora. She served me these 'Earl Jeelings,' as she calls

them." Isabella indicated her cup. "Then she came around the counter and sort of spat the news into my ear."

"She does that." Molly aborted an attempted sip. "Christ knows
how they get this tea to stay so hot. What did she say?"

Isabella adopted a confidential air and mimicked the waitress's
rat-a-tat voice: "New place opening. East eleven. Says it's Russian.
But don't even go there. Totally fake. Totally disgusting. They pee in
the *pelmeni*. Waitresses illegal. All sluts."

"But the new place is not actually open yet?"

"No."

"So how does Dora know?"

"She's seen 'definite sluts' going in for interviews, apparently. And
she knows the chef. Famous for peeing in *pelmeni* the world over."

Molly drew a faux-macho breath. "What the hell is *pelmeni*, anyway?"

"Dumplings. Stuffed with cabbage, cheese, mushrooms. That kind
of thing. Gogol's favorite."

"Did Dora tell you that?"

"No . . . No, that was my mum."

"Useful."

"Very useful. Dietary preferences — I know 'em all, Turgenev to
Tchaikovsky and back again. Just in case you ever need me to rustle
up something for one of the great men of Russian culture." Isabella
wrinkled her nose. "I'd better jump in the bath now, if that's okay.
Wouldn't want to be late for the office. I've got opportunity matrices
to evaluate."

"Sure. Go right ahead. Help yourself to one of those fizz-bomb
things. They're glorious. Really . . . fizzy."

"Thanks. Don't wait up. I may be a few days."

Molly took a tentative sip of her milkless Darjeeling. She had a shrewd
enough idea of what lay behind Isabella's impromptu visit. For one
thing, something was going on upstairs. She suspected that Isabella
found Sasha unfulfilling — intellectually, emotionally, spiritually. Indeed, she knew for certain that Isabella found the general obvious-
ness of masculinity tedious, since a common theme of their concert
nights out together was Isabella being amusingly caustic about the
clumsy gambits of stupid men. She did a great impression of the coy-
but-almost-immediate way that they peddled inventories of their "in-
terests" — "the shit fiction, the shit films, the shit music, the clichés,

the clichés, Mol, the same old clichés." And yet Isabella also seemed
to do down the smart ones — for their dishonest charm, their self-
satisfied pride in playing the man-woman game, their "cultivated ec-
centricities," their "depth." All of which analysis Molly had much
sympathy for. Sasha and men aside, though, it also occurred to
Molly that Isabella's habitually sardonic chatter might be symptom-
atic of a deeper unease. The difficulty, however, was getting Isabella
to open up. Evidently this stuff about broken boilers was total crap.

Thirty-five minutes later, Isabella came back into Molly's bedroom,
dressed now in her trouser suit and businesslike despite herself.

"Thanks for the bath, Mol. That was just what I needed." She
fetched her cup from the little bedside table and dropped it into a
brown paper bag. Reality poured back into the vacuum of the vanished humor. "I'll call tomorrow."

"Do."

Isabella's eyes met those of her friend a moment and then traveled
around the room as if looking for further cups that required dispos-
ing of. "Shall I bring your laptop over?"

"Yes. Thanks. That's helpful. You'd better bring the power cable
too, though." Molly shifted her weight. "The battery connection
keeps cutting out. I'll plug it in down here."

The laptop was on the tiny desk by the window. Isabella moved
smartly around the end of the bed.

"You know," Molly said, her voice gentle, her head following the
passage of her friend. "You know, I've been thinking — you should
put on those mini-concerts we keep talking about. Keep the momentum going — find some musicians who don't look and behave like
social-problem children and persuade your friends to come along.
Your thing for Sasha's birthday was cool. How many people? Two
hundred. And everybody loved it. Everybody. And that was only piano and violin."

"I know," Isabella said. "But I'm not sure people would come —
not if it weren't some kind of a special occasion."

"Oh, they would. Definitely. You have a pretty big e-mail list already."

The wires into Molly's computer were all twisted.

"All these things start small," Molly continued. "You could use
the place on Eleventh again."

Isabella clicked her tongue. "Which one is the power here?"

"Sorry, Is — it's the thickest cable. You might have to unplug it under the desk and feed it back up — otherwise that adaptor thing gets stuck. It's a pain."

Molly was right about the concerts, of course. But Isabella did not believe her neighbor really understood that such a course was far from easy. In the past twenty years (yes, since the Wall collapsed, dear, crazy Mother) modern life had speedily (and rather gleefully) drawn up and ranged all its best and biggest guns against anything remotely vocational. (Molly was the exception — and it had cost her dearly to find her niche.) The arteries of the world were becoming more and more sclerotic: if you were not creating money, then you were not creating anything. And sure enough, down on her hands and knees, Isabella heard herself citing the hoary old defense: "I've saved quite a lot, though — one more year and, well, I reckon I'll have enough for a six-month sabbatical rethink."

"If there's anyone who could rescue that kind of music, Is . . . I mean, the classical audience is so pompous and self-regarding, such a bunch of pricks."

Isabella stood, glanced out the window, and leaned over the desk, trying to thread the freed cord up from behind.

"But you're not," Molly continued. "You're young and you're clever and you're . . . capable. The only thing . . . the only thing is to make a start."

So keenly was Isabella aware of her neighbor's change of tone (and the kindness behind it) that she suddenly felt embarrassed and could not bring herself to turn around. Embarrassed because she wanted both to embrace Molly and to run away from her at the same time. Embarrassed too that she might be guilty of in some way soliciting such sympathy. And worst of all, embarrassed because the acuity of the insight made her want to demur, deny, deflect, evade . . . when actually she well knew that she was only being cheered and re-assured — reassured that here was an understanding ear, if ever she needed it. And yet what was the point of talking about this or that, when really — the floor of her mind now cracked apart and rose up like a swarm of agitated wasps — when really the whole mess needed sorting: dropping out and then begging her way back into Cambridge; a false-start career in law — years wasted; a change of plan; unbelievable amounts of work; then not managing more than three months with the cultish children of Magog at Harvard Business School; this new farce of a career at Media Therapy, also very difficult to lie her way into, with these human simulacra for colleagues. Not forgetting a disastrous series of so-called relationships with infants, a violent cheating manipulative bastard for a father whom (subconsciously) she had crossed the Atlantic to get away from and whom she sometimes felt the urge to pretend (in her sickest moments) had actually physically abused her, so that at least she would have some factual and universally recognized problem to cite as the cause of all her ungovernable feelings of revulsion and nausea toward him. And now the letters. She turned.

"You're right, Mol, I know. I should call the guy again. That place on Eleventh is perfect. But . . . but it's not as if I'm going to do this job for more than another year, maximum. I think I just had to get the green card and, you know, find a proper footing here after all the arsing around. If there's one thing about America these days, it's that you have to be legal. Land of the free and all that."

She passed the computer with both hands.

Molly placed it beside her on the bed and looked up, her face a picture of understanding.

And instantly Isabella felt the urge to share something real with her friend. It was cruel to push people away all the time. *Give* something. Anything.

"I had an argument with Sasha last night, is all. After I got back from the work thing."

"Was it hard-core?" Molly was almost disappearing with delicacy and the countereffort not to seem overdelicate for fear of further drawing attention to any tenderness.

"No. No, not really. Just stupid." Isabella likewise was almost disappearing, but for burgeoning shame at having raised the subject at all. "He can be an idiot. And — you know this whole thing — he doesn't work. Well, I suppose he does. But not in the way that we . . . that is conv —"

"Happen often?"

"No. Hardly ever."

"Feel like a normal argument that a couple would have?"

"It was just about space. You know." Isabella found a rueful smile.

"Yes, well, it's tricky up on your floor. The apartments are half this size."

Though she knew the time well enough, Isabella glanced deliberately at the old clock. "Damn. I really have to scoot. Here, let me plug you in." She bent and then came up again all bustle and haste. "I'll message if I'm up Thursday morning. It's unbelievable — I'm going to be late again and I have a nine with the Snicker himself."

"Go, lady, go." Molly frizzed her hair. "Thanks for breakfast.

And really, come down whenever. If I am alive enough to make it to the door, you can come in."

Isabella looked sympathetically at the ankle. "You'd better take it easy on the ski-jumping and stuff today, Mol. You done with your tea?"

"Yeah. Thanks."

Isabella put her friend's cup into the brown bag for the recycle bin and collected the rest of her things for work.

"Okay. Bye," Isabella said.

"See you," Molly called after her. "Soon as I'm fixed we're going to check out those sluts."

Isabella let herself out, careful with the door and gratefully aware that Molly had chosen not to pursue her any further. One day, she resolved, she would sit down and tell Molly everything, instead of all this endless slipping and sliding around the edges. Sort Sasha. Sort work. Sort everything. Just get clear long enough to achieve a reasonable perspective and then . . .

It was twenty-four minutes from her building on East Thirteenth between Second and Third to the offices of Media Therapy on Greene. And she was in the habit of walking to work. It wasn't so much that she liked the exercise, or the routine, or the therapeutic affect of witnessing firsthand the sheer size and scale of the city's endeavors (indifferent to her own) — though all of these. It was more that in some only half-acknowledged way, she continued to take the visitor's simple pleasure in a foreign city. (What was her father's phrase? "Expats make the best natives." Something faintly sinister like that . . .) She had lived here in New York nearly two years and three before that on and off (as much as various visas permitted), and she had been staying with Sasha at his mother's place down on Murray on September 11. And though the wide-eyed tourist was long departed, there lingered a related sense of satisfaction at the recognition of certain places, or buildings, or institutions, or instances of what she sometimes termed to herself (for want of a better expression) New Yorknesses. No, it wasn't the Empire State or the Rockefeller or any of that stuff anymore, but instead it was the pile-it-high, sell-it-cheap furniture shop run by grumpy Poles. Or it was the fact that she could find what she wanted quicker than the ever-changing sales staff in St. Mark's Bookshop. Or that she liked to cross Third just here and walk through Astor Place where the East Village kids jostled around that big black cube. Or that she was as near indifferent to Washing-

ton Square as any New Yorker. Or that, best of all, she recognized
some of the owners at the dog run. Same time, same place tomorrow? So their glances seemed to say. And in her mind she would return their query with a most dependable civic nod.

You bet.

She was on Mercer not far from the Angelika — Sasha's favorite
cinema — when her cell phone started ringing. She didn't notice at
first because an ambulance was howling and her remaining attention
was partially on an English tourist buying a silly John Lennon beret
from the street stand (So *that's* who buys them . . .) and partially on
an advertisement for shampoo that infuriated her every morning
with its phony tone (Aren't we just such close girly-girlfriends who
just *so* understand each other, oh what secrets we share, oh how very
much we know about each other's lives — it was the insidious adver-
tiser's assumption of mutual intimacy that really killed her). And
then, when she did realize that it was indeed her own cell that she
could hear, she had to rummage in her bag (which she absolutely
must get around to emptying) before she could find it. And next her
mind became preoccupied with fabricating some excuse for being
late — and how ridiculous it was that she probably woke up before
all the other employees in the whole place and yet she was most
likely the last to get in to the office. And when she finally looked at
the screen, there was a generic message indicating that the caller was
unknown. And the line was terrible. And she had to stand still and
press the phone hard against her ear because of all the noise in the
street and all the noise in her head and that's how news comes:
standing on the street on a morning like any morning talking to your
brother, who's saying that your mother is dead. Is really dead.

3

Arkady Artamenkov

THE MOST SIGNIFICANT HOURS of Arkady Alexandrovitch Artamenkov's life had taken place two years ago, on a day when a cold and pelting rain was filling the million St. Petersburg potholes with a thick and sickly yellow mud and the air tasted more than usual of corrosion.

Late, silent, unshaven, he had splashed his way through the back streets to the appointed café, a recently opened place up from Moskovsky station near the Militia House of Culture, where women liked to showcase their hair and hold their mugs of coffee the wrong way round and never by the handles, the greater to emphasize their empathies. His own hair was wet and straggling. His greatcoat was sodden and heavy. And he knew full well that his boots and jeans were filthy and leaving marks of dirt as he made his way across the parquet wooden floors between the pale pine tables beyond the marble bar, water still streaming down his face.

"Arkady Alexandrovitch?"

It was the same fat, square-faced, red-haired woman who had called at his flat three days earlier. He stopped where he was but said nothing.

She came toward him along the length of the bar.

"Hello again. I'm so pleased you came. Good."

He did not return her greeting, nor take her hand (momentarily offered, instantly reemployed), but met her eyes until she looked away. He had guessed that she was some sort of professional finder, maybe even thought of herself as a private detective. She spoke with a slight Georgian accent, which she tried to hide. She had a flashy cell phone, which she clasped in her hand as if it were jewelry. And today the dark tracksuit was gone; instead she was wearing the usual bullshit with which ugly women tried to fight the truth: an expensive crocodile bag, matching shoes, designer suit. Obviously she hadn't been fucked in years.

Determinedly ignoring his silence, she continued: "Come this way. We have a quiet table at the back. I was only waiting at the bar because you might not have been able to see me."

She sounded relieved. She was certain of her fee now. He followed, still silent, ignoring the looks from the two women sitting with their department store bags.

"Maria is not here yet, but she will be joining us in a few minutes. What would you like to drink? Some coffee or maybe —"

"Nothing."

"Are you sure?"

A barely perceptible nod.

"Okay. Well . . ." She was at a loss for a moment.

He took off his greatcoat and placed it over the back of his chair. Then he sat down, leaving her standing awkwardly.

"Well, I am going to make a call and just check that Maria, your mother" — he watched her yank a false smile up across the rusting hulk of her flat face — "is on her way. So I'll be back in two seconds. Please order whatever you want. Lunch is on us today!"

He was silent and he made no move. He was here only because he had nothing better to do.

Back then, Arkady was living with two others — one a fellow musician in his band of that time, Magizdat, the other a friend from the orphanage — in two rooms next door to one of the hostels behind Ligovsky Prospekt. When Zoya (for this was the finder's name) had turned up at the door for the second time, he had decided to be in. He had come out with his shirt open, in scruffy jeans, unwashed, bare feet covered in powder. He had been in a good mood. He had been fucking the would-be actress from the cinema kiosk all morning. And he had been struck by the sheer physical difference between fair-skinned Polina and the swarthy pig-truck in front of him.

Zoya had wanted to go somewhere else, but he had said that he was busy and if she wished to talk, they could talk here. So she had sat down on the hall stairs and sprung open her briefcase and begun handing him photographs and documents, which he had glanced at without concentration and then handed back. All the while, the

sounds of a football match came through the open door. Russia losing again. Either paid to lose or losing because nobody paid them.
Hard to say. But then that was the main amusement in watching the
national team play.

Five minutes later, when he had reentered the room, he had not
told his friends anything but had simply laid back down on the floor
with Polina to watch the rest of the game. He had kept Zoya's card,
had agreed to come to the café on the day she suggested and nothing
else. He did not believe her story. The documents meant nothing
to him. Could be forgeries, could be fakes. The photograph of the
woman meant nothing. Could be anyone in the world. Because (as
he well knew) this sort of bullshit happened to Russian children
from orphanages a lot more often than the rest of the country realized. He had seen it himself: the time that Mongol had turned up for
Sako, an athletics star with shrinking balls from his dormitory, for
example — the point being that Sako had just come in third at shot
put in the Olympics and was all over the bullshit papers and the television. No — the reality of the situation was that ninety-nine percent
of the abandoned children in the Soviet Union were poor desperate
scum when they were born, the parents were poor desperate scum
when they fucked them into existence, and poor desperate scum all
parties remained. And scum seldom wasted its time looking for long-
lost more of the same. As far as Arkady was concerned, therefore,
the only calculations to be made were these: was there any money
and would it be easy to get without having to do anything?

Thus the single eventuality that Arkady Alexandrovitch was not
prepared for when he set out that morning in the acid rain was that
the woman he was about to meet might actually be his mother. But
that's what life is: one eventuality after another, and none of them
prepared for.

She came ahead of Zoya, moving swiftly between the tables. She was
a slight woman of a little less than average height, but there was a
certainty and pride in her aspect that created the impression that she
was taller, stronger, more intense and vital than the mere time-and-
space coordinates of her corporeal presence. Her hair was tied back
against her head and dark as sable. She wore a fine charcoal-gray
coat, but her black clothes were unostentatious beneath. There was
no jewelry — not even a wedding ring. She carried a slim, elegant bag
under her arm, also black, pressed in tight against her. And it was
only now, as she came right up to the table and stood before him,

that he became aware of the effort that was she was making to hold herself in check. Her cheekbones told of a tightened jaw, her lips seemed almost blue, and a dozen tiny needles were knitting cross-purposes in her brow. Her eyes, sunken and turquoise like his own, were scouring his face as if by this act of such determined looking she might find his entire history plainly written there.

"My name is Maria—Maria Alexandrovna."

Her accent was pure old Petersburg. He said nothing.

"You are Arkady Alexandrovitch Artamenkov?"

He nodded but he did not get up.

She turned. "Thank you, Zoya. Please leave us." It was an order —an echo from a time long ago, before the Soviet era—and there was no accompanying smile.

Zoya bowed, suddenly a servitor, before backing away in the direction of the bar.

He watched this Maria Alexandrovna sit down, resolute. Outside the wide windows, the rest of Russia was carrying on with its life.

She faced him directly. He said nothing.

She had no interest in ordering anything either. So their menus lay untouched. They simply sat, mother and son, staring at each other, a lifetime's silence, everything and nothing, between them.

"Arkady Alexandrovitch, may I call you Arkady?"

He remained silent. But his clothes were now drying from the heat rising within him.

"I . . . I wanted to see you. I hoped that we could . . . I hoped that we could talk."

And suddenly, surprising himself, surprising the very air that they were breathing, and because he knew already by the recoil and thrashing of his heart that this woman was indeed his mother, he asked the one question he would not have asked if he had thought her mad or another crazy liar seeking solace, the first four words that came to him: "How do I know?"

"Know?"

"How do I know?"

She kept her eyes steady on him, breathed in, throat tight as she swallowed, and he watched her gather herself.

"You were born here in Petersburg. Your father was a government official. I was not married. I was twenty-two years old. He came to my flat one night. He was a violent man . . . He died." She faltered a moment. Then the constricted rush to speak beset her again. "He does not matter. There were complications. But when you were born, my mother, your grandmother, took you away. She was trying to save my career, my prospects in the . . . in the Party. It was different then. Soviet times." She raised her jaw a fraction. "I was married very quickly afterward. To a British man. I defected. I lived in London with two children and my husband . . . I could not come back for a long time. They would not permit it. For many, many years. I could not risk it. Until the Soviet era ended. Even then it wasn't possible to remain for more than a few days. Not until recently have I been able to stay as long as I wish. So I found somewhere to live. And then I found Zoya. But I returned only to find you. It has taken too long. I am sorry." She indicated an envelope protruding from her bag. "I have proof that your grandmother registered you at the orphanage. And I have proof that I am her daughter. You must believe the rest." She paused. "I hoped . . . I hoped we could become friends. At least, I hoped you would tell me about your life."

Even as he sat there expressionless, even as he sat there in silence, his blood was spuming white in the deep gorges of his veins. He could think of nothing, could neither speak nor move, could only feel.

"What are you? I mean . . . do you have work? Are you married yourself, Arkady?"

The one human-to-human bond that should come as guaranteed, without question, given unto all, she had denied him. She had abandoned him. How dare she turn up now? How dare she turn up now and sit here like this? How dare she think that he would ever want to see her, even to know of her existence? The stupid bitch. The stupid fucking bitch.

"I know this is probably very difficult for you . . . And I'm sorry. I don't know quite . . . I . . . I want to know about your life. I want to help you . . . I can't change anything but I . . . I want to make up for what I can. We could begin today. Slowly, of course. Make a start. On becoming friends at least."

But all he wanted to do was hurt her as viciously as he could.

"Can you tell me anything about your life, Arkady?"

To ram her words back down her throat until she choked. To show her every second of it. All the years of bullshit he had been through. Every fight. Every beating. Every bruise. Do to her what had been done to him. Every last thing.

"Okay, well . . . let me tell you something about *my* life. After I left, I went to Paris with my husband . . ."

He was absolutely still, his face expressionless, steam visibly rising from his clothes. Yes, he was in the grip of pure, visceral feeling, but pulled in so many opposing directions that the net result was a kind of ferociously vibrating immobility. And the only cogent thought that he could register, the one thing he kept thinking, was that he did not want to give her even the impression that he hated her — no ledge of his spirit on which she might get the slightest purchase. Nothing. She had given him nothing. She would have nothing from him. She had not wanted him. Now he did not want her.

"... I did not discover my mother and my sister were dead until ten years ago. I knew nothing. I have lived another life, Arkasha . . . Arkady. For more than thirty years I have been another person. An exile. I wrote to them, of course, but I received nothing in response. Maybe they wrote back and their letters were stopped. I knew nothing. I did not know if I would ever find you. How could I know? I did not even know which orphanage they sent you to." She shook her head and raised her hands to press her fingers to her brow. "And it has taken Zoya a long time. My God, when we found the records, it was your grandmother's name on your certificate. Not my own name — as your real mother. Not my name. They tried to erase us both, but now here we are and we —"

He could take it no more; he stood up and said the only other words he would ever say to her: "I do not want to see you ever again."

"I . . . I understand." Now, at last, despite the strength of her self-possession, her alarm was visible. Though still marshaling her dignity, she was shaking with the effort; she was desperate, and her lips were taut as she spoke. "I would like to help you, though. How can I help you? What do you need? At least tell me what you need." She stood and faced him. "We don't have to see each other ever again. I do understand. We don't have to, but maybe I can make your life easier in some way. If you can just tell me a little bit about your life, then I could . . . I could . . . And Zoya will do everything. Between us. You don't have to see me again, Arkady. But please let me help."

Her face enraged him. Her voice made him deaf. He wanted to send her sprawling to the floor. He wanted to shout. To denounce her at the very top of his voice. That she should stand in front of him, to ask him one single question about his life. That she should think that he might care about her or any of this. It was all he could do to bend his rigid will to the single purpose of leaving without violence. But he did so. And only his eyes told as he put on his coat. He would give her no satisfaction. Nothing.

"You have Zoya's number. If you change your mind." She barred his way a moment, her eyes too, like those of her son, lit from within. "Call Zoya. She knows where I am. Anything you need."

Then she stood aside.

He walked out into the rancid rain.

She watched him go.

They neither saw nor spoke to each other again.

It was Henry Wheyland who did the deal. And it was Henry Wheyland who now, two years later, circled the main room of flat number 1327 on the thirteenth floor of tower block number two, Kammennaya Street, Vasilevsky Island, St. Petersburg.

Undeniably, and though only forty-two years into his allotted, Henry looked ill: his wheat-stalk hair was fleeing his forehead, twin valleys razed behind; and he was extremely thin, which made him appear taller than his average height and created the general impression of too many bony angles, of awkwardness, of sleeves too short, fingers too long, shirt too wide, shoulders too narrow, of elbows, knees, wrists, and nail. But in actuality, Henry was feeling fine — as fine, indeed, as only an able and happily functioning addict can feel.

The space around which he turned was low-ceilinged, box-square, drab, and spartan. In every one of the other 520 apartments in the building, it would have been called the living room. Here, though, in apartment 1327, living was music and music was living and there was no worthwhile difference between the two. Indeed, the only furniture consisted of an upright piano, positioned centrally and raised on six or seven layers of torn carpet; a piano stool, likewise raised; a tattered sofa, a stereo, two of the best speakers Henry's remaining funds could buy, and something like five thousand CDs, stacked, banked, and ranked along the dun-beige walls head high. And that was it. What saved the place from wretchedness was the vast window and the beauty of the view beyond: the Gulf of Finland.

Out there, unseen as yet by the rest of the city, a second line of rainclouds was smearing itself across the western horizon, advancing low and fast, a running smudge on the canvas where Baltic sky met Baltic sea. There would be another downpour before the afternoon was out.

Henry continued his circling, inclining in the manner of an academic before this or that pile of disks, matching inserts to boxes and returning the completed results to their rightful station in the library —a library without order or sense to any but himself. On such afternoons, he had come to suspect, Arkady Alexandrovitch's ill humor was not really ill humor at all but nerves. Or, if not quite nerves — Arkady, six feet, lean as the last Siberian lynx, could never really be described as nervous — then perhaps the outward manifestation of the arrival of whatever unknowable incubus took possession of his body in the hours leading up to a performance.

Arkady, who had been lying in his customary position across the sofa for the past thirty minutes, now raised the long index finger of his left hand and pushed up the peak of his cap.

"Everything is bullshit today, Henry. Everything."

"Surely everything is bullshit every day. This is Russia. This is life. What else do you expect?" Henry laid an errant disk gently in the case that he had at last located. "I'm afraid we're all just waiting for the next big idea, society-wise. Sorry I can't hurry it up for you."

They spoke in English — Arkady was almost fluent these days, though his accent was inflected not only with the intonations of his native tongue but with his native disposition. "Everything I see or hear — full of bullshit. Every person I meet — full of bullshit. Every place I go — full of bullshit." He let his head loll back on the ridge of the sofa's arm so that he was addressing the ceiling. Or a much discredited eavesdropper. "Every minute, more bullshit."

"It could be worse," Henry said softly.

"Yes. We could be fucking goats on the TV to get famous." Arkady pulled the English-language newspaper over his head. "Perhaps I will donate my balls to the war on terror."

Henry considered the top of the piano, where a foolscap-sized flier advertising the evening's concert had been placed carelessly over an untidy pile of sheet music. He picked it up, noticing again that all the scores beneath were perfectly clean — his flatmate never marked a single note for fingering. Arkady stared out from the color publicity picture. Large-handed, cragged, inscrutable: sunken and steady eyes, hollow cheeks (forever unshaven in light shades of brown that looked almost gray), unruly blond hair that straggled out from beneath the ubiquitous cap and over his collar — and all without the usual compensating vulnerability in the mouth or that carefully oblique invitation to would-be admirers in the artist's brow. Not so much defiant as distant. Unconnected. Arkady Alexandrovitch was neither handsome nor plain, so Henry often thought, but like some feature of the landscape for which such fastidious descriptions were beside the point. A face that it was as pointless to oppose as it was to champion or implore. The face of a rag-and-bone man or a prophet-king returned in disguise.

Henry looked up. "I cannot believe you mean what you say, Arkasha." He sometimes used the customary Russian nickname for Arkady, though he was careful never to say it with any hint of saccharinity. "Otherwise, why would you practice ten hours a day? But . . . well, even if everything *is* bullshit, I am afraid that the great dictatorship of the here and now continues. And as outraged and ill-equipped as we are, humanity is nonetheless commanded to get on with it. We have no other choice." Henry glanced toward where his friend lay. "What time are you supposed to be there tonight?"

"I feel like a Swedish wankpit."

"Around seven?"

"And it's going to rain again."

"What time are you supposed to be there tonight?"

"Half past ten."

"I'll walk with you — if you are going to walk."

Arkady batted off the newspaper and placed his cap firmly over his face.

Henry smiled his anemic smile again and wandered over to the window to take stock of the weather: immediately to the left, the other tower blocks; below, street squalor, gray decay, refuse; to the right, acid-rain-stained concrete and a tall crane, like some oddly skeletal single finger; directly ahead, rusted docks that had never taken themselves seriously; disrepair and dilapidation on all sides, and yet none of it detained the eye for more than a moment — because spread across the wide horizon beyond was the sea, light-spangled and sapphire-glorious in the still commanding sun. And now — just now — the beauty was truly extraordinary: the sea, angle-lit from the south and here-and-there sparkling, was nonetheless shading darker and darker, slate to a bluish black, as that resolute line of bruised purple clouds low-scudded in from the west. The island of Kronstadt and the dam had already vanished, and in a few minutes those clouds would obscure the sun altogether.

It happened like this. Though son and mother never did see or speak to each other again, Henry found himself acting for Arkady while Zoya continued to work for Maria Glover. Perhaps some sense of a secular mission prompted Henry to intervene. Or perhaps it was some new and bold reckoning in his dispute with the God from whom he could not quite flee. Either way, the deal had been struck.

Many an intention had blurred since then, but even at the time, more than two years ago, Henry had chosen not to examine his motives too closely — were not most human interactions thus shaded? Just the same, were he capable of being honest with himself on the subject, Henry had sensed then (as he sensed still) that desire was down there, lurking and smirking among the innocents, if ever he had mind enough to look. And yet he could not face bearing his torch so deep, for fear of discovering who or what held sway in these darkest crypts. Besides which, when he was in his lighter mood, such thoughts seemed like huge misapprehensions, echoes of a daydream from a time long ago, before he canceled himself out, before he shut down his sex drive and opened up his veins.

In any case, theirs began as a straightforward friendship. Henry had been out with a group of mainly English expatriates at one of Arkady's Magizdat gigs at the JFC Jazz Club. A veteran of a thousand classical concerts and five times as many recordings, he had thought that he recognized something exceptional in the Russian's playing. Later, Arkady had joined the table — there was talk of gigs in Vilnius and Tallinn — and Henry had translated. Though it was no business of his, Henry had then offered to teach Arkady English at half his normal rate — out of an unmediated eagerness to assist such talent in any way he could. But perhaps Arkady surprised him by taking his offer seriously, turning up twice a week at eight in the morning at Henry's old flat behind the Nevsky, well prepared and with the vocabulary learned. And perhaps Henry was pleased to be thus surprised.

Indeed, for the next six months, Arkady studied with the tenacious application of a last-chance student — far harder than the rest of Henry's pupils. And within a few months they were practicing English conversation. Initially Arkady told Henry only the barest outlines of his circumstances — that he knew nothing of his parents and that he had grown up in Orphanage Number 11, called Helios, and that it was "like a house for the fucking of pigs." But over the weeks Henry coaxed out the greater part of his history. (As so often happened, Henry noticed, Arkady was far more relaxed and open in his emerging second language. Curious, too, how quickly the Russians mastered obscenity.) Like a thick central pillar which alone supported the roof and around which everything else revolved was the main fact of Arkady's life: that he had trained as a classical pianist. This confirmed what Henry had felt must surely be the case when he first heard him perform — though "trained" hardly described the experience that Henry discovered Arkady to have undergone. His various teachers had well and truly made him a pianist — fashioned him, beaten him, worshipped him, forced him, encouraged him, praised him, hounded him, persecuted him, pushed him, cajoled him, inculcated him, taught him his art in the least compromising and most effective of all teaching methods: old-school Soviet style. For as long as he had been able to read, Arkady had been reading staves. It was not Russian that was Arkady Alexandrovitch's first language at all — it was music.

And it was no exaggeration to say that Arkady had been a child prodigy — the proud boast of Petersburg youth orchestras and the boy chosen to play for Gorbachev himself in 1984. "They love orphans for Soviet times, Henry. We do not have problem of mothers, fathers. We are heroes of the great state. No parents to take the glory away." Certainly by the time he was seventeen, everything was set for Arkady's smooth transition to the St. Petersburg State Conservatory and from there surely to Moscow and international stardom.

Then Mother Russia fell apart — again.

At first Arkady's rightful place was merely postponed for a year. "There were problems, so many problems, Henry. You just had to wait — this was the way. Always in this bullshit country, we wait. For what? For nothing." He was nonetheless required to leave the orphanage and seek what work he could find as an electrician, the secondary training they had given him by way of Soviet-style existential comedy.

Then, when the long year had dragged itself reluctantly around the calendar, the place was arbitrarily postponed again. But still Arkady could not bring himself to face the facts: that the nature of bribery and corruption had undergone a complete reversal and that advancement was no longer about the Party system or Party sponsorship; that in the new Russia it was all about the money and the guns. In 1991 the orphanage shut down. In 1992 his piano teacher died. He lost access to the last good piano he had been using. The second year passed and he was told to apply to the conservatory all over again — through the new system. He did so, this time without a sponsor. By midway through 1993, he knew he wasn't going to make it. Even then it took him half a decade to abandon the greater part of his hope. And so he spent the last years of the millennium selling smuggled stereos around the back of Sennaya Square by day and (as much as to sit by a functioning piano as to stay alive materially) playing bullshit music in the new hotel bars by night, hour after hour, his fingers aching like ten desperate would-be lovers trapped in ten deadly marriages for something real . . . the *Hammerklavier*'s embrace.

The shortage of playable pianos in Russia . . . Ah, yes — besides the English lessons, there was a second reason for the deepening of Henry and Arkady's early association. Or perhaps it was the main reason. At any rate, a few months after Henry had begun teaching Arkady, he bought an upright C. Bechstein. Henry himself had once been a competent amateur, and maybe he did genuinely intend to pick up where he had left off at the age of eighteen — and yet, even as he and the seller's three handsome sons heaved the piano through his front door, Henry knew well that Arkady would be the first to sit at the keyboard. Sure enough, as soon as the Russian saw it, he asked if he could play, and — the quagmire of the verb "to be" happily abandoned for the time being — Henry spent the next two hours sitting still at his teaching table, utterly rapt. Thereafter Arkady came around three or four times a week, practicing for hours on end, regardless of the lesson schedule.

Nonetheless, these two circumstances — teaching and piano — might not have led to their present arrangement in tower block number two had it not been for two further eventualities: the dwindling of Henry's money and the unforeseen arrival of the woman whom Arkady referred to as "the stupid bitch." Maria Glover changed both their lives overnight.

They were some six months into the English lessons. Arkady was now playing Henry's piano several times a week. And yet Henry found out about the meeting between mother and son only some days after the event. The idea occurred to him more or less instantly, though: arrange for the woman to pay for Arkady to go to the conservatory. And get her to keep Arkady alive while he did so. Arkady would have to reapply, of course, and he would probably have to suffer the indignity of several auditions, but . . . But if he could prove himself at least as worthy of the department's time as any of the adolescents he would be up against, then the main thing was the money. If need be, the woman, whoever she was, could pay in advance. Surely, Henry reasoned, it was worth a try. The problem was Arkady.

In all his other dealings, as far as Henry could tell, Arkady was as vulpine as everyone else in Russia, but on this one subject he was as silent and scornful as an anchorite. Henry pressed, but the Russian refused absolutely to contemplate a second meeting, refused to consider asking for anything through Zoya, refused even to talk about it. Eventually Henry offered to broker the question himself. Arkady merely shrugged — Henry could try if he wished, but it was nothing to do with him.

Thus meagerly enfranchised, Henry nonetheless set about his task with skill, a renewed sense of purpose, and no little interest, the only further Arkady-related difficulties being the finding of Zoya and the meeting with Maria Glover herself, for which he, Henry, was required to bring photographs of the Russian that he was forced (against his liking) to steal with the complicity of Polina.

In the event, the deal was relatively easy to secure. After a truly ferocious hour in the company of his friend's mother (during which he had to relate everything he knew about Arkady thrice over), Henry found Mrs. Glover suddenly tractable; she had been testing him, of course — interrogating him, or perhaps, as Henry later thought, mining him was a better way of putting it. Regardless, once her mood changed — abruptly, as if by a switch — she was more than ready to guarantee the funds in writing to the conservatory ahead of any audition. If Arkady won a place, she would not give the money to Henry (he did not ask for this, and he explained that Arkady would not accept it either), but she would pay the conservatory directly and in advance each term, the entire three years' tuition as well as any dining, books, stationery, or other bills her son might incur. This without further question, Mr. Wheyland. I am not surprised to hear that you have trained as a teacher. And I further hope you will look out for my son for the duration of his studies. I trust you to do so. You will let me know immediately of his acceptance at the conservatory. Now that I have heard what you have to say, I am sure that he will be accepted. And from then on, he must have no other work or distraction until his career is made. You understand this?

She struck Henry in those moments — sitting in the casement window of her apartment, back to the light, face impassive, lips set — as a woman of great will, an exiled queen charging her courtier with the full authority of her divine right; and perhaps already inclined to duty, he felt her wish much as a command.

Of course he tracked down Arkady at his favorite pinball bar with the news that same afternoon, but the Russian never actually thanked him — not then, not ever. All the same, overnight, Henry's old place became a twenty-four-hour rehearsal room. Which was all the gratitude he needed.

Though nothing was left of Henry's former life (buried, loathed, forcibly forgotten) save for the ever-decreasing remains of the money, there was nonetheless something vaguely pastoral about what happened thereafter. For it was Henry who had suggested that they find somewhere cheap together so Arkady could practice whenever he wanted and thus make the very most of the chance he had finally been given. Arkady was going to need a piano, after all. Further, Henry offered to pay for most of their food, the bills, and the rent, so that Arkady could concentrate full-time and give up the nights in the bars.

After a fashion, the arrangement worked. Arkady practiced all day (and disappeared most nights). Henry listened and listened and continued to help the Russian improve his English. And in this lopsided symbiosis, they lived.

Henry met Maria Glover only once more, some six months later, at her flat on Griboedova, as before — though this time ostensibly to check on the efficacy of their arrangements. Perhaps Arkady's acceptance at the conservatory (communicated via Zoya) had furnished them both with the required validation — Henry to pursue his vocation more explicitly, Maria Glover to feel her obligation obliquely eased. At any rate, Henry found her that day in a lighter, more expansive mood. Perhaps glad of his Englishness too, she offered him tea and told Henry a little about herself, what she called "her second life" in London, her family there, her work on the newspaper of record. And thus charmed, Henry reciprocated by confessing something of his previous life too. That he had trained for the Catholic priesthood before abandoning the calling and becoming a full-time secondary school teacher, a job which, he explained, was these days almost impossible to do without incredible resources of stamina and insensitivity.

She asked him how he came to be in Russia. He explained that he had left his teaching job on his thirty-fourth birthday and that after his mother had died he had used the money from selling her small house in Reading to set off traveling. He described how he had come to Russia (after three years, mostly in India) overland, from the south, and fallen in love with Petersburg on his first visit.

She nodded as if such a conclusion were quite understandable and told him — with great feeling — that she had been born here. She reminisced a little about how the city used to be when it was Lenin-grad. He asked her how she had left. She told him she defected. She told him she had effectively "started again" in London. She became more and more loquacious. She told him a great deal and much that was personal, though she left out the names; and he began to form the impression that she was in some odd way trying to unburden herself, and that she was answering his polite curiosity with some-thing like relief.

Then, precisely as the second hour ended, she put to him the ques-tion that he realized was the real reason behind her asking to see him again: did he, Henry, think it possible that she might hear Arkady play?

Henry was caught out. He was moved by her plea. And yet, know-ing Arkady as he did and fearing Arkady's reaction both toward Maria Glover and toward himself if he were ever to bring the two to-gether again, he considered that he could not risk effecting such a meeting, even covertly. Despite all that she had told him, he felt he had little choice but to answer no.

4

Gabriel and Isabella

A BRUTALIZED DOG whimpered in the shadow of the crumbling courtyard. Six P.M. now in Petersburg; eleven A.M. in New York; and this was just the fourth or fifth call of nine or ten between them. Gabriel sat by the window of Yana's mother's apartment, the telephone never in its cradle, the undernourished light lingering, the better to slip away unnoticed when he turned; Isabella heading uptown, battery running down, the New York morning like a set of freshly whitened teeth. She fixated, he terrified — real and unreal, one and the same.

"You have to go back there."

"I'm not going back there."

"You *have* to go back there."

"Is, I am not going back there. I can't. You can go when you come or tom—"

"Gabriel, I need you to go back there today, tonight."

"We'll go together. When you get here."

"Too late. It might be too late."

"I can't—"

"How was she again?"

"How *was* she?"

"How was she?

"I told you . . . I told you. She was on the floor. In the main room. What are you asking me?"

"There was nothing wrong with her?"

"Yes. She was dead, Is, she was dead."

"For Christ's sake. I know that."

"What are you asking me, then?"

"I'm asking you . . . I'm asking you if . . . She wrote me this letter . . . I'm asking you if it looked like she did it herself."

"Jesus."

"I mean . . . anything . . . was there anything strange about her? Anything that—"

"Is . . . Is, she had a stroke. That's what happened. That's all."

"How do you know?"

"Yana. The ambulance men said—there was dried saliva and other stuff—her skin was all mottled—they told Yana it looked like a stroke and I—"

"You sure? Can you check? Will there be an autopsy?"

"Is—"

"Did they say that there would be some kind of autopsy?"

"Is, *for Christ's sake*. She didn't want to kill herself. I spoke to her on the phone on Sunday night. She was . . . she was fine. So will you stop. Will you stop being such a crazy idiot. She's dead. She is just dead. She died."

Silence.

Gabriel again: "Shit. Shit, I'm sorry. I'm sorry. I'm sorry."

"No, it's okay. *I'm* sorry. I'll be there tomorrow night if I can get my visa. I'm on my way to the embassy now." Isabella breaking. "Sorry . . . I'm sorry. You are right—I'm being crazy and you're there by yourself and . . . Gabs, will you be all right? Is Yana there? Or Arytom? Someone you can stay with?"

And so Gabriel pulling himself together. "I'm okay. Just make sure you get the visa and a flight, Is, that's all you have to do. This had to happen one day."

"I know. I know, I know."

"And you were right about the consulate. They're helping a lot. I'm . . . I'm talking with them again first thing. A guy called Julian Avery. When I called, they knew who I was. They remember Grandpa Max. They know who Mum was too—who we are, I mean. They're going to help . . . with everything. We're lucky, in a way."

A long silence, and then Isabella asking the question: "Does *he* know?"

Another silence. Then: "Yes."

"They contacted him?"

"Yes. The hospital contacted the consulate before me. The consulate guy—Avery—seems to know where he is. And he's next of kin. So they got hold of him. They told him. He knows." Gabriel drew his heaviest breath. "But we're going to bury her here, Is. We're not going to fly her home. She wanted to be buried in Petersburg. We're going to do that as fast as we can. We're not going to tell him. We're going to do it before he can get here. That bastard can go fuck himself."

5

Nicholas Glover

NICHOLAS GLOVER had in fact spent his entire adult life fucking himself. However, estranged as they had been these past ten years or so, neither Gabriel nor Isabella could know this; and even before their antipathy ossified, Nicholas knew well that they could scarcely have imagined the ongoing mêlée in which he lived. Indeed, in the past twenty-four hours, Nicholas had come to an awful and existence-rearranging realization: that the only other person in the world who might ever have grasped the true nature of his lifelong war was his wife — Maria, Masha, Mashka, Marushya.

But it was too late now. Too late to confide. Too late to be open. Too late to start the one journey that he might have taken with any hope of reaching understanding at the end. Was this a tragedy? At present, Nicholas had no idea. Because as of the past thirty minutes, he was ignoring all such thoughts, ignoring them with a strength of will which, had it been available to most other men, would have sent them rushing from their dreary lives pell-mell in pursuit of their disappearing dreams.

Yes, Nicholas was ignoring all thoughts save those directly associated with process and procedure. In these, at least, there was a kind of ease . . . As six o'clock chimed back and forth across the steeply raked Parisian rooftops, there was even some satisfaction in the sound of his handmade soles upon the medieval cobbles of the Rue des Barres. Everything procedural was taken care of. Thank Christ. Her rent was paid for another six months and then the flat would simply be leased to another tenant and his problem no longer. Her possessions, such as they were, Gabriel and Isabella could have. Welcome to them. Under Russian rules, all the money in her bank accounts would be returned to him . . . And even if this was not exactly the law, his solicitors could be instructed to make sure that it was done anyway. Who would challenge him? Surely nobody was going to fight him through the double jungle of a U.K. passport-holder (spouse, defector, repatriated) deceased on Russian soil. Not even Isabella. The Russian system could be relied upon to be as opaque as he required it to be. And what a relief that all could be conveyed through the Paris office; he had no wish to return to London. Even the wretched ache in his neck — a residual crick from his travels — seemed to have eased.

Almost jauntily, then, as if to put this improvement to the test, he looked up for the first time in two or three years at the crooked façade of the old building on the corner of the Rue du Grenier sur l'Eau — the oldest building in the city, so they said, beam-warped and brick-crooked as the eight hundred years of history it had witnessed. Yes, sixty-two was not so bad. Still in good shape. Still in sound mind. Still thinking. And still very able.

Yes, indeed: *tout était dans l'ordre.* Had he been carrying a cane to match his tailored linen suit, he might have twirled a spry thanks at the tourists now parting to let him make his way between their collective craning. Had he had a hat, he might have doffed it to the venerable old sisters now entering the mighty church of St. Gervais opposite. Good evening, sister, good evening, and a fine one too. Paris is behaving itself? The delicate scent of scandal, the salt tang of corruption, the sweet savor of vice — all vanished, all banished? Excellent. But now I must hurry home to my young friend, who has promised Tanqueray and tonic for my ills. And I am so very fond of him this evening.

Slim and trim, neither tall nor short, with pale eyes and a thin mouth (which between them disguised a fine, disparaging intelligence and a lifetime of immoderate appetite), Nicholas Glover had the kind of demeanor that Dorian Gray might have developed if that asinine portrait had never been painted and the young fool had relied instead on the excellence of his genes and the incisiveness of his wit to see him handsomely through to his sixties. His hair was turning white, still thick but close-cropped; his skin was clean-shaven and well attended to. Indeed, the only thing Nicholas took pains to conceal was his crooked teeth, which in the upper case were uneven and shading to yellow, and which in the lower were at war in such a manner as to have forced one another into partial overlap and sudden protruding angles. For this reason, a smile seldom parted his lips.

He stepped sprightly past the early diners at the café on the shallow steps and sprightly too across the main road, up onto the embankment, and so to the Pont Marie. The light was softening and even the lazy Seine seemed a little less raddled—the city's favorite older woman come out once more, dressed in the flattering colors of the evening sun, slinking through the town again, turning heads, remarked upon, while her most loyal admirers, the distinguished old buildings on the Quai de Bourbon (likewise lit most handsomely in shades of pale sand and amber-yellow and *blanc cassé*), kept their devoted station. *Bonsoir,* Madame Seine, *bonsoir;* our compliments. The air, softening too, he thought, linen loosened by an afternoon of love . . . Ah, yes, he could see the satisfactorily large windows of his own apartment.

Alessandro would most likely be in the bath, drinking wine, no doubt (and not something cheap, the grasping little shit), listening to that terrible music of his. Dear God, how he loathed Alessandro's music: some thirty-five-year-old ever-adolescent would-be chanteuse who couldn't sing or play or write or dance, popping along with her pigtails and her pout for the benefit of whom? Seven-year-old girls and thirty-five-year-old gay men; it was so bloody . . . so bloody *camp.* And of course Alessandro would be singing out loud, planning all the while in that chichi little Soho head of his, planning what he wanted to extract from the evening. Nicholas sighed. Those childish emotional blackmails of poor Alessandro, those peasant clevernesses, which he no doubt considered compelling evidence of a subtle, emotionally attuned mind but which (*hélas*) were probably culled from the daily parade of inconsequence otherwise known as the "relationship" columns. Probably written by Gabriel. *There* was an irony. Nicholas narrowed his nostrils and exhaled slowly. He remembered (fondly) the time before that particular word achieved its current ubiquity; and he found it impossible even to think of it now except escorted by those two unyielding quotation marks: "relationship." Give me the sincerity of nakedness and the honesty of desire, O God, and deliver me from the turgid bourgeoisie and all their favorite phrases.

A shudder. He had reached the far side of the bridge—the Île St. Louis. Home. In the middle of the river. Two young policemen cycled by, and he slowed to watch their saddles until they disappeared past the Librarie Adelaide on Rue Jean de Bellay. Then he raised his small leather document-holder to return the wave of the waitress from the Café Charlotte, white skirt swaying above pretty brown knees. Would she let him paint her one day? He thought so, if he went delicately about it. And so he turned left, along the quay, until he came to number 15, once the residence of Emile Bernard, *Créateur du Synthésisme* (so the plaque said), where he popped the lock, entered the cool of the courtyard (cedar scent and the clove perfume of basil in bloom), and climbed the wide stone stairs of staircase D, dipped in the middle from four hundred years of just such footsteps.

But the interior gloom of the stairwell recalled the sorrow and heaviness of his recent journey (his mind racing down avenues he had not sanctioned, as it always did). Anger and sorrow. His deepest consciousness had always felt this way — a churn wherein anger and sorrow were mixed and remixed and mixed again with the ceaseless salt of his lust. Oh Christ, his wife was dead. Masha was dead. Marushya. No longer findable as a living and breathing woman, as the only woman to whom he might have confessed himself. And already, as quickly as the evening was falling through the sky, the entirety of more than three and a half decades of his life seemed to him implausible. All the things he had never said. Or rather, all the things he had said, all the things he was always saying, but only to himself.

I am a bloody fool, Masha. A bloody, vain, and self-denying fool. Could you have understood this . . . this idle carcass of mine? Or did you always understand, despite my silence and deceit? I think you did. Could I have told you everything? I think I could. Even the worst of it? The very worst? Could I have told you and would you have understood? I tried . . . once or twice, I tried. But I was afraid you would not be able to bear it. Not want to hear it. I was afraid you would leave me. I was afraid of everything. I lived in chaos. I lived through chaos. I lived on chaos. And Christ, you never asked. Masha, you never asked . . . And I suppose I was grateful for that. I loved you because you didn't ask. I loved you dearly. The others . . . All those hundred others, they always wanted something answered. Something settled. "How can you?" "Why do you?" "Why can't you?" "Why don't you?" They wanted me to provide "clarity"; they wanted me "to be honest." Clarity — can you believe it, Masha? Yes: you would understand. I know you would. Because you know how difficult it is to hold the line against the thousand daily surrenders this craven new world requires, to keep on coming back for more, heart in pieces, soul in rags. Clarity! Oh, Masha . . . As if I . . . As if I, one man shuffling through all the disgusting piss and filth of this twenty-first century, one man at the tail end of a million desperate and profoundly unclear generations, none of whom have ever known the first thing about who they are, why they are, where they came from, what they are made of, where they fit in, if they fit in, why they are alive, why they die — as if I could provide anyone with any kind of clarity. But time and time again, Masha, I have been forced to this conversation: "Oh, but you can't live like this, Nicholas," they say. "Like what?" I ask. "With all this uncertainty and — you know — messing around." "Messing around? You call this messing around? No, Christ, this is not messing around. This is the very opposite of messing around. This is as in earnest as it gets: you and I, naked and alone, here and now, in this bed, the rest of time and space irrelevant. The soul's exchange, the body's vow, the mind's reprieve. Our most human nexus. I take this extremely seriously. It's the only thing I take seriously. It's the only thing I can take seriously." (Is this hurting you? Should I stop? For four years I was only yours. I swear it. Not much in a lifetime, but it was four years. I swear to you. My best years.) "Come on," they say, "be honest with me, Nicholas." And then, Masha, I have to fall to silence as the questions rain down upon me . . . Because what you cannot say, what you must not say, is that you are living your whole life enacting the only honest, clear fact that you do honestly and clearly know: that nothing is honest and clear. (My God — you are smiling. You do know all this. You knew all along.) The cells, the DNA, the molecules of the blood — they all — they all — have different opinions, different opinions on everything, from euthanasia to the Hippocratic oath, from Israel to Palestine, from God made man to Man makes gods. They do not agree. There isn't even a consensus. Not within me. And certainly not out there. Half the world is screaming for water and freedom when the other half is ordering cocktails and complaining about the service. (Didn't you always say that, my Masha?) And what could I say to them about me? What could I tell them about what I feel? The head distrusts the heart. The heart ignores the head. The balls want to carry on regardless. It's a total and utter mess. Chaos. "Come on: be honest with me, Nicholas, tell me what you honestly feel about the situation." But what they really meant was "Be simple with me, Nicholas." Be uncomplicated. Be straightforward. And simplicity — simplicity is the new code for . . . no — what am I saying? — simplicity actually means stupidity. What they're really asking is "Be stupid with me, Nicholas." The only way we can get through this is to be stupid: work, marriage, the war, God, love, and television. If we can just stay stupid, it will be okay. We promise. Honesty! Honesty — Masha, is it not the most monstrous piece of excrement that mankind has ever come up with? Human nature, consciousness itself, is famously indefinable, mysterious, mobile, responsive — is gloriously less constant, less intrinsic than the imaginings of rocks, trees, sheep. That's the whole point. No, no, no — you get three goes at it, Masha: birth, death, and that little moment of both. The rest of the time you are fooling yourself and everyone around you. If you are alive and thinking and still interested in being alive and thinking, then you are necessarily unclear and you do not honestly know anything — you're guessing, hunching, hoping. And that's it. What I honestly feel — what I honestly feel! I could not write down what I honestly feel if I started now and did not stop till the last syllable of recorded time. And yes, I loved you, Masha, because you never once asked me to be clear or honest. Because you understood what being human actually means. And you weren't afraid of it. Were you?

Or maybe this was all lies too. Maybe he was just making everything romantic, as he always, always did (the true sign of a monster). At the end of each of the culs-de-sac down which his mind careered, there was, he knew, a gaudy theater wherein savage satires were ever being staged. And to whom was he talking anyway? There was nobody left to tell. His wife was dead. He could not trust himself one inch.

Vanished entirely now was Nicholas's dapper manner, and though dressed the same, he appeared in the doorway of his own bedroom like a man who spent every day of his life fighting hand to hand through Hades and back.

"You're home!" Alessandro came out of the bathroom, steam chasing him, a towel wrapped around his waist and a dressing gown draped over his shoulders — an unusual modesty, Nicholas registered, and a symptom of uncertainty. Truly the young these days were so very, very obvious. Like the puerile century, they lacked charisma. But here at least was relief: the old salve of younger skin.

"Did it take all afternoon?"

"Yes, it did." Nicholas put his slim diplomatic case on the polished marble surface of his dresser. Life, the great distraction, was stirring sluggishly in his blood. And Alessandro's black hair was still wet and water ran from the curls on his forehead, causing him now to wipe his forearm across his brow—a little too slowly, Nicholas noticed. Despite the robe and towel, there was still, as always with Alessandro, a flirtatious door ajar. Evidently, though, the poor man had no idea what mood to expect. Understandable. Nicholas knew well enough that people lived in constant trepidation of his moods. (Had his temperament always been so changeable, or had he made it so—in order that people would fear him? He couldn't remember. So much was dark beyond eighteen. All was secret and suspicious and . . . and bloody *Soviet.*) In any case, it was obvious that Alessandro was waiting for his cue. So, disregarding the infantile whine of the abysmal music, Nicholas forced himself to smile his tight-lipped smile.

"But the good news is that I do not have to go to London. They can do everything through the Paris office."

"That's great, Nick." Alessandro fastened the gown but let the towel drop.

"And so tonight we are going to celebrate. Forget cooking. Forget that bloody concert." Nicholas hated to have his name shortened. Either Alessandro did it deliberately to annoy him, or he did it because he wanted to insist on some sort of parity. What a farce. Through forty years of impatience, Nicholas still could not make up his mind which was more annoying, the guile of straight women or the wiles of gay men. They were as bad as each other. A tragedy, really, when what one really wanted was a straight man. But let Alessandro have his junior satisfactions; Nicholas's mood at least was recovering.

"Le Castebin, I think." Nicholas forced another smile. "Shall we? You can have your *langoustines façon.* And their new house Champagne—from Troyes, Gaston tells me—is sublime. We'll dispatch a bottle each—why not? It's a while since we got ourselves well and truly tight. Brahms is such a terrible bore anyway." Nicholas realized that he had better show some interest. "And anyway, you . . . you must tell me about Greece. I want to know all the details. Did you get to Delphi? Did the oracle have news for us?"

"I was in Santorini." Alessandro picked up the shirt lying ready on the bed. The dressing gown came off.

Nicholas looked, unreservedly. "You have caught the sun again."

"I topped up on the sun bed with Freddie at the gym while you were away." Alessandro enjoyed flattery more than anything else in the world and could tease it out of quick-drying cement if he applied himself.

The phrase "topped up" annoyed Nicholas, though. The word lurking behind it, the word "tan," annoyed him too. And the name Freddie somehow infuriated him. Campness. But the revealed body — ah, the naked body of this . . . this other . . . The naked body of this other human being entranced him, engrossed him, bewitched him like a river god rising in vapors of jasmine and myrrh with a different violin sonata for each of his senses.

6

The Disendowed

ARKADY AND HENRY EMERGED into the deepening twilight of the northern sky and set off along the potholed street that ran between the six dilapidated tower blocks similar to their own. With the exception of three old women dragging home their heavy handcart full of cheap fizzy drinks and expensive fake mineral water, weaving oddly on their invisible route through the worst of the ruts, everybody was drunk: the half-dozen old men sitting on the weedy verge around their upturned crate on legless chairs, seating ripped from abandoned cars; the heavily made-up girl now leaving block two with her infant in an improvised sling, her three-year-old and her five-year-old—cigarette cocked and burning—all in sullen attendance and ready for the ride into town and another night working together with the tourist bar spill; the gang of boys, nine- or ten-year-olds, standing around an old metal drum that they had somehow managed to ignite on the corner and every now and then reaching in with tar-caked hands to chuck fume-spewing firebombs at each other or any passerby they did not recognize, then swapping their vodka-spiked drink tins from hand to hand so they could blow cool air on their blackened fingers.

The two turned right, away from the few feeble streetlamps that would have taken them in the direction of Primorskaya metro station. Instead they walked toward the Smolensky cemetery, a woodland, half wild, half kempt, with winding paths, dense thickets, and sudden glades that sat square in the center of Vasilevsky Island—a shortcut on their way into town.

Still in silence, they came to the gap in the railings and the unoffi-

cial path, which led off the road and into the cemetery. Despite the
sudden showers throughout the day, the ground underfoot was damp
rather than muddy and they were able to walk with relative ease between the trees. Arkady carried his concert shoes around his neck,
dangling by the laces; he was still wearing his cap; and he had rolled
up his jeans a little to accommodate his boots. Henry, meanwhile,
looked as incongruous as ever, his hooded top inside his arm-patched
corduroy sports jacket, his black jeans cut too narrow.

At length they emerged onto one of the main cross-paths through
the cemetery and Henry felt the need to speak. "Will the newspapers
be there?"

"I forgot — Grisha came today," Arkady said, as if it were he, not
Henry, who had begun. "This morning, when you were teaching."

Henry's eyes went across, though his head did not turn. "Actually,
I wasn't. I was ringing up hotels and restaurants and nightclubs in
London for little Ludmilla." He had been supplementing his dimin-
ishing capital for five years with a haphazard income from teaching
English as a foreign language, but he'd let the contacts shrivel. And
though his habit was cheaper here than anywhere save Afghanistan
itself, he was now down to a few thousand and he knew that something had to be done about money and soon. "My last pupil is leaving to join her friends, and her mother needed her teacher to argue
room rates at the Covent Garden Hotel for two hours."

"All your little bitches go to London. The British must believe
Russia is made only of millionaires' daughters. Or whores."

"What did Grisha want?"

"A salsa partner."

"I do not owe him any money," Henry asserted, though whether
to himself or to Arkady wasn't clear. "He oversupplied me. I told
him. I have paid him for what I asked for. I don't need the extra he
gave me. I told him that three times. He more or less forced me. So
he can't get all cross now if I am —"

"You understand well what he wants."

"I don't even know these people he seems to think I'm friends
with. Not anymore. Most of the English, French, and Germans I
used to hang around with have left or gone to Moscow or run out of
excuses for doing nothing and returned home. People move on. Especially the foreign kids. The new crowd, whoever they are — Grisha
probably knows them as well as I do."

"Did you give him your shit back?"

"No." Henry wished that he had taken measures to rectify the hole in his old black brogues. "How could I? I just won't get any more for a while."

Arkady's eyes narrowed for a moment, then swept the sky. "I need a piss," he said.

He stepped to the side of the track, where a once grand but now untended grave with an elaborate wrought-iron Orthodox cross was being choked by weeds.

Henry walked on alone toward the crossroads where the track that led to the central chapel met their own. It was thoroughly dark now. Ahead, the trees overhung in a complete canopy, branches shifting, though Henry could not feel any wind. An owl was hooting somewhere close by. He thought he saw its shape perched on a headstone. But it was only a trick of the ivy. Some cat or rat, rabbit or badger — he had no idea what — was rustling through the undergrowth to his left.

Unexpectedly, a cast of primitive superstitions he believed long forgotten revealed themselves in the forefront of his imagination. He smiled nervously to himself, drew rueful breath, and shook his head. Silly. Nonetheless, there was something about the Smolensky (and the answering crack of a twig) that caused him to wonder whether the place affected Arkady in the same way. After all, here they were, in a cemetery thronged with the Petersburg dead, a cemetery that had been built on the agonized bones of all those who had perished in hauling the city up from the marsh, and a cemetery whose perimeter was this very night ringed by their living and disendowed descendents — the desperate and the diseased — here they were, and Arkady was pausing unconcernedly to piss on an unknown headstone. One thing for certain: these ornate Old Believer crosses seemed to afford purchase only to the weeds. More places to bind and swathe.

He reached the crossroads and stood waiting. He often paused here on his way into town, by the main track down which the hearses came, day after day, followed always, he had noticed, by that stubborn delegation of white-haired women, forever in black, forever wailing, as if there were not time enough left in the world to get all the mourning done. But how quickly the generations forgot: his own father's father, Henry had hardly known, and his great-grandfather not at all, no more who he was than where he was from. In so many brief years we become strangers to our own blood.

His pocket was vibrating.

Someone was trying to call him. No: there was a text message on his phone. Grisha. He thumbed it open. In Russian: "Your sugar bitch is dead."

But in the time it took for him to turn and look for her son, he made the decision not to tell Arkady. Not until after the concert.

7

The Double Life

TEN-THIRTY IN PETERSBURG. Seven-thirty in London. And the worst night of his life was squatting black and heavy in the shabby courtyard outside. He sat motionless in the window of Yana's mother's apartment, his face a picture of mute and frozen shock, staring out like some child marquis on the place where they had lately guillotined his mother. Opposite his vantage, the locksmith was closing up on the ground floor and the builders, two brothers from Belarus, worked with naked bulbs suspended from naked joists in the room above. A cat held mangy station at the bottom of the adjacent stairs, its back to the bags of sand. He continued to hold the phone in its cradle. Isabella would call back any moment and he would suddenly become animate again, everything would start over, everything would race and swerve and dart and fall. Yana's mother was due to return from her gathering of special supplies. After their surreal trip to the hospital, Yana had gone back to the CCCP Café. But she would be home soon too. As would Yana's brother, Arytom, carrying his endless manuscripts and proofs.

Gabriel let it ring once. His focus seemed to journey in from far away; his head lowered a moment, and abruptly he had the handset to his ear and he was back in the storm and swell of the present.

"Can you hear me properly now? Is this line better?"

"Yes. Forget my mobile. It —"

"I couldn't get through."

"Sorry, Lina. Isabella called again." This was only the second time they had spoken since the afternoon, and already he knew that

Lina was his savior and that he would never ever be able to do without her, not for one day, not for the rest of his life.

"Okay — this is definitely Yana's landline? I can use this."

"Her mother's, yes. Yes, I think it's fine."

"Will you be okay there tonight, Gabriel?"

"Yes . . . I don't know where I . . . I will be all right."

Her voice became even more measured. "Okay, now, listen. I have booked you into the Grand Hotel Europe, Gabriel, where we stayed. For tomorrow. It's all on my credit card. I don't want you to even think about the money. We can talk in the morning about whether you want to go there. But I think you should have somewhere as a base. I've booked a twin, so you can be with Isabella. If you prefer to stay at Yana's mother's until later, then fine, but it's there if you want. We can talk about it tomorrow."

"Lina. God, you don't . . . Thank you. Thanks."

"And you have spoken with the consulate?

"Yes. Yes, I have. A guy called Julian Avery there — he's being very helpful."

"So don't forget, I can call people from here too. I can call anyone you need — if it helps, I mean. I will be here on standby in the morning. There's a lot I can do from here."

"Okay."

Gentle now: "We have to be practical for the time being."

"Yes."

"You are sure that you are going to have the funeral in Petersburg?"

"Yes. It's what Mum wanted."

"Right. Well, I'll try to get a visa first thing tomorrow and I will be there . . . Thursday, Thursday night. Latest, Friday. Okay?"

"If you can. But don't —"

"You have enough money?"

"Yes. Yes . . . it's all right. I have money."

"You have some food for tonight?"

"I'm not —"

"I know. But you should try to eat something. Will Yana's mother get you something?"

"It'll be okay, Lina."

"Just don't . . . Just take care of yourself. You need all that fierce strength of yours. And try to focus on whatever you need to do. Try not to think too much, Gabriel. Sometimes just doing stuff is best—you know, fool the days, or you'll go crazy. When is Isabella there?"

"Tomorrow evening. She's getting her visa now and then she'll fly."

"Is she okay?"

"I don't know."

"Is Sasha coming?"

"No. I don't think so."

A pause. "Is there anyone here you want me to call tomorrow?"

This, he knew, was Lina's way of approaching the question of his father. He loved her for her delicacy and for knowing him so well. He loved her for her endlessly decent strong sensible saving kind humanity. He loved her. "No. There's nobody to call, Lina. But . . . But I don't know. Tomorrow we should . . . we should try to think. Maybe there's some of Mum's old friends or something."

"What time is it there?"

"Ten thirty-five."

"Okay. You go now. I am going to call again at eleven-thirty your time, okay, before you go to bed? I love you very much."

"Thanks. Thanks for everything, Lina. I love you too."

Lina's voice vanished but he did not put down the phone. There was stillness. Sudden. Silent. His eyes glassed again and he was gone. The courtyard outside seemed to him now a darkened rough-made stage set for some great play about to begin, the hero appearing in a shaft of light as the door was thrown open, the shadowy and conniving chorus ushering themselves off (never quite fast enough), chanting their collective exhortation: "Gentlefolk, behold this, our man, at such sore odds with himself and his times." His dearest hope had once been that he would become a director—some bold reinvigorator of the London stage, teaching the silly actors to stop their *acting*. It was his mother's most fervent wish for him too, though she had stopped talking about the prospect in the past few years. *In art we are in conversation with ourselves across the generations, Gabriel; this is the lodestar of our humanity. The rest is chasing food and money . . .*

When he came back to the surface, he found that he was snatching at his breath and there was the taste of salt in his mouth, but he saw that his fingertips must have lingered all the while on the handset. He had not spoken to Connie since the morning—already an-

other lifetime ago. And he dialed the numbers now as if they were inscribed above the secret door to the other chamber of his heart.

"Connie."
     "Hey, lover. Are you in Petersburg?"
     "I'm—"
     "Jesus." She sensed it immediately. "What's happened?"
     "Con, my mother has died."
     "Oh, Gabriel."
And somehow with her, with Connie, he could turn on himself,
reach up behind and sever the taut wires of control. Somehow with
her he had the strength to actually say it. Somehow with Connie he
could give himself up.
     "Oh, Gabriel." Nothing else. A whisper that contained all the
compassion that one person might feel for another; a whisper that
somehow understood the fragile geometry of his soul.
     "Oh, Gabriel." Nothing else.
     And at last his tears broke. A quiet, desolate crying that juddered
through him as if he were dragging a blunted plow through every or-
gan, every muscle, every nerve.

8

The Good Things Trick

S HE LAY ACROSS the central four seats at the back of the plane, the thin airline blanket pulled over her face, accepting nothing from the flight attendants, hearing nothing of the other passengers' stir and murmur. She had never in her life been afraid on flights before. But this time, although her eyes were closed, she was wretchedly awake, rigid with stillness, feeling every plunge and shudder of wing and fuselage, her mind contracted on a single image: a row of white-painted bolts working themselves loose, one after another, on some load-bearing metal strut 35,000 feet above the storm-tossed Atlantic. Only with an intense effort — by somehow ripping up her fixated brain by the roots and setting it to think of every good thing she had ever known in Petersburg — did she conquer her urge to beg for whatever it was the crew was rumored to carry for passengers who went insane.

The Good Things Trick was a mental discipline she had learned from her brother twenty-five years ago, one night when their parents were screaming at each other in the front of the car — late, lost, and circling in the dark, miles from the holiday cottage. She had practiced and honed it many times since then. But she had not tried for at least a decade. And she wondered if she still had the will.

The images came and went, came and went, came and lingered, came and stayed, illuminating the vast and vivid screen of her fine imagination . . . The new blini restaurant on Kolkonaya, behind the Nevsky Palace Hotel, with hot pancakes, savory and sweet, where she and Gabriel had sat one Christmas and wasted the brilliant blue of a Boxing Day sky reading the thin, out-of-date *St. Petersburg*

Times, ordering more and more, saying nothing, drinking coffee after coffee, plates piling up in droll testimony to something gross or affirmative or just plain alive; or here, years ago, Yana's grinning face and the endless varieties of vodka they were drinking together, true friends, after-hours at the CCCP Café, just opened, *Highway 61 Revisited* turned up as loud as the stereo would go; or here was her twenty-four-year-old self, before the millennium turned, having some sort of a thing with Arytom, and they had nearly fallen in the canal because they were so drunk and stoned — except it was iced over — and they had crept in past Yana's mother and Yana herself to Arytom's tiny room at the back of the apartment and made love in absolute silence, bedclothes forever slipping off her shivery shoulders, he looking up, eyes wide in the darkness, holding her head in his hands, lips parting without a sound when the moment came; or here she was during the White Nights of the tercentenary year in the middle of the sheer frenzy at Troika opposite those shabby-grand shadowed arches of Gostiny Dvor, the midnight sky, the long day's ghost; or, yes, the first time back to officially-Petersburg-not-Leningrad! as an adult, the January after her grandfather Max died, turning off the Nevsky, down by the Fontanka Canal, where she had walked that night with her mother, a girl of nineteen no more, and it had seemed to her then that all the old palaces were lit in great amber teardrops by the glow of the streetlamps, in pink and yellow, in silvery damask, in ivory and pearl, and there were skaters already dancing on the ice, torches lit and chasing back and forth like children's souls, and later it was so cold in the rented apartment that when she climbed out of the camp bed to find her coat to lay on top of her blankets, she could see her breath passing from her lips in the dim blue of the pilot light, flickering hopefully on though all the pipes were frozen tight.

The plane scored across the darkening sky like a misshapen crucifix tearing a wound in the heavens.

9

A Savage Freedom

L E CASTEBIN WAS all candle-flicker, cream linen, and chiaro-
scuro. Their supper, though, was a little less solipsistic than
usual. Partly because Nicholas allowed himself to become drunk
more quickly than was customary and thus was prepared to give unusual voice to habitually concealed thoughts. And partly because
Alessandro too was concentrating and responsive for once — eliciting
information, seeking to draw Nicholas out, though for reasons of
his own.

In truth, Alessandro's sole and busy aim ever since Nicholas had
disclosed the news of his wife's death was to work out the new situation with regard to money. His most itchy hope: an allowance. Now,
surely, given that Nicholas was no longing paying his wife's fat rent
or living expenses, there was a chance that the tetchy old tart might
be prepared to rechannel at least a portion of this expenditure in
Alessandro's direction. Those funds that he wasn't used to keeping
for himself he would not miss — something like that. The question,
therefore, was how much extra did Nicholas have with the hag out
of the way? How much to pitch for? Certainly Alessandro deserved
something regular. Because while this shitty little money thing with
Nicholas continued, his inventory of the balance of pros and cons —
the default loop of all Alessandro's thoughts — kept coming up nega-
tive. Yes to Paris. Yes to the apartment and the parties therein. Yes
to the restaurants and yes to the musical soirées and yes to opera
and blah-de-blah-de-blah. All puttable-up with — as long as darling
Nicky never got jealous of his trips to Greece. But having to ask for
money all the time! No. Having to explain that he'd run out *again*.

And oh the boring palaver with the fountain pen in the study—the silly old slut waving the check around for ten minutes, pretending to wait for the ink to dry. No. No. No. So if he could just get an allowance—even a small one for now—then everything would be as perfect as could be. Choose the moment, though. Be as charming as champagne. Actually (Alessandro was beginning to believe), it wasn't going to be that difficult: Nicholas looked quite handsome tonight, with his short hair and those straight white eyebrows—the brutal but very fanciable father-general in the film about the sexy slacker of a son who hates the army but eventually rescues America just the same.

As was his habit, Alessandro made great play of his winsome desire for sweetness by reading out each of the possibilities—temptations narrowly resisted—until, at length, he declared that no, he couldn't possibly have chocolate again and how about a coffee instead?

The waiter bowed—a man long ago departed from these shallows for distant oceans of indifference.

"How are you feeling, Nicholas? Are you tired? God, you've had the longest day. Thank you for this, by the way. I love eating with you."

"You don't have to say thank you. It's not necessary."

"Do you want to talk about your trip?"

"I'm not tired."

This was true. Nicholas was not tired, or not locally so, at least. He returned his attention to his glass—the lazy bubbles drifting languidly to the surface. All that fizz and fuss seemed so long ago. Apart from Alessandro's extraordinary physical beauty—and he really was Perugino-pretty—his great virtue was that he did not matter in the slightest. And occasionally Nicholas felt that he could say whatever the hell he wished to him, confident that he would neither understand nor reflect upon it.

Nicholas shifted his chair so he could pull his legs from under the table and stretch them out to one side.

"Life let her down, you know, Alessandro. Politics let her down. Russia let her down. London let her down. And I . . . well, I couldn't give her what she wanted, what she needed. Poor woman. Poor bloody woman." He shook his head.

"When did you two . . ." Alessandro swirled his remaining wine around his mouth, making it froth. "When did you two meet?"

"We met in Russia—in Moscow—at a party, actually. One of

my father's little get-togethers with his Soviet acquaintances. She had just started working in the Secretariat. She was a rising star and she was accompanying some idiot from the Party. She was . . . she was a very clever woman." Nicholas looked directly at Alessandro. "She defected to marry me, you know. Abandoned it all six months later: family, job, and friends. Her home. Can you imagine anyone understanding that now? Defecting. The sheer risk. The absolute finality of the severance." Nicholas set his glass down, two long fingers pressing at the base, and spoke softly. "Knowing you can never go back. Making a decision like that takes courage. Real courage."

Like all small-time egotists, Alessandro was in the habit of believing every remark to pertain in some way to himself—oblique praise or oblique criticism. And so now he sought to assert his own courage. But could see no obvious opportunity and so chose the next best thing—an indirect attack on what he perceived to be Nicholas's cowardice. "When did . . . when did she *know?*"

Nicholas ignored the question. "We had three or four good years —yes, it's hard to believe now, but we did. Even when the children arrived. We were always friends. Or at least we always understood each other. Understood the exact nature of each other's knots, even if we could not exactly undo them . . . You might find this hard to believe, Alessandro, but actually I think we were happy. Really."

Alessandro widened his eyes and said breathily, "In love."

But Nicholas was way past his usual irritation at his lover's illimitable falsity. "For Christ's sake, it was impossible not to be happy: young—*young* and in Paris, sharing a single room in Zola country with a Russian defectress who had left everything to be with me. My God, it seems like a different city . . ." He tailed off. The mention of those days had made him aware of how old he was, how old he suddenly felt. And the fact that Alessandro hadn't been born when he had married. *When he had married.* How in Christ's name did these things happen? Life passed faster and faster: whole decades racing by like rushing landscapes glimpsed from the window of a perpetually accelerating train. He finished his wine, the taste a welcome reminder of the present. He had never had money back then—or even the prospect, if he was to be honest.

"Did you always live in Russia?" Indulge the old bitch, Alessandro thought, lull him deeper into this softness of spirit.

"I was at boarding school in England, Alessandro. I lived in a dormitory full of boys."

"Oh yeah. I forgot about that. Sounds perfect."

"But yes, Russia was home. In the holidays, anyway. From the age of eleven until Cambridge."

"St. Petersburg?"

"No. Moscow, when my father was at the embassy officially, and then Leningrad afterward, when he was sent there to do whatever the bloody hell he was doing."

Alessandro tilted his head. "You never talk about your family."

"You know that I was married, you know—"

"No, I mean your—you know—your dad and all that. Your old family. The Glovers." Alessandro had glimpsed a path through the trees ahead. By way of family . . . to money. Family money. There was plenty of that, he was certain. He allowed himself a blink. "Your dad—*the spy.*"

"My father wasn't a spy." Nicholas returned his lover's gaze directly. "My father was a shit."

"Oh." Alessandro withered beneath the sudden flare of disdain. "I thought he was at Cambridge with all those others . . ."

Wearily, Nicholas suspected he was hearing the story that Alessandro liked to spin to his sun-bed friends at the gym. And suddenly he wanted to exterminate the myth once and for all, even where its peddling did not matter.

"My father was a bloody fool. He liked to pretend that he was friends with the big men, but he wasn't. I doubt they even knew who he was. He was peripheral, small-time, and he never got the top job."

"The ambassador?"

"He liked to believe he could have been the top dog if not for his greater use elsewhere. But it's bloody rubbish. He was like a randy little rat—and he got caught inseminating half of Moscow. Both sides can smell a man like that straightaway. Totally compromised from early on . . . And the others, as you call them—well, perhaps they were in it for principles, so one is asked to believe. But my father—my father, it turns out, was in it for nothing more than cheap Russian skirt. And bribes. Took it from anyone and everyone like a rent boy." Nicholas made a conscious effort to relax his jaw. "He was a cheat and probably a thief too. All those paintings we have are the rewards of his conniving, bribing, smuggling. He lined his pockets by lining the pockets of the people who let him line his pockets. The clash of ideologies could have been a game of bloody brag for all he cared. It only mattered insofar as he could bet on it."

Alessandro sucked his coffee spoon. "But he was still a sort of . . . mystery man?"

Nicholas shut his eyes a moment, determined not to allow the Italian's insistent banality to exasperate him. "I suppose . . . I suppose he must have been up to something, because the British let him go to Leningrad as the unofficial consul instead of recalling him. Which also means the Soviets must have let him go to Leningrad. Which means *something* was going on. Because — yes, you're right — ordinarily our Red friends didn't want Englishmen snooping around the naval yards. I doubt, though, that he was of much actual use to anyone. Probably only got away with it because he was so easily blackmailed by all sides and . . . Christ, you have no idea how very sick the whole world was then." He paused. "And my father was the sickest person in it."

"God, it must have been so weird."

Nicholas looked at the ceiling. That the great dark leviathans' struggle of the cold war should now be reduced to "weird" . . . His mind turned away. And suddenly he had an image of himself as a boy, playing backgammon with his nanny in the courtyard of the embassy, every single summer holiday afternoon of his adolescence wasted — not allowed to leave the house, not allowed to do anything but wait. That was Russia. Waiting for it to end.

"It was lonely," he said after a moment.

"Hmmm . . . I bet your father wasn't very good at expressing his emotions." Alessandro's face betrayed thought. "And you know, probably that's why *you* don't like expressing emotions. No, seriously. You were not allowed to feel, so you learned to touch. These things" — he rested his chin on his cupped hands — "they *so* get passed on."

Nicholas smiled tightly. Perhaps he had Alessandro wrong after all. Perhaps there was an intelligence in there, lurking beneath all the crème caramel.

"I have no idea," he said. "We hardly spoke to each other for the last thirty years of his life."

"Anyway," Alessandro continued, as if it were all part of the same thought, "I still think being an art dealer is pretty glamorous and enigmatic, and your father made a lot of money in his business, didn't he?"

"Business." Nicholas finished his wine. "What exactly *is* business?"

"You told me he even conned the president into swapping a picture. Buy them as bargains, sell them as treasures." Alessandro tilted his head first one way, then the other. "Equals make a tidy profit."

"The general secretary, not the president. And not the general secretary himself, but his dealer." Nicholas sighed. "Yes, he did, Alessandro. He made a lot of money shafting everyone. He understood corruption intimately and it was the one thing he was very good at. Probably because he believed in absolutely nothing. Nothing at all. Not even art. A curious sort of freedom. But he must have surprised even the Russians with his venality." Nicholas looked directly at his lover again. "Let's go to Berthillons and get an ice cream. I want to walk. I'm tired of sitting. And you are not really listening."

But Nicholas was wrong. Alessandro had been listening as never before. Indeed, as far as he was concerned, this was the most interesting conversation they had ever had — the first emotional confidences that Nicholas had shared. And the first real hint, therefore, that he, Alessandro, might have acquired some purchase on what was going on inside. (The display of feelings: very important.) The only problem being, Alessandro reckoned, as he now stood up and squeezed the side of his tongue hard between his perfect teeth, that the moment to ask for an allowance had gone. Maybe later, though — maybe on the walk down the quay. Or maybe tonight was a bad time altogether. Hard to judge. Maybe all of this was because Nicholas was — would you believe it? — upset. Now *that* was a new one.

The two men, thinking very different thoughts about their very different lives, walked side by side until they came to the Quai de Bourbon, where they turned left, homeward, once more along the river's edge. And now, oblivious of the covert impatience in Alessandro's self-conscious step, Nicholas began to linger a little, looking out across the river toward the Quai de l'Hôtel de Ville and the lights of the city rising red beyond. He had started feeling old again. His knees hurt with pain he dared not have confirmed or named, and sixty-two — *sixty-two* — sixty-two felt . . . plain elderly. Neither wiser nor mellowed nor yet magnanimous, but merely elderly. Infirm, unwise, uncertain — as though he personally had seen the world repeat the same mistakes too often, leaving him with no intelligent choice but faithlessness and nothing to do about it but await the onset of failing faculties.

They were approaching their entrance when he stopped and exhaled slowly. "You go on in, Alessandro. I'm going to wait out here.

I want to . . . I think I want to watch the river or go for a walk or something."

"Are you okay?"

"Yes, I'm fine."

Alessandro nibbled at his cone. "What do you —"

"Or go out, if you want to. Out to a club, I mean." Nicholas raised his hand to his lover's back, aware (with the slim fraction of his mind that he allowed to think about it) that Alessandro would be secretly relieved by this sanction but would have to pretend not to have had the thought. A thin grimalkin disappeared beneath a fat black car. To hasten the process, Nicholas turned to face Alessandro and found his most conciliatory tone. "I'm serious. I'm no good tonight. Go. Phone your friends and have fun. I don't mind. Really."

Alessandro was now at a loss. His earlier reading of the evening was melting with the last of his ice cream. Yet still he was beset by the urgent need to achieve his goal while everything remained possible. He bent his head childishly toward Nicholas's chest, a gesture executed for no better reason than to buy time in which to decide whether or not now was the moment to ask. Oh *God*. No. No — discretion was the better part of, he thought, best to leave it. Best not to risk it. And so why not? Why not go out? After all, maybe Nicholas actually wanted to be alone. A bonus evening! But best not to get back too late and better make sure nothing happened. God, the old general might even cry in the night, and he'd really better be there for that.

Nicholas fed him what was left of his own ice cream, wanting the whole charade over quickly, wanting to save Alessandro even the necessity of saying anything else, wanting desperately to be alone. "There's a cab coming. I'll stop it for you. Here, take . . ." He reached for his wallet.

Alessandro would have liked to have changed but realized that the delay would seriously annoy Nicholas. He patted his pocket, seeking the reassurance of his mobile phone. "Are you sure, Nicholas? I mean, I am happy — I had no plans to —"

"I'm probably going to walk . . . down to Notre Dame or something."

"That will be nice. Clear your head."

"Yes."

Alessandro accepted the money with studied casualness.

The cab pulled up and wallowed by the curb.

"I won't be late." Alessandro kissed the tips of his fingers and placed them on Nicholas's cheek.

And Nicholas turned back to the river.

The Seine was as dark as history itself, and only the faint sound of its lapping at the embankment below gave the lie to its seeming stillness. Nicholas leaned forward onto the stone wall so that he could see down to the narrow bank-side path. The trees had been pollarded that afternoon and the night air was scented still with sap. He raised his eyes. The severed branches like great misshapen agonized limbs. And above them, the brightest of the stars — names he had learned and forgotten, learned and forgotten — needling their pinpoint antiquity through the city sky. Paris would be cooler tonight. But he knew he would not be able to sleep, and he knew that neither whisky nor coupling would help. For the first time in more than thirty years, Nicholas wanted the company of his blood — not the amicable converse of friendship, not the parley of a lover, but the marrow-talk of kin and consanguinity.

But there was no kin anymore. No kin save for Gabriel and Isabella, and neither, he knew well, could be persuaded to say so much as a single word to him, even were he to pay them in sweat or tears — not in letter, not by telephone, and never again in person. And he could not blame them. He had never once tried to talk to them.

Though wasn't it true that he had not been allowed to talk to them? Not about anything that really counted. Masha had strictly forbidden it. And she was their great protectress. (In some way, he thought, her Russian pride actually measured its strength by keeping secrets.) Then again, he could never quite be trusted. Whatever the cause — fatally distracted, indifferent, drunk, indolent, dissipated, dissolute, or preoccupied, he knew not what — the fact was that he had surrendered all familial sway to her in return for his savage freedom. Ah, grandest of all ironies: that she had been the one to care for them — their minds, their health, their hearts, the well-being of their twin susceptible souls. And thank God, for that was perhaps the only noble act in his entire life that he had managed to stand by. But still, perhaps a call . . . No. It was too late, and there was no way to begin. Profoundly, Gabriel and Isabella did not understand him, did not know him — neither as a man nor as a human being. Did not even know who he really was. After all these years . . . Christ, the bloody madness of it all. The bloody mess.

He stood up straight and walked another few yards, eyes tracking from one lighted window to the next. He suspected himself of maudlin self-indulgence. But the truth was, he had not thought it would affect him. Or not like this. His own tedious egotism, he knew, was causing the forefront of his mind to think about her death as a prelude to his own. But deeper than that, behind the facile and the obvious, there was something else, something intangible but real and hitherto unperceived: a hollowness he had not known the shape of before; a hollowness where his conscience should have been, perhaps. And somehow this emptiness, though composed of nothing, had prickled and tremored through the day like some forgotten disease. Slight but certain. Hardly anything. Nothing.

He turned back to the river and now — as a nameless night barge came stealing by, floodlights fore, freight unknown — now her face came back to him, not as he had last seen her but young: black, black hair, those wide turquoise eyes full of tenacity and temerity, the easy disparagement of her cheekbones, the thin cracked lips, the high-bridged nose, the proportions of her frame, taut, wiry, flat-chested (the better to wear her impenetrable breastplate in battle, he had realized) — she struck him in this moment's vision as if she were some princess of the tundra come south for obscure reprisals.

He looked up. Two lovers were walking toward him, the young man with his arm strong around the woman, seeking the Seine's blessing and a quiet place to kiss. They stopped a little way along, his hand on the contour of her body. Ah . . . now this he *did* understand. The sweet mercy of lust. The day's anxiety was but a passing mood after all. And what was conscience but mood wearing a uniform?

10

The Chernobyl Mongeese

BARBARA WAS BUSY amid the flurry and congestion of the ticket desk but she waved him through over the heads of the people in the queue. He was a regular at Fish, though less and less these days, and she had once been his student. He passed inside, inching like a stick insect along the bare wall of the congested corridor, excusing himself in Russian as he entered the cavernous main room, treading gingerly around stretched-out legs and vulnerable hands spread on the floor, squeezing between chairs, picking his way toward the miniature wooden table that was reserved (as promised by Sergei, the manager) in the center of the second row, directly beneath the low vertex of the brickwork arch above his head. Here the acoustics were as good as the room allowed.

He sat down, shut his eyes a moment, then opened the complimentary mineral water provided, which of course was neither complimentary nor mineral — Sergei's "table tax" and the back-room tap giving the lie to both claims. But there was no chance of attaining the body-soaked bar, all the way at the far end of the room. So he took a deep gulp.

Now that he was alone, his mind scrambled to reach a clear understanding of what the news meant — for Arkady, but also for himself. The source was depressingly reliable: Grisha, messenger (dealer) for and associate (henchman) of the even more indeterminately extracted Leary — full name Learichenko — the syndicate-sanctioned regional controller of all matters poppy in Petersburg and the man who usually knew most things most often most quickly. Yes, Maria Glover was definitely dead. No doubt about it. Presumably, therefore, Grisha (and so Leary) thought that he, Henry, was also living off Maria Glover and that her death was the blow that would send him into their arms.

It was Grisha who had twice asked Henry to push among the ever-growing but ultra-cautious expatriate community. Henry knew the reasons why well enough: the money from many of the Russian addicts was desperately difficult to come by, constant work to extract and easily dried up (into corpses), while the better clients — the seriously wealthy Russians — were more than likely connected and went over Leary's head via Moscow or direct; so what Leary wanted most of all was Eurotrash, wealthy expatriates who would trust only a Western dealer.

But of course Grisha and Leary were wrong in their suppositions about Maria Glover's support. Henry had in fact been using his own money — what was left of the fifty thousand pounds he had made selling his damp little house. (Not much now, not much. He picked at the label of his water with his fingernails.) And yet . . . and yet they were also right. Because what mattered most to Henry was what mattered most to Arkady. And as far as the Russian was concerned, Henry realized, the whole edifice had collapsed this last hour (with the cold and unforgiving instantaneousness of death) into a sudden rubble of questions. Had she left a will? Was Arkady provided for? Arkady had just started his second year. This term's tuition would probably have been paid already. They'd know soon enough if not. Certainly, without her funding, the corrupt members on the committee (in the papers again for embezzlement this very week) would refuse Arkady his place for the remaining year and a half, regardless of his teacher's petitions. If he were not given some kind of a legacy, then Arkady would be out. No final concert. No launch. No expectation and no concomitant resource or opportunity. No graduation of any sort. More or less back where he started. Good. Brilliant, even. But amateur.

Unless — Henry's mind began to move forward again — the wider family might be persuaded to help. (How many more people was Sergei going to cram in here?) Henry cursed himself. He couldn't remember what anyone in Maria Glover's family was called. Idiotic of him. He should have developed the acquaintance. She had seemed open enough — willing. But — damn, damn, damn — he could not now be sure if she had mentioned a single person by name, let alone where they lived or what they did. Where were her "new" children? Was her husband dead? She had never said one way or the other.

Would any of them know anything at all about Arkady? He very much doubted it. God, he had been a fool; but then, you don't expect people to die—no matter how often it happens, you just don't expect it.

Sitting there at his tiny table (label now shredded, cheap glue sticky on his fingers), Henry could think of only one thing to try: call Zoya as soon as possible, during the intermission. Make inquiries. Discover what she knew. A shameful thought slipped nimbly through the door after the others: that Arkady might never get out of the flat after all. Henry cringed involuntarily, glanced around, almost as if to see whether his mind might have been somehow overheard, and then began to survey the room more thoroughly to distract himself.

Over by the entrance, a clutter of students were having their hands stamped with the indecipherable fluorescent insignia of the club. Sergei himself—a startlingly faithful doppelgänger of Mussolini if ever there was one—came bustling through the door again and started remonstrating with them (all jowls and chops and slather) to move farther inside, though clearly there was nowhere farther inside for them to move to, since along both brick walls, all the way back to the buried bar, people were standing three deep. It was now quarter past ten and Fish was as full as he had ever seen it. Fifteen minutes to go. Clearly the word was abroad: people were not here to see the support acts.

The lugubrious hum and chunter of a hundred Russian conversations reverberated off the curve of the shallow-arched ceiling, making individual exchanges impossible to catch or follow. Henry saw that additional chairs were being sneaked between the tables, blocking the way, so that latecomers could cram in with their friends. He assessed the crowd. Most were younger—the students and those whose dress indicated that they would be going on afterward to other clubs. But by no means all. Fish could seldom have had such a mixed clientele. The real surprise was the number of older people. A group of weathered old-timers sat immediately to his left—aficionados, judging by their modest glasses of beer and heavy brown suit jackets worn over sweaters despite the heat, men who must have tiptoed through the dark decades listening to their heroes with the volume down. Even more unusually, right at the front there was a table drinking champagne—unheard of in Fish—the women with their dedicated approximations of the latest Hollywood hair, bedizened in designer jeans and jewelry, and the forty- or fifty-year-old men in Armani or Gucci; either business or the government, Henry thought. Institutional mafia. His mouth felt dry. He took the last gulp of water. The students were laying down newspaper: they had decided simply to sit on the floor right in front of the stage; he watched as one filled his glass covertly from a flask while another, a young woman, demonstrated with her arms what she obviously felt was the ostentatious posture adopted by some pianist or other — music students, then, from the conservatory.

Aside from the erroneous plural of "mongoose" (which he would have taken a teacher's pleasure in correcting), the irony of the entire concert, Henry realized, was that Arkady himself was the only person uneasy about the numbers: one of the Russian's few articulated fears — and the reason he had disbanded Magizdat — was that he might become well known for jazz before he had finished his course and had the chance to establish himself as a concert pianist. And Henry could now see that Arkady was right: this was the Chernobyl Mongeese's first night in nearly a year, and already he was in danger of gathering a following again — locally, at least — for his hobby rather than his true work. The *Petersburg Times* was almost certainly here. Arkady used a stage name, but there would be a picture, unless he had somehow arranged for that to be prevented. (The stage dimmed and Henry felt a tangible charge of anticipation enter the room, seeming to draw energy to itself.) And yet if everything were about to collapse again, would Arkady continue to cling to his ambition? Would he stick to his self-imposed rule — that the Mongeese would live for three nights and three nights only? Or, if the money stopped, would Arkady's desire finally give out as well?

The house lights went all the way down. The room shrank. And suddenly, waiting in the dark with three hundred other eager bodies, Henry felt the piercing needle of his conscience followed by the all-consuming flood of his duty. Obsessed compulsion or sober free will, he did not care; this was what he must do. Keep trying. Find a way. Don't give up. Not yet. Make Arkady finish the fucking course. At least ask the family first. And he, Henry Wheyland, would be the man to tell his friend of his mother's death — right after the concert.

There was an agonized whine. Then an amplified voice asking for quiet sounded from the stage. Sergei stood at the principal microphone, his pate glistening beneath the spot and his tormented T-shirt straining against his bulbous stomach as he spoke. He completed his introduction by naming each member of the band in turn, then raised his arms and began clapping above his head. The charge leaped the gap, the fuel was ignited, and the answering applause ricocheted off the brick. Someone with spiky hair came out from the back of the stage, hand up against the glare of the spot, crazed shadow on the black wall behind. He was followed by another, taller figure. The other stage lights went up. The clapping was redoubled. Sergei jumped heavily down. And one by one, the Chernobyl Mongeese came forward, looking less like musicians than men accustomed to breaking rocks on some forgotten desert chain gang, long days of thirst and shuffling — unkempt, ruefully aware of the intimacy of their work, determined to look anywhere but at the audience.

Despite their individual talents, Henry could tell they were conscious of the fragility of their impromptu ensemble. Since last year's series — also for three nights only — he knew well that they had rehearsed only twice all together. They took up their various positions: Yevgeny (the drummer, and the only other from Magizdat) dragged his snare closer; the double bass player settled, then resettled his spike; trumpet player and saxophonist, instruments lowered, fingers already flexing over valves, looked away from the audience, inward, at Yevgeny, as though aware that his patient placings and careful rearrangings — stool a little to the left, cymbal a fraction to the right — were the necessary rites by which their observances must begin. Arkady, meanwhile, unable to adjust his seat up or down, simply sat there, waiting, staring blankly at his hands.

There was a moment of pure silence.

Then, suddenly, there it was, manifest among them: the age-old miracle of music. Where before there had been people-din, chair-scrape, glass-chink, fractured, fractious, fragmentary sound, now there was only the startling beauty of harmony and rhythm and order, of tone and skill, the compelling narrative of human talent expressing itself.

They began by playing something that Henry did not quite recognize, something with a walking bass line that beckoned insolently to the putative soloists on either side of the beat, daring them to cut loose. From the second row, his gaze could settle anonymously on his friend; but for the moment he shut his eyes and channeled his entirety into listening, seeking to recalibrate his classical English ear, to appreciate the slip and the shuffle, the skid, the slide, seeking to understand better what this free form of music meant to Arkady, for whom all kinds of playing were part of an endless continuum. He was reminded now that he had first fallen in love with his friend's gift when he had heard Arkady performing jazz, not practicing sonatas or concerti. There was the extraordinary clarity of his articulation and his breathtaking improvisational skill, but neither of these qualities had appealed to Henry the most; rather, it was Arkady's *generosity*. Then (as now — for here came the piano, dancing to the fore again), there was something deeply affecting about listening to a man with such an evident gift play so selflessly with and for (and even through) musicians who had a fraction of his ability. More than that: over time, Henry had realized that when Arkady was performing in an improvisational environment, he seemed somehow to participate in his fellows' struggles — to savor their triumphs, suffer their mistakes — as if all of this were part of the wider effort of musicians the world over to help one another understand the mysterious syntax of their language.

In no other part of his life did Arkady exhibit even so much as a warm mood. Yet Henry could hear him now as they entered the second number — something careful and more intricate, with less swagger and more intimacy — could hear him taking care not to impede the others, nudging along with the bass (elbow to elbow at the back of the class), joking with the trumpet (after you; no, after you), playful rival to the saxophonist (beat that, pal), but never intrusive. He was everywhere and nowhere; he was forward, he was back; he was side to side; all the while conducting an urgent but underlying conversation with the others that somehow mattered absolutely but never distracted from the main oration.

Henry opened his eyes. He recognized this second tune. Something he knew in another context — something he had heard Billie Holiday sing, perhaps? A version of "Loveless Love"? Maybe. Arkady was in his usual loosened-up posture now, leaning back, sitting deep in the music, playing easy progressions, letting the saxophonist lead. But it was a deceptive relaxation, for in reality, Henry knew, his friend was using the easy wandering of the song to acquaint himself with the various deficiencies of the strange keyboard, quickly adjusting the weight of each finger to compensate for the odd ash-burned felt or random vodka-soaked damper, all in preparation for the time when he would break loose and make the instrument sing on its own. Almost as much as the music itself, Henry liked the intimacy of this knowledge, observing something he alone could see. Sometimes Arkady appeared to coax the keys with the flat-fingered elegance of Horowitz; sometimes he came at them with the near-vertical attack of Thelonious Monk. By the end of the song, though, Henry could tell that the Russian had learned the entire keyboard; notwithstanding their variously tendered sick notes and excuses (as the band swung straight into the third number), Arkady Alexandrovitch now had the notes running up and down in perfectly produced lines, as though they were the very specimens of good health and endeavor.

Henry disliked intermissions — the whole of his life was an intermission. He didn't drink, and there was no chance of gaining the bar in any case. But he was glad of the air.

Outside, Moskovsky station was more than usually heavy with police; something was happening, or somebody suspected that something was about to happen. The open wound of the terror-torn south, blood seeping up the railway lines, dripping into the cities one bead at a time, and the same solution here as everywhere else in the world: tighten the tourniquet. With one finger in his ear against the remorselessly careering traffic, Henry could not raise Zoya in person. Her number was ringing, which was something, but either she was asleep or she wasn't answering. It was getting late, but still . . . you would hope that of all people, private detectives would pick up after-hours calls.

He drew a lungful of the damp air; tonight it felt as if the sky itself were weighed down by something vast and alien above. There would be a proper thunderstorm soon. The weather made him nervous. The police made him nervous. The cars swinging madly around the war monument made him nervous. Maria Glover's death made him nervous. Everything made him nervous. Everything — except his fix, his boy. He tried again and this time left a message. This is Henry Wheyland. I met you last year regarding Arkady Alexandrovitch. I understand that Maria Glover has passed away, and we wondered if you could . . .

To the people hurrying by, he looked more like the glimpse of some Grimm-conceived scarecrow than a human being, standing there in the half-light of a cigarette shop, the letters of the station illuminated behind him — MOSKOVSKY VOKZAL, his jacket hanging slack on his frame as he murmured things into an ancient cell phone in a slightly academic Russian, for whom?

From the moment the Mongeese came back on, Henry could see that Arkady knew his mother was dead. Something in his manner told. Told that everything in his world had been detonated again. Told that here was a man changed — changing — even as he took his seat. Though they could not know the reason, the whole room seemed to feel the change too, seemed to be craning forward collectively, as if the rumor had gone around that they were about to witness some pivotal moment of nature.

The band played ensemble for a few bars. The saxophone took a short solo over the chord sequence. The trumpet followed. And then, almost hurriedly, they were back together. This was a song not so much fast as urgent, a song of avowal in an importuning six/eight.

One by one, the other musicians began to withdraw from the tune, like a ballet chorus inching toward the wings in anticipation of the grand jeté of the principal male. The horn players stepped back from their microphones, a quickened fade; then, stealthily, the bass player likewise dropped away, leaving just Arkady and Yevgeny. Old friends, these two, and Henry found himself leaning toward their play along with everyone else. Arkady began to let his fingers work a little faster, running mini-scales around and around and up and down, loosening the knots of time, until the beat itself began to crumble away and Yevgeny likewise disappeared into silence.

And suddenly the piano was alone.

There was something tight in the lines of Arkady's brow that Henry had not seen before. Something strange was happening to Arkady's relationship to the piano too. It was as if he had begun to live — breathe, talk, move — only through the keyboard. As if the instrument were becoming part of him, the keys no more than an extension of his arms and his arms merely a lateral articulation of the keys, the dampers, the singing wires themselves. To eye now, as well as to ear, pianist and piano were one and the same. As a man might inhabit his own body, so Arkady appeared to inhabit the mass or density of his instrument, as if he had assumed command not only of sound but also of the space and time that the piano occupied — could ever occupy — as if every capability of the instrument was known and understood and all alike were his to deploy or withhold on the instant. As if the quick of his will was alive in the grain of the soundboard.

At first he stayed with what was familiar — clearly recognizable variations on the tune, each bowing decorously and paying due respect to its progenitor; but bar by bar he began to stretch convention, risking more, straying further. The room's breath was stilled and the tune was unrecognizably transformed, and the notes were shimmering and shimmying, pouring and pouring, cascading out of the piano in great glittering waterfalls of sound, dazzling, dancing, and yet each individual purposely lit in its own special livery of color and tone. He was playing as Henry had never heard him play: back

and forth across rhythm and time signatures, the first beat of the bar
long ago discarded (though hiding somewhere, Henry could sense, in
between notes). And yet the Russian seemed determined that no single person be left behind on his journey, so he kept doubling back
to the almost-forgotten tune, sounding echoes in adjacent registers,
raising finger posts, urging the whole club along with him, stragglers
too, all bound, faster and faster, for some new upland of music that
he wanted to show them . . . And now, just as they were all arriving
on the very summit, just as people were raising their hands to clap,
as if by magic, he was gone. Vanished through some secret trapdoor,
only to reappear somewhere far below them all . . . And where did
all this sudden sadness come from? Or was this the tune again? Not
quite. Not quite. Something else, something heartbreaking, something profound, something solemn . . . And then, just as Arkady
seemed lost for good, here he came once more, racing back with his
left hand to greet the momentarily beleaguered audience, a wide gri-
mace spreading across his face that became now almost a grin, and
in three quick figures he had brought the whole swirling madness under control, and — astonishingly, astoundingly — there was that old
beat again, that importuning six/eight, and one by one the other musicians picked up their instruments and stepped forward and Arkady
was back in the original key and his arms were open wide in warm-
hearted musical invitation, and in they all came in perfect formation,
because yes, there it was again — beat number one, and only in that
moment of resolution, somehow, did the entire solo make sense, and
the old men in their Soviet jackets were clapping and even the endless self-appraisal of the Gucci couples was finally vanquished, and
on the Mongeese went, all together, Arkady looking around, catching the eyes of the others, finger briefly raised to poke them up a
semitone from F to F sharp, the nightmare key, but no matter or fear,
for all five of them were playing as if there were nothing else in the
world to say or do but sound these very notes this night in this very
order, and neither Henry nor anybody else in the club ever saw or
heard anything like it ever again, because on learning that his fragile
world might be about to collapse back into the misfortune and misery from which it had so briefly risen, Arkady Alexandrovich had
taken a private vow: to free himself from the endless agony of these
contingent circumstances, to never again sit down to play another
piano until he knew for certain that he could play forever or not at
all and be damned.

11

The Narrow Angle of Dead Ahead

A T NOON THE FOLLOWING DAY, Wednesday, Gabriel walked due west along Nevsky, passing among the crowds clustering at the metro station, looking neither right nor left but waiting self-possessed in their midst to cross at the lights, then on again, stepping up the high curb and so to the Kazansky Bridge — cries in coarse Russian from below, the canal-tour boats, a tout shouting in English, the muddy water silent. Glancing neither down nor across the dusty road at the great curved colonnades of Kazan Cathedral, he went on, the narrow angle of dead ahead all that he permitted himself.

The crowd congealed, forcing him to slow almost to a halt. He felt as if he were deep underwater now: he could not hear and people loomed, swam at him, disappeared on either side. He seemed to have lost time and connectedness too: the day past, the day present, all days future — impossible to believe in, impossible to experience, minutes swollen to years, hours shrunk to seconds.

He had hoped to appear anonymous today, in blue jeans (wallet in the front, following the manner of his father, to counter pickpockets real or imagined), in cornflower blue shirt with breast-pocket cigarettes, in light brown running shoes, with black backpack over one shoulder, in sunglasses. A would-be tourist. Except . . . except that it was such a beautiful day. And how could all these people not be aware? How could they not guess? He brought the heel of his hand to his cheekbone and dropped quickly into the dim underpass, away from the sun, moving to the outer stream of the throng, slowing, then stopping, then trying to press himself unobtrusively into the side shadow of the illegal-CD seller's stall, turning his face to the gray nothing of the wall, removing his glasses, bringing thumb and forefinger to bear additional pressure on his eyelids, already squeezed tight shut against this new leak.

He was horrified that he had started. Somehow, with Connie tears were limitable, containable, there was someone to pull him out; but on his own — Christ. There was no control. He was terrified that he might cry forever.

He had not slept a single moment. For all its kindness, the careless *life* of Yana's bedroom had become a kind of torture. The soft pillows, the posters, the photographs, the ancient teddy bear, the casual tangle on the dressing table. And so all through the long night, all he could think to do was smoke at the window. Because . . . because it seemed as meaningless to speak as to cry, to pray as to wish, to sleep as to stare, meaningless even to feel. Nothing changed: she was dead, forever dead.

No one in the underpass had noticed. But soon the storekeeper was sure to wonder what he was doing, part the side curtain, peer around and ask him what he wanted. No matter. He was already moving on, already emerging into the enthusiastic sun, already stepping past the old woman's cart of drinks, placed deliberately athwart the pedestrian stream on the pavement.

There were bound to be bad moments, of course. On the first day. And it *was* only the first day — yes, it was bound to be bad. This much he knew. Had he not edited an entire issue of *Self-Help!* on this very thing? Grief comes in tightly bound packages, his experts said: vast at first — mighty deliveries that take days and nights to unwrap, waiting on the doorstep of consciousness first thing each morning; but they become gradually smaller, less regular. Or at least you learn how to deal with them. How to go on living despite.

But if this wisdom meant anything, which he doubted, then he understood it only in the abstract, as a man understands that the Earth is hurtling through space. Simply, he did not feel old enough for this to have come to him yet. And he wished to God that he weren't so alone today. He just had to make it through until Isabella arrived. That's all he had to do. Hold it together.

Most of all he wished he could trust himself again; he wished that his heart would stop playing tricks on him: one moment he was sure of it, the next a new reality would unveil itself and beckon him further within and he would find himself in a completely new place — suddenly steeled, or suddenly destroyed, or suddenly businesslike, or desperate, or resolute, or resigned, or full of a new despair, or madly joyful. And each time he thought he had entered the right and final chamber. And each time it was not so.

Just now — past the bank and the tourist-crammed Literaturnoe Café — just now, for instance, he had felt as lucid as he could ever remember feeling in his whole life. His mind as sharp and clear as a ten-year-old swimmer's. Then he had turned right, off the Nevsky, the Triumphal Arch ahead, and suddenly he was fogged and reeling and seasick again. It was the other people passing by that did it — seeming to him to be no longer individuals, nor even crowds, but merely animate reminders of the context of his mother's death. It was all this evidence of birth, of life, of soon-to-come death, all this evidence of the teeming world that somehow made it worse, somehow drove the swelling sadness harder down the channels of his heart. And it was the sun in the great square ahead, the uncontrived beauty of a day she would never see — the incongruity (for surely there could not be such a loss on a day like this); the very azure of the sky; and yes, there ahead, before him now, the pale beauty of the Winter Palace. *Let's see one more painting today — let's see what Mr. Rembrandt can show us about human nature.* It was the other people. It was the sun. It was the Winter Palace. It was people, sun, and Winter Palace that sent him desolate against the cold stone walls and held him fast in the shadow of the arch.

Then he came jolting and shuddering and shaking out of it. And he was standing in the queue for his ticket, noticing details of other people's clothing, breathing his way determinedly out of whatever latest insanity he had been in, and a rational coping-calmness suffused him. Not clarity this time, nor nausea, but yes, a curious, coping, soft-focus calmness. And he believed (with fervent relief) that he knew himself again. Christ, this must be shock, this must be it! And he realized that of course these others did not know his mother had died — how could they? — and that they did not suspect him of crying or grief or madness or anything else, and that they were just a happy French family, standing in line like him for a ticket to the Hermitage Museum, just a group of German students, just two old — what? — Poles, Czechs, Lithuanians, he had no idea. Simply other people, neither hostile nor friendly.

A ticket for one, please. No concessions.

And then he went over everything coolly again, forward and backward: Lina, Isabella, Julian Avery (he jogged up the wide Rastrelli stairs), his gratitude to Yana. He must do something to thank her

and her mother, and Arytom too. (Left past that ludicrous ceremo-
nial coach that the tourists loved.) And Jesus — Yana's face as she
told him to leave the room and collect some of his mother's fresh
clothes while she wiped his mother's body clean of dried saliva and
the discharge he had pretended not to notice. (Left past the tapes-
tries.) Then Yana, so young, urging him to leave the clothes, which
smelled of his mother on the floor, and go! go now, Gabriel! go! and
wait in the kitchen. And those unreal minutes staring at a Chinese-
patterned tea caddy. (Ignoring *silly little Cézanne*.) Then Yana shouting that it was okay to come in now. (Moving from Winter Palace to
Hermitage.) Then Yana in solemn, solemn Russian on his mother's
phone. The world's most solemn language. (Toward the Peacock
clock, which always made him smile, and so self-consciously forcing
himself to do so three steps early, dreading that none would otherwise come.) And then their arms around each other (hanging garden
to the left) as they sat there on the window bench in the middle of a
rainstorm, waiting for the ambulance, his mother lying on the floor
because he couldn't bring himself to move her and had no idea where
to move her to, except the bed, which seemed as pointless as the ambulance itself.

Turn right.

Rembrandt.

Portrait of Rembrandt's mother.

*Acquired for Catherine in 1767. Gabriel, look at her eyes: very
slightly askew. Thin lips. Black silk dress. But she's not looking directly back. And I don't think she was really his mother.*

He sat on the chair on which his mother always liked to stop, and
closed his eyes.

12

Night Watch

T HE NIGHT WAS SCRATCHED forever on the thin varnish of his childhood; its exact disfiguring pattern likewise etched on every single pane through which he might look back. In the drafty old-fashioned kitchen in the basement of the Highgate house, the half-past seven radio had predicted fog, predicted cold, predicted bad conditions for motorists. But father and children and the children's two friends were all in other rooms, unconscious of flights grounded or the murky freeze fingering its way up the Thames.

It began just before eight.

First the record jumped; then the needle broke and the dancing stopped; then, slowly, the ruptured stump began to drag itself across the vinyl. The newly purchased speakers clawed, rasped, snarled, screeched, but all the same, he heard his father's fury before Nicholas had even left his study in the room above.

Gabriel stopped dead still, his sister the same. A sidelight fizzed, then appeared to brighten, and the room seemed to stretch itself taut in terrified anticipation.

Next, too much rush and panic.

And somehow, as they scrambled over the improvised disco floor, Gabriel (in Superman socks) lost his footing on the polished parquet and — hands flailing to counter the slip — knocked the actual stereo, bounced the needle back onto the record, scratching the shiny black surface a second time and causing the speakers once more to yowl. Even as he was losing his balance, he saw his sister's teeth sink into her lip in pursuit of a plan that might alleviate the worst of what was to come. By the time he had bounded up again — less than an instant later (denying himself even the luxury of a complete fall) and now with the same aim as Isabella — she was already moving past him toward their father's vast vinyl collection. The needle was broken, but at least they could hide the record.

He fumbled with the deck. His father was on the creaking stairs. The needle arm wouldn't lift for a moment, then freed itself. He swung around, looking for the sleeve. He wished with all his heart that he might magic his friends away. Instead they were frozen quivering-still, the realization that there was reason to fear out of all proportion to the damage done beginning to thumbnail itself into their faces.

Too late. As the storm broke through the door, Gabriel was only halfway to putting the ruined disk back in its sleeve and his sister halfway to setting a replacement on the turntable.

In truth, as Nicholas entered the room, he had already abandoned any adult restraint and was borne in a riptide of childish emotions. The evening's wine had thinned his blood, flooding the labyrinths of his intelligence all the more easily. His evening hijacked, even in the midst of its resentful torpor, he had caught them at it: deceit. Deceit — on top of their standing on the furniture, on top of their dancing about the place when he had expressly told them it was forbidden for this precise reason, on top of their willful inability to play fair when he had chosen to ignore their disobedience for the past hour. On top of everything else. At moments such as these he felt too young to be their father, too close: a dangerous rival, not custodian. And he was quite unable to command himself, even in front of eight-year-old children. He stood glowering on the threshold, gripping the door handle with long fingers, scouring one face and then the next.

"What the bloody hell is going *on?*"

The children could find no place to look, so bowed their heads.

In three infuriated strides he crossed to his new stereo.

"What the bloody hell have you done?" This spoken under his breath but so that the room could well hear — as (with his infinite sympathy for inanimate objects) he detached the broken needle, revolved it between finger and thumb, and laid it gently down.

He turned, his voice rising in a steady climb to a furious shout: "I've just bought this, Gabriel." This was true, though the money was not his and had been meant for a very different purpose. "And it is not for you to be messing about with. Do you hear? Have you any idea how much these things cost? Have you any bloody idea?"

Only now did he see the ruined record in the boy's hand: two deep scores the color of sun-bleached bone in the shape of a jagged *V.*

"You little *shit.*"

Though Gabriel knew well what was coming, he was caught by the speed of the strike and took the first blow full across the ear. The second caught him awkwardly coming the other way, across the opposite cheek, before he could raise his arm to protect himself. The pain delayed a moment, then rushed at him. Tears surged to the corners of his eyes and he was lost to the torture of fighting them back in front of his friends, face spun toward the wall.

Fury was heaving through Nicholas, gorging and swelling on itself, raging back and forth far beyond this moment, out across his whole life, annihilating all ancillary thought save for the resounding certainty of his own outraged conviction: that this — this night after night of staying in and looking after these bloody children — this had never been part of the bargain, that he had been cheated, that he (and he alone) was the victim of gross and iniquitous injustice. He was visibly swaying. Isabella was standing still in front of him, clasping the replacement record two thirds unsleeved across her chest, her wide eyes looking up at him, unblinking. The effort required not to say what he bloody well wanted to say almost defeated him. *Serve the old bastard right.* And yet . . . and yet, as always, something — something about Isabella, perhaps, or something in the expressions of the other two, or something residing in the deeper terror of what he would do or become or have to face without the money, without the house, without the daily collateral — something held him back. Instead he cuffed the girl lightly across the top of her head.

"Right, get your bags, get your things — you two, Susan, Dan, you are both going. Right now. Bloody move."

The friends had been motionless in their terrified tableau vivant since he had come in: the one standing unnaturally upright with hands strictly by his side, a child soldier traumatized to attention in front of the old fireplace; the other on the sofa, aware that her feet had been all this while on the furniture and so awkwardly half crouching as if in the act of disguising this fact. Now, released from the spell, the two gave themselves fully to efficiency and haste, as if unconsciously glad of the emotional cover they provided.

And already Nicholas felt himself tiring. His wretched circumstances at the age of thirty-eight, the thought of his wife out at her self-righteous work all night ("My own money, Nicholas, I make my own money, to spend how I will"), the house itself—all of it pressed in on him now, corralling him back to the more subdued ire of his habitual corner. The torrent was receding. His intelligence was re-emerging, asserting itself. And he could sense the shadow of his rage smirking at the histrionics of its master. Still, he had bound himself into the entire tedious performance—furious parent disciplines disgraceful children for the duration of an entire bloody evening. So he set his face.

"What the hell are you waiting for, Isabella? Get in the bloody car."

Gabriel sat in the front, the seat belt too high and chafing at his neck. His father was driving—the contortion of face and body far worse for being imagined rather than directly looked upon—driving with undue gesture and haste, braking too hard for the pedestrian crossing, accelerating unnecessarily as he pulled away.

Nicholas swore, then swerved hard into a petrol station. He got out to dribble another teacup's worth into the tank; he ran the car perpetually on the brink of empty and there was never enough for there and back.

Gabriel shifted for the first time and took the chance to look into the back. His sister's gaze was fixed on his seat, as if she expected smoke to coil any moment from the point of her stare. The others too were unnaturally still: a grazed knuckle on the armrest of the door, a disco girl's polka-dot-painted fingernail digging into the fake suede of the upholstery.

"Your dad is mad." White-faced, Susan mouthed the words and whirled her index finger at her temple.

There was nothing Gabriel could say.

They drove on. And the silence in the car seemed a worse agony than the shouting and the striking that had gone before, seemed to hold them all rigid as surely as if they were each pinned with a hundred tacks through pinches of the skin. And Gabriel felt instinctively, without the restrictive formality of articulation, that it was neither fear nor resentment that kept them all from meeting any other's eye; it was the shame. The livid, writhing embarrassment of every moment now being lived through: the shame of the blows—witnessed blows — henceforth indelible in their individual histories; the shame of what lay ahead, of what he and Isabella must both face at school, of what would be known about them; and, worst of all, lurking beneath all these like some poisoned underground lake, the shame of the discovery that their father — champion, guarantor, backer — had turned out not to be the idol of their public boast but a public betrayer instead. This the most painful shame. And a shame he felt without the adult luxury of the long view, of independent resource — though immortal all the same for that.

But it was not the ride to Acton that Gabriel remembered most of all when he shut his eyes. It was the rest of the night.

Nothing had been eased and nothing spoken ninety minutes later, when the vast Victorian house reared up in the headlights. His father turned off the engine and stepped out of the car, his distance the shortest to the front door. But Gabriel sat very still, watching his sister walk around the hood while Nicholas fumbled for his key. Without looking back and expecting him to follow, they both disappeared inside, leaving the door ajar and a narrow triangle of light on the frayed gray mat.

But Gabriel did not move. Something held him there.

It was not exactly his conscious intention. But a minute passed and he simply remained motionless.

Then another minute came and went.

And still he did not shift to unbuckle his seat belt. But found himself staring dead ahead: the porch light, at this exact position of parking, somehow revealed the otherwise invisible smears on the windscreen left behind by long-vanished rain.

Three minutes passed in this observation and his attitude did not change — upright, legs together, as if ready for a new journey, self-consciously breathing through his nose. And though yet without plot or purpose, the more he sat, the harder it was to move. And with each additional second, his resolve seemed to be hardening; yes, the more he sat, the more he knew that he had to go on sitting. And the more he sat, the harder it was to move. And that was all there was to it. Somehow he had become a fugitive from his own decisions — a boy in an adventure story, locked in the basement, stock-still, ear to the door, listening to the baddies decide what they were going to do with him.

The porch bulb was extinguished like a dare. The driveway darkened. He refocused on the opaque semicircular patterns left by the wipers. To his left, the rhododendrons shuffled outside the passenger window. To his right, he could sense his father ducking down a little to get a look inside the car from the steps. And even though he could not see directly for fear of turning his head, even though the narrow angle of dead ahead was all he permitted himself, still Gabriel knew at once that this was the moment, that this was the test—that he must not move at all, not even the shiver of an eyelash; he must remain as still as the headstones in Highgate Cemetery.

His breathing stopped. And he summoned all the will he had in his eight-year-old soul. He would not breathe again until. He would not breathe again. He would not breathe.

His father was gone!

The front door shut.

He had done it.

He was alone.

For the next five minutes triumph surged through him. But just as quickly as it had arrived, his jubilation began to seep and shrink away, his veins to hollow. Pins and needles attacked his foot. The trees shifted again, disturbing the shadows. And all of a sudden he felt uncertain and scared. He tried to rally. He bent everything he had to the single purpose of containment. He sealed off his mind. He shut his eyes. His foot was killing him. Needle pin, pin needle. But the pain was something he could concentrate on, at least. The spasm must pass. If only he could survive the next minute. Survive the next minute. Count up to sixty.

He was totally convinced an hour must have elapsed, maybe longer. He was okay, though. He had come through it in some sort of waking sleep or trance or something. And the cramp had disappeared. And he reckoned he was good for the full adventure, whatever that might be. He allowed himself to relax slightly. Yeah, it was like he was in the book he was reading about three boys who ran a detective agency somewhere in faraway San Francis—

Shit!

His sister's light was on, directly above. And now off. And now on. And now off. Signals . . . No, Is, no. Don't wreck it. *Please* don't wreck it. Off. On. Off. On. Off. Off. Staying off . . . Of course, she would be able to see him better with no light. She must be looking out right now. All he had to do was signal in return. He could sense her face, just above and beyond the ceiling of his self-permitted vision. But once again he knew that the movement of a single nerve would mean mutiny and total collapse, and he would be up and out, and she would sneak down and open the front door, and he would run straight to his room, and she would come running after him, asking him all kinds of Isabella questions. So don't look up. How long would she be there? What was she doing? Was she waving? Don't look up. Don't look up.

The engine had cooled completely when the first serious shiver passed through him and the night began in earnest. The house now loomed like a phantom liner. He was sure of less and less. He could not tell the murmuring of the trees from the murmurs inside his own mind. Voices he had not sanctioned muttered rival commentaries in his head. Familiar faces came and went behind shadowy windows he could not see. And there was only his own stillness left to be relied upon.

His last conscious thought came as dead midnight fell. His chin dropping to his chest and the shivering properly upon him, he became dimly aware that Highgate church bells were chiming — twelve? Was it twelve? His feet and legs had long gone but it was still quite warm beneath him. Nestle into this warmth and let it spread up through him like a hot fountain. Count the church bells.

He was a stranger to the world after that. The fog rose as forecast from London below, creeping and stealing up Highgate Hill, whispering forth blind comrade the frost, until the windscreen rimed and the red hood turned all to pearl. But Gabriel was no longer looking through conscious eyes, because a feverish waking sleep had overtaken him and he was a pilgrim now, wandering through a bone-strewn valley in the story of a dark and evil land. Several times he thought perhaps he could make out the shape of Isabella's face again — his mysterious twin watching at her window, by his side, or over his shoulder — but he could not be certain. And anyway he did not want to lose count on his journey.

He was still sitting there at four, when Maria Glover's headlights swept the driveway. At first she dismissed the evidence of her own copy-sore eyes; then she thought it must be a thief. But when the shape still did not move (a bowed head silhouetted through silvered glass), she killed her engine and stepped out of the car, leaving the lights on. The three seconds that it took to cross the gravel were filled with a mother's horror — she could not guess what or how or why, and surely it could not be Gabriel? But it was. Even then, she put her hand to the door handle expecting to meet resistance — he must be locked in. And yet, save for the adhesion of the frost, there was none.

She said his name. First in a question, then almost a shout, then in her most tender voice. "Gabriel? *Gabriel.* Gabriel." But he was too far gone to turn or to speak, in a convulsion of sleep and starts, shivering and staring and stiff in all his bones, and long past answering even if he had wanted to. So then she tried to pick him up, as if he were still a baby, and somehow she managed to lift his legs enough to get them outside the car and swivel him around and raise him toward her, all this while saying his name over and over. But one step backward and his knees gave way and she had to catch him. His hands were frozen but his forehead was searing hot.

13

A Plan

I F YOU THINK you can do it, then do it," Henry said.
"I can do it." Arkady was hunched on the piano stool, his back
to the keyboard.

"But I don't like it."

"I do not ask if you like it. You tell me that she has family. This is
how we find them."

"How do you know there is nobody there?"

"I know."

Henry met the other's eyes but found no reciprocity and so sent a
scrawny hand back through the point of his widow's peak. It was
Wednesday, early evening, and this was the first time Arkady had
said anything other than monosyllables all day.

"I can go and see Zoya. Maybe she will give us something — an
address — if I go and see her in person."

"Zoya does not care one fuck about it."

"I could pay her."

Arkady did not respond.

Henry raised himself from the sofa and walked toward the window. Though he kept it out of his voice, he had little enthusiasm and
less money for this idea. (He must find some new pupils. Build it up
all over again. How had he let his teaching shrivel so far?) Things
were still okay: he had just over three thousand dollars in cash, plus
a few more scraps and scrapings in his old English bank account. He
had paid Grisha for his regular score — though, admittedly, he had
not settled for the extra so enthusiastically advanced and Arkady

was right: he should not have accepted it. He planned to skip a pickup and use the oversupply for the two weeks after his regular ran out. Still, he knew he should sort things out soon if he wished to avoid falling into Leary's debt, through contrivance or otherwise. He probably should have gone down to Stavischek a few days ago. But too much of immediate importance had been happening: the canceling of the weekend's follow-up gigs and Arkady's subsequent silence; a delegation of Mongeese (minus Yevgeny, who perhaps knew better) arriving in the morning and nobody getting anything out of Arkady; Sergei himself turning up at lunchtime, waving a newspaper review (to no effect) and then weighing in with various threats and bribes and curses until Arkady finally manhandled the fat manager bodily out the door while Sergei, suddenly afraid, started bleating and moaning until he was safely outside, whereupon he began shouting and swearing again — that he would get his money back on the lost takings and that Arkady would never play again in Petersburg. So Henry had contented himself with sending Grisha a text message. He'd be down with the money for the rest on Friday. Dear Lord, he loathed it that the wretched creature was so much in his life. When those moments of clarity came, it was Grisha's face that spoke most powerfully for coming off.

Henry turned back to face the room. "I could pay Zoya to give us whatever she has on file relating . . . relating to Maria Glover." The name sounded horribly grating as he uttered it.

Arkady took off his cap, leaned forward, and balled it in his fist. "Zoya is bullshit. You leave message and message. She never phones you. She knows nothing. Because if she knows something, then she calls you back so you know she is ready to be paid again. This is how it works." He raised his eyes and spoke through the fall of his hair. "She knows nothing. If you see her yourself and you pay her, you will only find this afterward. Forget Zoya. She is Gypsy scum. You should have made friends with the real bitch when you had your tongue in her ass."

Henry sat back down on the sofa and seemed to fold in on himself like a bat trapped in a room too long in daylight. He did not know what to do, or how best to be, or help, or anything. And he was becoming agitated. It was past his time.

"This term is almost certainly paid," he began again. "Therefore I reckon we need . . . we need twenty thousand dollars, more or less, to get you through to the end of the third year."

Arkady was staring at the backs of his hands, which were still clasped around his cap.

So Henry continued. "Twenty thousand may not be so much to them. Or it may be that she has left it to you in her will. We should hold on. She's only been dead a day or two. We should see what comes next. Her relatives might get in touch any time now." His words were sounding prissy even to his own ear. He pressed on hastily. "We have until Christmas — assuming the money *is* settled for this term. We should wait for news."

Arkady straightened up, the better to scoff. "We wait for nothing. We do something. Or we sit here playing with our balls like fuckmonkeys." He turned around to face the keyboard. Slowly he shut the lid. "This family, they do not know me. Nobody knows me."

Henry had never felt Arkady's anger hang so full and naked in the room; the air seemed to be choked with emotional cordite. A power of projection he had not properly understood until now.

Arkady addressed the score open on the stand. "I do not continue if I cannot finish. I do not waste my time and my life anymore. It's bullshit." He stood up. "We write a letter to say I cannot play for a month. I hurt my hand. I will go only to theory lessons. And in the meantime, we do what we must do. This way we find out what there is to know. We get information. Then we decide. I am tired of wasting time."

"But you can still play. You can still practice. Why do we need to pretend that you —"

"No."

Henry's right hand patted rapidly but softly at his knee. There was no point arguing anymore — about Arkady's hand, about the plan, about anything; it was like disputing with the weather. "Okay. If you can do it without risk, then do it."

Arkady went into his bedroom, then reappeared a moment later wearing his greatcoat. "I have to find a friend of mine and see what he is doing tomorrow night. A man called Oleg maybe will phone your mobile. Take his number."

Henry nodded, hand still patting, conscious that the credit on his phone was running out. "You coming back before? Or shall I meet you at the ground?"

They had a long-standing plan to watch Zenit Petersburg play. Arkady, Yevgeny, and a few others were going.

"Meet there." Arkady picked up and pocketed the few ruble

notes that Henry had put down on top of the piano and then turned on his heel.

Henry listened to the Russian leave, feeling the sudden amplification of self-recrimination now that he was alone. He had no tolerance for his own emotions. He simply could not endure them, their terrible power to consume him. He rose quickly, passed into his bedroom, and closed the door.

14

The Ratchet

AYS IT'S BEEF on the packs, Is, but we did an undercover defrost and it's not."

"What, then?"

"Larry says it could be some kind of rat from Peru. They got big fuckers out there."

"Wish I had taken a year off. Sounds brilliant."

"We're going to try and write about it for the local paper."

"Thought you wanted to be a theater director, not a journalist."

"Larry's secretly filming it — for a documentary. I'm telling him what to film. How is it going at college? What's it —"

"So why write about it?"

"Fund the documentary."

"Yeah . . . bet the local paper pays big for pieces from undercover student meatpackers. I'll tell you when you get here."

It was December 1991. Isabella had just (unofficially) dropped out of Cambridge — failed to complete even a single term, appalled beyond reasonable doubt by her fellow students' staggering mixture of naiveté and smugness. But she'd been home for only one strained (though mercifully meal-free) Sunday evening with her mother, who was clearly suffering from a fervently denied but virulent depression of her own, when the news came that Grandfather Max had died on an unholy bender in Scotland. A distillery tour, a walk on the Black Cullin, skinny-dipping. His heart.

Gabriel, meanwhile, was working double shifts with his friend Larry, packing frozen foods in Southampton, trying to earn money to fund what remained of his year-off travels, because "Dad won't

give me a penny and I wouldn't take it from the bastard anyway."
Though Isabella calculated that by the time her brother had saved
enough to make it across the Channel, it would be next September
and he'd have just a month before he started at university himself.

Gabriel clicked his tongue. "I'll be back Friday . . . I'll just have to
take the afternoon off. They're not going to like it. We're not supposed to have any holidays, and the bosses get their hard-ons from
firing casuals. The service is definitely on Saturday?"

"Yeah."

"Jesus, Is, it's so brutal, isn't it?"

"I just can't believe he's actually dead."

"Do they know anything about what happened?"

"It was a series of heart attacks, apparently. Mum says that the
people with him told her he kept trying to crawl across the mountain
— even when it had started. He wouldn't lie down. But he had been
swimming or something, so he must have been half naked." She
paused. "I just wish I had gone to see him more often — you know."

"Me too."

She cupped the receiver. "I'm trying to persuade Mum to get Dad
to pay for us to fly to Petersburg and deal with anything that needs
to be dealt with. It's an excuse, but — you know — I reckon that
Mum will be allowed back soon. I can tell she'd love to go."

"Is she upset?"

"Kind of . . . yes."

"Is Dad back?"

"No."

"*No?*"

"Mum doesn't know where he is exactly. We can't call him."

"Jesus Christ. What the fuck is he doing?"

"We don't even know if he knows about Grandpa."

"Where the fuck is he? Oh . . . oh shit."

She heard the pips and then the receiver clattered.

"Oh bollocks, the money is running out again. I've got no more
coins." He spoke quickly. "Tell Mum I'll phone tomorrow and speak
to her again."

"Okay. See you at the weekend. Bye bye bye bye."

The old house stood at an odd diamond shape to the road so that it
met visitors with a corner angle and seemed to present two different
aspects, both designed to be the front. The modest, badly kept lawns

gave no clue. And nobody was sure quite when Max had bought it. Sometime during the war, was the rumor.

Isabella sat with her mother in the long basement kitchen warmed by the ancient cooker, neither of them knowing where Nicholas was —Paris somewhere?—passing the time watching the portable television, waiting for him to show up or call and trying to measure the mightiness of history in two-minute segments between show biz and sports. And all the while the telephone kept ringing with Foreign Office officials, the odd MP, old friends, clipped-speech men whom neither of them had ever met, asking for Nicholas and wishing them sincere condolences in his absence; and her mother furious and sarcastic half the time, nostalgic and maudlin and tearful the rest; and Isabella panicked and petrified half the time, thankful and relieved the rest, that the overwhelming stupidity or wisdom or madness or vindication of her leaving Cambridge had somehow been overshadowed.

"Grandpa Max gone, Izzy. Dear oh dear—*there's* a chapter finished. Hard to believe, isn't it? Very hard. And just as the Soviet Union is finally put to death as well. Can you believe it? Can you believe anything?"

"Shitting hell."

"Please don't use bad language."

Isabella looked away from the screen. "I quite liked Gorbachev. Is he going to stay with us in some capacity?"

"He's better than the fat drunk." Her mother paused. "But poor Gorby was finished a year ago, Is. And now there is no Soviet Union to rule—even were he able to cling on, which he isn't. Now we have this CIS," she scoffed. "The Commonwealth of Independent States. But of course it's rubbish. There will be chaos. We need a great man now, Izzy, if Russia is to survive. A strongman."

"You mean a tyrant?"

"Exactly so."

"Mum, your worldview scares me."

"Yours me, Isabella." Her mother lit another cigarette. "Yours me."

"I don't have one."

"Exactly. You don't believe in anything. Which is understandable." She waved out the match. "You *cannot* believe in anything—if you have learned your history lessons. But still, you are the rising generation."

"And we want marzipan and chocolate." Isabella rose, her chair scraping on the floor.

Her mother gestured at the television. "So here—we bequeath you this desperate, flailing, lopsided world, in a worse and better state than we ourselves received it. We ask only that you look after it as best you can. And make sure that when your time is over, there's something to pass on. For truly, Izzy, this unlikely blue ball is it. This blue ball is all there is."

"Anything else you need to tell me?" Isabella tried a second cupboard.

Her mother looked across and smiled. "Whenever you have the chance, try to raise your head from the busy living of your life. And if everything seems compromised or unworthy, then remember the simple and fundamental aim: to reduce human suffering wherever you find it. At least you can be sure that this is a good plan, regardless of God, money, fashion, and the bloody news."

"Please don't use bad language, Mum."

"I meant news of blood."

"Aha!" Isabella eased the bar out from behind a wall of condiment jars. "Toblerone. Jesus, Mum, you must be the only person in the world who still buys this stuff. Not quite what I was after, but there's no sense being all judgmental about things before we've tried them, is there?" Isabella came back to her chair at the table.

"Your father's favorite," her mother said softly. "Half each. You break, I choose."

Isabella snapped the bar in half and said, "I can't believe that they are going to let all the states split off."

"Do not be so sure. Soviet times are over." Her mother took the smaller piece. "But now we see what happens when Russia wakes up."

"Do you reckon there's going to be fighting?"

Her mother nodded. "Lots of things will happen in the night, and we will never know."

The television cameras left the Kremlin and returned to the studio in Shepherd's Bush where assembled experts prepared to expatiate.

"Oh, Isabella, will you look at their smug faces. They're disgusting, these people. Where do they come from? And my good God—listen to that stupid newsreader's voice! She can hardly read the cue. No idea what she says or what any of it *means*. These people make me sick. Even that pretentious buffoon of a reporter in Moscow is better than this silly tit. Surely you have some intelligent people in

this country somewhere? They can't all be like this. For the love of
Pete. And they think the good guys have won—ha. Idiots. Idiots. Idiots with their *news*. The KGB will win, you fools. Oh yes—and I'm
sure Mr. Bush and the baby Jesus and the World Bank and the pope
and all the lovely boards of directors are delighted tonight. Singing
into their swill. Well, I leave you in their very good company and
care."

The two fell silent for another while, sitting at the kitchen table,
watching the screen together, sometimes turning the sound up in curiosity, sometimes down in disgust, their minds on the different matters of their different ages, though all the while conscious of their fel-
lowship and common cause against their precisely identified private
array of culprits, major and minor. The chocolate disappeared peak
by peak.

By and by Isabella asked, "How will Dad know?"

"He will find out."

"Do you think he'll be back in time?"

"Of course he will."

"I don't understand how you can be so sure."

"Because . . . because when that bell goes, Izzy, your father is up
and out of his corner as hard and as fast as any man you will ever
meet."

And find out somehow Nicholas did. The following day he arrived
home at noon, having cut short his "business" in Paris. "I bloody did
call. About fifty times from the hotel before I set out. But the bloody
phone was engaged all the bloody time, so I decided to stop messing about and get in the bloody car." And throughout the crema-
tion, the obituaries in the newspapers, the formalities with the solicitors, the surreal service and wake (organized not by Nicholas but
by Randolph, an old friend of Max's whom nobody quite knew)—
throughout all of this, it appeared to Isabella that her father took
no trouble at all to hide his relief—his *glee*—that finally, "at long
bloody last," the paintings, the Jaguar, the houses in Leningrad and
Scotland, were all 100 percent his. And all the money. The greatest
fear of his life, he was happy to proclaim—to strangers, friends, and
family alike—was that "the old goat would shaft me one more time."

Thin as a corkscrew but outwardly as cool as any eighteen-year-old
woman had ever been, Isabella wound in and out of the many shadows of the weekend.

Gabriel returned from Southampton on the Friday night and there was an almost immediate row, Nicholas having volunteered Gabriel to go around to Randolph's house (halfway across London in Holland Park) to help out first thing in the morning, Gabriel furious that he had not at least been consulted before getting to the real point of his anger: that Nicholas was now disappearing for weeks on end without bothering to tell their mother where he was going.

Her mother, meanwhile, continued to whisper about "returning" and — unbelievably — taking Isabella's father's side against her brother.

And for the first time, with the fresh eyes of the returning student, Isabella began to consider her parents' relationship for what it truly was — fractured, incoherent, erratic; mutually critical, disdainful, dismissive, emotionally terse, emotionally *illiterate*. And yet, she observed, there was a bilateral understanding, which, though never explicit or remarked upon, was near absolute — lived out in a series of elaborate codes and oblique conversational procedures. In fact, she now realized, her mother was always pretending to her father's view, as soon as he showed up, though all parties knew her avowals to be utterly false.

In the car on the way to the service, for example, Isabella's secret was detonated out of the blue and her mother suddenly pronounced: "Izzy, don't expect us to support you, if you intend to live at home." (The sheer distancing cruelty of that "intend.") Then, next minute, her father was blithely affecting the opposite — considerate, thoughtful, compassionate: "Is, this is the great opportunity of your life. You need to think very carefully about what you are doing." When in fact Isabella knew full well — they *all* knew full well — that her mum did not care one kopek about money and would have supported her forever, until the last drop of her working blood, and that of course her father did not care one idle flick of his contemptuous wrist about Cambridge as a "great opportunity" or otherwise, having been there himself, to the very same college, and having declared on several painfully public occasions, including the day that she had got her offer of a place to study modern languages, that the university was a convenient depository for "the most boring people in the country — a mini-Australia for the criminally tedious."

On the Sunday, the day after the funeral, when they were all four alone, the ratchet wound itself up another notch. Isabella could hardly believe that they were going to attempt to dine together as a family, but this indeed was the stated plan for the afternoon. "Lay the table,

Is, we'll be back in an hour" — delivered with total *Pravda*-like conviction as her mother put on the green raincoat that she wore four
seasons around and made for the heath with a silent Gabriel . . . leaving Isabella and her father alone together in the large room at the
front of the house, Isabella in the tatty chair by the empty grate,
Nicholas standing by the window, watching out for she knew not
what.

It was one of those days when no matter where she sat or how
many layers she put on, Isabella found that she simply could not
warm her bones. The whole house was cold. (Her mother was pretending that the heating was necessarily rationed via the timer and
had in fact been on all morning, her father that it was broken. Both
were lying — someone had simply switched it off.) There was also
something wrong with the workings inside the grandfather clock, so
that each movement of the minute hand was accompanied by a just-
audible scrape. She was downstairs only because she was awaiting
the imminent arrival of her boyfriend, Callum, whom she had told to
come over and pick her up, with the idea that they might go down
into Camden and see one of his rival Brit-pop band's gigs, and whom
she did not want intercepted by her father. Though going out, she
knew, would aggravate mother, father, and brother alike. Or maybe
nobody would care at all.

She was pretending to look through the neat file of official-seeming
documents left behind on the small table by Walter Earnshaw, solici-
tor and new best friend of her father's. Somehow or other her father
had arranged for everything to be transferred to him; she was dimly
aware that she and Gabriel should be studying things more carefully,
but leaving aside their utter naiveté and hopeless lack of resources, it
seemed ridiculous to check up on her own father. In any case, her
real attention was swooping, perching, and beating its wings elsewhere — far, wide, near and back again. After another minute she
abandoned the charade and addressed her father's back, thinking
that this was at least some kind of an opportunity to communicate to
him the sincerity of her mother's hopes.

"Dad, you know . . . you know, you should get Mum a place in
Petersburg. I bet you can buy stuff there now."

He did not turn around.

"It'd be a great investment. Everything is opening up again." This
wasn't true, or if it was, Isabella had no way of knowing it to be so.
But she said it to appear insider-informed in front of her father. And
to provoke him. The word "investment," she hoped, would do that.

"We have our own priorities," he said to the windows.

"Mum has been talking about it nonstop since I got back. Honestly, you should see her — she's glued to the news, and every time there's a picture of Petersburg she starts pointing at the TV. She really, *really* wants to go back — even if it's only for a while. You know she does. She was planning a trip with me in any case. We could search for flats. She would love to be able to go there a few months every year." Not looking up, she added, "Now you have all that money, you probably won't even notice some of it gone."

That did it.

Her father turned. "Oh, don't worry, Isabella, as soon as I die, you —"

"You *know* that's not what I am talking about."

"You can all go and hang around Leningrad as much as you like." He fixed her with his eyes. "Why exactly have you left Cambridge? And please don't tell me that it's got anything to do with that bloody boy. What is his name?"

They were speaking to each other directly now.

"Jesus." Isabella was conscious of a heat rash on her chest. All her life she had been caught between these two sufferings: the one — trying to goad her father into engaging with her, and the other — her hurt at his cruelty when he finally did so. "I don't care about the money, Dad. I'm just saying that you should buy Mum somewhere to live — or rent something. And why not back in Russia? We can sell Grandpa's house and buy a small flat. She hates this place. It . . . it's cold and it's empty. And I know you are away more or less all the time — fair enough — and she needs some new thing, you know — something she cares about in her life. Just imagine: she's not been back since she was . . . well . . . well, since she left with you. She'd *love* to see Petersburg again. She'd love to stay there. I really think —"

"Isabella, I want to be clear about this." Seemingly insensible of the cold, he stepped forward, his shirt, as ever, without a single crease. "We're not paying for you to hang around here. If you're at Cambridge, that's a different matter. We've always said that we're prepared to support you until you finish university. But that's it. After that you are on your own. So if you are serious about leaving, then don't think that you can waste the next three years finding yourself here."

"What the hell makes you think I want to live here?"

"I have no idea what your plans are — that is your business. You can live where you please, of course. Here included."

"That's very kind of you."

"But if you are not going to complete your degree and if you do expect to live here, then I will expect you to pay maintenance to your mother. You can't just swan around the world as you please. You're an adult now."

"Dad, for Christ's sake."

"Isabella, please."

"I am talking about Mum." She was aware that her anger was increasing in direct and dangerous relation to her father's calmness — affected or genuine, she could not tell. But her eighteen-year-old self had no capacity for restraint — and so she went on harder, her throat as red as her knuckles were white.

"I'm not *going* to live here. So don't worry. I'm just asking you to consider being decent to Mum — helping her — just once. *God*."

"That is between your mother and me."

His expression, his measured tone, even the way he was standing there looking at her was as patronizing as she had ever known. She wanted now to rouse him to outright anger. She wanted it more than anything. She wanted to prize out his feelings — any feelings.

"I don't care, I really don't fucking *care* what you have to say about me or my life or anything else. I don't care what you think or what you do. I just want you once — once — to consider someone other than yourself."

"Isabella, please stop being so tiresome. Your life is entirely your own. To fail with exactly as you please." He sat down slowly, crossed his thin legs, and reached for the documents, pulling them across the table toward himself.

"Don't talk to me like that. How dare you? Not one thing you ever started have you finished. You've never done anything. You've spent your *entire adult life* swanning around. You're a total fraud, Dad. A fraud, a failure, and a small-time bully." She had him now. She had never ever said anything like this to him. She went on, her hot fury the counter to his cold. "Just look at you, sitting there like a pompous little prick — how do you even live with yourself? Well, let me tell you something: I don't care about your crap either. Whatever it is. I don't care. Maybe it is too late for Mum. But I — I don't need you. I don't need to hear your pathetic little lectures. I don't need your money, which isn't even yours, or your control-freak attempts to use it. Gabriel thinks you're an arsehole, Dad. But I — I think you're just plain mediocre. So — you know what? Fuck off."

She made as if to get up. She was rigid with the effort not to cry.

"Isabella, sit down."

"Why?"

"Sit down."

"What's the point?" Her voice was cracking. She wanted to run from the room.

"Sit down."

All the same, she sat back — suddenly feeling like a child but holding her face tight as stone.

He leaned forward, his voice quiet and deadly clear. "I am sick — sick to the back teeth — of you and your bloody brother. The pair of you. You seem to think just because you feel a thing, that makes it externally true. You — you in particular — seem to live at the mercy of whatever juvenile emotions you are suffering. And please don't kid yourself, Isabella. Because in this you're just like all the others out there, all the earnest young women scraped into the polytechnics to do their ghastly gender studies and sociology courses, heads stuffed full of daytime TV and magazines, all the whining Princess Diana housewives who have conveniently forgotten how stupid they were at school and how stupid they continue to be. No, don't kid yourself — you are just like them. Just because you *feel* upset, they assume that it's your right to *be* upset. Just because you aren't intelligent enough to do anything but feel, you want the rest of us to live within the tyranny of whatever the insecurity of the day might be. You . . . You go away for a couple of months and you come back with your head stuffed full of all this rubbish. You disappoint me."

"I've got nothing to say to you, Dad."

"Nothing intelligent, clearly."

She was crying and there was nothing she could do to hide it. "You are full of shit."

The doorbell was ringing.

"Your boyfriend? What's his name?"

She was determined to walk slowly, not run.

"I sincerely hope you have not left Cambridge on his account. Apart from being embarrassingly slow-witted and a terrible musician, he's queer. That's all."

15

Grisha

A WEARER OF GRIEVANCE, a bearer of grudge, shaven head slightly too large for torso, torso slightly too large for legs, and legs slightly too large for feet — this was the squat figure who trod the grimy corridor on the thirteenth floor of tower block number two, Kammennaya Street, Vasilevsky Island, St. Petersburg. Grigori, Gregory, Gregol — known variously here, known nefariously there, in Brindisi, London, Bucharest, but passing these past few years, on and off, in Russia, under the general name of Grisha. A man for whom all the million eddies and currents of human interaction had long ago been distilled down to a single granule of conviction: that the world owed him, so fuck it.

And tonight was just more grist to that rutted mill. Henry Wheyland had not paid what he was due. That was bad enough. (He swapped the angle grinder he was carrying from one hand to the other.) Worse, though, was that Grisha knew the delay was not the result of Henry's having a lack of rubles but the result of Henry's having a lack of respect. And if there was one thing that stuck in Grisha's gullet, it was lack of respect. Indeed, for Grisha, respect was everything. He would have retraced his steps and faced down a mongrel dog if he came to suspect that it might have sniggered as he passed. And anyway, he was acting on orders.

Now was that everything?

He put down the angle grinder and addressed his Slovak employee in Russian: "Gunt, what the fuck is that?"

Gunter heaved up the indicated power tool from the floor and brandished it like a mighty sword.

"Tyrannosaw," he said with a smirk.

Twenty minutes later, and a little to his own surprise, Grisha (groping unconsciously for his groin) found himself entering Arkady Alexandrovitch's bedroom with a degree of trepidation. Though he was 100 percent certain that at this very moment the Russian was with Henry, watching Zenit's Wednesday night game, still his mind seemed to be on tiptoes and his toes themselves a little ginger inside the stretched and swollen udders of his fat white Nikes. Yeah: something had him jumpy in here, no doubt about it.

He sighed.

It wasn't right.

He stopped just inside the threshold and eventually located his cigarettes in one of the front pockets of his twelve-compartment combat trousers. He raised the packet as if to swig from a bottle and let the first to slide out lodge between his sticky lips before shaking the rest back in. He then set about tracking down his Zippo, patting first one leg, then the other, up and down, forward and backward. Combat — a very compartmentalized business. Keep stuff separate, that's the thing about combat. Where the hell?

At last the zone just above the back of his left knee grudgingly relinquished the required tool. And so, relieved and taking considerable comfort in the procedure, he now lit up with stagy deliberation.

Better.

Much better.

How did he ever manage before cigarettes? Life must have been terrible. No wonder he'd started smoking at ten. In fact, come to think of it, maybe that was why his childhood was such a piece of shit. Should have started much earlier, should have started at two. He flipped the lighter shut.

Now then: what we got?

The room was more or less bare: a double mattress on the swept concrete floor, bed neatly made, thin cream blanket, white sheet folded over at the top. And that was just about it. No curtain or blind on the window (which, like those in the lounge, looked out on the Gulf of Finland), no mirror, no wardrobe, no desk, no chest, no chair, no posters or pictures, no pinups, nothing. For fuck's sake, these two lived like monks. He pivoted. There were five or six serious nails hammered into the wall behind him, on which a few items of clothing hung flat: two white shirts, a gray greatcoat, a pair of black trousers, a dinner jacket. Beneath these, two wooden boxes, both containing what looked like underclothes. A pair of shoes. Nothing else.

Grisha exhaled thoughtfully through flared nostrils — twin off-road exhausts under heavy acceleration — and approached the wide window, walking carefully by the side of the bed. It was upsetting, was what it was: the room had a scrubbed and dusted feel, as though someone had washed everything only an hour ago. Shifting blood, lifting DNA. He looked about him. There was no money in here. (Grisha could intuit money in a place, like a water diviner sensing that delicate underground tremble.) The windowsill yielded neither residue nor discoloration to the pink of his stubby finger. The floor was everywhere stripped and bare. And the pillow, which he now bent to touch, was freshly laundered. Grisha saw that Arkady would be able to look up through the window into the sky from his bed — very nice. Grisha was tempted to lie down himself and stretch out, think, smoke, have a piss.

Hello . . . There was something that looked like a book in the bed, slipped in between the sheets.

Filth?

Curious, comforted, Grisha dropped to his haunches, picked it up, and flipped through.

No . . . it was music. Fucking music. No words, no pictures, no tits, no pussy. Just notes. Not even a rogue arse. Grisha's expression grew distant, thoughts developing slowly but steadily, like graffiti declaring itself letter by letter on a waste-ground wall. Wait . . . Yes, that was it. The answer he had been looking for. How to fuck everything even faster. No need for any further consideration. Leary would love it. Grisha grinned grotesquely. He replaced the music, stood up, flicked his ash carefully into his cupped palm, and left the room.

And so to the main business.

Grisha next entered Henry's room, smashing the door hard against the wardrobe inside as he opened it. Much smaller in here, and darker too. Almost messy by comparison. Now then — where? A single mattress, likewise on the floor. A small window. The free-standing wardrobe. A high shelf heavy with books running down either side of the room. A chest of drawers. A school desk and a chair covered in clothes. Two boxes of needles stacked with the hospital insignia on the side. A black garbage bag under the desk. Where would a skinny little shit-stabber keep his money?

Grisha surveyed the ceiling, hoping for giveaways. No breaks or cracks or panels. Nothing. The floor was the same flat Soviet-crap concrete as Arkady's, save for a rug. He bent and flipped it: nothing. The stunted baseboards were all intact. He dragged the wardrobe out from the wall. Nothing obvious back there. He turned to face the room again. Surely not under the . . . He upended the mattress. Nothing. Ripping off the sheet, he checked all the way around. No slits. No pouches. Nothing.

All right then, so be it, let's do this properly. Grisha ground his cigarette into the twisted rug and unsheathed his prized Uzbek knife.

For the next fifteen minutes, he devoted himself to a thoroughly efficient and concentrated search in which everything, absolutely everything, was tipped out, tipped over, upended, yanked, emptied, slit, spilled, split, dumped. And all things passed beneath Grisha's eyes—gravel-gray piggy little nugget-sifters—and many through his greasy palms, but nothing for more than the second it took to ascertain their status as harborers of money or otherwise.

He worked with surprising energy and the absorbed gibbonlike strength that his odd dimensions gave him. Truth be fucking told, it wasn't often these days that he got the chance to go back to basics, and he had to admit that he rather enjoyed it . . . Enjoyed it too much, maybe, because, as he now realized, he hadn't been thinking. Grisha grimaced. That was the problem: you got carried away; you forgot yourself. Good job Gunter was on guard and not here to witness this minifailure. He drew breath.

Time for another snout.

He lit up, sucked in, and sat down, resting heavily on the corner of the overturned desk. With Henry it was all very straightforward: find the money, find the man; take the money, destroy the man. And no amount of ancillary damage would really matter two bitch's shits to Henry once he discovered the money was gone. Leary's work was easily done. Grisha could chainsaw the walls in half if he felt like it. Henry wouldn't notice. Because money was what guaranteed Henry's supply and protecting supply was all the poor bastard was capable of caring about. (And also, since he, Grisha, was Henry's supplier, finding the money was all that was necessary to bring him in.) But where?

The fucking books!

A moment of genius.

Butt-*fucker.*

Obvious, yes, but that's genius for you — a mixture of the obvious and the inspired. Grisha rubbed his cupped palm back and forth across the stubble of his razed number-two scalp. He could not be sure where exactly these moments of brilliance came from — there was some unknowable black magic going on deep in the sightless coal mines of his interior, and every so often news of a diamond would come smoking up some unexpected shaft or other and he would be as amazed as the next man.

Almost ruefully, he stood on Henry's creaking wooden chair — a compact titan towering above the shredded landfill — and began working his way quickly along the shelf, picking up each book and dangling it by the spine, pages hanging as he shook them back and forth, hurling the rejects at the wall when he was satisfied.

It was the Bible that first gave up the booty. Twenty-dollar notes flapped out and fluttered to the floor. He stepped down and began carefully to gather the scattered bills, smoothing them as he did so.

He ran the painful ulcer on the tip of his tongue along the jagged range of his molars, considering. Then, with a feeling of almost embarrassing mental communion with his prey, he clambered back up and began work on the opposite shelf.

Right.

Again!

No doubt about it: he really was on a roll. The vegetarian cookbook yielded another minisquall. But it was the dense immensity of the English dictionary that really delivered the goods. And this time the notes fell heavier, having long been pressed together.

So there was an additional degree of sway in Grisha's shoulder-dipping walk as he made his way down the short internal corridor toward the front door. Three thousand two hundred dollars all told — Henry Wheyland's only future.

With an atypical flourish, Grisha put down his ergonomic backpack (containing the money), stuck his mighty head through the man-sized hole in the thin wall that separated the interior of the flat from the dim communal hall beyond, and greeted his colleague in Russian again.

"All right, Gunt?"

Gunter was sitting on the floor to the right of the hole, away from the pile of dust and debris, with his back to the undamaged and still thrice-locked front door, keeping watch by playing a shooting game

on his cell phone. He held up his hand to indicate that a critical moment in the action was upon him. Then he hit Pause and turned his
head, which, like that of his employee for the evening, was shaven,
scarred, and substantial, though Gunter could at least claim the req-
uisite physical frame to go with it.

"Yeah," Gunter said. "All right."

The bulb at the end of the corridor by the stairs was blinking on
and off.

"Anything?" Grisha asked.

Gunter nodded across the hall in the direction of the opposite
apartment. "Piglet dick and his fat whale opened up to see what was
going on."

"And?"

"Shit theirselves." Gunter smirked, indicating the range of power
tools that lay around him. "You got everything you want?"

"Yeah," Grisha grunted. "One more job, though." The halogen
light in the hall of the flat gave him an odd sort of halo, as if he had
just broken out of heaven.

"What?"

"Gimme." Grisha pointed at the masonry chainsaw with diamond-
tipped chain and hydraulic power pack (pure diesel — for reinforced
concrete and serious brickwork) and then backed away from the
hole so Gunter could swing the heavy tool through.

And thus armed he made his way back.

The bulb in the main room blew as he reentered, and everything
was cast into the uncertain near-darkness of the residual light pollution. But Grisha did not pause, pulling at the ripcord of the engine even as he walked, power pack slung casually over one brutal
shoulder.

There was a moment, though, just before the engine caught — a
moment when the pale moon rode out above the low clouds over the
sea beyond and bathed the keys in the ivory light of one last benedic-
tion. A moment when the piano seemed to inhabit its shape as never
before, gathering luster to its grain as if some innocent pausing for
one last prayer before she sweeps her hair from her neck and in-
clines her head for the axe. Then all was noise: the whine and whir of
chain blades cleaving unresisting wood, the scream of a sundered
soundboard, the crunch and snap of collapse, dust, debris, splinters,
shards, then the crazed twang of severed notes passing away on the
instant into so much dead, tangled, voiceless wire.

16

The Grand Hotel Europe

WEDNESDAY EVENING. And in all his life, Gabriel would never again await the arrival of another human being with such anxiety. He was tired in a way he had never believed possible. Coming out of the lifts, past two armed security men, he had thought about sitting at the bar, but as he had approached (and then stood staring at a free stool), he had been forced into the audience of two suits, not even drunk yet, talking loose and loud about *their* plans for tackling Chechnya, talking in the abstract, inhumanly, as if, like everything else in the world, death and destruction were best dealt with in the manner of a forthright marketing campaign, nothing that a few PowerPoints couldn't handle. And he had seen the eyes of the Russian barmen as they turned away to mix the drinks.

So now he was sitting alone, as far away as possible, in the far corner of the Grand Hotel Europe's belle époque lobby bar, beneath walls of burnished gold and an unreachable empyrean of mirrors, bolt upright in the capacious desolation of his lounge chair. He dreaded having someone drop into one of the three adjacent seats. He dreaded having to interact with the waitress to order a drink. He dreaded how much his drink might cost. He dreaded the impossibility of the night ahead, the desertion of sleep. All he could think to do was to smoke. Listening to the poor pianist summon spirit for his nightly schmaltz was out of the question; reading the endless masturbation in the international business papers was out of the question too. Eating was out—the expense aside, his appetite had completely disappeared. (Indeed, the very thought of food made him feel sick, as if it were some kind of insult or transgression against the ever-ravenous dead.) The television — the television was *utterly* out of the question . . .

There had been another bomb and the pictures had been coming through all afternoon: sons lying on the ground, legs twisted and half covered by bloodstained blankets; fathers carrying their bruised, limp-limbed daughters across broken glass; yet more mothers crying. There was fresh violence in the air. Barbarity and a cold-skinned fear. Even in the hotel, police and security men — newly authorized, self-assured, righteous — were everywhere: on the doors, outside his window, in the lobby. The whole city (country, world) felt as though it were under imminent threat, besieged and bewildered. By whom? For what reason underneath all the other reasons? The news was deeply unreliable. What would happen next was uncertain. And where the hell was Isabella?

All he could do was smoke.

It was almost eleven, and she was therefore an hour late. And so . . . And so he lit another cigarette from the previous. He wanted a proper drink but did not dare, for fear of not being able to stop, for fear of being drunk when she finally arrived. Oh God. Probably just a delay. Her phone didn't work outside the U.S. He checked the time. Julian Avery from the consulate was coming at eleven-fifteen. He had gratefully made the appointment earlier in the afternoon, assuming that they would be able to go through everything together with Isabella as soon as she arrived and utterly forgetting (or not thinking about) the convenience or otherwise of the late hour to Avery himself, who had said nothing of it but calmly promised to be there as though it were all in a day's work, which perhaps it was. He had thought Isabella would have time to shower and change. Now he didn't know whether to call Avery and cancel or see him on his own. Give it five minutes.

He looked up. In the mirrors above his head he saw a man, much older than himself, sitting upside down in a chair, looking back at him as if he were about to fall and smash his face open on the floor. He fidgeted with his virgin mary. He fought the war with his desire to order a vodka. He closed his eyes.

Earlier that afternoon he had returned from the Hermitage to find the light on his bedside phone flashing. Another message from Isabella, Isabella-brief as always: "Hi, it's me — hope you are okay. I'm at Tegel. And I am on a Petersburg flight. Thank Christ. I don't have to go via Moscow. Arrives at eight-thirty your time. Be with you tennish. See you tonight. Grand Hotel Europe. Take care."

So then an almost crazed euphoria had seized him. He retuned the radio to the Russian thrash-rock station and smoked thick and deep out the window, looking at the Russian Museum — a strange echo of the White House or vice versa, he did not know. He did not know anything. (He had said this all his life, facetiously, but now at last he knew he really meant it: he did not know *anything*.) But it didn't matter. The worst that could happen was that he might die — not so bad. Happens to everyone. If she could do it, so could he.

Five minutes later he had calmed, gathered, reordered, found some Chopin, and lain down. But just as sleep was ushering him away from himself, Avery had called, and he had begun (absurdly) pretending to have a cold as he rehearsed his thanks over and over, insisting on being as well as he could be, in the circumstances. Holding up. In the circumstances. And unthinkingly, mind all over the place again, surfing his mad excitement that Isabella was coming, he had made the arrangement to meet up with Avery at eleven-fifteen in the lobby bar.

So next, feeling freshly vulnerable, he had called Connie . . . And had been so touched and taken aback at her sheer human kindness and wisdom and perception and support (when really all he had ever been to her was a pointless heart-clawing complication) that he had begun to choke again — not this time for his mother, but because he couldn't believe that Connie could be so good to him, couldn't believe that he knew a woman this selfless and compassionate. And soft-spoken Connie had talked him all the way back to steadiness, so that when he hung up he had felt able to call Lina again and thank *her* for everything and tell her, in a stable voice, that he was okay and the hotel was such a huge relief and that Isabella was due and that the funeral was already being organized, and that they hoped for this Friday, and that if it went ahead on Friday, then she, Lina, need not be crazy and fly out because he'd be home Saturday, in three days, since there was no way he was going to hang around, and had she got her visa back yet? And yes, he was okay. And speak again tonight, before Isabella arrived.

After that he had taken a bubble bath, listening to the news on BBC World — wars, famine, armies on the march, and then all of a sudden the bomb, and hell seemed loosed again, outside, inside, everywhere—and so he'd climbed out to see the pictures, and then, exhausted, distraught, appalled to the point of epilepsy, he'd turned everything off and tried once more to sleep. And that's when he had fallen to thinking that perhaps his mother's death had begun directing his only-just-subconscious in a new and unwanted direction . . . that each reluctant step he was being forced to take away from her as a living reality was in fact leading him back toward the shadow of his father. But not to sleep. Not to sleep. Rather, it was as though grief's corrosion had somehow rusted over his eyes so that he couldn't open them even had he so wished.

"Hey, Gabs, you awake?"
    He started, catching his knee on the table.
    "Is—Jesus. You scared the shit out of me."
    He stood up, drowsy and confused.
    And so they faced each other, standing in the selfsame square meter of the swarming planet at last, the selfsame genes, the selfsame history: Isabella with her hair longer than usual, curling a little against the pale cream of her scarf; Gabriel with his shorter than when they had been together last, clean-shaven and thinner too than he had been for a long time.
    "I made it," she said.
    "Jesus, Is, I think I passed out . . . I thought you had . . . I thought something . . ." But he could not marshal words to sense.
    "I'm sorry. Security stuff." Isabella speaking softly, her usual hint of subversive humor banished entirely. "How you doing?"
    "I'm actually okay—I'm just . . . I'm just really tired. I should have slept this afternoon. But . . ."
    And for the first time in their adult lives, brother and sister embraced. There was no thinking; it was pure compulsion—too quick for the ruthless intellectual habits of their nature, their nurture. But when they parted, neither was visibly distressed—Gabriel's dark eyes ever unguarded, Isabella's slightly smiling—as if they had silently agreed that for tonight at least, process and organization would be their joint enterprise. As if tears were for people much less tired than they. As if all that might have to be said could wait.
    Instead, Isabella smiled, openly and freely, as she did only in her brother's company.
    "Sorry, Gabs. My phone doesn't work, or I would have called

you again. There was a security nightmare in Berlin. Some complete wankers on a stag jerking around. And we lost another hour. But I couldn't face going back to buy another phone card. I just wanted to get here."

"You seen the news?" he asked.

"Yeah, it was on the TV while we were waiting to board. And Pulkovo was like an army barracks when we landed. It's awful — weird."

The nature of death itself, or death's meaning, had somehow changed.

"The Russian TV has stopped showing it," Gabriel said. "Nobody knows who is in charge or what is really going on." He shrugged heavily, and Isabella saw how extraordinarily tired her brother was. There were broken blood vessels in his eyes. And his face was blank. He really was exhausted. She had wondered how she would behave when she arrived. Now she knew: a reaction to her brother's evident wretchedness — she was going to be all competence and coping.

They were still standing. Isabella glanced around. "Okay, well, I think I'm going to grab a shower and then let's get —"

"Julian Avery is coming over," Gabriel interrupted, still a little frenetic but seemingly unable to moderate anything. "Now, in fact — in five minutes. We're meeting him here. Sorry, but I wanted to —"

"The guy from the consulate?"

"Yes. They've been — they've been brilliant. I mean, Christ knows what would have —"

"Don't." Isabella bit her lip.

"Shit. I think that's him."

Isabella looked behind her. A short, surreptitiously overweight man was crossing the lobby toward the bar. Julian Avery moved with surprising alacrity, his walk a double-time waddle. He had not seen them.

Isabella drew a deep breath. "Okay. Right. So . . ." She hooked her hair behind her ear. "Shall we all get some coffee, then?"

"Good idea." Gabriel nodded. "I was wondering what to drink."

"Hang on a sec." She put down her bag on one of the chairs.

Gabriel spoke softly. "They are being very can-do. Because of Grandpa Max, I suppose. God knows how they have even heard of him. It must be fifteen years since he left."

"They remember everything in the Foreign Office." Isabella took off her scarf. "They will have known exactly who Mum was too, since she had a British passport. You know how it is. They always know everything, somehow. Okay, let's go."

Avery had begun flicking through his briefcase, which he had propped on a stool. Now he stood smartly to greet them. He wore a blue, round-necked, fine merino wool sweater and beige slacks, and Isabella guessed his age as late thirties, but he had one of those fair English faces that appear to change hardly at all between the loss of freckles and fifty-five. His features were genially unremarkable, she thought, save for his hair, which was wound in the tightest possible curls, and his unusually large ears.

She introduced herself, her name sounding strange as she said it out loud. She felt suddenly very British, the granddaughter of Maximilian Glover.

"Julian." He took her offered hand with a demure nod. "I can't say how sorry we all are. My condolences. It must be a very difficult time."

"Thank you."

Gabriel presented himself and said, "We thought coffee, but please, feel free to —"

"Coffee is fine."

The barman nodded and they went back to Gabriel's table and sat down, Isabella taking the chair opposite Avery.

"Thank you so much for coming over here tonight — it's very kind of you," she said.

"No, not at all."

Almost businesslike, she opened her bag for pen and notebook. She was conscious that this was overdoing it but could not stop herself. Since she had taken Gabriel's call outside the Angelika, a renegade part of her had been noticing the increase in unintentional words, involuntary actions. "We were only now saying how grateful we are for your help. Thank you so much for coming out."

"It's the least I could do."

"I've only just arrived from the airport, I'm afraid, so we haven't really had a chance to catch up. And we're both pretty much at sea. With more or less everything we need to be doing . . ."

"Of course." Perhaps taking his cue from Isabella's pad, Avery adopted an air of quiet professional practicality, leaning forward a little, small hands joined, fingers loosely knitted, thumbs pointing toward the mirrored ceiling. "Okay. Well, first of all, the good news is that we have managed to jump the cemetery queue and short-cut some of the other bureaucracy — with the kind help of your father. Your mother can be buried at the Smolensky graveyard on Vasilevsky, which is, I understand, in accordance with her wishes. That's official as of close of play today."

Without needing to look over at him, Isabella felt the entire force field of her brother's attention change direction. So now she spoke quickly, fearful of what he might say if she did not. "Sorry, I'm totally behind here. I live in New York." This was also unnecessary, but she felt the need to invoke the strength somehow resident in the city's name.

Avery had a way of moving his head from one side to the other every so often, as if he were required to hear things with each of his ears in turn in order to quite believe them.

"I've been on flights for the last God knows how long," she explained. "And I haven't had a chance to speak with my father. I don't think Gabriel has either." She did not look across but kept on as casually as she could. "Is our father helping?"

"Oh, I'm so sorry. I had no idea. I assumed . . ." Avery hesitated, but only for a second. "I assumed you had all had the chance to talk."

"No. Not yet." Isabella smiled adeptly. She could not tell how much Avery was reading into their strange lack of familial communication. "We were going to go through everything after we had spoken to you."

"Right. Well, I should . . . I should fill you in." The coffee was set down, and Avery was silent until the waiter had left. "I had a conversation with your father earlier today. Just after I spoke with you, Gabriel, this afternoon. Actually, he rang me. I'm sure he will tell you all of this . . . He was calling to confirm that he would be meeting all the expenses. Unfortunately, there is something of a cemetery . . . er, shall we say a cemetery *system* operating here in Petersburg, and, well, certain people have to be paid . . . Though as I say, everything is now settled on this score, as of this afternoon." He sipped his coffee. "Once that side was sorted out, the rest was just a matter of contacting the relevant people at the hospital and the undertakers — and, of course, the people who organize the service itself. I have passed all three sets of details on to your father's solicitors. I understand that it is his intention to meet these expenses as well. But as I say, once the cemetery is confirmed, and the service, the rest is comparatively straightforward. So Friday should, fingers crossed, be just a matter of details."

Again she spoke quickly. "That's really great news — about getting a space at the cemetery, I mean." Only now did she risk a glance at her brother. He had his hand to his forehead and she could not see his face. "And it's a massive relief to know that it's all being done so quickly. Is it okay if I give you a call first thing tomorrow and check if there is anything you need us to do — once I've had a chance to catch my breath?"

"Yes, of course." Avery raised a manicured finger and thumb to his stiff shirt collar. "I can be the liaison, if that's helpful — in case your father gets through to me first, or you need a man on the ground, as it were."

His eyes expressed genuine sympathy; an intelligent man, well used to dealing delicately with distressed human beings. And she was grateful for that kind "gets through" — as if there would really be any trouble with their father "getting through" to his children if he, or they, had wished it.

"Thank you — that might be useful." She knew that the natural end of the conversation had been reached. She paused a moment and then asked, "Will there be an autopsy?"

Avery turned his head a fraction, as if to allow his left ear a chance to confirm the impressions of the right, but if he was surprised at this ambush, neither his face nor his manner betrayed it. "No. In the case of an older person's death, where there are no suspicious circumstances, then there is not usually an autopsy."

There was a moment's silence. Avery slowly rotated his head. Though he had sensed the disquiet previously, Isabella had now taken him into a much murkier place altogether. And she realized that rather than adding anything to his statement, he would wait until she spoke again. Silence was his natural holding pattern; he was a diplomat, after all. She was just about to ask another question when suddenly, to her complete surprise, Gabriel sat forward for the first time.

"And there's no problem with her being a British national . . . who defected and all of that?"

Again without changing tone or manner, Avery directed his attention to her brother. "Yes . . . you are right — it's a strange situation. There might have been an issue with nationality. I was talking to your father about this. But . . . well, the truth is, I think we can assume that the Russians know who your mother is and that they don't have a problem." He finished his coffee, pleased perhaps to be back on familiar consular ground. "I would be amazed if they didn't know her. They knew your grandfather of course, very well. And they will have known your father too. And all defections were treated with extra-special . . . er, *attention,* shall we say? So even if she used her married name when she came back, I'd be surprised if they did not know that she was Maria Gavrilov originally. In fact, your own surname, Glover, might well be flagged on their computers—I know it's a common enough name, but they might well cross-check. Again, I wouldn't be surprised."

It was a clever putting-at-ease question of her brother's, Isabella realized. He had interrupted only to move things on after her autopsy inquiry—as if to take over now that she had gone crazy. Perhaps she had.

Avery continued. "My guess, for what it's worth, is that they used her original return application politically—granted her a visa to show that the new Russia was not the same as the Soviet Union. If anything, they will quite like the fact that as a Russian she wanted to be buried here. I don't think we need worry about all of that."

Isabella cut in. "Did my father say that he would be coming on Friday?" She knew this was brutal, but she also knew that the question had to be asked and that if she left her brother to his own devices, he would never ask it.

And this time Julian Avery's hesitation was obvious. "No. No . . . Actually, he didn't mention it. I . . . I presume he would want to be here, but I can't—"

"Not necessarily." It would be better if she just said it. "Our parents were separated."

"I see."

Gabriel did not allow the silence to lengthen. "And will the service be in the Russian Orthodox tradition?"

"Yes. Was that your mother's faith?"

"Mum didn't have any." This from Isabella.

"But," Gabriel pursued, "I assume that we have to have a Russian Orthodox service at the Smolensky?"

"Yes." Avery nodded slowly. "It may be possible to arrange something else, but not before Friday."

"Oh God no, don't worry." Isabella gave a wan smile. "Everything you have done is . . . is really helpful. We don't want to change anything. We're just grateful that it's all going to be dealt with so painlessly."

The security man passed behind them again, his face set and seeming to say, *Terror does not sleep and neither do I.*

She had dropped her bags in their room and now sat waiting for Gabriel to return. He had gone to fetch yet more cigarettes. This did not feel like the Russia she knew. Indeed, this hotel, this lobby bar, wasn't her Russia, her Petersburg. In countless visits to the city, she had been here — what, twice before? Once with her grandfather, as she recalled. She looked around: two escort girls, laughing quietly and sipping their mineral water at one of the narrow tables in the corner; two slack-bellied businessmen drinking untidily at the bar, lecturing the blank-faced barman. An elderly American couple. It was past midnight. But something like midafternoon as far as her body was concerned. She knew for certain that she would not sleep, not soon, probably not at all. Indeed, ever since she had arrived, her brain had been moving so quickly that she had experienced the peculiar sensation of not being able to rely on reality, as if she were driving so fast that the scenery ahead was only just managing to construct itself in time, as if she were having to do far more than merely read the road, as if she were having to guess how the world was going to fashion itself. Their father had certainly outflanked them thus far — not only did he know about the death and the funeral plans, he was paying for everything already. But would he come? Gabriel's only thought would be how to keep him away. And her brother was right: their father was all corruption and tarnishing; their father could find a way to taint even the truthfulness of sorrow. And yet she could not help wondering what he would feel — as a human being, if nothing else. What was her father feeling right now, for instance?

She smothered these questions quickly with the thick blanket of her loyalty as Gabriel reappeared, and in doing so had one of those odd moments which come only infrequently when you have known someone forever — longer: she suddenly saw her brother clearly as a stranger might. Yes, he was handsome in what she always thought of as his famous-for-something-but-nobody-is-sure-what look, but now his slight scruffiness, his tousled hair, his loose shirt, his jeans, his battered boots — they somehow told against him. Where before there had been a casual confidence dressing down, she now saw anguish dressing up. His manner no longer said, "I don't care to manage any better — take it or leave it," but instead, "This is the best I can manage."

"How you feeling?" she asked.

"Fantastic. All go."

Isabella smiled. "I mean, can you take a drink or are you going to crash?"

"I'd love a drink. I would absolutely *love* a drink." Gabriel eased into his seat and grimaced. "I didn't sleep last night — in fact, I can't remember when I last slept. I'm totally wasted. What you thinking?"

"I'm thinking vodka. It can only help."

"Tonics separate?" Gabriel found a lopsided grin.

She smiled in return. Vodka that was worth tasting — it meant they were in Russia together again.

Gabriel put up his hand to catch the attention of the barman and unwrapped the new packet of cigarettes. "But if I burst into tears, get me to the lifts. I'm serious. It's been happening all day."

"You won't. You're too tired." Isabella held out her palms. "Chuck the cigarettes, then."

"You smoking again?"

"No."

"Me neither."

After that, everything external slowly faded away until there was just the two of them talking to each other, moving slowly across the ice toward the discussion that they knew they must have. On any other subject they could be as frank and as open as it was possible for two human beings to be; but on the subject of their father — and on this subject alone — there was convention and even taboo between them.

"What are we doing here, by the way?" Isabella asked.

"Lina. Lina sorted it all out. She says not to worry about anything . . . and I was too . . . I was too battered to argue . . . so I just checked in."

"Right." Unlike everyone else, Isabella understood without judgment the exact nature of her brother's situation. And above all her other concerns on the subject, she worried about the hidden damage it was doing to him. But all that was for another day. "Is Lina coming?"

Gabriel shook his head. "Probably not, now it's looking like Friday."

Isabella considered. "I'd better go to the flat tomorrow. I suppose we're going to have to ship Mum's stuff home. Maybe not the furniture. But all the rest — her private papers, her books and everything. We should start."

Her brother smiled sadly. "We'll spend the day. Go through it to-gether."

She watched him sip his vodka, then hold it on his tongue for a few seconds, tasting.

"She had begun to call quite a lot," he said. "It was getting pretty mad. Every night."

"Mad?"

"I didn't mean that. Not mad. I mean she was becoming more roundabout—she was saying more and more roundabout stuff that always seemed to imply other things." Gabriel raised an eyebrow ruefully. "As well as all the usual lectures on how to live your life and the state of the world."

Isabella swallowed and felt the burn. "Hard to know whether or not to take all that stuff seriously."

Her brother sucked his teeth. "She did," he said.

"Yes." Isabella nodded slowly. "You know, in the last few months she kept writing to me about Thomas Jefferson." She affected a de-clamatory voice. "'All attempts to influence the mind by temporal punishments, or burdens, or civil incapacitations tend only to beget habits of hypocrisy and meanness . . .' You know the routine."

Gabriel nodded slowly.

The vodka was working its magic on their willful blood. Isabella took another sip. "Do you ever think about those summers when she used to drive us around Europe—on her own in that old car?"

"All the time." She saw the lines around her brother's eyes as he spoke. "Nothing but concentration camps and art galleries for weeks on end."

"And don't forget every house that the great composers ever lived in," Isabella added. "Mozart's cradles and Beethoven's death masks. Jesus, she must have driven us a thousand miles every summer."

Her brother shut his eyes a moment and screwed up his face—against the vodka's bite, perhaps. "You know she was ill?"

Isabella looked away, momentarily taken aback, though this was one of her suspicions. "Ill in what way?"

"She was coughing—coughing really badly on the phone. The last time she called she had this . . . this *fit*. I'm not joking—she was coughing for about five minutes." Gabriel straightened and extended his arm before him, his cigarette between fingers. "You know what, Is? I think she had cancer and I think she knew it. I think that's why she was ringing me. I think she found out recently. I think the stroke might have been a blessing."

Isabella forced herself to relax her forehead.

"She smoked all her life. It happens, Is. It happens all the time."

"Yes . . . yes, I know." Isabella tipped tonic into what remained of her vodka. "Actually, I've been thinking the same."

"You have?"

"Yes . . . I mean, not specifically cancer. But I've been thinking that she might have been ill." And now Isabella saw what she had been looking for: a chance to take those last few steps. "It would explain something that she wrote in her last letter. She said that I should make sure that I visited her here, in Petersburg, before I . . . before I visited Dad."

Her brother was silent.

Isabella asked, "Do you think he's going to come?"

"Who, Dad?" As if she meant anyone else.

"Yes—Dad."

But Gabriel, either too tired or past caring or vodka-quelled, surprised her again by speaking in a flat and emotionless voice. "He's only been back here once since they got married. And that was to sell Grandpa Max's house and plunder all his stuff. He hates this place."

"Yeah, you're right . . . But this is slightly different, isn't it? It's not like they're divorced."

"Is, Dad doesn't give a fuck about Mum." She watched him put out his cigarette. "All he will care about is recouping the money we made him give her. They haven't spoken properly for ten years."

Isabella wanted to ask her brother how he knew this. But she guessed that he didn't, that it was a belief, a quasi-religious assertion. Gabriel loathed their father as much as he loved their mother, and to such an extent that he could not countenance the fact that the two of them had ever got on at all. Their marriage was opaque to him—an abomination he refused to consider. And now was not the time to dispute this or indeed any of the hundred credos of their family lore.

"Are you bothered about his paying for things?"

"Let him pay. Even if he is trying to make us feel guilty. It doesn't matter. The result is that Mum gets buried where she wanted to and has a decent funeral."

"Do you think he'll try and get in touch?"

"Not with me."

She felt the challenge behind this and automatically rose to it. "Well, he's hardly going to call me direct either, is he? The last few times I saw him, I took good care to tell him he was a bastard and a failure."

"He won't come. He won't try to get in touch. He'll just do every-thing through his brand-new puppet at the consulate."

"That's not fair. Julian is a decent bloke."

"Maybe." Gabriel finished his drink. "Why did you ask about all that autopsy shit?"

She was caught out by the question but knew she had to tell the truth—and immediately, because even in his current state, her brother wouldn't miss the hesitation. Sometimes the speed and accuracy with which he read people reminded her of . . . her father.

"I had this mad idea Dad killed her."

Gabriel shook his head. "Jesus, Is. You are more fucked up than I am."

But this was her other suspicion.

17

A Plan Enacted

THERE WAS NO POINT in locking the door. The cardboard they had tacked over the gaping wound in the wall would fool no one. In any case, there was nothing left to steal. So he pulled it shut and made his way into the darkness of the unlit stairwell.

Once on the street, he paused and looked around for a moment, as if assessing the fighting weight and shape of the night. He set off at a slow jog, following the same route they had taken two nights previously on the way to the gig — through the gap in the railings and into the cemetery. His muscles felt loose and limber and he moved with the ease of fitness, listening to the fall of his own step, the rasp of his own breathing. Above the swaying trees, a gibbous moon seemed to follow him, slipping from cloud to cloud.

On the far side of the cemetery, he saw a group of figures gathered by the gate on the corner of Maly Prospekt. He slowed. Ordinarily he would have taken the most direct route and run straight at them, through them, beyond them. But tonight he did not want any distraction. So he ducked left, soundlessly crossing first one grave, then another, careful with his footing on the wet stones, until he came to the small parallel path. Here the trunks were thick and the way was darker and he had to slow for fear of low twigs and thorns scratching at his face, unwilling (from lifelong habit) to use his hands as protection. Dogs were barking somewhere, discordant, out of time.

He climbed the railings and emerged onto the roadside opposite the canning factory. In the shadow of an overhanging pine, he paused a moment to check that the envelope had not slipped out of his pocket. He was an anonymous figure dressed in dark colors: Henry's V-neck pullover over gray T-shirt, his old tracksuit bottoms, his boots, and his playing shoes around his neck. The money was still there.

He went on through the mostly dead Vasilevsky streets, stray cats all that he saw, until he reached the river. Then he slowed his jog to a brisk walk and crossed the Neva on the Leytanta Bridge, the river as black tonight as liquid obsidian.

Entering the central district, he stiffened a little, continuing at a more casual pace, ready to appear drunk should a car slow or show undue interest. Soon enough he was sloping along the banks of the Kryukova Canal by the pitchy water of New Holland—a derelict place, unvisited by all but small-time criminals, addicts, and the gangs of homeless insane. Though he kept his head down and his gaze on the pavement in front of him, he was listening, his meticulous ear primed for the slowing note of an engine or the fall of another step. He knew well that it was in these dead hours, when Petersburg slipped off its creamy European robes and revealed itself a mean and swarthy peasant once more, that the real business of Russian life got done. Boy and man, he had seen it: the black Mercedes rolling down the half-lit street, the tinny police car idling, smear-faced street girls slipping like sylphs along the railings of the canals, and the drugged and the drunk always watching from their darkened doorways, glassy-eyed and desperate, crawling back and forth between heaven and hell, one scabby knee at a time. And all of it dangerous. He glanced up.

A figure had appeared on the pavement ahead.

"Arkady."

"Oleg."

They did not shake hands but, after a moment's mutual assessment, fell swiftly into step, walking side by side in the direction of the Mariinsky Theatre. The other was a man of average height but on the brink of irreversible obesity, balding, with a puffy, pastry-fond face, small eyes, and the fastidious manner of the superfluous employee.

"You've not changed, Arkasha."

"You've lost your hair and you are fatter."

They spoke in the most familiar Russian.

"I was married. There is nothing to do but eat and talk about food. You have the money?"

"You should do some exercise," Arkady said. "Or you will die even faster. Yes, I have the money. Not here, though. Do you have what you need?"

"Yes." Oleg raised the hand that was carrying a dark sports bag a fraction. "But you know, I can't do the security gate. I told you that."

"You did."

Oleg was already regretting that he had agreed to meet his old school friend again — and fuck the money. He had forgotten: like nobody else he had ever met, Arkady Alexandrovitch made him immediately nervous, made him feel as if everything he said or did was somehow a low-down lie. They had shared bunks in the final two years, which was as close to close as anyone came back at the orphanage. Arkady was somebody that most of the others left alone, even the ugliest of the bastards — someone you couldn't change, reason or fight with, someone who would always go crazier faster. And Oleg had felt priv- ileged to be one of the few that Arkady spoke to about anything. Then they'd been *phartsovschiks* together in the 1990s for a while, trading small-time contraband on the black market, Arkady bring- ing him the stuff to sell from God knew where and no questions asked. That had been a frantic time. And even now, years later, there was something flattering about Arkady's asking for help. Plus the money. Okay, not fuck the money. The money was good. But the in- escapable truth was that he, Oleg, had not actually picked a single lock in five years. And somehow he sensed that Arkady knew this. Still, if it came to it, he could just give the banknotes back. Arkady wouldn't kill him, and he could live with five more minutes of the other's scorn. There was curiosity too: what was it all about? Arkady Alexandrovitch was no common thief.

They jinked left, waited at the lights, then walked out in the open, across the wide courtyard in front of the Mariinsky. A police car was crawling toward the river, window down, cigarette glowing, but it was following a group of tourists fresh from one of the clubs, stag- gering along with their arms around their prostitutes. The Russians would be ignored.

Arkady had not said where they were going. And Oleg felt it would betray too much anxiety to ask. So it was only when they had circled around the back of the conservatory, crossed the Gribo- edova on the bridge of lions, and entered the narrower streets where Arkady began to slacken his pace that Oleg guessed they must be getting closer.

"Are we breaking into one of the Dostoyevsky flats?" Oleg spoke too loudly, smirked, and shifted his sports bag again.

But Arkady seemed not to have heard. Instead he now slowed right down, as if to maximize the walk-by time, and motioned casually toward the building on the corner, facing the next bridge.

"The first-floor apartment," he said softly. "With the balcony."

Oleg nodded, glad of the semblance of professionalism.

The street itself was mercifully quiet. They passed slowly along by the walls, both men peering up at the window. Arkady was listening, Oleg glancing around. There were very few lighted rooms in any of the other apartments on either side of the road. They drew level with the gated entrance. Arkady gripped one of the metal bars and pushed sharply. The lock rattled but nothing gave.

"Come on." Abruptly Arkady crossed the canal without looking back and walked straight down the stairs that formed the entrance to the CCCP Café.

Oleg caught up with him and they stood together while their eyes readjusted to the heavier darkness of the stairwell.

"Here's the money." Arkady slipped an envelope from his tracksuit trousers. "It's all there."

Oleg hesitated. "How are we going to get past the gate?"

"I don't know."

Oleg drew a deep breath, shrugged, and put the envelope in the breast pocket of his jacket, unwilling to count the notes or stow them within, given what he saw as the unlikelihood of his actually being able to do anything to earn them. It was not his fault if Arkady was insane. In fact, a good part of him was rather glad that his old business partner had clearly failed to think out any sort of plan, since they'd probably just have to forget about the whole job and that would be that. He wouldn't hear from the mad bastard for another seven years or whatever it was. Get back to his little locksmith's hole in the wall. Cut honest keys.

Oleg located his cigarettes and with them a mislaid cache of self-assurance. He exhaled. "We can't just stand around and hope someone goes in or out. It's nearly three now — nobody is going to come home at this time. Nobody nice, anyway."

Arkady had his hands wrapped around his playing shoes. He said nothing. They climbed a few of the café steps together and looked across the bridge at the balcony. There were no lights on in the entire face of the building. The moon was behind clouds for the moment. Some sounds reached them from Sennaya Square—drunks, raucousness, shouts, not too far away. A car turned onto the embankment and began coming slowly toward them. But the headlights brightened with the acceleration—some old piece of Soviet-made shit and nothing to worry about. All the same, they dropped back down beneath street level.

Arkady half turned. "If we get up onto the balcony, will you be able to get us in through the windows?"

"Yeah, I—"

"How long?"

Oleg affected a businesslike whisper. "Depends. If it's bolted, then I might be able to cut through them. But that could be twenty minutes. Depends. If it's only locked, then I don't know. Quicker. I can't tell until I see. Is there an alarm?"

"I don't know."

Oleg exhaled a heavy jet of smoke.

"Okay." Arkady produced some leather gloves from one of his pockets and began putting them on.

"But we can't get onto the balcony, and even if we had some ladders, which we don't, then we can't just piss around breaking in up there. The whole street can see that fucking balcony."

"There's a ladder in the courtyard behind us. It's padlocked, but that won't be a problem, will it, my friend?"

"Is there?" The realization that Arkady must have been here earlier after all caused Oleg to fall back on his mettle. "Okay. We're still going to be seen by anyone who comes up or down either side of the canal."

"Only while you are going up it." They were standing close, and Arkady was looking directly into Oleg's face for the first time. "We'll get the ladder. You go up. I take the ladder away. You get in. You open the front door from the inside. You come down here. You let me in through the security gate. I get inside. You can go."

Oleg climbed two steps away—despite the gloom of the stairwell, the other's eyes seemed to sear through him, as if to accuse him of lifelong cowardice and shirking. The moment of decision had come. He looked across the canal to reassess the balcony. The returning moon seemed to light the window in question. He hooked his thumbs to adjust his belt, which felt suddenly tight. The window would undoubtedly be easier than a quadruple-locked front door, which he had been dreading. There was at least *that*. In a way, the window would be a relief . . . But what if there was some sort of alarm? He turned back to Arkady. His chest had tightened with the smoke. He had asthma. He flicked his cigarette. "Okay, let's get the ladder."

"Good. Once you are up, I will take it away and nobody will know. I will wait. If you have a problem, whistle. Don't worry. I'll be listening." Arkady grinned. "I have very good ears."

He was leaning close to the gate beneath the shadow and he heard Oleg coming long before he saw him. He stood up straight and peered through the rails, his boots swinging around his neck, the playing shoes now on his feet. A moment later he made out the heavy shape of the locksmith walking hurriedly through the shadows of the inner courtyard.

Arkady's voice was calm, to counter the agitation he sensed in the other's footfall: "I think the button is over there."

Oleg grunted.

Even in the penumbra of the streetlamps Arkady could see the sheen of sweat on his companion's high forehead.

The gate began to jerk open. Oleg had to stand back to let it swing inward. His voice was close to a hiss: "It's the staircase in the corner. I propped the door so it can't shut. There is nobody there. Everything is quiet. You'll be —"

"Good." Arkady was already slipping through.

For a moment their eyes met.

"Right, well, I'll see you, Arkady Alexandrovitch."

"Yes."

And with that Arkady was gone.

Oleg turned on his heel and walked as quickly as he could in the direction of the demented anonymity of Sennaya Square.

Arkady stood alone in the darkness of her hall, his face expressionless. The front door was shut behind him. For a long while he remained quite still, listening for any sound of movement coming from the other apartments in the building. But aside from the muffled cough of a distant pipe, there was only silence. Gradually he was beginning to be able to make out the shapes of photographs on the wall.

He lifted his boots off his neck, put them down on the mat, turned to his right, and walked noiselessly toward the open doorway at the end, the direction from which he guessed Oleg must have entered.

He wanted to be sure that the curtains were drawn before he began his business here tonight.

He found himself in a large room with high ceilings. Lighting from the street relieved the darkness, and he looked about at the unfamiliar shapes and their stretched shadows: a deep chair, a chaise longue, a large desk against the far wall, and a table to one side, in the shallow bay of the window. He walked over, treading as lightly as he could. Cold air was coming in at waist height through a small circular hole in the glass. Arkady cursed violently under his breath and drew the curtains. Evidently Oleg had been unable to deal with the locks and had cut through the pane to open the balcony windows from the inside.

Arkady's business: he wanted names and addresses . . . He wanted contact with her family. And through contact, he wanted money. Not just a few thousand stolen rubles but the kind of money that would change his life — money to pay for the next two years at the conservatory, of course, but in his fiercest imaginings more than that: money to pay for a decent apartment, a proper piano, travel in Europe, flights to the U.S., big hotels in which he could fuck and sleep until four in the afternoon after all the hundred concerts he would play . . . The kind of bank-account-swelling money that the shit lice at the British and American embassies would consider enough to make him "safe" for visa approval. No more of this bullshit existence. He wanted the full life that was rightfully his. He wanted the life that she had denied him, the life to which he was entitled. Legitimacy. Everything or nothing.

With the curtains closed, there was no sense working in the dark. So he crossed over to the desk and bent to follow the flex of the lamp, his gloved fingers seeking the switch. His eyes had grown used to the dimness and he blinked a little when the room suddenly declared itself in detail: paintings of landscapes and a portrait of someone he did not recognize on the wall, a chandelier, thick rugs on the floor, another lamp by the chaise longue, a stack of English-language magazines on a low table he had not seen between the chairs, an expensive stereo with twin freestanding speakers in front of the wall opposite, which was, he now saw, one vast bookcase, crammed and bursting.

He turned back to the desk. The surface was empty save for a map of the Moscow underground and some lens-cleaning solution. There were no photographs . . . Another car was passing along the embankment. He stiffened, listening. But the engine note did not change; it was not stopping. He breathed in sharply through narrowed nostrils. He opened the drawers. They were all empty. He slid them shut, stood back, and looked around. A single courier's shipping carton lay on the floor by the side of the desk. The label simply displayed the number six. He took off the lid: newspaper clippings, bills, official-seeming letters in English that he did not understand, but no personal correspondence. Obviously somebody had already been here and started clearing up.

He walked around the room, treading softly in his soft shoes, searching more closely. A small wooden box on the bookshelf caught his eye, but inside was only an expensive-looking mahjong set. Fuck. It felt like she lived here alone. Was she divorced? Was her husband dead? It didn't matter: someone close to her had been here . . . And whoever it was — child, husband, friend — they would see that hole in the window when they came back. So now he would have to take something valuable to obscure the real reason for his coming. Thanks to that fat swine-fucker. Because if they thought that the burglar had come not for money but some other reason, they would be alerted, and when he later turned up asking for a new life, they might just work out how he had come to find them. He could say that she had given him their names and addresses, of course, but he could not afford for them to think of him as even possibly suspicious.

The heating pipes stirred again, but this time he paid them no heed. Frustrated, he began to go through the books, hoping for a handwritten name inside one of the covers — a gift which the giver had signed. He had a dangerous urge to find some music — to play something as loud as the stereo would go. He bit his tongue. He cursed Oleg again. He'd try the other rooms, but chances were that boxes one to five were already gone. All he needed was names and addresses. What about the kitchen or, better, the bedroom? Or — or maybe the photographs . . . for names, at least.

The light in the entrance hall did not work, so he had only the residual illumination thrown through the doorway from the main room to see by. But it was enough. He had not realized the extent of the display before. The entire wall was covered — a big map, pictures of dancers, icons, the Romanov family, a clown, other figures from history he did not recognize; but it was the photographs nearer the light that drew him, held him.

He knew nothing of the people framed there — nothing save that which he now saw for the first time. His eye devoured these pictures:

a family, the moments of a family's story captured. He stood close in, his head turning this way and that, transfixed. He snagged again on the faces of two children in school uniforms — a boy and a girl, no more than seven or eight, both smiling, the girl in front. They looked strikingly similar. Next, a photograph of four people taken, presumably, on holiday — this time the boy and girl were awkward and not smiling, thirteen or fourteen, and there was a thin man with fair hair and tight lips staring back into the lens, and *her* . . .

He stood back again. Here it all was on the wall in front of him: the life he did not have, the child he had never been, the story that was not his . . . Here was the boy in a university gown. Here, the girl in a red bridesmaid dress — long dark hair, pretty. And again the four of them, outside a big old house, the boy and girl grown up, none of them smiling this time, the thin man in jeans looking away, a sports car. Here was the thin man talking into a telephone — older this time, smoking, white hair. Here *she* was with the thin man when they were both very young, sitting somewhere on a bench, with a pram. Here the boy with his head sticking out of a tent. And here a woman about his own age, with short black hair, standing facing the photographer with the sun in her eyes and her arms spread out on railings behind her — it was the same girl as in the other pictures. And behind her — that was New York. His eyes swarmed the wall. He read the words below the pictures — Nicholas, Gabriel, and Isabella. Names. At Cambridge. Down in Devon. Highgate. In the study. Paris. Camping in the Black Forest. Moscow. New York. He leaned in again. And his eye settled on the smallest photograph of all, just off the center of the display: a portrait of . . . of his *mother* — proud, clear-eyed, and untroubled in some uniform he did not know from the old times. She was young: twenty, twenty-one. More than a decade younger than he was now. The thought whispered in his blood: she may already have been carrying him inside her. His mother. His mother. He had never allowed those syllables to form, even in the deepest caves of his most secret mind. He turned away.

His throat felt tight and he wanted to screw up his face for some reason. He . . . He . . . He needed something to steal. Down here must be her bedroom. Where was the light switch? This place was so dark. He had the names. Fuck the addresses. Maybe there was some jewelry in here. Take something valuable. And get out of this terrible place . . . He found the switch and the light came blazing on, horribly bright, and he forced himself to take another step into the room, squinting a little, and then . . . And then he saw her piano.

But even now, standing stranded, motionless in the bedroom of the mother he had never known, Arkady Alexandrovitch Artamenkov did not recognize the prickling in the corners of his eyes for what it really was. Like everybody else in the thinking world, he assumed he was going mad.

18

A Funeral

T HEY WALKED BEHIND the funeral cart in a deep and painful rut of self-consciousness. The wind was harrying in from the east, causing the clouds to race and the sun to come and go and come and go as if dashing from one to the next. Neither Gabriel nor Isabella could absorb or respond to or even quite believe what was happening in front of their eyes. Instead they made their way — reeling, disciplined, half apologetic, half aghast — like two intelligence agents plunged unexpectedly into the bloody bayonet business of life-and-death on the frontline. Indeed, the whole extremely-bright-sunlight-then-sudden-shadow day had thus far been as alien as any they had ever experienced.

A wiry gray-haired man wearing a threadbare liveried tunic sat up high, driving two skin-and-bone black horses, all three reluctant: the horses to walk, the man to use his whip. The horses pulled a cart. And on the cart was a pale wood coffin, in which the body of their mother must surely be feeling every jolt. Gabriel came along behind and to the right, dressed in hastily bought cheap black trousers and a dark shirt; Isabella was on the left a little way off in her black work suit, black hose, and her office shoes — used to cabs, sidewalks, and lobbies, not gravel, not potholes. Behind the twins, Yana and Yana's mother, both in the long skirts of Russian mourning. And behind them, four near-strangers all wearing their most svelte and somber tailoring — Avery, officially representing their father; Avery's wife, Sophie (in sunglasses); and two others from the office, whom Julian had introduced but whose names neither twin knew nor would ever remember.

Surprised alike by the formality of what the rite required and the Dalíesque actuality of the horses, and yet way past both surprise and actuality, the twins had met with the others at the main entrance to the Smolensky cemetery. They had now been walking five minutes and already it was absolutely unendurable and absolutely had to be endured.

Gabriel had desolately (and happily) concluded that everything that ever happened was far, far beyond his control. Likewise, he had long since abandoned any attempt to apprehend the narrower significance and implication of what losing a parent actually meant. Each moment manufactures itself into a vast and hideous writhing universe-wide reality regardless, he thought; what business could it be of his? Nobody had the slightest idea what was actually going on. The horses were sweating steadily and the smell came and went on the gusts of the wind. His mother had always hated animals. *We have enough excrement in our cities.* Meanwhile the cart bumped and banged and the coffin shifted an inch here, back a few centimeters there, and he worried that perhaps it might slide right off and dive nose-first onto the gravel, splintering the wood, two dead legs shooting out the end, buckling, body following, crumpling, snapping, folding under its own weight. What was the flexibility of lifeless human sinew? What was the elasticity of death? At any moment he expected his mother to sit up and harangue them for such uneven treatment.

If anything, Isabella was even further away from reality, her thoughts droning around and around like a maddened bee trapped in an empty jar—amazed, upset by, resigned to, and yet bitterly angry with the numbness of her own head as she smacked it repeatedly against the invisible borders of her new circumstances. Give me something in here to sting and I will gladly give up my life to sting it. Only this *has* to stop. (Besides that, her feet were starting to hurt.) Her only real feeling, she felt, was that she could not feel. The best she could manage was the strange sensation of imagining that she was an old woman, older than her mother, sitting somewhere on a retirement home couch watching events as if they were footage of her thirty-two-year-old self in Petersburg—footage that had somehow become part of a documentary film about the legacy of defection. Or estrangement. Or the working life of animals. They were passing under trees, and another cloud had obscured the sun, and the semidarkness was as mad as the intense light that had caused her to squint only a second ago. The horses had become even more reluctant, so that the pace slowed even further . . . They might as well have crawled to the grave on their hands and knees. Would have been quicker. She wanted it over. She wanted it done.

But perhaps it was not the horses, nor the threadbare livery of the driver, nor the uneasy trees that most prevented the two from finding a way to access whatever feelings they had both imagined the funeral of their mother would evoke. Perhaps instead it was the old women . . . For waiting ahead at the main cemetery crossroads were five such, swathed in heaviest black. And without acknowledgment or query, these old women now filed slowly into step on either side of the coffin, flanking bewildered Gabriel and furious Isabella. Who they were and where they came from, nobody appeared to know. Neither did anyone wish to take responsibility for asking, or for telling them to go back there. (Part of the arrangements? Part of the package? Normal? Not normal?) And for the next ten minutes, these five walked beside the cart as well — now sighing, now incanting, now silent, continually crossing themselves. Some final delegation dispatched from the twilight fringes of the living to murmur Maria Glover to her judgment.

And for all anyone cared, Isabella thought, they could indeed be her mother's sisters. Because the fact was, they knew next to nothing about their own mother's family. They had never met a single living soul who shared their mother's blood. (How much farther? How much farther?) Just an austere photograph of a severe woman: Russian Granny, Oksana. That a life could end like this. That this is what it all came down to. Who *was* this woman they were burying today? Who were all these people already buried? It was all too hasty; there was no time even to attempt to find her mother's family, no time to do anything; the whole business felt mad mad mad and Isabella wondered if Gabriel was right to insist on having it all done here and so quickly. But then, what did it matter? And where else could her mother be buried? And what family? And what friends? At least they knew for sure now that their father could not show up. Not unless he was planning a surprise at the open grave.

And for all anyone knew, Gabriel thought, these old women might simply be actresses sent in as part of the day's skillful conspiracy to subvert its own crazed reality — a conspiracy of which he was well aware but could do nothing. (The October wind was fresh, though, and took away the smell of the horses, and that was good. They must be nearly there. How much longer? How much longer?) And it was amazing how swiftly life could come at you when it felt like it. You thought you were moving fast — seasons passing unmarked, anniversaries barely celebrated, numbers careering forward on all the checks you had to write — but then these sort of things happened and you realized that Time hadn't even got out of first gear. You realized that when Time really opened up and hit the gas, there was no telling how fast it might go — famine and floods crammed into the working week, entire lives passing away and forgotten in five short days, the heavens and the earth fashioned in six. Jesus, the incredible speed of it all — a routine Sunday night in Tufnell Park, the telephone, Monday in the visa queue, Tuesday hop on a plane, and by Friday *this*. And when time was racing, everything became impossible to understand or process or deal with. Of *course* it did. And, dear God, the utter intolerableness but utter necessity of what he had been required to talk about, consider, decide upon these last days — and mostly through Yana's honest and well-meaning translations: "Do you like that we see your mother's face for our praying, or do you like she keeps a special mask, like a wail, for the dead faces — so we can see but Masha is still little bit covered, like a wedding . . . a wedding material from the brides . . . It's a wail, yes? You understand?"

They came around a shallow kink in the path and out from beneath the trees again. The way ahead, the last few hundred yards, was smoother underfoot, or so it seemed — marked out by manicured roses and thorns and fourteen crooked white headstones. If he did die up there on Calvary, then the last thing he would have wanted was resurrection. Not this, Father, not this shit *again*.

There was an awkward delay before they were allowed to enter the chapel. (Lid back on one coffin and haul it out the back; lid off a new one and haul it in the front.) So for a while they were all required to stand around outside, at a loss, as the sun kept on coming and going, coming and going, and the swaying trees appeared taller than ever. Nobody knew the name of the black birds that wheeled against the sky. But something like a robin settled on an iron cross close to where the twins now stood a little apart.

Isabella spoke first, her voice low but clear, as if she did not really care who heard: "Why can't we just bury her? What's going to happen in here? How long is it going to be? I want it to be *over*."

Gabriel was cold in his shirt now they'd stopped walking. "I think they have to . . . I think it's part of the service or whatever. Avery said you choose a rite and you have to go along with the whole procedure if you want a site here. Maybe the church people insist. Or the owners. God knows."

"I wish they would keep God out of it. It's just such *horseshit*. And it's making me hate. And I can't, I can't —"

"I know, I know, but Is . . . Ssshhh." His voice was oddly calm. "It doesn't matter. You know that. Nothing we say or think or do here now comes even close to what is actually happening or what anything actually means."

"I feel like I'm dead. I feel like Mum's living and we're dead here. Stuck."

"It's just us, Is, and what we think she thinks. It's just her thoughts imagined in our minds. And . . . I think . . . I think she'd laugh. She'd laugh. At this. At us two. Wouldn't she?"

"I can't stand that fat priest or those awful women pretending to mourn. She's *my* mother." She bit her lip. "Why do we have to wait out here while they do whatever they're doing in there? She belongs to us, not to that fat bastard or those fucking witches."

"Sshh. Is, come on." His arm found his sister's shoulder.

"They're only here because they want someone to be there when they croak themselves." Her voice was thickening. "They're shit scared, all of them — cowards. I want this to be over. I feel like we're being buried here. And nobody is noticing."

"Hey, I'm noticing. I'm always noticing. I notice everything."

"Me too."

He bent his head and smiled gently at her. "That's the problem."

She blinked against her tears. "You're right. We should stop noticing everything."

"Learn to get over it," he murmured.

There was a pause, filled only by a snatch of wind. Then Isabella said, "I can't get over anything."

"Me neither. I can't get over anything at all. Not one thing that happens in the damn world can I get over." The doors scraped and clattered open and another cadre of black birds took to the sky. "You were right, Is — we should have done it ourselves. Driven out somewhere quiet and far away. Burned her body on the steppe. It's not as if there's a shortage of lonely places."

Inside the small chapel, the walls were covered in dark icons. The priest walked around and around the open coffin. The old women held their candles in their left hand so that they could cross themselves with their right. And the chanting swelled and fell in a minor key that seemed to have journeyed west with the wind from far away, wherever the heart of Russia lay, somewhere in some sacred valley. Now and then, partially obscured by the trees as they moved outside, the sun came streaming in through the plain windows high above, so that there were dappled patches of shifting light on the floor, the walls, the mourners, the priest, on Masha's immutable face. She wore no veil.

Part II

NOVEMBER

Susanna (da se):
  Scusatemi se mento, voi che intendete amor.

Susanna (aside):
  Pardon me if I lie, all you who understand love.

— MOZART, *Le Nozze di Figaro*

19

A Message

AN EIGHT-THIRTY wind was howling up and down the darkened canyons of New York and seemed to eddy and squall on the corners, rapacious for like dominion over the cross streets. November — month of storms: men and boat lost out on the Grand Banks, ashen newscasters (laconic veterans of murder, blood, Israel and Palestine) finally in earnest, satellite pictures of clashing fronts, colliding systems, circling depression.

She had made up her mind.

All the same, it was almost impossible to move forward: the wind flattened her trousers against her legs, her hair was flung this way and that, and her skin felt as though it were being stretched. The worst storm since the last one. Skies of bitumen and creosote. There could no longer be any doubt about it: the planet was finally becoming angry — the wildest beast of them all goaded, poked, insulted once too often. You looked out of the grime-smeared office glass — what, once, twice, five times a year? — and sure, the Earth was still out there, but flooded and drowning, or frozen and blizzarding, or parched and burning up. She could smell the rain now, racing in on the wind.

What to say, though? What to write?

Never mind — see how it goes. Let's just get this done. She could always store whatever she typed in Draft and come back to it tomorrow.

The first rope lashed at her face just as she ducked inside the store advertising free coffee, magazines, and Internet. Perhaps it was the thought of Sasha, the cramp and claustrophobia of the apartment, of his childish neediness; the lack of personal space. But she knew that she could not do this at home, and work was likewise out of the question. Whatever the question, she had noticed, work was always out of it.

"One." She nodded in the direction of the back room. "Please."

The guy behind the till was talking on his cell. She guessed he was from Yemen or Saudi Arabia. He made a note of the time in his book, held up five fingers, and pointed to the second bank of terminals. She wondered what he was making of the American Dream.

Ignoring the coffee stand, she went over and sat down at the computer. The place was busy and smelled of cheap damp carpet. She shoved her bulging bag under her feet, slipped off her shoes, double-clicked, and waited for the sluggish connection. The young Muslim guy to her left — beard barely grown — was surfing what looked like soft porn in a double agony of pseudo-jocularity and not wanting to be seen; she could feel the waves of his embarrassment. The woman to her right, desperately out of condition and with her asthma inhaler beside her keyboard, was playing online poker with melodramatic intensity. Isabella typed in her password and clicked.

The woman broke off suddenly and made as if to throttle an invisible neck just in front of her screen. "Bitch. Bitch. Bitch." She looked over, shaking her head. "Another bad beat. How's your luck holding up?"

Isabella screwed up her nose. "Luck's okay. But my decisions suck."

The woman nodded. "Where you from?"

"London."

"Wanna play a hand for me? Can't do any worse than I'm doing. My ass is being beaten all over the planet by people I don't even know."

"Sorry. Not today." Isabella smiled sympathetically. "Gotta ask my dad if he killed my mum."

The woman nodded slowly. "Yeah, well, I need a fried chicken cool-me-down." She swiveled her chair around and looked directly at Isabella, taking a slow toke on her inhaler as if it were the last cigar before the shootout. "My advice: gets to the river and looks like there's some shit might be going on, then walk away. Walk right away. First lesson of life: walk away." And with that she stood up, put on a huge pair of sunglasses, and walked away.

Isabella's in box asked her if she needed a bigger dick and then offered her a loan to finance it.

All day she had sat through meeting after meeting, frustrated, irritated, exasperated, and finally bored beyond the realization of boredom. There was nothing quite so depressing, she had thought, as the slow November darkening of the stale-aired office afternoon.

Media Therapy had been attempting to seduce new clients, and the achingly pedestrian attempts of the men from the client firm to show off were matched only by the tedious duplicity of Marissa and Jo (her immediate boss and junior, respectively) in hoping to be desired. And then, of course, when eventually the men finally read the signals and began to come on to them a little, Isabella had been forced to suffer her colleagues' restroom pretense of being insulted and outraged, when in fact they were — Marissa and Jo both — very obviously brimming with satisfaction, affirmation, whatever it was they needed from men. Finally, at seven, concealing her indifference behind an expression of concern, she had closed the door behind her and taken the offered chair for the long-awaited one-to-one (conducted nonetheless for his part in the first-person plural, she noticed) with the head of the department, Timothy Robe — straight blond hair, expensive open-necked shirt, the smug manner of an exclusive tennis coach, ex-professional, ladies a specialty.

"We'll come straight to it, Isabella — we're worried about your attitude, especially in front of the clients. At the moment this is probably a perception problem. But maybe we also have aptitude issues to address in the short term and performance issues going forward. So, to be frank — I know you appreciate candor in . . ."

Robe was one of those people who found himself insightful because he considered the human emotions as if they were a range of competing brands, honesty being his proud brand of choice. And yet there was something about the word "frank," she always thought, that vociferously signaled its opposite.

". . . We just wanted to see if there's maybe something we should be doing. That we are not doing. From our side. Maybe there is a way we can all work together to try and help you get your focus back . . . It is a focus thing, right?"

She hadn't told them the whole story — i.e., death. She had left it at "ill" and come back without changing the news much beyond an upgrade (as Robe might say) to "seriously ill." As far as she was concerned, her mother wasn't the issue. Or rather, she was, but not in a way that could be unraveled for these people.

To the question of focus, therefore, Isabella bit her tongue and tried to think of something appropriate to say, some complaint that maybe Robe might have come across in one of his management "away days." She settled on the word "unchallenged," since she had heard Robe himself use it during some hideous life-insulting inanity of a presentation. And sure enough, "unchallenged" did the trick. Robe hit his stride almost immediately and talked thenceforward without the need for any further reciprocation.

Meanwhile she absented herself entirely from the situation and returned to the troubled Kremlin of her mind . . . remembering a phrase of her father's that had not made sense to her before (delivered in a rare good mood after one of his innumerable firings from some magazine or other): "Watch out for the clichés, Izzy. They're not lazy, they're malicious — they're out to get you." Something to that effect. Only now did she realize he was talking about the clichés of life rather than those of speech. And how strange, she thought with a jolt, that so many apparently random things that her parents had said to her (and that she did not remember for years), how strange that they came back like this. Her mother too, in the midst of one of her ludicrous anti-West rants, delivered (she now recalled) with punctual timing on receipt of the news of Isabella's acceptance to the Harvard MBA course: "One day they may just about persuade you to believe that business is the engine and money the fuel, Izzy, but whatever they say, you can be absolutely certain that neither is the journey and neither is the view. Remember that. Who would you rather be listening to on your deathbed, Bach or the chief executive?"

At first she had thought that nothing had changed, that the death of her mother was having next to no effect on her. Indeed, for the first few days she had entertained the view that maybe she was just one of those ascetics who didn't (or couldn't) respond to loss — or, for that matter, anything. Emotionally cauterized, to use one of her brother's less glib phrases.

Not that she was entirely fooled by herself: she was wise enough to recognize shock for what it was, and she saw too that it must eventually wear off. So regardless of the temporarily blank screens, she had been monitoring herself with close attention ever since arriving back in New York. But it was the stealth with which shock slipped away and the disguise in which grief arrived that had caught her out. Because of all grief's many masks, she had not expected anger.

It had begun as an almost friendly perplexity at her own numbness, which had increased somehow to impatience with herself, increased again to resentment against her mother — for the cryptic distancing, the idiotic, adolescent, unnecessary attempts to manipulate and pose with those bloody letters when, oh God, she must have known that she was seriously ill; until finally, yesterday, it had become the tumultuous fury from which she was now suffering. And yet only this lunchtime, during an e-mail exchange with Susan, her oldest friend back in London, had she realized — bang! — that this was it: that fury was the reaction. At last. And only later (while smoking on the fire escape to get away from the Jimmy Choo chat) had she recognized her error, that the precise opposite of that which she had imagined was in fact true: when a parent passes away, the family demons do not retreat but rise from their sarcophagi and move out across the borders of the mind, swearing in their puppet regimes as they pass. And from here on in, it would be frontline, hand-to-hand: her against them. You think that your journey from birth to death is a journey away from the clutches of your parents, but in fact it's the reverse. Life is a journey *toward* mother, father. Because as a child, though you live by their hands, you understand not a single one of their decisions, not a single action, not a single response. But each year that passes, through adolescence and beyond, you begin to grasp more and more, you grow a little closer, start to see what they see, think what they think, realize what they have realized, believe what they have believed. Am I right, Mum? Am I right, Dad? And don't it make you sick.

The Internet café continued its very global and yet simultaneously very local existence. She curled and uncurled her toes. Then she clicked on Compose — a button designed to flatter if ever there was one — and began to type, careful to avoid the greeting because she knew that she would not know how to start, deliberately trying not to think, aiming only to communicate the essence of what she wanted to say.

I just wanted to let you know that the funeral went okay. Some people from the consulate turned up. You know this, of course. Gabe is okay, I think. I'm in New York at the moment

—surviving. E-mail to this address if you ever intend to visit Petersburg. I'll give you the details—it's the Smolensky cemetery. Is.

It was the work of less than two minutes. And it was all she could muster. Her face was burning with the thought of betraying her brother. And she could feel her heart beating against the unforgiving conscience of her sternum. An image of her father careened into her mind—his face livid with the drunken discovery of her and Gabriel trespassing in his office, trying his locked drawer.

She forced herself to return to the top of the screen. For five further minutes she typed one greeting after another, deleting the words as quickly as she entered them: "Dear Dad"; "Hey Dad"; "Dear Nicholas"; "Dad—"; "Hello Nicholas"; "Hello Dad" . . . Nothing felt right. But nothing had ever felt right. After all the years of silence, she simply did not know what to call the man. She remembered that once, when he had hit her so hard that she could not hear, she had called him a "shoevanist pig."

In the end, fearful that she would lose her courage (or fury, or the need of a child to know, or whatever the hell it was that was driving this), she just left it blank. No greeting at all. Feverishly, she picked up her bag, rummaged until she found the e-mail address that Julian Avery had given her (and what a conversation *that* had been), and typed it in . . . And then, for a few seconds, she allowed herself the costly luxury of the truth—that it was actually communication itself that she wanted to establish. That the content was merely a means. And that in this subterfuge she was . . . She was *just like her mother*. And that her father, the cleverest man she had ever met, would see through it as surely as if she were made of glass. But— shallow breathing—maybe that didn't matter anymore. Banish thought. Banish games. Banish play. (Another image—of her father swimming with Francis, his friend, in the men's pond on Hampstead Heath while she and her brother stood by the railings, scared of dogs.) The point was to get the journey started. Take the bastard on. Do it. Send.

20

An Old Master

WHY, IN THE NAME of heaven's fat white rolling arse, is everything I attempt so utterly wretched? Were I one fraction less indolent, then I might improve. Were I one fraction less idealistic about my endeavors, then I might be content. Were I one fraction less intelligent, then I might fool myself into thinking I was better than I am. Instead, I am triply cursed. And still, after all this cursing, the fact remains: I am bloody awful at portraiture, Chloe. I stand before you as beside the point as a businessman in an orchestra pit."

The pure white canvas had become a wretched oozing swamp. Nicholas had long ago lost sight of the painting itself, so cleanly sketched and proportioned in a deft burnt umber only two hours ago. But now even the local details on which he had fixated were disappearing; his representation of the nose, for example, had turned to sludge; whole patches of the picture were swimming in paint, and the only colors he could conjure were tertiary. He simply could not place his brush with any kind of precision; it was all too slippery and oily. And all the while, nature continued to mock him from where it lay, propped up on its little lilac pillow, feminine beauty indifferent as ever to the effort of man.

In the first few weeks he had felt anxious, dislocated, shaken, and saddened by turn, but these reactions had soon given way to an indistinct but abiding sense of annoyance with everything, and most of all with himself. As if he had been consistently putting off an important job or failing to give up smoking day after day. These feelings were familiar to him, of course — he had suffered from something similar for most of his life, but in recent years he had managed to block it out, to beguile time with such single-minded commitment to his own amusement and pleasure that the days had not been able to round on him. This was the peace deal he had negotiated with himself and he'd grown accustomed to living contentedly under its terms: in return for a program of unstinting indulgence, he had promised to stop the self-antagonizing. Now, though, even his most tested techniques (of which painting was one) were failing him: distraction, denial, diversion — nothing was working. Life had reneged. Death had interfered. And hostilities with himself were resumed. He saw now what a flimsy little sham of a deal it had been all along.

He suspected that his blood pressure was higher than normal today — whatever normal was. He turned to glance out of the great window behind. Even the light refused to be precise — the morning's watery sun had given way to heavy, sullen cloud, as if Paris were about to enter one of its long winter sulks. The traffic on the opposite bank rushing on, endlessly urgent. But the heavy Seine between was a sluggish thing this afternoon, a sluggish thing of surliness and sullage.

He returned his eyes to the room — or rather, his studio-study (as he called it) — and they carried slowly across the ephemera therein: his stack of canvases in one corner, the desk he never used, magazines and papers, articles unread or unwritten, rags and paintbox, his easel; too small to be a studio, really, and the only thing he had ever studied in here was failure. He held up his brush and squinted. He wanted to scrape the whole head off with his knife, except that long experience had taught him that scraping never worked quite well enough and that at this stage the only thing to do was to wait until the paint stiffened and became compliant. Or start again.

Start again.

How many times must he start again? Blood and sand: surely it was possible to paint what he saw, at least. Those pretty toes pointed toward him, one leg up and bent, her arm above her head, the other arm loosely across her hips, a sort of lying-down contrapposto . . . The canvas should *smell* of her naked body. Instead, foreshortening had defeated him — even the basic proportions now seemed wrong, making her look freakish, steatopygous, when she was anything but. And then there was the big problem of the perspective of her face — totally counterintuitive, since her eyes in this pose were almost lower than her nose, itself an odd triangle of nostrils and nothing else. He had found himself transforming the never-ending wonder of animate human features into an ungainly and geometric thing in order to map it doggedly onto the slimy mulch of his canvas. He shut his eyes completely. All hope of capturing the intoxicating mingle of her expressions had now vanished.

If nothing more, Nicholas was honest with himself on the subject of art: he knew rubbish when he saw or heard it (as he did, often); he could recognize genuine talent even when it was confusing itself; and he saw mediocrity clearly for what it was. His own first and foremost. But like everything else he had done in the past forty years, Nicholas was doing this entirely for himself, so the success or failure of the work didn't matter beyond his own struggle with it, and the fact that he was a profoundly mediocre painter might not have bothered him at all except . . . Except that every time he closed his eyes, he could see quite clearly what it was that he wanted to achieve. Except that he did possess artistic vision. And — here, today, again — it was the very fact of this vision that made his abiding lack of skill or talent or stamina (or whatever it was that was needed to render artistic vision into reality) so infuriating, so demeaning. Worse still: this problem was an old problem. Indeed, he sometimes thought it was the defining problem of his life. The artist's vision without the accompanying artistry: the cruelest curse of the gods.

The only way forward was to stop. The only way to stop was to escape. And the only way to escape was to lose himself — physically lose himself — in the very body that was evading him artistically. There was one distraction left to him that never failed.

He addressed his model in French, which, curiously, still included the occasional suggestion of a Russian accent, an echo of the much heavier intonations of his private tutor during those long confined Moscow summers of his childhood.

"Chloe, I think we'll leave it there for today. I am making a mess of it. The paint is too wet. I need to let it dry." He stepped back from his easel, as much for effect as anything. "We can carry on next week. Or in another lifetime, when I have learned how to paint."

"Are you sure?"

"Yes, I think so."

"Okay, you are the artist."

"I wish that were true. Unfortunately, I am merely yet another commonplace toiler in the mud."

Then the old magic began to happen: as she sat up, she disappeared altogether as a model and became Chloe Martin once again — sometime actress, sometime real estate agent, once a little famous, twice divorced, an auburn-haired bob cut woman of a flat-chested forty-three, wide-wide mouth, all gum and marching molars when she smiled, freckles, crow's feet, translucent skin (which she ill-advisedly exposed to sun whenever she could), and eyes as green as pale nephrite. And watching her rise, he felt desire surging back to reassert its hegemony over his emotions.

"I'm going to have a drink, Chloe. I think . . . something white and chilled. What would you like?"

"Apple juice first. I am thirsty. But bring me a glass of wine as well." She smiled a smile that began sincerely but became false as she caught herself evincing impromptu sweetness and belatedly tried to capitalize—to witness that subtle transformation alone, Nicholas thought, worth the one thousand euros he paid her to be his model. Oh sweet Jesus, the hours he had spent covertly watching people as they so vigorously sought to disguise themselves, while their every expression and mannerism bellowed out the giveaways. It was almost funny. Just a shame there was nobody with whom to share the joke. Not anymore. He put down his brush and rag.

The drawing room was pleasingly Alessandro-less as he entered, and his irritation was further alleviated. The Italian was away in London, pursuing his ambitions in musicals: some audition for some piece of terrible shit based on the terrible shit of some terrible shit's life in a shitty and terrible rock band. The evening's rubber might even be enjoyable—untainted by moping, melodrama, or huff. Nicholas almost smiled as he entered the kitchen: Alessandro could not sing, could not dance, could not act, could not even mime . . . and yet, like more or less everyone under thirty-five he met these days, he firmly believed he had talent, a precious and precarious gift that needed sensitive nurturing in order to blossom into the hardy rose of genius. Dear God, who was telling the young all these lies about themselves? The poor fools had no chance. Their serfish heads so filled with false promise and misleading encouragement, their eyes wide with Hermès and Prada.

You are peasants, my friends, of peasant stock and loamy soul, only lately freed from your bonds—muck and ignorance cling to your every desperate venture. Desist. Relax. Go easy awhile. Ease into your emancipation. For I tell you this: the democracy you live by, this freedom, these rights, they are so many cruel jokes being played on you by your old rulers as they snigger and snort behind their latest disguises. They're only pretending you are equal, for their amusement. They *want* to see you struggling with it all—too fat, too

thin, crazed on exercise, crazed on junk food, bewildered and belittled, arms full of ghastly designer shopping (Cambodian tat, I'm
afraid) from the pages of their ghastly magazines. It's a cruel, cruel
joke. And alas, those values you are so proud of, they're no such
thing; they're but a confection of silly little sayings they smuggled in
with primetime so that you could be mocked all the more for repeat-
ing them. They have you running in all the wrong directions again,
my friends; they've set you off on the wrong track as surely as they
ever did when they called themselves your bishops and your barons.
You must hope for more insightful leaders or plan for another revolution. The world is yours awhile yet, if you would only seize it back.
Oh yes — and you, my dear, dear, Alessandro, please try to understand: your gorgeous arse is your one and only card. You have nothing else. So be sure to use it well when Herr Direktor turns his gaze
on you, my darling boy.

And yet, Nicholas reflected as he took out two clean glasses, who
could blame Alessandro and the millions like him? What was the desire for celebrity but an age-old ache for some kind of externally
verifiable significance? Testimony from somewhere other than the
self — relief, reassurance, reinforcements — even if the testimony was
a vapid and quick-vanishing lie. He bent for the Tokay, which he had
been keeping in the fridge for the evening's bridge but which now
struck him as far too good to share with anyone but Chloe.

She had that particular female shape to her inner thighs which
caused that certain little triangle of space to form between the tops
of her legs when she stood up straight, as now, framed in the far
doorway of the drawing room, shirt undone, naked otherwise; that
certain space, just beneath.

Sexual chaos — that was the only way to describe it, the whole of
Nicholas's life from the age of sixteen. One long rolling, roiling, rol-
licking sea of sexual chaos; magnificent, frightening, awful, sickening, mettle-testing, perilous, heartbreaking, audacious, and glorious
by turn. No, his was not the common journey. But, as he had always
religiously maintained, who, on their deathbed, actually wished to
say (with a satisfied sigh to ceiling and gathered loved ones), "Ah,
mine was the common journey — excellent."

The odyssey began in earnest in a grand but threadbare hotel
room (that would never recover from the loss of the empire) when he
was barely seventeen. He'd enjoyed a three o'clock lid-full of his

mother's secret scotch, and as ever, he was supposed to be studying quietly, waiting for the rest of his family to return, preparing himself to follow in his father's footsteps straight into Cambridge (classics) and the Overseas Service. It was Easter, Max was back from Moscow and in London for the week (some reprimand or other), his mother was God knows where, and his little sister was out spending the money he had stolen from his father's wallet precisely for the purpose of sending her out.

Antonia Grey, his little sister's friend, however, was very much in . . . In his mother and father's bed, to be dogmatically factual about it: freshly undressed, sixteen, and giving it the full actressy adolescent treatment. But not for Nicholas's direct benefit. No no no: he'd already had quite enough of the straight stuff from Miss Grey, his first model. ("Toni, I think we should try something. You know we can't paint it unless we see it, unless we *experience* it . . . so will you, if I promise to stay quiet?") No. Instead, his sister's friend was faking her way through her second orgasm of the session with Stephen or Jonathan or Benjamin or whatever his name was, captain of rugby or boats or some such. Young Nicholas Glover, meanwhile, captain of nothing but fucking, was stationed in the walk-in wardrobe, looking on from the darkness behind his mother's favorite evening gown with the kind of unqualified attention more befitting a newly fledged heart surgeon taking final instruction from the senior consultant.

As he recalled later, he'd had thoughts even then that more conventional creatures might eschew. Thoughts along the lines of *I like that she's faking, I love that she's faking, I like the way they look together, man and woman, woman and man, I love the way they look together, I like the geometry of their combining and recombining limbs, I love the movement, the struggle, the ache, the sound (ancient, ancient), their skin, the smell . . . the honest reality. I love the unequivocal reality of this.*

And of course after a few minutes he'd had to slip out of the closet and join in . . . And Antonia, to her credit, was almost okay with it. Almost. She caught sight of Nicholas from atop her charge as he tiptoed through her peripheral vision, and her wide eyes said, Oh. My. God. What are you *doing?* But they did not ask him to stop — not necessarily, not definitively, not so that he felt he should actually stop. On the other hand, as his fingers slid around her rocking torso and made their clever play with her girlish young breasts, and as the narrow eyes of Steve Jon Ben opened from their boyish pleasure to bear witness to this development, there occurred the most almighty eruption. A second for Ben Jon Steve to apprehend and process the undeniable evidence and then — *you fucking bastard* — the captain of boats, rugby, and so on exploded in a triple frenzy of orgasm, rage, and shame.

And it was this more than anything else, this precise moment, that Nicholas remembered forever. Because (over the folded angel's wings of Antonia's fragile shoulders) Benjamin Jonathan Stephen's face was the most absorbing thing he had ever seen: anger, jealousy, belligerence, shock, righteous affront, guilty aggression, childish embarrassment, manly shame — all of them flying across his otherwise even features, one after another, like so many kamikazes. It was this precise moment that Nicholas remembered forever, because the involuntary movement of their nakedness was so powerfully enthralling: Ben Jon Steve's beautiful young body bucking up (stomach muscles proud as Coldstream Guards) and shoving itself with such rude and sudden surprise into rearing Antonia, and she (half winded, half ecstasized) crying out involuntarily, her nails digging into a bare and blushing boyish chest. It was this precise moment that he remembered forever, because in those three astounding seconds, satirical Nicholas realized that he had seen more kinetic humanity than most people would manage in their entire lives.

For seven dedicated years after this it was flat-out sex — a game of volume and frequency in which he balanced his requirements for deviation with the overwhelming need to get as much as possible of any sort.

Then came the mercy of beautiful, dark, endlessly enchanting Masha and the only years of his respite. In the early thick of his marriage, he thought he might move on, he thought he might be past the worst, he thought he might be just as others were — the oats proverbially sown (wild, wild, wild) and the ensuing happy reconciliation to a life of monogamy and fulfillment in other areas. (What *were* they, these much-vaunted other areas?) And certainly Masha's influence was strong. The more so perhaps when they had only each other, totally without money, two exiles in Paris, talking late into the night, stealing food, he painting, she writing her pamphlets, hurrying through the awakening streets together, fervently believing that no other man and woman in the whole history of men and women had ever made love with such pure intensity as they.

And then the deal was done. And with it came the children and London and Highgate and domestication in its truest sense. The change was shocking and absolute. Within a fortnight the man was no longer a man but a servant—at the beck and call of the infant-rearing righteousness of his wife and every cry or whim of the two helpless infants themselves. Desire's flame began to sputter, the eye to cheat upon the heart.

Even so, Nicholas continued to steer through the gathering swell by the red star of his remarkable wife. And for a while longer he thought that perhaps he might make it, that what interested him most of all in life was trying to understand the exact shape and weight of other people's inner selves, the architecture of their spirit. Perhaps Masha herself led him to this conclusion. Certainly they agreed that this was the nub of things. This was what fascinated them. Perhaps they could march together into their middle age with this in common. Man, woman, children: the old happiness formula. After all, it was true. A certain very particular form of honesty did obsess Nicholas—just as it did Masha. Not a person's honesty in the prosaic sense of telling the truth about this or that, but rather that a person should inhabit his or her humanity truthfully, fully, with commitment. This was the quality that they both sought out and re-sponded to in other people. As he moved into his mid-thirties, Nich-olas found that what he wanted to do (more and more with each passing year) was duck beneath the usual farragoes of "I do this" or "I do that" and get as quickly as possible to the quick . . . Yes, but. Yes, but. Yes, but. What sort of human being *are* you? What do you really think, feel, want, fear, like? How is life for you? Any insight? Any new thoughts? Any new feelings? Any feelings at all?

And, curiously, he became very good at eliciting due response, charming some and offending others in roughly equal measure. But he found no name for this preoccupation. Neither medical nor so-cial. Neither did he find an occupation—a job—that required such abilities. (That his bloody father must have been in counterintelli-gence struck him around this time with the renewed force of sudden certainty; what else could you do with this particular skill set? Oh, it was all in the genes—here was the proof; his own existence seemed to be entirely about counterintelligence.)

Such inquiries did not save him, though. They merely led him back to the same path by another, longer route. For sometime in his mid-thirties he realized that merely asking people these questions was not enough. Partly because they lied, but mostly because the rev-elation of this kind of detailed truth (had he not always secretly be-lieved?) was to be found only . . . in bed.

Hitherto unformulated suspicions now crystallized into a firm conviction: that in order truly to understand the essence of another human being, it was necessary to make love. Because sex was the only vantage from which to view the *whole* truth, all at once. The central act of coition was the only time that body, mind, spirit came out and showed themselves all together.

The vows gave way.

And now he went at it as if in a frenzy. Men, women, husbands, wives. He had money. He had no job. He had time. Masha was at work on the paper all day long. Masha was on the night shift. Masha didn't mind if he stayed away for the odd weekend with friends.

There were years of rush and flurry. There were years of danger and caution. And there were years of relative stability — a steady uncomplaining mistress for eighteen months, a fond youth up between university terms on whom to squander the money his father sent, a bored sub-Bovary of a wife desperate to feel the prickle and blush of romance again, a needy American dancer, a famous actor stuck in a bad run and a worse marriage. There were even one or two professionals with whom Nicholas struck up sexual friendships. A beautiful Chilean man whose dark eyes occasioned the only lines of poetry his soul ever permitted to the page. A plump little Estonian whom he visited for three years, taking her books and teaching her English via Russian between the epic mania of their lovemaking. But there was never any peace.

Indeed, since he had left the city more than three decades ago, these last few years, living on the river back here in Paris, were the closest to contentment that Nicholas had come. And, a little to his own surprise (aside from Alessandro), Chloe Martin was the only person Nicholas had slept with for the past eighteen months.

Thus his journey so far.

"Nearly, very nearly." Chloe's coy finger traveled the short distance between their sweating bodies, parted his lips, passed between his crooked teeth, and so was greeted warmly by the object of its target. "As close as it has ever been."

And he let himself lie back, his heart calming beneath the white hairs of his narrow chest. Her intention was sincerely to pay him a compliment, but of course she could not be aware of the true grotesqueness of his complaint. Nicholas had heard this kind of thing many times before — the it's-not-work-with-you assurances from all the professionals, the best-lover avowals from all the lovers, and the when-you-use-your-tongue declarations from all the wives of his friends that he had taken great care to satisfy well and truly by way of compensating them for the unforgivable ordinariness (sexual, mental, spiritual) of their variously defeated husbands — had heard it so many times, in so many beds, and in so many states of mind that he had long ago decided that he, and he alone, would be the judge of whether or not any of it was really, empirically true. An extra dimension of his madness, this: that he trusted nobody but himself as the true pleasure-level arbiter of any encounter — not only on his own account, but on behalf of his sexual partners as well. Not without reason, though, as always with madness, as always with Nicholas. Not without reason. For the fact was that he knew exactly how close she had been — knew it through every soft fingertip he had touched her with, could hear it trapped like stifled song in the deep well of her breathing, could smell it rising like rare musk in her pores, could taste it in the salt-shiver of her skin, could see it in the pleasure-ache of her face, the dig of her heels, the clench of her womanly fist.

And actually, she was not lying.

But not there.

Not quite there.

What a woman. He couldn't paint her. And he couldn't make her come. Someone to hang on to, for certain.

"Let's drink more." Irritation vanquished, mind at ease, he reached across and plucked the wine from the bucket of thinning ice.

"What are we listening to today?" she asked, stretching lazily for her glass.

"Mozart, *Marriage of Figaro*."

He poured — the angles awkward, since neither of them could be bothered to sit up straight.

"And this bit?"

"This is the duet between the Count and Susanna. *Crudel! Perche finora farmi languir cosi?*"

"It's beautiful."

He replaced the bottle and settled himself. He liked to look at her every way — and sometimes, as now, her body changed back again into that of artist's model: laid out beside him, propped on her elbow, face close and glowing, freckled shoulders and that hip jutting heavenward. Pure artistic provocation.

"Yes, it is beautiful." He took a refreshing draft. "But it's also a lie."

"What do you mean? Why is it a lie?"

"Because despite all the glory of that angelic voice, I'm afraid that

Susanna—she's the one singing—has absolutely no intention of meeting the poor Count—that's him—even though she is right now promising repeatedly that she will. The plan is for the Countess to disguise herself as Susanna and take her place at the rendezvous. So all Susanna is doing is luring the Count into their trap—and making sure that he pays off Figaro's debts along the way. I'm afraid her part in the whole exquisite duet is a lie—from start to finish."

Chloe shook her head. "The most beautiful music we have—a lie."

"Yes. And all the honest toil in the world not worth a single bar."

He noticed that Chloe sipped her wine like a fish—lips pursed in an unselfconscious pout. And he realized that in twenty minutes he would have to make love to her again as a direct result of this observation.

She narrowed her eyes, but playfully. "Have you always been a liar, Nicholas?"

"Yes."

"Why?"

"Because it is the only way to get myself into situations like this."

"Is it?"

"Yes. Honest men have very little fun in life. It's a well-known fact." His lips parted in a rare smile.

"And women like lies?"

"Men, women. Everyone wants to be seduced. Even the coldest blood will warm to a little solicitation."

"And seduction is always lies?"

"Of course . . . it takes us away from the real world into something fantastical and compelling."

"Maybe. But still, lies are not the only way." She sucked her lips. "You could, for example, pay someone far too much to be your model."

"True. But then she must believe, at least in part, that she is being paid genuinely to model. Or else she might lose her self-respect. Or demand much higher wages. So even here, lies come into it."

She wrinkled her nose so that her freckles took up new lines of defense.

"And what's it like being such a liar?"

"Interesting. Exhilarating. Amusing. Transcendent."

"Like Mozart."

"Yes, that little bastard told millions of them, you just *know* that he did." He sat up in the bed, holding his glass high above his stomach as he rearranged the pillows. "Once you cross the line, you can't go back. And why would you ever want to? Everything else seems gray, leaden, unimaginative, plodding, bound in. Did you not lie to your husbands?"

"No. I tortured them with the truth."

"The worst form of torture there is."

"But in those days I was acting all the time, so I suppose the rest of my life was a lie. Lies to get the parts, I mean. Lies to play the parts." She held a sip in her mouth a moment and met his eye as she tasted. "And yet . . . and yet you are an honest man, M. Glover."

He too allowed the wine to linger on his tongue, but said nothing.

She spoke cautiously into his silence. "You mean it — whatever you are doing, you mean it. You're here because you mean to be here. You do not do things you do not mean. Every sip of your wine, you mean it. Or . . . or this." She pointed with her little finger, glass now raised, indicating her nakedness, his nakedness, the bed itself. "You fuck me like you mean it. Always."

"I do."

"And then there is the fact that you know your painting is terrible."

"Thank you."

"My pleasure."

"I feel a lot better now than I did a few hours ago," he said. "My painting doesn't matter."

"Then I am a success. A top-up, please." She propped her chin on his chest, holding her glass out in the direction of the bottle.

For the first time, and with all the attendant surprise of a new idea, it occurred to him that he could remarry. *There* was a novel thought. Move Alessandro out, move Chloe Martin in. He could get by on a single piece of tight male arse a month, say. Or even pay Alessandro a fixed fee to visit. (The idea of turning that deluded little Roman into a whore certainly appealed.) Though would Chloe Martin actually say yes? He thought not. Except, perhaps, for the money.

"Did you lie to your wife when you were together?"

"Every day. Every hour. Every minute."

"You have never said anything about her."

"Ask — if you wish to know."

"Where does she live?"

"My wife died a few weeks ago." Nicholas drank more deeply.

"I am sorry."

"We were separated for the last ten years or so. We didn't speak for most of that time. But — to answer your next question — I loved her dearly. I never said it, of course. But then you must hold something in reserve against the final reckoning, wouldn't you say?"

"No."

"Ah, but in reality you do . . . you hold many things back." He scratched her back with gentle fingers.

"You never saw her again after you left?"

"Actually, I did — just before. I was lucky — I was able to spend a few good days with her. She lived in Russia. You can still buy the necessary pills there. They ease the pain. She had cancer. I bought her a whole stack. She was going into hospital. I had arranged for the best doctors."

"She lived in Moscow?"

"St. Petersburg."

"But you didn't tell her that you loved her then — when you saw her, I mean."

"No. I . . . I assumed I would see her again. We hardly said a word to each other while I was there, in fact. I regret that very much now. There was a great deal that I would have liked to talk to her about. I suppose I thought it was the start of . . . of our reconciliation. I tried to persuade her to come back to our old home in London — to be treated there. But she said she would not leave Russia again. She was the most stubborn woman I ever knew. Would die to prove her point. In a way, she *did* die to prove her point." (Why? What perverse gene had made it thus all his life: so much easier to speak to friends than to family, to his lovers than to his wife?) "Anyway I booked my flight back two weeks later. I was going to surprise her — visit her in the hospital. She died a few days after I left."

"What did you do while you were there?"

He found himself admiring the lack of melodrama in Chloe's voice: that she did not become stagy or overcareful or otherwise false-toned around the subject of death. Odd, especially for an actress. Perhaps she had lost someone. Odd too how close to Masha he felt, just talking like this. He realized with some shock that he hadn't spoken properly to anyone since. Since.

"We went to the Hermitage once, when she felt she could make the trip. She was in a lot of pain. Though the pills helped — helped enormously. The other days we just played these six-hour games of chess and listened to music. Sat together. Nothing much. I went to see the doctors to arrange things with the hospital." He raised his glass but paused to speak before he drank. "They feel as if they were the best three days of my life. Just to be near her. She might have been going slowly mad all her life but, my God, that woman had *so* much raw courage."

"Why didn't you live together?"

"We did. For a long time. Until the 1990s. Until the children were gone."

"And you were close?"

"Always."

"Why? I mean, you say you were separated. So why do you feel you were always close?"

He had never asked himself this question, but now he was struck by its importance. And suddenly, at ease here in his soul's only rest, he could see the answer quite clearly.

"Because my wife understood the geometry of things."

"I don't understand."

"She understood how people are — how people are *really*. She understood what lies hidden beneath . . . and how our falsities are more eloquent than our truths."

"This was the reason you loved her?"

"This was the intellectual reason, I suppose."

"And in your heart?"

"If you are asking me the emotional reason . . . I would say because . . . because the shape of our needs always seemed to tessellate. To fit together, wherever they met."

"Like crazy paving."

"Exactly so."

"Did she lie to you?" Chloe kept her eyes on his, a frown of sincere concentration on her brow, her glass pressed down onto the bed in the space between them, her little finger free and circling his thigh. "Did she deceive you as you deceived her?"

"We deceived each other throughout — from the very beginning. Yes, in a way she deceived me as much as I her. She did not realize, for example, that I knew she had a child before we were married. I waited for her to say something . . . but she never did. And so I assumed that the child was dead or that she simply did not wish to talk about it. I felt no need to pry. There were a thousand things I did not tell her in return — many, many things about myself, about what I was doing, more and more as time went on. But the lies never mattered — they often don't. That's what these psychologists will never tell you. Indeed, that's what the new world will never understand about the old. She recognized mine, and I hers. And we both sub-

tracted them from what was really being said. We could never remark upon this recognition, though. It could never be explicit. Instead we lived out our complexities and our mutual understandings,
as if they were continual tributes to each other's love and at the same
time continual tests."

Her finger circled. "So why did you split up, then?"

"She had become too mad for me—there was no meaning left in
any of our conversations. Not mad—that's not quite right. I mean
obsessive and compulsive—obsessive in her need to repeat and repeat these prejudices and opinions, these fantasies about what was
happening in the wider world. And yet . . . and yet she knew well
that she did not have any idea what she was talking about—and
worse, that the opinions she pretended to were not real either. She
didn't believe a word of what she herself was saying, but she was
compelled to go on saying it. It's a strange thing, Chloe, it's . . . it's
very *Russian*." He shook his head. "And somehow we just lost our
route back. I found that my own sense of sanity was going in her
presence. I could not listen to her anymore. Marriage is a generosity
contest, and she won. Perhaps I was going mad in a different way.
And I was . . . I was—"

"Mad . . . physically."

"If you like."

"Were there many others?"

"Yes."

"The reasons for your lies?"

"Not the reasons. The occasions."

Her knee found his leg. "The occasions."

"I always felt the need to be free."

"Why?"

"I don't know. Perhaps this is what drove her mad. I couldn't live
with her in the normal way, I suppose. I . . . When my father died, I
had the money and . . . after a few years of trying . . . I . . . I took my
freedom."

"You needed these others?"

"I needed them."

"Because . . ."

"DNA."

"No."

Nicholas raised an eyebrow. "No?"

She moved her knee softly up and down a fraction. "You needed
them because . . . if you believe that you can still make love with

other women, then it feels as though not every issue is settled — that your life isn't bound in iron."

"Something like that."

"That you are still *alive*."

"Perhaps." He wanted to drink and fuck and talk and drink and fuck and talk forever. And why could he not paint this pretty, ugly, pretty, ugly, ugly-pretty, pretty-pretty face? He would bet that Chloe had passed the first thirty years of her life entirely innocent of the damage those pale dreamy green eyes could do; rather, she had grown into this look, this manner. All the same, it worked. He wanted her, wanted physically to be inside her, to go and fetch her consciousness and compel her into the moment with him. Share the endless present.

"And you did not love these others?"

"Very few."

"How many?"

"There were some I did love. Never as I regarded . . . as I *loved* my wife, though. But there are as many kinds of love as there are people. You know that."

She finished her wine and smiled. "Do I? Some people would say that love and sex are one and the same. You are not loving your wife while you are sleeping with another."

"Only the ignorant or the childish."

"Unfair."

"I have nothing against the ignorant or the childish."

"And that's another lie." Her knee moved over his leg all the way so that he could feel her warmth against his hip.

"No, they are not half so bad as the dinner-party vermin who believe they are sophisticated and who claim to think that sex and love are separate things."

"And you, Nicholas, what do you think?"

"Really what do I think?"

"Yes, really. Tell me."

She bent to kiss his stomach, the base of her empty glass now cool on his chest.

"I would say that sex and love are like . . . like the two principal dancers of the ballet: sometimes they are magnificently, beautifully, indissolubly together, through the great centerpieces of the pas de deux — and make no mistake, this is what the audience pays to see; but sometimes the one will dance while the other watches in the wings; or sometimes they will dance in parallel, on opposite sides of the stage, together yet apart, a curtsey for a bow, an arabesque for a *tendu;* sometimes one is alone while the other is forgotten for long acts at a time; sometimes the one dances with the chorus to make the other jealous; sometimes one leaps on moments after the other has left; sometimes one dies while the other lives; and of course sometimes they go on separate exhibition tours."

She laughed.

He took her glass, half turned away, let it fall noiselessly to the floor. He held a last sip of his own and reached for the tiny pill that he had already popped and readied discreetly on the walnut side table.

When he turned back, her hand was on him, her eyes bewitching him. And his kiss was chaste as pure intention.

21

The Bastard of Everything

THE CRANE OUTSIDE the window had begun to sink into the mud below, or rather had begun to subside, so that the long skeleton finger no longer reached true to heaven but listed dangerously toward their tower block as if enacting some strange and terrible slow-motion death strike.

Everything was sinking.

Everything was always sinking.

Back into the Neva. Back into the sea. The people, the city, St. Petersburg itself, forever sinking. And Henry's guilt was as raw and saturating as the sewage marsh into which everything sank.

In those few moments back from the football — that gaping and ragged hole in the wall, the taste of grime on his lips as he opened the front door, the corridor strewn with masonry and rubble, his bedroom trampled and destroyed, his money stolen, the semidarkness as he entered their main room, the smell of sawn wood, his eyes adjusting, the piano vanished, Arkady on his knees — in those few moments, Henry had known that he must give everything he had left to his friend. Complete divestiture. Because that heap of jagged shards and the Russian's ghostly face were the last scene of his life in its current incarnation. Nothing worse could happen. It was over. Something else must now begin.

Though he continued to lean against the wall and look out at the docks and the sea beyond, there was therefore urgency in his voice as he addressed his flatmate: "How will we know if the passport and the visa look real enough?"

Arkady lay on the sofa, half dressed in jeans and open shirt. "We won't," he said.

"Can we order a passport without specifying where we want the visa for?"

"It does not work like that. It is not a pizza."

"I appreciate that."

"Anyway, forget Paris. The bitch divorced him. He divorced the bitch."

"Not necessarily."

Aware that it was pointless to do so, Henry had found himself repeatedly pushing Paris as Arkady's putative destination. Partly because that was the only sure address they had been able to Google immediately—through an expatriate bridge club. Partly because any conversation with Arkady was better than the ever-expanding silence, whatever the price. And partly for mortal fear that the Russian's resolve would slump, that somehow there would be born between them some whelpish failure of nerve.

"Not necessarily." Henry turned. "And you know, it might be easier to get into France for . . . for a Russian."

"She lived here." Arkady began to button his shirt. "He lives there."

"We don't know why they split. We mustn't judge. There are —"

"Divorced. Separate. Different lives. They don't f—"

"Actually, many people who are divorced remain in amicable contact with each other." Through the crack in Arkady's bedroom door, Henry caught sight of the woman moving inside. Suntanned legs. Dark pubic hair. He looked away and began walking in irregular circles around the sofa, stepping carefully over the fallen disks. "You don't know, Arkady. And we have to try everything."

"He is not my father. I am his wife's virgin-fuck child. He gets a letter from me. He does not even wipe shit with it. Why would he care?"

"There are a million good . . . good people out there." Henry stopped and retraced his steps around the back of the sofa, wanting to stay out of Arkady's line of sight. Somehow, with the centripetal pull of the piano gone, the room felt hollow. And even as he continued to speak, he could hear the priggishness of his old self recolonizing his voice. Pompous Henry, prudish Henry, prim Henry—these old Henrys, they were all openly pursuing him now. He began again. "We can at least try a letter."

"I think he does not know I exist."

"We don't know that."

"We don't know anything."

"We do." Henry could smell her cigarette.

"And if he does know that I exist, he does not *want* to know it." Arkady's voice became pure cynicism. "'Hello, Mr. Glover—I am the bastard you do not know, the bastard of your wife, the bastard of everything. Very nice to meet you, sir. Now, please, I want money. Immediately.'"

Arkady adjusted the buckle of his belt.

Henry forced himself forward and approached the window again. He wiped three fingers through the film of wood powder and grime to make a new square to see through. The sea was covered in something not quite fog, not exactly smog, just a nameless haze that would soon itself be smothered by night. Thirteen stories below, he could see the drunks and the vagrants hunkered around their afternoon fire. They were still burning the larger splinters of the piano. Black smoke rose.

On the day after their break-in, and after nearly six hours of passport verification and bureaucracy, Henry discovered that he had just over nine hundred pounds left in his English bank account. Shocked to his core (and frightened now), he had that same night given Grisha everything he owed. Grisha had taken the money with a cheery leer that all but celebrated culpability. And immediately advanced him more. Henry took the extra, paying for it there and then, peeling off the thinning notes.

Henry's new and panic-stricken plan was to buy passport and tickets for Arkady as soon as possible, to give everything he had left, to see his friend gone, and then . . . to quit. He had therefore accepted enough heroin for another twenty-five days (longer if he rationed it), because he knew that he needed sufficient to see the Russian well on his way. Without a good stash, he was certain that he would enter the scoring trance, he'd be crazy again, and he would not be able to trust himself to stick to this plan. No chance. He absolutely required the security of having lots of the drug to help him get off the drug later. He must take the drug to quit the drug.

After he had left Grisha, Henry had gone straight back to Vasilevsky to wait for Arkady to return from Maria Glover's apartment. But Arkady had not come home. So the following day, the Friday,

Henry had spent a windy afternoon staking out the canal while the clouds raced overhead. But he had seen nobody come and nobody go.

On the Saturday he had at last tracked down Zoya and paid her for her Maria Glover "file" — an utter waste of time and money. Stuff on orphanages, pages and pages of notes, times and dates of searches, bribes dispensed, a list of children called Arkady at Veteranov, and almost nothing on Maria Glover's ersatz English family save for half a page in Zoya's bad Russian scribble confirming what Henry already knew from his own conversation with Maria Glover: names, no addresses.

Arkady eventually showed up on the Sunday but did not utter a single word. So Henry, biding his time, retreated to his room and counted out his remaining funds. The Zoya file and his angel both paid for, he had less than two hundred pounds left. He realized he would have to borrow to secure the passport and visa. But so be it, he thought. This is where his long flight had led him. In his right mind or not (he did not care), Arkady was his vocation, and it now no longer mattered how that vocation had begun, whether the vocation was real or imagined, or what purpose the vocation had beyond itself. If this duty hastened him to zero, all the better. He would meet himself there afterward, when Arkady was on his way. He would meet himself there and try his mettle in that clear and empty ring. So be it. But momentum was all. For both of them. Momentum. Keep going.

He left his peephole at the window and set off on his circling of the room again. The tight dance of love and guilt.

"In my experience," Henry said, "children often become very curious about their parents after they die. It is part of their grief. Shock, denial, anger, guilt, anxiety, depression. And curiosity. If not —"

"You have no experience. You are a narkoman."

The Englishman felt his blood freeze and a chill sweat seep into his palms. He could not look over and meet those eyes. He forced himself to keep moving along the wall. Never, not once, had Arkady called him a junkie. And he did not wish to know if this, at last, was it — the moment when Arkady's scorn finally turned on him. He'd rather not be sure. He'd rather circle the room until the end of time. Keep moving. He squeezed his resolution all the harder to his threadbare breast.

"Either way, we need to get you this passport. And we need to be doing that as soon as possible." His own voice was loathsome to him. "I am assuming you know the right people."

Arkady said nothing.

Henry could hear her trying to open the window. He wondered if she could understand English. He passed Arkady's bedroom door and came around in front of the sofa again. He had the sudden idea that he would shave his head. His hair was lank and ridiculous. Widow's peak, bald patch. Penance.

"You do know people who can get us a fake passport?"

Still the Russian said nothing.

"We should have the documents they need ready — the photos and everything. For the passport. We'll get the visa separately . . . when we know if it's Britain or France. Now, the good news is that they didn't get all my —"

"*Grisha* did not get all your money."

"We don't know that it was Grisha. Okay, he's . . . he's a dealer. But he's not a . . . not a psychopath."

Arkady swore in Russian.

Henry rushed on. "I have around a thousand pounds sterling left in another bank account," he lied. "And we can use this to buy the passport."

"Whatever you have, you need."

"Please, Arkasha. Let me finish." Henry drew shallow breath, coming past the window again. "I am not sure how much the passport will cost, but I assume this is enough. And I am not *giving* you the money. You can pay me back in a few years, when you are taking your huge concert fees. Or maybe right away — when you come back from meeting them! If it goes well. Who knows? Regardless. It doesn't matter. The point is that you have to go now. And I can help you."

"You need your money for your shit."

Henry came to a halt at the top of his circuit. He said the words quietly, addressing the back of the Russian's head. "I am stopping."

Arkady laughed out loud.

"I am stopping."

"You are never stopping. Nobody ever stops."

Henry passed the bedroom door once more and stood at the foot of the sofa, meeting the other's eyes for a second before taking off again along the far wall. He spoke quickly now, his bony arms jerking as if he might sheer off from his desperate orbit at any moment.

"Arkady, listen to me — I don't want to have any money left. And I don't want to have *anything*. I . . . I have a bet with myself. If I have nothing left and I can't buy any more, then I will give up. Pull myself together. Yes, okay, yes . . . I will buy enough food and water to last until you are back. I will spend what I need to get that. Water—some food. And we will fix the hole. But that's all. After that, I don't want the money in the bank because I don't want to burn it all—and that's what *will* happen. I will burn it on the shit. Every penny. So this . . ." He indicated the room with a throw of his arm. "This is a blessing in disguise. Not the piano. But I mean all my money gone. Everything taken. Because I would only have spent it on shit . . . shit, shit, and more shit. And it would have gone on and on—until I ran out of money, anyway. So all that has happened is that I have the opportunity to stop sooner. To stop when you go to find your family. And I don't *want* to have any more secret money in the bank. I don't want it there. I don't want it, because I tell you: I will go and I will spend it on shit. So you *have* to take my money. I want you to take it. I need you to take it. It's a loan. That's all. A loan until I am off. And then you can give it back to me."

Arkady was watching Henry closely.

"Do you understand, Arkasha?"

At last the Russian sat up. "You say this now because you know there is so much more hidden in your room. But when the time comes, when you have no more, you will do anything. The money or the no-money is not the difference. When the time comes, you will do anything—you will sell your body, you will kill if you have to."

"If it makes no difference, then take it. If the money is not the difference, then take it. Please. Let me try."

She came out of the bedroom barefoot, wearing nothing but one of Arkady's T-shirts. Henry tried to nod a greeting, but her expression reflected only a sudden aversion back at him. He walked quickly past the sofa and entered the wreckage of his room.

The faster he used, the faster he ran out, the faster he would get to zero.

22

Self-Help

THERE COMES A TIME in every man's life when the fucking around just has to stop. Operating (as ever) in the murky, muddy, potholed, all-sides-fired-upon, no man's land of modern secular ethics (which might, of course, be no ethics at all), Gabriel could not be certain whether it was his mother's death, his life stage, or the quasi-religious ache of some ancient human gene that had brought him abruptly to this realization. But once beheld, this flinty truth, he realized, could no longer be avoided. And he knew for certain that he must now make some decisions about his life — ideally, good ones, though he recognized with stolid candor (as he faced down an unnecessarily confrontational lunchtime sandwich) that any decisions at all would likely be greeted with much emotional bunting as a sign of progress.

The telephone interrupted his thoughts.

"Hi, Gabriel. Francine."

"Hello, Francine. I was about to call you. How are you?"

"Fine, fine, fine."

He detected more than the usual vinegar in the various acid ratios of her voice.

"Hang on . . . I'm in the car." There was the sound of an ill-timed and aggressive gear change. "You know, I'm not being funny, but I really don't think that the . . . the *Indians* know how to drive."

He twisted the proofs around so he could read them. No, she was not being funny. Francine O'Brien was never being funny.

"Gabriel, I wanted to say that I personally am really looking forward to 'Toxic Parents.' And that — get this — Randy himself is taking an interest in this one. His assistant called last night from Los Angeles. Have you met her? Caroline. *Lovely* girl. She's had surgery, of course, and I think it's affecting her skin, but she's got such a great smile in her voice. Do you know if they've shut the M40?"

"Haven't heard anything here, Francine. Are you off to somewhere exciting?" His eye fled to a quarter-page advertisement for one of Randy K. Norris's herbal "rescue remedies." "Fight Stress," it screamed. But surely, he thought, that's exactly what stress wanted — a fight.

"I've got this half-day of brand-new treatments. Sumatran Indulgence Therapy. It's that seventies singer's ex-wife — God, you know who I mean, she's in all the mags at the moment — it's her new place."

"Can't think who you mean, offhand." Gabriel knew exactly whom Francine was referring to. He'd spoken to the woman in question on the phone. Yet another avaricious, harrowingly insecure, narcissistic little claw-wielder who had recently about-faced into a guru of well-being and life balance. How did any of these people expect to be taken seriously? At least Francine let the toxins flow.

"Davina Trench. That's her. But anyway, they're trialing in bloody Maidenhead. I mean — hello? — who ever wants to go to Maidenhead? It might as well be in . . ."

"Indonesia."

"Wherever."

"Be great when you arrive, though. You can really relax and pamper yourself." He hated the word "pamper" almost as much as he hated the word "indulgence," which in turn was almost as much as he loathed the word "treatment," with its wretchedly inane pretension toward medicine. Even more dispiriting was that this kind of idiotic vocabulary had become his daily vernacular; most of the people he dealt with these days could not even imagine him employing such words sarcastically, never mind noticing any nuance in his voice. No more than they could imagine the seven solid years of round-the-clock blood-and-agony life-and-death slog that it *actually* took to become a doctor. "Are they just an indulgence outfit, or do they do other stuff too?"

"Yoga."

"Expensive?"

"Very."

"Well, three-sixty inner calm is priceless, I suppose."

"Oh, you *cow* — that fat cow just cut me off." There was the sound of a horn. "This is a freebie. Said I might do a write-up for them."

And he hated the word "freebie." And the thought of Francine never doing any of the write-ups for all the million "freebies" she accepted, and the thought of how excruciating it would be to have to run one of her pieces if ever she did.

"Anyway," Francine said, "I just wanted to be sure that you are taking the feedback on board from the last issue. I know both of our teams agreed to move on —"

And "feedback." And especially "team"; he never ever wanted to be on anyone's team for anything, ever. But it was his own fault: clearly the rest of humanity was on a journey to some other place he did not understand.

"This is going to be a top-level-watched issue, Gabriel, and I need to be sure that the lessons we learned from 'Depress Your Depression' are going to be implemented for 'Toxic Parents.'"

The engine note was climbing. "Francine, I'm looking at the proofs right now and I can tell you that all the design concerns have been dealt with. This is a much more readable edition. I think my *team* just got a little bit too . . . too creative — and maybe we left some of the readers behind. So, yes, we have made sure to . . . well, to row back with this one."

"Great. Good. Excellent. Okay, we'll speak again Friday. Have to dash."

The line went dead. And with it, another fraction of his soul.

Without ever for a single minute intending to, Gabriel Glover worked for Roland Sheekey Ltd., a medium-sized contract publishing outfit operating in the nether regions of the Paddington sump, responsible for some thirty-five titles, ranging from in-flight and supermarket tie-in magazines to trade press via corporate brochures and cat-club newsletters — each unnecessary in its own way. But to all intents and purposes his immediate boss was Randy K. Norris, or rather the Randy K. Norris Organization. Gabriel was the editor of *Self-Help!*, a monthly spinoff from the embarrassingly successful series of Randy K. Norris self-help books, "translated into sixty languages and the first step on the road to recovery for millions."

Francine O'Brien was the woman in charge at Norris HQ UK (South Kensington). Gabriel was pretty sure that even her own blood cells loathed her. All the same, it was now Tuesday afternoon, and it was to Francine O'Brien by Friday at 0900 hours that Gabriel had to deliver the twenty-four deliriously interesting pages of next month's *Self-Help! In Association with Randy K. Norris.*

The job in hand: *Self-Help! Number 29: The Toxic Parents Issue.* As yet, all but eight pages of the two dozen were nowhere. Four were so badly written that they would have blushed to serve as toilet paper during the siege of Leningrad. Another four, likewise the work of ridge-browed illiterates, seemed to be about things entirely unrelated to the professed subject of the cover (itself in need of radical attention). The eight pages that were okay were all prepaid ads, mostly for variously lamentable Randy K. Norris products (as if every line of the whole magazine weren't pushing his crap already). As to the remaining eight, they were as yet entirely and formidably blank.

He sat back from the layouts on his desk and once again considered running away. (Mexico? Skye? Shepherd's Bush?) How did it happen this way *every single time?* Did he have the courage for the second sandwich? No.

Instead he opened up his e-mail screen: something from his friend Kolya, about a 1920s party (remember to grow a mustache); something from Larry about a new TV show ("Fuck and Run"? Surely not?) that Larry's company had just commissioned for some TV channel he had never heard of and a celebratory drink being in order. An internal round-robin message, someone from one of the travel magazines advertising a room to let in a shared house in Chalk Farm. Some bulk mail inquiring as to whether he needed help maintaining an erection (no, it's the getting rid of them that's problematic). Something from Isabella about could she crash in a few weeks' time? (Was she coming to London? She hadn't mentioned this. Odd. Very odd.) And something from an address he did not recognize.

Dear Gabriel Glover,

My name is Arkady Artamenkov. I was a friend of your mother, Mrs. Maria Glover, here in St. Petersburg. I am hoping to come to London in December and wondered whether I might meet up with you.

You mother shared a great deal with me before she died and I would very much like to talk to you. Unfortunately, I am not sure where I will be staying just yet but I will get in touch when I am in London.

Hope to see you then.

Yours sincerely,
Arkady Artamenkov

Jesus. Some friend of his mother's . . . Now that was interesting. He typed an immediate reply. And for the thousandth time, he tried to imagine her life out there. What did you do all day, Ma? Where did you go? Why didn't I come and see you more often? He blinked. She was gone, forever gone. And he missed her so very much.

Like his sister, from the moment he had returned home after the funeral, Gabriel had become sensible of the feeling that he had left the reserves, that he was suddenly frontline, and that it was all about to become a great deal uglier and more real. (How ugly could it get?) But he also knew (when the recollection of Isabella's last half-hour of graveside intensity came to his mind) that he did not have his sister's singular sense of psychological purpose, her focus, or her fury. Instead the war his mother had bequeathed him seemed vast and vague, fought across many fronts, stretched out across time zones, idiotic, agonizing, senseless, and terrible by turn, locally fatuous, everywhere critical.

Most immediately there were his conscious wars — sectarian, inane, and petty. There was the war against cigarettes, for example, a war of hard-won and commendable open-air victories overturned in seconds by cellar-sprung ambush and subsequent rout. Or there was the war against food — a trench-trapped grind through the calendar, the fat canons of greed facing the sniper rifles of fitness across the elaborate slop of a million senselessly expensive eating occasions. There was the war against booze — a game of false friends and alliances betrayed, in which he vowed over and over never again to trust the sleight hand of camaraderie (offered with a lopsided grin) and yet found himself somehow suckered like an ingénue three times a week. There was the chemical war on drugs, the war on terror — two or three episodes of utter annihilation every year and a lifetime of anxious vigilance and security checks the never-ending price to pay.

But these were only the conscious wars, the phony wars. Deeper down, closer to his heart, the real war was now pressing: the war against his father. And here hung the shadow of the mushroom cloud. For this was indeed a cold, cold war, all about areas of influence and control, posturing, troops massed, invisible borders drawn, crossed, and redrawn, blanket-smuggled exchanges on shivery bridges by night, years of watching, listening, propaganda, betrayals, chronic suspicion, and the endless, endless silence. A war that felt as though it too were now shifting toward some new point of crisis.

But deeper than even this, at the very bottom, never spoken, never admitted, was the loneliest war of all: the war against despair. This last a solitary staggering struggle that took place in the freezing darkness of the polar night, a struggle from which he could not rest but for which he must be forever on the lookout, perpetually exhausted and perpetually tensed, peering hard into the blizzard, ready for the shape of that hooded foe emerging, ready for the three furious minutes of nail, tooth, and blood that would decide it.

The worst of it was that these wars (and many more) were all being waged simultaneously. Had he been fighting any single campaign in isolation, he would have required all his available resources to prevail. But en masse, he had no chance. And so, like every other human being alive, Gabriel now found that his only free time was filled with craving for more free time so that he could gather the space and energy to engage his foes. Pick them off. (Deal with the cigarette problem at the very least.) Since he had returned from Petersburg, though, he had found that day-to-day distractions pressed in on him from all sides all the more. Considered thought, intelligent resolve, emotional balance — there was no chance. Weaknesses faced, dilemmas considered, relationships weighed — there was no time. No chance and no time for anything other than the blind and foolhardy living of it all.

And the nightmare scenario was already happening: since the death of his mother, his enemies had started talking. Smoking, for example, seemed to hijack his evenings under the casual pennants of his mother's lung cancer (for that, he was sure, was what she had been suffering from), and then, just as he was raising his arms in surrender, some leering little corporal would swing the main banner around and he'd be looking at the insignia, not of his poor mother, but of his father. Yes, cigarettes now reminded him of his dad. Simple as that. A cigarette in itself — white, thin, blithely toxic — said "father" to him as noisily as if it were able to speak out loud. Worst of all — and irony's perfectly curved scimitar this — his father had managed to give up. Easily.

Another thing: he had become curious about — no, fascinated by; no, preoccupied with — his mother's life. Not her life with his father (though this too) but her life before that, her life around, behind, beneath the life he thought he already knew. (What did this Russian guy know?) Related to this was his panic that he would forget what she looked like, what she sounded like — hence his need for hourly mental checks. And related to this was his quest for pictures, for mementos, for anything at all that he might gather, hoard, treasure. And somehow — somehow — related to *this* was . . . was the strong sense that he had to sort his life out. Sort his bloody life out.

He dialed Lina's cell phone. Her office phone was usually diverted, and he didn't want to speak to her secretary.

"Hi, how's it going?"

"Busy," she said. "I'm supposed to have written a presentation and people keep coming in and asking me stuff. And the phone keeps going."

"Shut your door."

"I do. Then they knock and I can't think of anything else to say except 'Come in.'"

"How about a sign — 'Fuck off unless you are giving me money or can do interesting tricks.'"

"Gabriel."

"Sorry. Do you want me to check through the presentation?"

"Yes. That would be nice, thanks. It's a pitch."

"When's it for?"

"Friday. Will you have time?"

"Yes . . . yes, if it's important." He paused. "Are you out tonight?"

"No. You?"

"I'm on the radio. It's the late show again."

"Okay. Don't wake me up. I have to catch a train at eight-thirty." She changed register. "Quality Kitchens just rang, by the way."

"I love those guys."

"They're sending someone new to start next Monday." She shuffled something. "Frank Delaney."

"Can't wait."

"Okay — I have to go. I'll put your pajamas in the lounge so you don't have to turn on our light. See you later."

"Bye."

The afternoon arrived like an aggrieved trade unionist. Not a single one of his so-called writers had filed their so-called copy on time. And what he did have was universally shit. *Unbelievably* shit — even by the standards of modern journalism, even by the standards of contract publishing, even by the standards of *Self-Help!* Further, there was no single person among his staff to whom he could appeal for help. He looked out across the empty office floor. Ten to three, and they were all still out at lunch—probably drinking in the Alfred. Not that having them back would make things any better . . .

His chief (and only) picture editor, Pablo, was a pouting Portuguese prima donna who accused him of being antigay every time he ever so gently suggested that an additional effort of the imagination might be required on such and such a spread, or whenever he delicately pointed out that perhaps a cover picture of Charles and Diana circa 1986 was not the best idea for the "Toxic Parents" issue; his one (and only) copy editor, Craig, was now openly smoking cannabis during his many screen breaks and only last Friday had declared to all comers at the Alfred that he "couldn't be arsed"; his features editor, Annabel (home counties, public school, Durham), had some sort of trouble with her thyroid and was as maniacally ambitious "to make a national" as she was utterly unsuited to her chosen career— completely unable to cope with any kind of decision-making or pressure and totally incapable as an editor, designer, or, he sometimes suspected, even as a reader; his deputy, Maureen, forty-seven (and forty-seven a day), was probably the single most bitter and poisonous woman ever to scratch a living in the miserable secondhand dirt of the profession—in an industry riddled with rancor, rashed with resentment, choked with bile, gall, and spleen, Maureen Wilson was head and shoulders above everyone else, by some distance the most noxious human being Gabriel had ever called colleague, she spent her days whispering on the phone to the National Union of Journalists or lying in wait for just the right moment to take him to an employment tribunal—a woman outdone only by Francine O'Brien in sheer pound-for-pound toxicity; Wendy, meanwhile, his one and only in-house staff writer—aside from the fact that she was Chinese and English was her fourth language, behind Cantonese, Mandarin, and Japanese—simply could not be made to understand that interviews with fashion gurus and Tokyo pop stars, however hard to get, had no place in the magazine unless there was a clear self-help angle and so continued (on her own initiative, at her own expense, and at the expense of the jobs she was supposed to be doing) to file three-thousand-word pieces on the latest glamour boy of Japanese death metal—only to break down in tears when he had to explain why they could not run her stuff before she sprinted off to the toilets to lock herself in for the rest of the day.

The job in hand.

He conjured the current cover onto his computer screen. There was the masthead with its familiar exclamation mark: *Self-Help!* (It was company policy that every title that belly-crawled out of the building did so under the distracting fire of that exclamation mark.) Beneath his own subtitle, "The Toxic Parents Issue," a youngish Prince of Wales and a near-teenage Diana stared back at him, unhappiness drawn in clear lines across their faces. Both photographs had been tipped slightly sideways and were overlaid by the transparencies of two test tubes, as if about to pour and mingle their contents.

What the living fuck was Pablo trying to do? Gabriel sighed. He was going to have to go it alone. Again.

The cheerless reality was that twelve times a year, working night and day as each deadline approached, Gabriel commissioned, designed, wrote, copy-edited, illustrated, captioned, laid out, and proof-checked the entire magazine. In truth, *Self-Help!* was a one-man operation. Yes, the others — Pablo, Craig, and Annabel, at least — did their stuff eventually, however unprofessionally. But he had never once felt able to leave their work unchecked. And almost without fail, he found himself rewriting, revising, redesigning, reworking, later and later into the night as the deadline approached.

The problem was one of conscience. For even though he could not stand the Randy K. Norris Organization, even though he thought Randy K. Norris himself one of the greatest charlatans alive, Gabriel nonetheless felt a crushing sense of responsibility toward the people who read *Self-Help!* The people who might — Jesus Christ — actually turn to the magazine for succor and guidance in their genuine distress. Despite himself, he was trying to make a go of it.

He looked up. His colleagues were returning. Maureen — heels high, chin low — walked straight into her office opposite (far larger than his own), shut the door, sat down, and lit the cigarette that she had readied in the lift. Given the flurries of rain, she would soon be joined by various pinch-faced delegations of fellow smokers from other magazines in the building, whom she welcomed with sardonic zest throughout the day, and who had grown used to using her room as the only alternative to the stairwell or the street. Pablo, meanwhile, sat down at his desk opposite Craig, who did the same for the count of three before standing up again, wedging his armpit with newspapers, and heading in the direction of the men's room. Ominously, there was still no sign of Wendy. For a foolish moment, Gabriel considered calling an editorial conference. But really, there was no point; it was way too late for that. No, his only chance was to try to pick them off one by one. (He must remember to phone Annabel at home, too; check if she was okay; maybe she was genuinely ill. The hours that he had spent counseling that girl . . . and oh man, what do you say, what *can* you say?) He drew breath and got to his feet.

"Hey, Pablo."

"Hello. You seen the layouts?"

"Yes, I looked through them over lunch. And the new cover. I really like the two test tubes things — clever."

Pablo sucked in his cheeks. "Yes, it's very oh-my-God. Mum and Dad, like two poison test tubes, pouring down into one bottle" — he mimed the chemist's concentrated decantation — "which is you."

"I see that." Gabriel had the sense that he was being personally compared to a newly mixed tube of poison. Perhaps it was paranoia.

Pablo clicked his mouse and made as if to return his attention to the screen. "Okay. So, great — send me through the copy when you have it. You got anything ready now?"

Gabriel was unsure whether to perch on the desk or ask Pablo to come over to the big table so that he could talk directly over each of the alterations he required. He glanced up. Craig and Wendy's absence argued in favor of staying put. He perched.

"I've got some changes." He put the mocked-up cover on the design desk adjacent to Pablo's terminal. "First, I don't think we can use the Prince of Wales and . . . and Princess Diana on the cover of the 'Toxic Parents' issue."

Instantly Pablo contorted his face, as if Gabriel's stupidity were beyond the merely unbelievable and on into something that might be medically interesting. "That's everything. Just, like, *the whole cover idea.*"

"No — not everything. As I say, I love the concept. We just need different people in the test tubes. What about some celebrities from . . . from one of the soaps. A famously toxic couple. There must be one."

"And, like, you would know."

This seemed unnecessarily aggressive. Though, perversely, Gabriel was flattered. Which only served to remind him how far apart they were as human beings. He feigned a measured hurt. But Pablo was now staring dead ahead at his screen, busily clicking on pages as if to suggest that *some* people around here had work to do.

"Come on, Pablo—change the cover. If you don't, you know I will."

"Diana sells."

"She is also dead."

"But her painful legacy lives on. That's the whole point. Duh. Every single person who picks this up"—Pablo indicated the print-out with his finger but without taking his eyes off the screen—"will know exactly what this issue is about. Instantly. In one visual hit. They'll think parents. They'll think toxic. They'll think William and Harry's struggle. What more can you ask from a cover?"

"Charles has remarried," Gabriel returned. "This is cheap. Worse than that—it's nasty, it's lame, it's offensive, it's lazy, it participates in everything about our national life that we should dislike. Come on, Pablo—it's also more than twenty years old, and hardly a scoop or a particularly new image." He held the proof up, his tone still just about jocular. "It's tired. It's worse than tired—it's unimaginative, it's ill-judged, it's childish, it's without taste, it's a slight on the dead and an insult to the living, it's—"

"Iconic."

Jesus. Argument was futile. Power was the only recourse. "And it's never going to be approved by the client, or Hamish"—the group editor in chief still signed off on everything individually—"or anyone else who has to approve every single thing we do here."

Pablo now turned in his chair so that he was facing his editor with folded arms. "Well, let's fight for it."

"Pablo, our readers do not think of Diana as toxic. They love her. They love her to death."

"Fight for it."

"For Christ's sake, Pablo, I—we—we are not going to fight for this shit . . . We're just going to get on with it and stop wasting fucking time."

He had never cursed in anger at the office before. And for a moment Gabriel could not think of anything acceptable further to say. For the first time in his working life, he found himself wanting to lash out at one of his colleagues. He found himself wanting to say something truthful for once: Look, you utter penis of a man, we're in *contract publishing*—there's nothing to fight for. We've lost every claim to dignity already. Let alone art. We're totally and utterly beaten. Christ, they're *all* beaten, even the bastards on the nationals. Journalism is over. Art is over. Design is over. Publishing is over.

Fact is fiction. And fiction is fucked. Money won. We're here because we're slaves. And the only claim we are permitted to make
is to tug on the chains of our wages once a month. That's the deal.
I get to buy my girlfriends overpriced tapas every so often. You get
your tight designer T-shirts and a night out at Cream or Lube or
wherever you go on the weekend by way of forgetting. So shut the
fuck up and get on with it. Or get out there and start your revolution.

Somehow, though, he controlled himself, ignored the echoes of
his mother's voice (you would say it, wouldn't you, Ma — you'd just
come right out and say it), and tried to take advantage of Pablo's
horrified attention.

He repeated himself slowly. "We are not going to fight for this,
Pablo. And it's not just the cover."

Pablo straightened his back and set his jaw, as if to arrange himself against the moment of his life's greatest indignity.

"Also, I can see what you're trying to do with the center spread,
but it's . . . it is all image, Pablo. The copy just has to be bigger than
this." Gabriel ran his finger along the bottom of the page, where
Pablo had reduced the point size of Annabel's (wretched) interview
with a celebrity famous for forgiving her parents to something that
resembled a slapdash massacre of starving ants. "Nobody is going to
be able to read it."

Gabriel began to turn through each of the layouts at speed. "And
— I'm sorry, but we have to have headlines at the top. So pages five
and seven, can you redesign? On nine, you've got the body copy running sideways — I think it's sideways. We can't do it. Sorry. Hamish hates all that space. So do I. So does everyone. Okay? Right.
Readers' letters should be the same font size — at least the same font
size for each individual letter. And Spirited Away has to go back
around the right way . . . Our readers won't guess that they have to
turn the magazine upside down for those pages. They're desperate,
Pablo. Let's not make it any worse."

Pablo's eyes were two slits.

But Gabriel had moved beyond care. "The neobrutalist stuff, or
whatever it is, that you want to do on the back — well, okay, I'll allow that on the inside back cover. But. But Inner Space can't stay in
this . . . this galaxy effect. Yeah, I know what you're trying to do — I
get it. It's just totally unreadable. And not really that clever. Spiral
text — it's for kids' mags."

"I'm not doing it. I'm not changing anything." Pablo was actually crying.

Tears. *This* was a first.

"I'm sick of . . . I'm sick . . . I'm sick of you squashing my creativity."

Gabriel felt the surge of his furious blood. Beethoven was creative, Pablo — Mozart was creative, Dickens, Dante, Kant, Dürer, Newton, Raphael, Aeschylus, Balzac. Yes, there have been a good few genuinely creative human beings. But you're not one of them. You are not in the least bit creative. You are not even talented. You just have a computer. That's all. The same as every other mediocre fucker whose terrible shit we all have to suffer every second of the day. So let's leave that word "creative" alone for a few decades, shall we? Let's all stop pretending. There are *no* creative departments in London. Creativity is not copywriting or art directing, creativity is not interior, graphic, or fashion design, creativity is not mimicry or doodle, is not gesture or token, is not a clever text message, a new and even sillier pair of trousers, or an unmade bed, it's not your shitty computer music, or your shitty homemade films, or your shitty Web site with a flashing cock. Creativity is . . . creativity is a massive and serious lifetime's endeavor to further humankind's fundamental understanding of itself. Creativity is 154 perfect sonnets and 38 immortal plays, creativity is 1,126 masterworks of music, every note perfect, creativity is $E = MC^2$, the Rougon-Macquart cycle, the discovery of planets. What you do is total horseshit. Got that? Total and utter horseshit.

And suddenly it came at him like a whetted knife slicing out of the fog in which he was living: he wasn't thinking like his mother at all, *he was thinking like his father.* The journey that he had feared in Petersburg was already under way. Thinking like a nasty, bullying, cowardly, small-time little bastard.

"Pablo — I'm sorry. No further argument about the changes. Just —"

"I really . . ." He was fighting through the tears. "I really do not respect you, Gabriel. You are a fucking fascist. A fucking homophobic fascist."

"I'm neither of those things, Pablo. And you know that I am not." Gabriel handed his colleague some tissues. The distress of others had always distressed him more than his own distress. He reached out his hand and put it on the other man's shoulder as gently as he could manage. "I apologize, Pablo. You are a great designer. I mean it." He spoke softly. "But please, can you make the changes? If not, if you still feel upset in half an hour, then let me know and I will do them."

The fat taxi wallowed west on the Westway. All through the late afternoon he had been chasing so-called experts for quotes, opinion, insight . . . To no avail. Even down in the thickened sedimentary murk at the bottom of the journalistic swamp, the same rusty old rule applied: anyone worth speaking to was impossible to get hold of, and anyone free to talk or write wasn't worth listening to or reading. He made a vow to go in even earlier tomorrow and track down at least one serious human being whom he might ask for information and guidance with his piece.

November nighttime London rolled by his window — white strip lights in the places of work, amber low lights in the bedrooms, the flickering blue of a thousand TVs.

His mind would permit him no rest.

Everyone said that it was unsustainable. Mother, sister, and the few friends who knew. But, Gabriel told himself, none of them could really understand it, or feel it, because none of them were inside the circumstances. None of them had the day-to-day experience. None of them lived it. No, Gabriel alone knew the truth: that it was *utterly* unsustainable. Because he alone had been sustaining it. For the past eighteen months.

Different parts of the heart — this was the way he explained it to himself. Indeed, this was the way he tried to explain it to everyone. You can love a sister and a mother, both entirely and at the same time, correct? But the love for them seems to come from different parts of the heart. One does not replace or override the other. Like the love parents evince for one child simultaneously with — yet separately from — the love for another, for son *and* for daughter. Or the love for closest friends. All of these loves — real, sincerely felt, ready to be tested — they all seem wholehearted in the individual case, and yet they all seem to come from a different space within the whole. I love my mother with all my heart *and* I love my sister with all my heart. These two statements are not mutually exclusive; one does not render the other nonsensical; rather, they are both meaningful, simultaneously. We all know this, intuitively.

But to take this a stage further, Ma, perhaps it *has* to be this way — necessarily, mathematically. Perhaps this is what it means to be truly human. Because, first, the human heart, where exercised, is found to have infinite capacity. (And if not exercised, then what is the point?) And second, because there are infinite infinities in just one infinity. This is the great paradox in the laws of our universe, and this is also the great paradox of the human heart. And these paradoxes are as necessary as the consistencies they defy. And that's how it is for me with Lina and Connie, Ma: the love for one comes from a different place from the love for the other. And though I agree — of course, who wouldn't? — that it may not be possible in practice to live like this, still, in terms of the heart, in terms of the reality of my feelings (the only terms that really count, Ma), I tell you it *is* possible. So please, consider deeply. We must all respect feelings. Do not say that it is not possible — a paradox, yes, a very human paradox, but not an impossibility. Quite the reverse. An affirmation of my humanity. Yes, believe me, it *is* possible. Different parts of the heart. I know — I live it: I am the proof. Every day of my life; every day of my life, Ma, I live it.

"Here we are, mate. This is it."

Radio Rabbit was run from the basement of a converted Victorian school in a part of town that some people thought of as Ladbroke Grove and others Shepherd's Bush — nobody was quite sure, least of all Gabriel. No other city that he knew of had quite so many half-secret but long-established side roads, each one of them a great tragicomic story all its own. The car came to a halt. He signed the chit and stepped out. The night was uncommonly dark; the streetlamps did not make it this far up the cul-de-sac, and the rain fell so finely that he felt it only as a gentle film.

He pressed the buzzer at the side of the shiny door. The lock sprang. He felt his heart lighten, then quicken. A security man, a stuffed bear that someone had thought amusing to dress in a suit, nodded him through. Or might not have moved at all. Gabriel was a regular, and after eleven the bear did not seem to bother to sign people in or out. Not that it mattered; they could always burn together live on air. Be fitting, in a way. He passed down the familiar corridor hung with the fifteen or so faces of Radio Rabbit, including, right at the far end, the one with which he was in love.

Honey-highlighted hair that fell straight in careless strands about her pretty brow; blue-green eyes that appeared a little melancholy and yet forever just about to wink; high cheekbones, but rounded rather than sharp, so that when she smiled (and a smile was the natural set of her lips) she had the cheekiest face of any woman he had ever met — a face full of friendship, mischief, passion, and vitality, collusive, playful, understanding, a face forever caught between laughter and a kiss . . . And yet there was also a distancing cool there — resolve and firmness in the rise of her chin, in the slight sideways angle of her head to the camera, most of all in the way those eyes came at you from somewhere deep and old as the pool of life itself.

He pushed open the familiar door and mouthed his hello to Wayne, the lone producer, assistant, researcher, screener of callers, or whatever it was that he titled himself. In the studio, behind the glass, cans on her head, eyes on her computer screen, Connie was absorbed in the technical business of her job. She did not see him arrive. He watched her a moment, thirsty as a hermit for her beauty and her being.

There was a song playing. Something by Tom Waits. Wayne motioned for him to wait. So he helped himself to some of the vending machine coffee (which always tasted of acorns and cinnamon) and stood sipping it — the spy about to board the plane that would drop him deep behind the iron curtain. Then the red "on air" light went out as they cut to some ads and Wayne waved him in.

Connie looked up as he opened the heavy padded door and greeted him with that smile that women reserve for men they love but cannot love, which of course makes men love them even more. He took his seat opposite hers.

"Hi, you. We have three minutes five," she said. Then, a little softer, "Hmmm — you look tired, Gabriel Glover. Have you been sorting your life out?"

This was her perennial question — faux-comic Connie code for *Have you either proposed to or left Lina? Can we therefore end the misery-exhilaration cycle of our relationship and either never see each other again or live happily ever after somewhere in the countryside?*

"Of course not."

"Well . . . no rush." She was mocking him but not with her eyes.

"Are we still playing it cool?" he asked.

"Yes. We're learning to become friends." She nodded slowly, as if ticking off a wayward pupil. "As we should have done in the first place."

"I think I am addicted to you. I've been missing you like . . . like . . . like something I am addicted to."

She smiled. "Well, sort your life out and you won't bloody have to."

"I am doing."

"Feels like it."

"Connie."

She raised her eyebrows. "Don't try to be cute. You know how much I hate all this mess. I really hate it."

There was nothing he could say. There was never, ever anything he could say.

She relented. "Are you okay?"

And she meant it. She felt for him.

"Yes. I'm fine." And her generosity and understanding and inexhaustible patience made it worse. "I brought the stuff — I've read it through and made some suggestions." She was writing a script for some radio and awards thing she was hosting. He'd taken unbelievable pains to imagine her voice and edit accordingly.

She beamed her thanks. "Good job Wayne is watching or I'd have to kiss you. A lot."

"Does Wayne ever fall asleep?"

"Gabriel."

"Sorry. You started it."

"Never. Wayne never sleeps."

"That's a shame." He smoothed the piece of paper on which he would write the callers' names. "I mean, that's a shame, *mate*."

"One minute, thirty seconds. No, *mate,* you started it — if you remember."

"Mate, I remember everything."

She said, "I keep thinking about when we went to Rome. I think about you all the time."

He said, "I get scared when I am thinking about you that it's getting in the way of thinking about you."

"Soulmates."

"Soulmates."

Even though the red light was off, they were talking in hushed voices — partly because they were in a radio studio, partly because the excitement of being in each other's presence again demanded it, and partly because they were lovers and here they were, somewhere half secret, and it was the dead of night and it felt like they were the last people awake in the middle of a great city and only hushed voices would do. The song played on.

"Fifty seconds."

He said, "We could try breaking up completely — after this."

"We're not together, so how can we break up?"

"We've done it before."

"Yeah . . . about a hundred times, and it's never worked."

"We could try extra-hard this time. No calls. No texts. Nothing."
He took out his favorite pen. "No sudden collapses. Not even any
action."

She made a suspicious face, then lightened. "Okay . . . Okay.
Good. It's a deal. We leave each other alone. You take some proper
time to work out what it is you want and what it is you're doing."

"But I can't stop wanting you, Connie, and I can't imagine my life
without you."

"Nor mine without you. So."

"So?"

"So *sort your life out,* Gabriel—for the love of Jesus, sort your
life out." She gave him an expression that mixed exasperation with
desire. "I'm going to introduce you in the usual way, okay?"

"Sure."

"Signal me if it gets too heavy and we'll move on to someone
else."

"Okay."

The song ended in applause. The red light came on. And her voice
spoke softly to the hearts of three thousand sleepless Londoners:
"You are listening to Radio Rabbit with me, Connie Carmichael,
and that was 'Strange Weather,' by Tom Waits. Who I still haven't
met, despite the celebrity-stuffed life I lead. Well, it's midweek and
it's midnight and that means it's time for our self-help phone-in.
With me in the studio is our regular guest, your friend and mine, the
editor of the Randy K. Norris *Self-Help!* magazine, Gabriel Glover.
How's the week shaping up for you, Gabriel?"

"Terrific, so far."

23

Comrade Masha

THE RIVER SLUNK and the city slept. Parisians dreamed in three million darkened rooms. But Nicholas was still awake, sitting alone in his high-backed leather chair.

The pipes groaned, and the wood seemed to creak in the beam. He had the window open a fraction for the night air, though the flames of the false fire were turned up as high as they would go. He set down his malt, took out the letter from its cheap Russian envelope again, and held it to the angled light. His eyesight was as good as it had ever been. And yet, although he was alone, it suited some indefinite part of him to act as if it were fading.

The English, he thought, was surprisingly lucid — though lucid in the old-fashioned elegant manner rather than merely plain in the modern way. The handwriting, however, was quite unable to stay within the confines of its institutional origins. He read the letter through again. The opening sentence began with the specific use of his name: "Dear Nicholas Glover . . ."

The writer was intelligent enough not to commit any specific threat to paper. He merely asked for a meeting. But it was there, Nicholas was sure, betrayed perhaps by the square hook of those gallows-shaped *r*'s — the grim Cyrillic Γ in thin disguise.

He allowed the letter to dangle between finger and thumb and played the whisky through his crooked teeth.

My God, Masha, your bloody son is alive after all. You knew this all along, of course . . . Christ, why am I always so slow-witted compared to you? Only now do I begin to see what has been under my vain nose all along. You went back to find him. Didn't you? This was the reason. Only now do I begin to see. It was not the call of your country at all, was it? It was the call of your blood. Alive all along. Known about. And yet . . . you did not tell me. Even when I came to you at the end. Even as we sat together. Your quid pro quo for all the things I did not tell you — was that it? Ah, but what a shame that we played chess with our secrets like this. A shame, dear Masha. A shame on our lives.

Somewhere down on the embankment a drunk had started sobbing like a child bereft. Nicholas rose to pull the window shut, the flames wavering a moment in his draft as he passed. He eased the frame up a millimeter or two on its old hinges so that it would close more easily and turned the handle through ninety careful degrees. Then he fetched his bottle and returned Bach's harpsichord to its beginning so that he would not have to move again.

> I was very close to your wife here in Petersburg and I wondered whether or not it might be possible to meet up as there are a number of important things that I wish to discuss.

And what exactly am I supposed to do now that the bastard — sorry, but we *are* all bastards, Masha, except you — now that the bastard has tracked me down? What is he to me? Or I to him? And what kind of man are we dealing with? Is he our everyday comrade — brutal, avaricious, mercenary, desperate to get out? Or is there some of your nobility in his character — is it just a meeting he wants, friendship, a lifelong correspondence about Turgenev?

Or will it be money?

Wait, though. Wait . . . is this what you were doing in Petersburg, Masha, giving him money? After everything was said and resaid and asserted and defied, did it come down to money for you too? Oh no. Wait. I know you, my Mashenka!

He leaned forward in his chair, childishly enlivened by the rare excitement of a thought he had not had before.

My father's money was stolen from Russia. It came to me. I gave it to you. You gave it back to Russia. That's how you will have seen it! That's exactly how you will have seen it! Oh Masha, did this become your life's project? This son of yours and his birthright . . .

A young woman rising in the Party, you see this Englishman gallivanting through your cities: Maximilian Glover, whoremonger, embezzler, art thief, traitor . . . Or, my God, perhaps you were sent to him . . . Perhaps you were sent to my father.

Nicholas sat back, let the letter dangle again, and swallowed slowly, concentrating on the burn of the Talisker down his throat and into the pit of his stomach.

But you . . . you . . . you marry the son instead. You can serve your masters better that way. My God. Surely you weren't spying after all? How many times did we talk about this? Laugh. Fantasize. Pretend. You loved to make things up, of course, and this I celebrate. But was the final joke on me? Was I distracted? Was I double-fooled? Oh, Masha, is this your little secret?

He drank again and this time held the spirit in the cradle of his tongue. (The chain of thought was long familiar to him. But he fingered the links now with a new concentration.) You study your ruffian English so very, very carefully. You take your terrible job as a lowly copy editor — a miserable checker of grammar and facts on the newspaper of record, as you liked to call it. You work the night shift. You work weekends. You work whenever you are told. And there are whispers, of course, in the canteen, up and down the editorial floor, there are whispers everywhere; more than this — there are tales and conversations and rows, all the hundred truths that cannot be printed are heard out loud, bandied back and forth across the desks every day; and then there is all that copy they cannot run; and you see it; you sift the in box while you're waiting for the idiots to file their illiteracy; and you hear the political correspondents boasting in the lifts and the diplomatic editor confiding on his way to conference; foreign desk, crime, health, and defense — you hear them all; and there are politicians and there are artists and there are captains of industry, stars of this and experts in that, and they are all in and out of the editor's office, day and night, like Japanese businessmen through a brothel. And you are there all the while, as decades pass, listening, reading, sitting quietly at your workstation, Maria Glover, the efficient copy editor.

And I wager you never took a penny. There would be no trace of it. No money. Just love. You passed without being asked to do so. And I wager you never asked if any of it was useful, or appreciated, or even relevant. You simply passed information. Dutifully. Loyally. Even when they stopped acknowledging your drops. Because, yes, one day, just as you are sitting there, the Wall comes down. And it seems as though it has all been for nothing.

What then? Do you go on regardless? Or do you turn slowly from the great struggle to the personal? Is there one last thing, a private thing — though the bourgeois scum are teeming gleefully through — is there one last thing that you can still accomplish? You can return the money to your son. You can return what is owed to Russia. You would enjoy that last bitter little irony, wouldn't you, my clever, clever Masha?

He weighed this new idea, pleased to have hauled it from the mirrored lake of his life, pleased that there was hidden treasure at the end of the chain after all.

If this is the way we must play, then play this way we will, you think. If it's all about the money, then let it be so: let's start again, but let's start fair. Yes, let's start again: oil, labor, and technology — the East will rise once more in a monstrous aping of the slobbering West. Harder, careless, and more ruthless yet. And this time the West will beg for mercy.

Or am I wrong? Am I wrong about all of this?

His eyes reflected the flames. The ice had melted in his glass.

24

Scorched Earth

WORK WAS EASY.

She asked for a sabbatical.

They refused.

She said that she was sorry but she was going back to the U.K. to deal with some family issues anyway. And that she would therefore be tendering her resignation.

They said, oh, they hoped it was nothing serious, they would be sad to lose her, but she should definitely drop in when she got back and they would see where they were then.

She said that, yes, it was serious, her mother had died.

They looked at her with faces of sudden concern and expressed their sympathy. They asked her when her mother passed away.

She took a private moment to dislike their choice of euphemism and then, as planned, said that her mother's death had been yesterday rather than almost four weeks ago. This so that they could not stop her from leaving immediately, now, this very lunchtime.

They did not know whether to comfort her or become even more professional.

She could tell they were alarmed at her calmness. She wanted to say, Don't worry, so was I; it passes.

They shook their heads and meant their platitudes.

She was sorry for them for having to deal with this. Death gave them focusing issues to address in the short term and mortality issues going forward.

They asked her if there was anything at all they could do to help.

She told them no, thanks, and that seeing as she would be dropping by in six months, and given the circumstances, she wouldn't be working her notice and she had to go pretty much straightaway.

They said, oh, and then, of course.

She didn't gather her small collection of things at her desk. And she did not stop to consider whether it was she or they who had the perception problem on her way out.

Her father, though, was the hardest task she had faced in her life. The hardest task since the last e-mail. Her twenty-second draft read:

Dad,

I am coming to London. Please don't feel that you have to write back. I really don't wish to interfere in your life in any way. I suppose I just wanted to let you know that I will be dropping in to Highgate to see Francis—I assume he is still there; neither Gabs nor I have heard anything to the contrary. I need to store some stuff if he is okay with that . . .

I have to admit, it feels strange to be writing to you like this. I'm not even sure you read e-mail. (Forgive me btw: Julian, at the consulate in SP, gave me this contact. I suspect that you still prefer letters but I'm afraid that I don't have your postal address.) I know we haven't been in touch for years . . . and yet, now that Mum is dead, it all seems a bit sad. Of course Gabriel and I talk all the time. But you knew Mum before we were born, you knew Mum when she was a young woman, you knew Mum better than anyone else. And I think this whole thing is affecting me more than I thought it would. Time will pass, and I'll get used to it. But I suppose I would like to know more about Mum—and, yes, you too, Dad.

At the funeral, out there in Petersburg, I became more conscious than ever of who I am: half you, half Mum. And how little I know about either of you really . . . Dad, I have been thinking back a great deal—it's natural, I suppose, at times like this—and if there is anything you would like to say to me now, about your life, about who you are, then I want you to know that I am ready to listen. Just that.

Yours,
Is

But having gone through the e-mail again, for the twenty-third time, she found it a cringing agony still. No matter what she did, she could not rid her words of their phony tone, their dishonest designs, their awkwardness. The plain truth was that she could not plainly ask her own father anything that she wished to ask him. She squeezed her eyes shut. What was it with some people — that the very idea of them prohibits certain questions from ever being asked? How does their power, their charisma — if that's what it is — cast such shadows in other minds, even if they are halfway around the world?

Shitting hell.

She was back in the same Internet café. And this time, as well as the rotting carpet, she could smell the milk turning sour where someone had spilled it beside the help-yourself coffee stand.

Hey, Dad, are you gay? I've suspected it for years deep down. Francis is an old boyfriend, isn't he? Well, good. Great, in fact! It's fine. It really is. Nobody cares anymore. That's one victory we have won. You can tell me. You can trust me. If trust is what you need. Anyway, it explains a good deal, and thank you for your honesty.

Oh yeah, and were you in Petersburg before Mum died? Your friend Mr. Avery nearly gave you away, you know. Did you go to see her die? That would suit you, wouldn't it? The ultimate combination of pain followed by histrionic displays of affection, you sadistic bastard. See, she suffers almost to death! And see, I love her after all! All you who doubted my capacity for compassion. You were wrong. I held it back behind these castle walls of cold gray stone for dire moments such as this. So now . . . now see the iron man's bleeding heart! See how I demonstrate my love. Hitler fondles his dogs. Stalin pats the children's heads.

Well, understand this, you vainglorious little shit: I'm not fooled. Because I do see, I see it all clearly: because still, still, still, it's all about *you,* isn't it? Even your own wife's, my mother's, cancer is nothing more than a stage on which you can strut and preen your narcissism. Admire me, admire the drama of the strongman's unexpected kindness. Admire his great reservoir of love released. Count yourselves lucky to see such a glimpse. Because you never ever forget how it plays, even if only to the rapturous audience in your head, do you, Dad?

Oh Christ. Christ. Christ. She felt the grief kraken rising from the deep, sending ripples through the underground lake of her tears.

Shitting hell.

She looked around. The Internet café was almost empty this afternoon. She bit her lip. This was going to be a long, painful process. She must ask her questions singly. She must win her father's trust. She must persuade the portcullis guard one ratchet at a time. Only then . . . With a tremendous effort, she gathered herself. And then, falsely calm, she deleted everything except the first paragraph (as she had always known she would) and let the phrase "I don't want to interfere in your life" stand as the most oblique invitation to a father's frankness that had ever been written.

Next, Sasha.

Though maybe she didn't plan to end it forever. After all, she liked the guy. He was sweet. He was intelligent. He was on the same side. Lazy, immature — yes; but good-hearted beneath all the pretentious film-industry jargon he talked; and all he needed was some confidence, someone to take him seriously out there so that he could take himself seriously too.

When she had met him, he had just sold a scene from one of his screenplays — something to do with a dog being set on fire by accident — and he was riding high. He made her laugh — properly, wholeheartedly, like the young Woody Allen made her laugh. He had a nice line in existential incredulity. Since then, he had seemed to grow younger or more puerile. And either she'd begun to see the banality of the form for what it was or he had started to write more banal things. In any case, his work had foundered. And his mother, she knew, was now giving him money. Which wasn't good for him. He was turning in on himself. She suspected he was spending hours online in chat rooms. He needed someone to draw him out again, to love him without secret reserve, to whisper reassurance to him in the night.

Their recent antagonism, which had started a good few months before her mother had died, was officially about space. Sasha worked at home, and he needed some undisturbed zone of his own: namely, the main table. This she duly ceded, accepting the piles of papers, the ostentatious laptop, the stacked books, the newspaper clippings, the printer on the floor with its wretchedly too-short cable stretched lethally taut from desk to socket at shin height. In return, the sofa was hers. She lived around his mess. She did not complain.

Beneath this, though, she had known that there was a second and more truthful level of the argument. Sasha thought that she did not believe in his efforts. Did not really believe in his talent. Did not believe in the persona he wanted her to believe in. Did not, in fact, believe in him. And the more he thought that she did not believe, the more the paper and the mess expanded, as he tried to seek her affirmation by subconsciously forcing his work again and again back under her retreating nose. Because in some furtive way, Sasha also knew that this was the real argument, and so he wanted to prize her out into the open to challenge her. And yet he was also a coward. So, having goaded her out with his mess from time to time, he would then devote all his energy to pretending that the argument was only about space after all and what the hell was she getting so crazy about when, sure, if it was a problem, he'd tidy up every night and she could use the goddamn table.

All this changed in the weeks after Petersburg. After Russia—dear God, the endless false floors—after Russia, a new and even deeper level had gradually revealed itself to Isabella: that Sasha was beside the point. Simply, she didn't care. She didn't care about the space. She didn't care about his work. Not really. Not in the way you are supposed to care about the people you love. All of it was . . . was irrelevant. Because really this argument was with herself: where she was, who she was, what she was doing. And she was determined now to fight her way clear of the emotional wreckage of her parents (and their whole spineless generation), and Sasha would never understand this. She could neither count on nor confide in him. Either go in repetitive circles or break free: this was the choice. Fondness but not love.

Having left work in the morning and despite the hours at the Internet café, she was home early—it was only just three. She climbed the narrow stairwell with no plan of what to say but knowing that she must say it.

Her keys caught him out. She put her bag down by the sink. She did not look over again, to save him that indignity at least. Instead, leaning against the doorjamb, she bent awkwardly, her skirt restrictive, and removed her wretched shoes as slowly as she could, while he did himself up.

Fifteen bad seconds passed. The apartment smelled close, fetid.

"Hi, baby," he said.

He was crimson. Torn between candor and dissembling. Uncertain of her reaction. Trying to click screens shut surreptitiously now.

"Sasha, I resigned from work today and I'm going back to London as soon as I can. I'm not sure for how long." She did not advance but remained on the threshold. "I don't want you to wait for me, though. I don't want you to wait for me to come back, I mean."

His face was blank, then bewildered. His attention divided. He was still trying to shut down whatever it was he had been looking at.

And she could see that he was not sure what exactly she was saying. Understandable. So she had better just say it.

"Sasha." She had him now. She had never said his name like that before. "Sasha, this is over for me."

"What?"

"I don't want to say . . ." Clean break, cruel to be kind: she felt the clichés gathering like a circle of bitchy teenage girls. So she stood her ground. "I don't want to say that this is about me and not you, because it isn't. This is about our relationship together . . . coming to an end." She almost said "for now"—anything to make this easier. "But it is true, I have so many things I have to get straightened out— on my own. Partly about my mother and father and all that, but I think also about me. My life has been on pause for too long. I feel like I can't move on until I have . . . okay, until I have sorted out who I am. And until then, I can't be anything to anybody. I can't be anything to you. I'm sorry."

Though it was true enough, she hated herself for the way it was coming out.

The poor man was visibly reeling. "Is . . . Is . . . Izzy, where did all this come from? You *resigned?* What are you saying—what's happened? I mean, come on, baby, you can't just walk in and do this, just say all this out of nowhere. Out of totally nowhere. Jesus. Baby."

He sat back, shaking his head, white-faced, his hand still on his mouse. But even in this moment she thought she detected a hint of melodramatic self-indulgence in his aspect. And already he was trying to make out that she was mad, an irrational woman. That old, old male gambit. And yes, it *was* all gambits with Sasha. She let this feed her determination.

"What I have just said is a little bit bullshitty, Sash, I know. I'm sorry. I do have a lot of stuff to sort . . . but that's not the reason I'm saying that I want to bring this to an end. I—"

"We have to talk. Like, we have to talk right now." He was up, reaching for his jacket. "Let's get out of here. Let's go somewhere. Right now."

He was coming toward her. She had to say it. She had to stop him before he tried to hold her.

"I want to end it because I am not in love with you. That is the truth. Sasha. I am sorry."

He was very close now—suddenly handsome again, suddenly

sweet, suddenly a man she could learn to love after all. But she met his gaze directly. Ordered the ducts of her eyes dry even as she felt her tears rising. Continued to hold his eyes with hers for a moment. Let her words find their way in. Let him hear. Let him know. There was no way back from that sentence.

Then she was passing him, heading by the sofa, carrying her shoes, exhausted. And in that moment, their bedroom was the saddest thing she had ever seen. Their shallow closet, their clothes mixed up on the chair, the cartoons that they had bought together, their photos, Sasha and Isabella swapping cocktails, Sasha and Isabella arm in arm on the cable car in San Francisco, Sasha and Isabella kissing for the camera she was holding at arm's length, Sasha and Isabella dancing together, this duvet they shared, these pillows, this bed, this life.

Over.

25

The Kitchen Sink

"ELLO."

"Hello. Gabriel Glover?"

"Yes."

"It's Frank. From Quality Kitchens."

"Hi."

"Erm . . . can you come out? Don't want to leave the van . . . Have you got the parking permit?"

A minute later, in jogging top and shorts, he was face to face with Frank Delaney himself: fifty-five, swept-back, dyed black hair, string vest, and hand-rolled cigarette; six-two, big hands, big shoulders, potbelly, long, fridge-carrying arms, wearing the default smirk of a man who has seen it all before, knows a thing or two (especially about women, so he'd have you believe) — a maverick, but still the best in the business, and already right at home in Gabriel's entrance hall.

Without really thinking (he *couldn't* think), Gabriel confessed that he did not have a parking permit. He must have looked blank or panicked or in need of leadership or something, because Frank nodded slowly and then said, "Oh, bollocks. Well, you'd better go and get one, mate. I suppose I'll have to wait here in the van."

"Right. Where do you get 'em?"

"Kentish Town. Spring Place. You know it?"

"No."

Three minutes later, knees creaking to the off-beat of the never-oiled chain, he was cycling crazily across, through, between the furious morning traffic — rigid arms, rigid knuckles, rigid handlebars, rigid face set against the rigid city's petrol rush.

Fifteen minutes after that (head like a sack of sickened Moscow rats), he was queuing with fat sassy gasmen, stick-thin chippies, wiry sparkies, bum-wielding builders. He was the only private citizen in the city, he noticed, to be collecting a parking permit on behalf of his workman.

Twenty minutes more were lost (and forty much-lamented quid) before he had filled in all the forms, signed everything, survived the looks, the jibes, the scorn, and was back on his bike pedaling furiously home, fearful both that Frank would have departed in disgust at the delay and that Lina would have arrived off her dawn flight back from a weekend in Stockholm. And perhaps these thoughts or the sudden rain (or the memory of his mother's war on cars) distracted him.

As he came off a curb, plastic-covered parking permit in one hand, house keys in the other, the front wheel somehow jerked left and he hadn't sufficient grip on the handlebars to correct it. He lost control and down he went, hard and sideways onto the pavement — clatter of bike, scrape of limbs, pain, and yet more disbelief. To counter the embarrassment, he had, of course, to jump back on as quickly as possible, though he was well aware that this was in many ways more ridiculous than falling off in the first place. Ladies, gents, I assure you that the accident you have just witnessed was all but planned . . . As if anyone cared.

They lived in Tufnell Park, North London, and not bad. They had four rooms: big bedroom, big bathroom, a small nameless room (that screamed in certain cartoonish nightmares for a child), and a decent lounge, down one side of which was their kitchen. Given that to live in the city was for the vast majority of Londoners to live in a dark, vole-sized hole, they were lucky. Ridiculously small and silly by any other standard, in London of the twenty-first century, their flat was modestly desirable.

Or rather, used to be, before they (Lina) had decided to get the kitchen "done." Now, alas, all was dust, rubble, and dereliction. Week six, and everybody involved, including the flat itself, was showing signs of having had enough. In one sense, and as past participles go, having the kitchen "done" described the process well — though maybe not quite robustly enough to Gabriel's mind. Rather, it seemed to him that under the pretense of "installing" the new kitchen, the

fitters were actually serially *abusing* it: shoving it up against the walls
and banging it every which way they knew how — as hard and as often as they could; ripping it apart, pushing it down, forcing it into
places it did not want to go; hurting it, flipping it over this way and
that for their brutal pleasure; breaking it, smacking it about, calling
it all the filthy names they knew; scratching it, breaking off its knobs,
dropping its drawers; fucking it forward, backward, side to side,
good and proper, once and for all. And when one guy got tired, another took over and went at it again, as hard as he could for five days
straight.

All of this, plus all of everything else, as well as the need to stop
all of this and stop all of everything else, was on his mind as he came
haring up his street, bike clanking unnaturally loudly. Haring up the
street to find Lina looking every bit as fresh and pristine as the face
on the North of Sweden Tourist Board's 1992 press campaign (clear
lakes, snow-white mountains, nature's undiminished purity), which
job she had in fact held when she was seventeen. Haring up the street
to find Lina standing beneath an umbrella, giving instructions in her
measured and sensible voice to Frank, who, unbelievably, was taking
down notes as she spoke.

His brakes squealed him to a histrionic halt. There was pavement
muck on his trousers, blood on the elbow of his jogging top, white
skin-scrapes on his hands, and rainwater on his nose. He tried his
best to smile. He was staggered by her . . . her competence. Nobody
was angry or crying or about to die. Nobody was talking about
Leonard Cohen or the appalling adolescence of the new world leaders or why they were still tearing down the Amazon or anything
remotely like that; they were actually talking about the kitchen sink.
And in the chaotic and unpredictable way these things happen to
men, as she looked up at him, he was struck by desire. He wanted
her there and then. He wanted her as he always wanted her — at
the least appropriate moments life could conjure. To kiss those lips
now. To hold her *now*. Shut the door against Frank and all his kind.
Fall on each other in the hall. Cast off clothes as best they could.
Raise her skirt. Go at it like Olympian gods made mortal for half an
hour only.

Their relationship had begun with the best taxi ride of his life. He
had just flown back from New York. She was standing at the baggage counter. He had always found it easy to talk to women, his unconscious secret being that, unlike so many men, he naturally talked

to them as human beings and not as women. Even so, looking back, he realized that it was probably some magical and unrepeatable combination of his tiredness, his mind's emptiness, his confession of fear, his unfakeably relaxed I'm-not-after-anything manner (which a man gets when he's had attention from another woman recently), his genuine feeling of camaraderie with her after the turbulent flight, and maybe even his sincere desire to get a cab at half price that made her feel comfortable enough to let him continue asking questions, carry her vodka through customs, share the ride.

They sat quietly side by side as they drove in, watching that gentle miracle of the dawn: steadfast old London emerging from a quiet rain, gray and wet, street by street — prewar terraces of solid brick, modern low-rise offices, the high white stucco of West London's prosperity, newsagents on corners just opening up, the Victorian railway lines, the Georgian canals, the early-shifters already afoot, making for the nearest tube with umbrellas, headphones, privately preoccupied. The drizzle zigzagged down their windows. The car's heater hummed intermittently, as though a tiny piece of paper had been caught somewhere. She sat with her shoulder-length dark hair tied to one side at the back in a mini-ponytail that wisped sideways, long legs twisted around each other in her heavy black tights, buried otherwise in her coat; he sat, also looking out but thinking thoughts that mingled the history of his city with a tingling awareness that he was slipping under the encounter's gathering spell. That somehow there was a fragile affinity between them that may or may not come to anything, something intimately shared beyond the immediate ride — something, he thought, to do with that mysterious old alchemy that happens when a man and a woman find that their journeys coincide for a while.

When they turned from their windows, they met each other's eyes. And he eased the moment's silence by asking for her number, saying it would be fun to meet up again and discuss customs regulations. And she gave it to him. And the next day he called her.

In the weeks and months that followed, he probably fell in love. Lina was twenty-six, two years younger than he at that time. She was half Sami, half Swedish. Her limbs were all long and thin, so she had the occasional gawkiness of a slightly taller woman. She had ice-blue eyes, snow-sunned skin, sleek, dark, silky black-brown hair, which she was forever tying up this way or that. Her lips were almost colorless, though shaped and full, as though designed by some high seraphim of kissing. And the soft light of the midnight sun was in her smile.

Indeed, hers was a sorcery of the genes that no other combination on earth could hope to conjure. When he sat down to think about it, which, in those early days, he did more often than sanity might require, he calculated that there could be fewer than a thousand like combinations alive—how many pure Sami people were left in the north of Sweden, and of those, how many had married the southerners, and of those, how many had produced female children who turned out like Lina? She was one in six billion. And yet it was impossible to place her without knowing where she was from, for her eyes had only the faintest rise of the far north, her dark hair and skin suggested the south, while her smile was as wide and white-toothed as the west itself, and her manner was almost oriental.

Her mother—now married to her stepfather (her "plastic dad") and living in London for the past two decades—looked as though she had just stepped out of a 1970s holiday brochure advertising happiness and free love in Sweden: the cheekbones, the head-to-one-side smile, the true blond hair, the ever-honest self-reliant Scandinavian eyes of steady azure. And it was from her mother that Lina had received the gift of living in her body with ease and openness—not so much the tawdry modern "confidence," more a deep and unconscious surety in the authority of womanhood—and the gift of competence, a steady practicality and equilibrium that found life for the most part exactly as it should be.

Her father had abandoned an existence of fur trapping with his father to go the long way south to Gothenburg at nineteen. Lina's grandfather, meanwhile, had lived his entire life bound in ice and liquor. She had a picture of the old man, grinning broken-toothed from inside the layers of his furs, standing on the edge of a white forest, white mountains behind, white sky, surrounded by dead animals neatly fanned out in the red-stained snow before him. And so it was from her father's side that Lina had received the gift of tranquility—or, more accurately, the gift of silence. For Gabriel knew that she was without doubt the most silent human being he would ever meet—not silent as in "a bit quiet" or "sometimes shy" but silent, when the mood took her (twice, three times a year), as in utterly wordless for days at a time. He had known her to say nothing for entire weekends, wrinkling her nose, smiling, and blinking after they made love and then wandering off, towel loosely held like an afterthought, to find a drink, her bath, her music. And it wasn't erotic primarily, or even sexy (though both these things), but it was somehow ancient and intense.

The relationship deepened. Lina was kind, unbelievably generous, and supportive. She gave him all the freedom he wanted. She was as honest as Archean rock, and almost weirdly straight — quite without artifice or any sort of emotional deviousness. For a while Gabriel wasn't sure if this was a side effect of her being forever in her second language, but her English was perfect, better than her Swedish, she said, and the only errors that she made — "tempting faith," "a leap of fate" — were too few and far between to bear any wider significance. So next he wondered if it might be that in fact she was entirely normal and it was just his own background that caused him to consider everything short of fabled espionage, intrafamilial hostility, and deceit as "straight." But eventually he came to see that she was indeed wholly guileless. She was clever, but logically so, clever in straight lines, clever at recognizing the trail; she was quick-witted, but not witty; she was insightful, wise, socially observant, but somehow tone-blind, or rather blind to the effect she was having on the people around her. Then again, she didn't actually care, which he found more and more attractive.

Except, perhaps, when this blindness translated itself into the Lina who would notice (and comment upon) the shabbiness of a pianist's shoes after he'd just finished playing the last three Beethoven sonatas from memory. Or the Lina who would be talking about the lack of good customer service at the petrol station they had just left as they drove north for their holiday into the purple-peaked Pyrenees with Elvis playing on the radio and the sun sinking in the west like Cleopatra's barge burning for the beauty of its love-struck queen.

True, the correlative of this was that she was the most capable woman he had ever met — a facilitator. There was nothing she could not sort out. (After college, she'd joined the same advertising agency that had previously made her the face of Swedish Lapland and sorted that campaign out too.) Indeed, so much of his life did she ease and improve (as the first three years disappeared) that he sometimes felt as though he were being corralled, trained, domesticated according to some grand plan that he could never know. And now and then he did resent being managed as if he were an awkward account. He suspected that if he were to allow her to do so, she would get up an hour early every morning to wash, dress, groom, and perfume him. Her man-doll. But then, not one of her requests was in the slightest bit unreasonable: dry his feet before he left the bathroom, stop eating everything at three hundred miles an hour, be on time when he said he was going to meet her, replace the garbage bags when he carried out the trash. And so on. She was never, ever unreasonable.

They walked together now, beneath November skies of pond-sodden bread. The rain had stopped since he had been out for the permit, and London seemed to be prepared to make a go of it again. It was not yet eight-fifteen. Already Frank was assiduously under way with the plumbing and Gabriel was feeling a little better. He knew Lina well enough not to try anything when he was covered in mud and bleeding. So instead he had merely told her how pretty she looked, then dutifully taken a shower, dressed in his favorite shirt, and asked her about her trip as they moved around the bedroom, before telling her that he had transferred all her music to her new MP3 player, which won him a kiss.

Lina took his arm and he crooked it for her, as he always did. They crossed Tufnell Park Road, solid at this hour with precious mothers off-roading precious children to precious schools, and began to make their way toward the main junction. Traffic wardens were swarming on the corner. In the middle distance, the sirens sounded like eight-year-old girls making fun of their friends' boy stories. Gabriel could scarcely believe that he was the same person who only an hour ago had been cycling, bleeding, having a breakdown. And it wasn't anything Lina had said — it never was; they seldom talked about feelings, his or hers — but now, for the first time, he smiled rather than flinched as a memory of his mother entered his head: a policeman parking illegally to nip in and get a pizza in Highgate village, his mother remonstrating, he embarrassedly waiting so that they could hurry up and buy the promised tennis racket, policeman catching schoolboy's eye, mutual sympathy. Yes, though light on his arm, Lina felt steadfast and certain. He was glad to be with her this morning. Glad the world contained her. Glad that she was here with him. Maybe it was because she had been away for a couple of days, but he was struck again by how calm and together and resourceful he felt in her presence. There was nothing he could not do with this woman at his side. Oh God.

Breakfast was already well under way in Martha's Café. His hangover was hungry. They were greeted by the welcoming aroma of fresh-ground coffee as they opened the door, which gave way to a delicious smell of bacon toward the kitchen at the back. They sat at one of the miniature tables under the blackboard on which the menu

was scrawled. They had been coming here most days since the work
on the kitchen had started.

She ordered some inscrutable confection of muesli and he went
for the half English, which, after all, was what he was. Conversations of football crises, of such and such a figure in the news getting
exactly what he deserved, of so and so needing to get her act together, of problems, rumors, plans, and hopes reached his ears. To
Gabriel, the whole experience already felt as though it would be
something that they would look back on and remember . . . Some-
day, twenty or so years from now, when visiting one of their children
at university perhaps: breakfast at the local college café, newly independent child assuming parents had never dreamed of eating such a
thing, mute parental complicity as child talked through the menu as
though it were the most recent thing on earth.

Lina reached up to remove a stray eyelash from his cheek and
took the opportunity to hastily rearrange his hair more to her liking,
a habit that he vehemently disliked.

"Lina. Pack it in."

"What have you been up to, then — apart from throwing yourself
at the local pavements?"

He grimaced. They had only talked about her trip so far — her
real dad's birthday.

"Larry came up last night," he said. "It was terrible. He's an alcoholic. He's definitely an alcoholic."

She smiled. "What did you do?"

"We went to the pub for a quiet one and then into Camden . . .
Ended up drinking in some pig-packed shit hole until Christ knows
when."

"Fun?"

"At the time."

"Sounds it."

"Actually, it wasn't."

"When did you get in?"

"Two."

"Larry meet anyone?"

"No, he just got a cab home."

"At least none of your friends can stay over when they're drunk at
the moment, so you don't have to go through all the rigmarole with
the futon."

What she really meant was not all the rigmarole of turning the
futon into a bed but the secondary rigmarole of putting a sheet down

—one of her pet insistences. She was the most hygienic woman in the world. She would physically cringe at the thought of a man falling asleep on their furniture without the prophylactic of a clean sheet, duvet, pillowcase. And yet there was never a word of censure about what he was *doing* until two in the morning. He could have turned up three days later without his trousers and said that he had been in Rio judging the Miss Porniverse Pussy-Pumping Pageant and she would have been just as calm. And he loved her for that.

Her coffee (decaffeinated) appeared, his tea hot on its trail with a jug of milk. There was a sudden sizzle of sausages arriving for the workmen on the next table. She spoke over the top of her raised mug. "You should get him a girlfriend. Then you could both go out and do something you actually enjoy."

"What do we enjoy? I've lost track."

"Swimming on the Heath."

"Lins, it's absolutely freezing at this time of year."

"Joke." She eyed his hand, gauging his minor thumb injury as he gingerly removed the teabag.

"He wants *you* to get him a girlfriend."

"Me?" She raised her eyebrows.

"He thinks you know loads of beautiful Swedish women."

"What? From ten years ago?" She affected consideration. "Well, there's Anya—she's thirty-one and about to have a cesarean any day. She's my oldest friend and happily married, but I could ask if she'd like to give it all up for an overweight TV producer."

"No. Forget it. She goes out clubbing. Larry only goes out eating."

Someone swore at a bottle of ketchup that could not be bullied into dispensing its chemical treasure.

"I could have a look at the office. What type does he like?"

He also loved it that Lina wasn't on some phony high horse about womankind; he loved it that she could talk about other girls—minds, bodies, behavior—without all the invidious ancillary crap that so many women had to shovel into such conversations all the time.

"Medieval barmaid type."

"Blond?"

"Yes. Blond, big baby eyes, breasts . . ."

She wrinkled her nose. "It's such an easy look."

". . . comely, honest but saucy, daughter of local miller, weaver, wainwright. You get the idea."

"I'll do a round-robin e-mail."

"You still want me to order your mum music for Christmas?"

"Yes. Thanks for doing that, Gabe. Choose things she would *like*, though. Nothing too weird. Maybe those cello pieces you listen to."

"Nothing too weird."

"I'll give you the money."

Their breakfast danced into view. He was starving. Having poured her milk — she always swamped her cereal, causing Gabriel to think that what she really wanted was muesli-flavored shake — Lina did not start eating but instead began to watch him with mild disapproval (which she never could hide) at the sheer speed with which he was devouring his food.

"Try not to eat so quickly, honey — it's really bad for you."

"I know."

Maybe that was it: the fact that she couldn't hide a single thought that came into her head . . . This relentless compulsion for honesty, transparency, as if the epitome of human goodness was merely the willing ability to broadcast every last waking thought, no matter how trivial. Was it actually possible to resent someone for being so honest? What kind of a monster was he becoming? Anyway, why was he attacking her all of a sudden? Her request was perfectly reasonable. Slow down, Gabriel. Slow the fuck down.

"I've got an easy couple of days," he said.

She made a start on her muesli. "What's the next issue again?"

"'Inner Voices.'" He forced himself to stop eating. "I should try to make this one better. I think . . . I think I lost it a bit with the last one. I'm already struggling with the whole idea, though — I mean, how can anybody trust their inner voice when inner voices are universally famous for coming and going at random? And when they tell you all kinds of contra —"

"What you should do is take a break from living and thinking on behalf of the rest of the world." There was concern as well as humor in her tone. "Leave it to someone else for a while — the pope or the president or someone."

"People in power *can't* think on behalf of anyone else. They get cut off. That's the problem, Lina. Power may not corrupt every time, but it always isolates." He raised a fist to his chest in a gesture of mock heroism. "That's why everything is up to you and me."

She smiled but shook her head. "We should go on holiday and you should not be allowed to think about anything except pizza top-

pings and ice cream flavors. Have you thought any more about doing the play?"

"No. I need to call the man in Highgate again."

"You should do it."

Care, consideration, and total, unquestioning support.

"I know."

"I think May is perfect," she said. "And I was working it out on
the plane this morning . . . If you can start everything at the beginning of your working month, like now — just after an issue is out —
then you can probably get loads done from your office and sneak out
for rehearsals. Then take your holiday for the next fortnight, while
the issue is actually coming out — let your deputy do some work for
once — and then put on the play the week after, when you are back
at work but when it's easy again. That way you get a six-week run.
Have you thought any more about which play you want to put on?"

"Steven Berkoff." He picked up his fork.

"You've gone off the Shakespeare idea?"

"No. Just . . . not the first one."

"Shakespeare is not necessarily very commercial anyway." She
nodded. "You want something that the audience can get to grips
with easily."

Maybe that was it. Something lurking behind that "not very commercial" or that "get to grips with" — that attitude. Which, again,
was fair enough.

"And if you have to take a month off unpaid, then you should do
that. You know the money is not an issue. I'll support you."

Or maybe *that* was it: maybe the money was an issue — though
not in the way Lina thought. He had never borrowed; the house and
the holidays were strictly fifty-fifty, his expenses were his own, but
she paid more restaurant bills than he did, paid for more tickets, furniture, food. He finished his breakfast as slowly as he could manage.

"You need a new coat," she said.

"I know."

"How come Frank managed to persuade you to go and fetch the
permit?"

"It just kind of happened. The buzzer went and he let on as if I
was supposed to have organized it all . . . and I . . . I said I would go.
I don't exactly know how it happened."

She laughed lightly. "Well, don't bother becoming friends with
him like you did with Bernie. It doesn't seem to help. You don't have

to be friends with everyone in the world. Let's keep Frank at arm's length. I have given him pretty strict instructions, so we'll see . . . He's doing the new sink, then he's going to sort out the dishwasher, and I've told him not to fit the new surfaces until he has properly sealed them."

"What time is it?"

"Eight forty-five. I'd better get going. I'm going shopping with Fran at lunchtime for at least two hours. I'll keep an eye out for coats you might like."

Or maybe there was no reason. Maybe there was no reason at all. Maybe he just did not like safe harbors. Maybe he was the sort of idiot who enjoyed throwing away the best things that he had found. Nothing would surprise him these days. They finished their breakfast and he put down money enough to cover their food.

Their lines parted at King's Cross. She continued south. He had to go west. He kissed her and jumped off. He put on his headphones—Martha Argerich playing Bach's Toccata 911. The Hammersmith and City train was first to arrive. He stepped inside, eyed the other madmen a second or two, dropped into his favorite seat at the end of the carriage, and closed his eyes.

Marriage, commitment, clever wife, pretty wife, dependable wife, capable wife, children, one, two, three, love and money coming in, love and money going out, security, the family breakfast table, homework help sessions, holidays, hobbies, barbecues with friends at the weekends, picnics in the summer, occasional reflections on politics, television, exhibitions, mortgage paid off, holiday home, grandparents, contentment . . . How had Lina come to represent these things, and why did he alone in all the world think that this wasn't what life was all about? Why did he alone find it so nauseating and depressing and escapist a proposal? What disfigured gene of contrariety was he carrying? Why was he furious with her for noticing that pianist's scruffy shoes? Why was he miserable because she bought him a sweater that matched his socks? And what were these minor, minor things beside his own persistent deception and monumental cruelty, which had now been going on for *ages*? Oh, Ma. All he had to do . . . all he had to do was get it together. And there it was ahead of him, the motorway through the mountains, the best of the Western human being's life—laid out, smooth as freshly smeared tarmac in all its satisfying, fulfilling, familial glory, and yet . . . And yet here he sat, knuckles white, looking desperately this way and that for another route, determined to assert the other, eager and willing as a fool for love, chaos, pain, any kind of feeling that would lead him away, off this main road; here he sat, implacably ready to oppose whatever was asserted and to assert whatever was opposed, steadfastly determined to champion the antagonist, the great adversaries, the counterlifers, to ask the same questions again and again despite knowing that they were probably meaningless, despite knowing that such questions were *the wrong questions to ask;* here he sat, searching the rain-smothered crags, hoping for that moment when the sun might slice its brief light between the heavy clouds and show him some other way. Some steep and shining path.

26

Club Voltage

T HE OLD PIPES must have cracked or backed up somewhere. The stink was foul. And the sound of their squelching made him want to retch. Someone appeared to have laid a makeshift pathway of plastic carrier bags across the rancid courtyard; but, torn and thin, they were of no use at all, and the slime simply engulfed them with every footfall. Henry cursed the hole in his sole. The freeze, when it came, would be welcome here. Hard ground. A filthy gull barked as it circled in the cold gruel of the sky.

They passed into a stairwell opposite—a door banged high up above them, there were drunken shouts and then the sound of two or three coming down. Then they were out in the daylight again, into a second, smaller courtyard beyond. This one was muddy too, but not so bad underfoot, mostly broken cobbles, miniature steppingstones. The smell here, if anything, was worse. Fate seemed to have shackled them together, as if two prison friends escaped Sakhalin and slogged these three years three-legged all the way across Siberia in ever-deepening silence, all but abandoning any hope of severance.

They entered the dimness of the building on the far side, crunched on broken glass, and turned down the dark and crumbling stairs below ground level. They walked along a scarred brick corridor, under a low beam, around a corner, past a bare bulb; stepped over bags of damp cement; went past a second light, around wires that stuck out sharp and bent and crazy from the wall, like the severed tendrils of some grotesque creature whose body was trapped on the other side —wherever that was. They went further into the gloom, a jink right, a correcting jink left, and three final steps as far as the third bulb,

which illuminated a Lenin-red rusty iron door square across the pas-
sageway.

Arkady pressed a half-hidden button to one side, then stood in the
glare of the bulb. There was no sound from the buzzer itself and no
sound from within. Henry leaned against the wall. Neither spoke.

There had been nothing back from Paris. But London — London
was good. London was hope. London was their chance. All Henry
had to do was hand over the down payment and there would be no
turning back. Arkady would be on his way.

Henry prayed. And he didn't care that prayer was as big a joke as
communism. He prayed with fervor and dutiful urgency, as if he
were thirteen again and trying not to touch himself and come top of
the class in Latin and not be punched in the arm by Mark Rolke on
the bus. He prayed without a second's counterthought, prayed to
God's only son, somehow both fully human and fully divine, somehow born of a virgin, died (definitely died), and somehow resur-
rected for our sins — he prayed that they would have enough money,
that there would be no problem with Arkady's friend of a friend of a
friend, that the passport and visa would be ordered and collected
safely, that Arkady would go, would not delay or stall, that the Russian would make it unhindered to London, and that his family
would treat him kindly.

And so far it was damn well working: his prayers had been answered. Okay, so Paris was a nothing. Perhaps Arkady was right —
what man wants to hear from his wife's long-forgotten love child?
Perhaps the address was wrong. But Henry's assiduous Internet
fishing for Gabriel and Isabella had finally produced results: too
many Isabella Glovers, and no matches at all for Isabella plus Maria,
but a single match for Gabriel and Maria Glover — an article from a
local newspaper. A godsend. From this Henry had learned that son
had "followed mother's footsteps into journalism." So, a search for
journalists called Gabriel Glover. Disregarding the Americans and
subtracting those listings attributable to the same person, three pos-
sibles. Next, some very expensive calls to receptionists at the compa-
nies most recently served by these Gabriels to "confirm the e-mail
because I have to send something . . ."

Then nothing for five days.

So more calls.

No, Gabriel Glover did not work here anymore, try the *Camden
Journal*. Passed about like a pedantic reader. Until someone on the

news desk said, Oh yes, that Gabriel Glover used to work here, on features — God, that must have been about five years ago now. Ask Jim. But Jim was off on holiday.

One week later he had found his lead again: try the contract-publishing firm Roland Sheekey Ltd., Jim advised. Another call to another receptionist, another e-mail pretending to be from Arkady. This time, despite the cost, Henry waited at his desk in the cheap-Internet-and-foreign-calls café near Primoskaya, hoping. Three hours later, he had his man.

> Sure, by all means, get in touch when you arrive, look for-ward to talking very much.

It was enough. It was hope. Arkady was going to London.

The red door remained shut. Henry dared not suggest they press the buzzer again, and Arkady seemed content to wait. The bulb hissed periodically. Three minutes must have passed before, with a shock, Henry realized that Arkady was standing in the middle of the pas-sageway because a camera was set up high in the lintel. He wondered who might be looking at them and what they were looking for. He noticed afresh that his friend was growing more ragged. That great-coat, those tattered jeans, those boots, the frayed collar on that fa-vorite shirt, fake Armani. When the time came, Henry knew, he would not have the courage to suggest that Arkady clean himself up: cut his hair, shave, find a new shirt at least. And yet it was his duty to do so. To improve Arkady's chances. Simply, there was nobody else to say these things. No other person who could see beyond the strug-gle of their own circumstances as to what goodness or salvation the wider world might yet bestow if only they could keep on believing. He *must* say something. What did it matter if Arkady came to de-spise him, as long as he made the best possible impression when he found his family? The danger was that on the streets of London, Arkady would simply look insane or worse — frightening. Besides everything else, the Russian had his right index finger wrapped and bound in a fat bandage, which he had recently taken to wearing all the time, even though he had not been near the conservatory this week or last, as far as Henry knew. And the injury looked gruesome. Violent. Henry understood — up to a point — that Arkady had to live his lies religiously once asserted, had to actually believe in them himself, had to *perform* them. (There was something especially Russian in this, he thought.) But all the same, Henry hoped that the grimy bandage would come off as soon as they had the passport.

Without warning, the door started to move. There was a whir-ring, as though the hinges were motorized. The corridor within was better illuminated; a series of doors—some shut, some half open—led off, right and left. They passed a filthy toilet, a bedroom of sorts with the floor covered in mattresses, a decrepit shower with its head dangling loose, and, last of all, on the left, a big kitchen—gas rings, saucepans. Ten more paces beneath weak multicolored light and they emerged into the wide cavernous low-lit room—the spider's den: Club Voltage.

The place was almost empty and there was no music, but then, it was only eleven in the morning. They were in a vast cellar. Like the passageways, the walls were all bare brick; a glowing row of yellow, orange, and red light bulbs set in two plastic bulb racks was wedged up by a series of nails hammered irregularly into the mortar behind the makeshift bar, the cables looping down like ossified tapeworms. There were no drinks on display save sample cans or bottles of the range available—one Russian beer, one Polish beer, vodka, vodka, vodka, cheap, cheaper, cheapest—standing strangely spaced across the solitary shelf. Aside from a few other bulb racks and one or two random strip lights, the decoration was limited to a series of poster portraits that had been lacquered like fliers for forthcoming gigs to the bricks of the far wall—poster portraits of famous Soviet athletes in various attitudes of exertion, muscular repose, or medal-winning triumph. In English, across the face of each, someone had sprayed the words "Drugs are for winners" with scarlet paint. High up, be-hind the bar, there was a second series, these much smaller, pages cut from magazines rather than posters: presumably the bartender's true love, some model never quite dressed.

Sitting just inside the door to the right on the threadbare sofa and chairs were four or five youngsters—couples, friends, strangers, it was hard to be sure—all as thin as coat hangers, their faces oddly blue beneath the fizzing of one of the strip lights. One girl sat for-ward, her banknotes ready, clutched thick and tight in her scrawny fist.

Someone came through the door behind them, sped past at an incongruous jog, and circled back behind the bar. Arkady moved forward and spoke in Russian.

"Hello, Genna."

"Piano." Offering a raised fist (held sideways for Arkady to knock

with his own), Gennady, the teenage tender, greeted Arkady from behind the makeshift bar with a grin.

He could be no more than fourteen years old, Henry thought.
Eyes like flattened lead shot, flared nostrils, skin like congealed lava.

Arkady declined the fist, enveloping it in the mighty palm of his
left hand instead.

"How you doing, Genna? Still running. Next Olympics is your
Olympics, I just know it."

"If I can get the invisible drugs that the pussy-boy Americans use,
then I'll be the fastest man on the planet." Gennady sucked in a
sharp breath. "Whoa, shit, you bust your finger."

"Yeah — stupid. Should have known. Never try to fuck two fat
girls at the same time. Some shit is just too dangerous."

Gennady's laugh caused him to screw up his face.

Arkady raised an introductory thumb. "Henry."

Gennady paused, self-consciously rehearsing the look that he had
laboriously formulated from the hundred films that informed his
every expression, then raised his fist again.

Henry had no choice. Embarrassed, he raised his own bony knuckles, his long sleeves hanging lankly from his scrawny bones.

"We will take two vodkas. And you can pour them," Arkady
said.

"Sure."

All customers had to order a drink — one of the rules. This was a
bar, after all. Some just paid the money and Gennady knew not to
bother opening the bottle. Henry rubbed his hands together, agitated. He was suddenly anxious that Arkady was actually going to
drink. He'd never seen the Russian have so much as a sip of beer.
And yet he dared not speak. So he pretended to stare into space instead, careful not to glance up at Tatiana. He sensed that Gennady
would die rather than allow anyone even to touch these posters. But
he felt stupid and panicky watching the teenager pour the vodka, so
he turned away to face the room, hoping to appear casual.

The main wooden tables were all empty save for one over in the
corner beneath a barred and blacked-out window, where two men
sat: the one with a hollow face, a decorator by the look of his paint-
streaked overalls, who seemed straight enough; the other a fat man
with a black beard, dressed (without irony) in sports shoes and tracksuit, who was slouching sideways on the bench, his head nodding
back and forth. This was the cheapest shit you could buy in Petersburg; God knows what they mixed it with, but it was supposed to be

safer than the street. They sold clean needles too. And people came back. The place was busy nights, Arkady had said, passing itself off as a normal club. Part of Henry, the sickest part, was actually grateful to Arkady for the inadvertent introduction. If he needed to, he could now return alone.

Henry paid. And Arkady picked up the drinks.

"So, Genna, when your uncle is free, tell him I am here to speak with him."

Gennady made two guns with his fingers and thumbs. "I'll tell him."

They sat down at the table nearest the bar, the Russian leaning back with his arms stretched out in front as if he were about to play, the Englishman with his shoulders folded, hunched in, sharp as vultures' wings.

Gennady passed them again at speed.

Arkady swilled his vodka around, looked at it a moment as if another—maybe better—life was therein contained, then sloshed it out onto the sawdust floor.

Voice low, Henry asked, "Has this guy done a passport for you before?"

"I have never left Russia."

Henry felt himself recoil involuntarily. Idiot. Keeping his sallow face blank but suffering cringes within, he cast his glance away as if to reassess the room.

The fat man suddenly came to life and began snapping his fingers, his upper body bobbing about to music only he could hear, chant-sing-talk-murmuring some kind of maddened song that sounded to Henry's ears as though it were memorized word for word without the speaker understanding the language, the subject, the meaning, anything. The man kept up for a minute or two, then collapsed forward; his friend, the decorator, helped himself once more to the other's drink with a scowl.

"The guy's name is Kostya," Arkady said quietly. "He is Gennady's uncle. He is from Kyrgyzstan. He can get anything. He is the man who let us in. Speak only if he speaks to you. Then be nice. No fucking English."

Silently grateful that Arkady appeared not to have taken any offense, Henry turned back and gingerly tipped his own vodka out onto the floor. Stop being such a fool. He watched his vodka soak away. Stop saying such stupid things. Of course of course of course Arkady had not left Russia: Arkady *was* fucking Russia.

The smell of spirits mingled with chemicals was overpowering. You had to be an addict or an alcoholic simply to breathe in here. Henry widened his nostrils a moment and then began patting his leg involuntarily.

Arkady stared with narrowing eyes at his finger.

Henry spoke again. "Do I hand over the money in here—at the bar?"

"No. And wait until we know the exact price. You have it in separate hundreds, yes? If we don't have enough, then fuck it. No promises you cannot keep. It does not matter."

"Okay. But it *does* matter. You need to go to London."

Arkady said nothing.

A happy thought was occurring to Henry . . . He had started to wonder again whether he might be able to buy a hit. Try it out. It looked to be working for the fat man. (And, dear Lord, he needed one—cutting down was *hard*.) He shut his eyes a moment. Even thinking about his boy gave him strength. He leaned his head forward onto his fingertips and felt the bones of his skull. Then he faced Arkady directly, whispering.

"Is there anyone else who can do it, if—if Kostya says no?"

Arkady grinned his hollow-cheeked grin. "Leary."

"No."

"Yes, Leary can do it easy."

"Not now."

"Yes, now."

"Not—"

"Yes, more now." Arkady shook his head and kept his voice low. "You do not see the plans all the way, Henry. You do not see anything."

"Why . . . why would Leary help us? So far he has sent Grisha to smash up the piano, stolen all my money, and left us with nothing but an arse-shaped hole in our wall."

"Because he doesn't give a fuck about me." Arkady's face was scornful. "Because he wants *you* to owe him. For the sake of Jesus. How many times? He does not do these things because you are a few days late to pay him. He does not give a piss about a few days late. He does everything to bring you to nothing. And if he thinks you are spending whatever you have left on a passport, then he is happy to help. The sooner you are desperate, the sooner you work for him."

Henry patted at his knee. "I'm not—"

"Listen, Leary will buy you a brand-new suit if it helps. He'll rent you a big apartment on the Nevsky. He'll get you a fucking *Russian* passport. And if he is bored with waiting or you don't do as you're told, he can just tell the police about you. And then you are really in the big shit, my friend."

"I'm quitting." Even here, even now, Henry loved to talk about it: the subject warmed him, made him tingle, killed the remaining wheedle. They were leaning close together now. "I'm not a dealer, Arkady."

"You will do anything when the time comes."

"No. I told you, I'm going to stop." He meant it. But the strange thing was, he could say it with any kind of strength or conviction only when he was thinking about his next hit. "When what's left runs out, that's the end. You will be gone by then."

"So you hope."

"I believe it."

"Great. We hope and we believe. We are impossible to defeat." Arkady curled his lip. "Here he comes. No English."

Eyes red, nose streaming, face like a suppurating pumice stone, Kostya looked as if he had been at the baths all his life—beaten with the birch, then steamed, frozen, steamed, plunged, and steamed again. His gray-white overwashed Doors T-shirt was loose and clung damply here and there about his massive frame where the sweat slicked most copiously. He wore long, loose shorts and sandals, and the flesh on his feet, like the skin of his nose and ears, was cooked red and cracked.

They spoke in Russian.

"Kostya."

"Piano." He embraced Arkady and then took a seat.

"This is Henry."

"Hello." Henry nodded. No hand was offered. Kostya's attention left him almost immediately and came to rest on Arkady's finger.

"You fucked your finger."

"Yes."

"Bitch motherfucker bullshit."

"I know."

"What you going to do?"

"It's okay. I can play most things with my cock."

Kostya laughed out loud. Gennady too, from where he was hovering behind the bar.

Arkady said, "We have money. We need a passport. How much?"

The humor in Kostya's face disappeared like water into volcanic ash.

"Good. I thought it might be about the shit." He waved about his head, indicating his surroundings, his customers, his life. "And that would have made me sad. Where you going?" Kostya looked at Henry.

"Not him, me," Arkady said. "London."

"Do you have a passport already?"

"No." Arkady shook his head. "Not an external one."

"Okay. Well, you're better off with a false identity anyway. Otherwise they can always check who you are. Better to be safe — be nice and rich so you are good to go." He shook his head. "But it's difficult these days, Arkasha. They have bar codes now. Computers are fucking everything up for everyone. It has to be right or you get yourself in a lot of shit. Only the . . ." He plucked at his T-shirt, separating it from his skin. "Only the networks get in and out easy."

"Fuck." Arkady ran his hand back and forth across the beginnings of his beard, keeping the bandaged finger extended out of the way. "Maybe it's a stupid idea anyway."

Henry cut in, speaking in Russian. "But can you do it?"

Kostya turned to face him.

Henry felt Arkady's eyes on him too. Searing. Henry's right hand was tapping rapidly over the knuckles of his left.

"We can pay now," Henry said. "If you can do it."

Kostya continued to scrutinize Henry for a long moment. Henry knew that the Kyrgyzstani would already have him down for a user, but he was counting on the fact that money counted. He knew that much about Russia.

Kostya turned his heavy head slowly away and addressed Arkady. "The honest truth is that I cannot do it myself anymore and be sure. Not with the computers and not to Britain. If it was for someone we did not give a shit about, to some butt-fuck country, then yes, maybe. But it's you. So . . . I myself cannot do it." He raised his finger and thumb to his red nose. "But if you are serious, then I know people who can do it — properly, I mean. But of course you have to pay their price — expensive."

"How long will it take?" Henry interjected again. He wanted this done and no escaping from it; then he wanted to leave, to fly home to his ruined bedroom. His flesh was itching and crawling and cold.

"A few weeks." Kostya only half turned this time. "My contact is coming here today—I can ask him to start immediately. Do you have the photographs with you?"

"Yes. How much?" Now Henry had him.

"Four hundred dollars today. Four hundred when you collect. Identity. Passport. Visa. Safe."

"Okay." Henry reached inside his pocket.

Arkady hissed, "Not in here. Sorry, Kostya. Can we go somewhere . . ."

"Yes. Come." He pushed back his chair. "You *are* serious."

"We are serious," Henry echoed.

The fat man was singing again.

Once outside, Henry went ahead, desperate to return to his room and walking as fast as he could. A little way through the larger courtyard, the sound of the gulls began again. He glanced up. A short, squat figure in a hood was coming toward him, walking squarely on the plastic-bag path.

Henry stepped aside, ankle-deep in the filth.

Grisha grinned. "Hello, cunt," he said.

27

Grandpa Max

I T WAS THE NOVEMBER WEEKEND of the twins' sixteenth birthday. The family was gathered at the Highgate house. Nicholas was back from his latest business venture in Edinburgh (an art magazine that he was setting up, editing, publishing, sort of). Masha had taken a few days off and resynced herself to the daytime hours. Most exciting of all, Grandpa Max was over from Moscow — partly for the occasion, partly for some meeting with a select cabal (chaired by the lady herself) about perestroika and the implications thereof.

Unusually, Max was also staying the night in the master bedroom, which was always kept ready for him in case he so wished, but which he rarely occupied, more often preferring residency in one of the old London hotels. He was traveling with his secretary, Zhanna, a dark-haired, dark-skinned woman with the carefully tended comportment of a wronged princess and a limitless silence to match — a silence that seemed to harbor disapproval until directly examined, at which point it was always found to be entirely neutral and somehow pristine.

"Probably Armenian or Azerbaijani," Nicholas had conjectured, in answer to Gabriel's question.

"No more than thirty-five," Masha had added, in answer to nothing that anyone else had heard.

Zhanna was in the spare room. They never discovered if she spoke English, as Max addressed her only in Russian.

The twins' main party was, of course, elsewhere — guest-listed later that night in a place called K-Rad, a filthily cool nightclub near South Kensington, famous most of all for the queues outside. But

five of the twins' closest friends had also been invited over for a
birthday lunch that Masha had spent three days assembling: some
delicious blini topped with mushrooms, cheese, and herbs unknown,
followed by *kulebyaka,* a salmon pie with more mushrooms, spinach, rice, kasha, all topped with smetana and fresh tomato sauce — a
challenge that only Gabriel, his friend Pete, and Grandpa Max himself had really engaged with in any meaningful way. Nicholas had
left his untouched, pushed back his chair, and started smoking almost immediately. Isabella had refused more than a single slice, her
plate deliberately full of lettuce and spinach from the salad bowl
to frustrate her mother's vigilant generosity. Susan, Isabella's best
friend, was allergic to fish and so was having another course of blini
— a route through the meal of which Zhanna (cutting the *kulebyaka*
with much concentration into smaller and smaller pieces) was quietly jealous.

In the way of sixteenth-birthday gatherings, the entire day had
been excruciating, and then absolutely fine (fun, almost), and then
excruciating again, the whole party sweeping slowly from exhilaration to tension and back again in the manner of an emotional sine
curve. On the up, Gabriel and Isabella were both excited by the occasion, the general busyness of the house, and, in particular, their
collusion (and that of their five friends) in the knowledge that the
hideously out-of-touch parents had no idea where they were really
going for the night or what they were really going to be doing there.
(Weed outside. Cocktails inside. Cigarettes throughout.) On the
down, both twins were in a state of residual agitation, if not rebel-
lion, as a result of the various confrontations of the week just past,
during which they were met with an ongoing and bilateral refusal of
permission to allow them to stay out until the club shut at four. They
were to be back by one-thirty, latest, no negotiation. The reason
given by both Nicholas and Masha — in rare accord — was that it
was not often they saw their Grandpa Max, and if they stayed out,
they would not be seen out of bed this side of Sunday lunch and
there would be no chance of a family walk in the morning.

In addition to these two amplitudes of euphoria and seething,
they were both suffering, despite themselves, from the generic difficulties attendant on turning sixteen: adult, not adult; precocious,
trying, but supersensitive to precocity and trying; cringing with embarrassment at everything, knowing everything; knowing nothing,
knowing that there was nothing more embarrassing than cringing itself, still cringing.

Thus the day so far.

Now they were all gathered in the lounge at the front of the house. Max, Nicholas, Masha, Zhanna (all smoking or between cigarettes), Gabriel, Isabella, and Samantha, the last of the lunchtime five to leave, since she was not going to be coming to the club and would not therefore be seeing them later.

Max sat in the deepest chair with his back to the windows, the smoke of his cigar so thick that Isabella was aware that she could really see him clearly only now and then, when the many house drafts conspired. Masha was handing out cake, though with napkins rather than plates, which somehow infuriated Zhanna, which in turn might have been the reason for Masha's refusal to make the trip back to the kitchen for crockery. Zhanna was beside Max but on an upright chair, dressed in strict secretarial two-piece, twenty-dernier pantyhose, shoulder pads, serious heels, and wearing eyeliner and big hair as if she might be called upon at any moment to represent the very distillation of fashion. Gabriel too found the lack of plates unreasonably annoying, but more on behalf of Samantha, toward whom he had adopted a self-consciously chivalrous air throughout the last hour. Like most of their friends, Samantha was seventeen, a year older. (To Masha's eternal satisfaction, both Gabriel and Isabella had been moved up a year at infant school.) And she was waiting for her boyfriend, Steve (eighteen, soft-top MG), to pick her up. Steve was late. He was a dental technician and (for reasons undisclosed) dental technicians seldom ran on time on Saturdays. But it was somehow clear — to the Glovers, at least — that the next phase of the day, whatever that was, could not begin until Steve had been and gone.

It was perhaps for this reason, and as if to apply the broom a little harder, that Nicholas now brought the conversation to Samantha directly.

"So when is the baby due? Have you thought about a name?"

"Not really, Nicholas. I mean, I have had some thoughts, but I dunno if it's a boy or a girl yet. Got a feeling it's a boy."

For what felt like the thousandth time that day, the twins flinched mentally — they knew their father hated their friends' calling him by his Christian name. And yet they loved Samantha all the more for doing so.

"Must be exciting." Nicholas seemed curiously untroubled, though — polite, interested even. "We are biased, of course. We like the Russian names. How about . . . how about Tatiana if it's a girl, Eugene if it's a boy?"

Masha got up and began rather noisily to pour the tea from the samovar on the side.

"I was thinking more like Dominic or Stephen . . . or maybe Alison. Dunno." Samantha smoothed her stomach, enjoying the attention. "It's going to be a surprise."

"Wonderful." Nicholas sighed. "A little tiresome, isn't it, though? That it's always one or the other — boy or girl, girl or boy. You'd think just once we'd come up with something new. Shame, really. Pregnancy is never *that* surprising in the end."

"Nobody takes milk, do they?" Masha addressed the room by addressing the wall loudly.

"Yes, Mum, I still do. As I always have. Since I was two," Gabriel answered. He turned to his friend. "Sam?"

"Erm . . . Not sure if I've got time, Gabe. Steve will be here any minute."

"Have some and just leave it if he comes," Gabriel said quietly, before directing his voice to where his mother stood waiting quizzically for the outcome of his consultation. "One for Samantha too, please, Mum. With milk."

"Okay." Without saying or doing anything at all, Masha somehow transmitted to the room her disapproval of milk-takers (a class of person quite beyond hope) and began to hand out those cups already poured to Max, Zhanna, Isabella, and Nicholas, the worthy ones.

"I think it's refreshing, anyway — having children young." Nicholas reached up for his and sipped immediately. He took some strange pride in being able to drink his tea at boiling point. "Good for you."

"Samantha doesn't need your approval, Dad." This from Gabriel. Masha left the room, presumably to fetch some milk.

"Oh God, no. Lucky thing too. Because I don't approve of anything, Gabriel, as you know." Nicholas winked at Samantha.

Gabriel shook his head in adolescent disbelief.

On the sofa, Isabella was torn between wishing that her brother would stop behaving so painfully and wishing that her father would shut up. And all of a sudden she was dying for a cigarette. Ideally, one of the thin Russian ones that her grandfather smoked when he wasn't on cigars. Perversely, the more the birthday normalized (and normalized all the people in the room), the more she wanted to escape, to feel and to *be* exotic. Indeed, from within the prism of her sixteen-year-old sensibility, it seemed to her a waste that her grandfather should be forced to witness such domestic tedium. She imagined that Zhanna felt the same and found herself empathizing with the secretary's scornful silence. Presents, parochial friends, cars, new computer, clothes, tea, cake, this dumb conversation, sixteen itself. She was embarrassed on Grandpa's behalf. And this new embarrassment lay uneasily, like a wriggling blanket, over all the other embarrassments she was feeling. A cigarette would help. It was strange, though: Grandpa Max could sit so still that he almost disappeared.

"I'm sure yours will be a fine child whatever you name it." This at last was Max himself, his voice deep, like sand in hot wax from the years of smoking. "You are young and you are fit. That's the main thing."

Zhanna pursed.

Masha reentered the room just in time to see her do so.

"It's Sikkim tea," said Nicholas as Masha came over with the last two cups, "scientifically proven to help in nine out of ten pregnancies. We all drink it religiously — just in case."

Gabriel reached up to take charge of Samantha's cup.

Masha did not sit down but returned to the samovar and began to cut secondary slices of the cake.

And Isabella was now certain that her mother was drawing out her tasks to avoid any serious interaction. But whether something in particular was causing this newfound domestication, she could not determine. Certainly it was unlike her mother not to come into the heart of the conversation, especially when her father was rehearsing his prejudices or behaving like an idiot. Perhaps it was Grandpa's presence. Perhaps it was the subject matter. Whatever, her mother's evasion aroused her curiosity. And so, believing her initiative to be a further example of mature social skill, she spoke up.

"Mum, nobody wants any more cake. Leave it. Come and sit down. You've done enough."

Of course Masha was unable to ignore her daughter's specific appeal, and so, balancing a few more slices on yet another napkin, she came over with a thin smile.

"I know you all like the marzipan and you're just pretending to like the rest of it, so here are some marzipan bits." She laid them out on the little table. "Samantha?"

But Samantha did not answer and Masha did not manage to sit down, because just then the doorbell chimed.

"That, we must assume, will be Steve," Nicholas observed, lighting yet another cigarette.

"Oh shit," Samantha said. "Oh, sorry. Excuse the French. I'd love some more cake, Maria. But I'm going to have hit the road . . . Thanks for the tea, though. In fact, thanks for everything."

"It's been a pleasure having you." Masha continued to stand. "Here, take this." She reached down and gave Samantha a huge slice. "They don't appreciate it anyway. They just pretend."

Isabella noticed the deeply disguised relief in her mother's voice that their pregnant young friend was finally going. Samantha rose. And there followed a chorus of byes and pleased-to-meet-yous as Gabriel escorted her to the door.

Masha sat down beside Isabella.

It was obvious that Gabriel was angry from the instant he reappeared in the doorway. It was also clear that he did not wish to confront any one individual — and was feeling the weakness of this — and so he addressed the room at large, raising his voice to compensate.

"I can't believe you lot. I can't believe you were all *smoking*. I just can't believe it. My friend is *pregnant* and you're all sitting there smoking in her face."

He remained for a moment on the threshold. But his self-consciousness as he stood there — sixteen, acne, too much wet-look gel in his hair, a face of aggrieved incredulity — his self-consciousness undermined the vehemence with which he spoke. Worse, he sensed this and felt compelled to raise the stakes.

"My God, you people are . . . are . . . bloody unbelievable." He wanted to risk saying "fucking," but something held him back; it felt like a cliché to do so on his sixteenth birthday. "I mean, at the very least you could have shown *me* some respect, even if you are too rude to give a toss about my friends."

"Gabriel, please." Masha returned to her tea, which, in contrast to Nicholas, or by way of obscure counterstrike, she prided herself on drinking when almost cold. "You sound like something off the television," she added. "Sit down."

"And asking her all those rancid questions and treating her like she is some kind of a freak. God, it's disgusting. Just because she is an unmarried mother. Wake up, people, it happens."

"Climb down off your cross for a few minutes, Gabriel, and have some more birthday cake." This from Nicholas, who was actually smirking. "Seriously. Take a break. It must be agony up there all year. You can pop back up this evening. Don't worry, we'll get you some fresh nails."

"Dad . . . just . . . just . . ." Gabriel held his hands to his ears and shook his head as though trying to rid himself of some terrible pain. "Just shut *up*."

But as ever, Nicholas's needle was exacting and precise as well as cruel. "It's fairly obvious that the only person who thinks your friend is a freak, Gabriel, is you. You'd imagine she was about to give birth to some new child of Zeus the way you're fidgeting around her. The rest of us couldn't care less if she was married, crippled, half Kazakh, or half pig. Look at us — your mother is a romantic old Marxist, I'm a lazy anarchist, your sister is a spiky little revolutionary, and your grandfather won't admit to anything. We don't give a damn. For God's sake, sit down. Have something to drink if you want. You are allowed."

"You're a bloody fascist," Gabriel muttered.

Gabriel was in the mood to have an individual fight with his father now. And these could be truly horrific. And above all else, Isabella did not wish to jeopardize the evening. She could restrain herself no longer. It was the first time ever that she had asked: "Dad, now that Samantha is gone, can I have a cigarette? And can you give one to Gabriel too? If you haven't guessed, we both smoke. And he's got really bad withdrawal."

Masha laughed out loud.

Max began to shake silently. "Now that is an interesting question."

Even Zhanna's face betrayed amusement.

Gabriel slumped back down, shooting his sister a dark look.

Isabella continued, a sarcastic smile hovering on her lips. "And don't give us all the not-in-my-house crap, please, Dad, because it really is pointless. We can just go down to the shops and buy them and smoke them all over the rest of the world if we want. It's legal. And you can't seriously be worried about the damage to the curtains. It's like a bloody diesel convention in here as it is."

For once Nicholas did not know what to say.

Instead Masha spoke, her voice hesitant and kindly. "No, Is, no . . . not just because it's this house; but because they are so bad for you and I don't want to encourage it. I'd feel awful."

"Hypocrisy reigns supreme." This from Isabella with raised brows and a look, which invited her brother to join in.

As always, Gabriel accepted his sister's olive branch and stepped back into the ring, though this time without real anger. "Apparently nine out of ten of the anarchists who were" — Gabriel made a sneering face — "on the barricades in Paris, on the barricades burning tires — nine out of ten anarchists are firmly against smoking."

Though as precocious as brand-new sixth-formers (which is what they were), the twins were a fearsome team when they got going. Which also made Masha secretly proud. She was smiling.

It was Nicholas's turn to shake his head. "Jesus, two minutes ago you were bawling at us to stop smoking. Now all you want to do is join in."

"We learn our consistency off you, Dad," Isabella said. "You are our beacon."

But Gabriel was still sore with his father. "That was different," he said. "We all have a choice."

"Oh yes, sorry, I'd forgotten. The little baby Zeus."

Max cut in. "How about this?"

All eyes turned to him except Nicholas's. Even when Grandpa Max moved his head, Isabella thought, it was as if something of incredible importance were happening.

Max let the silence hang in the air with his cigar smoke. "You are both allowed to have a cigarette — one of my special ones — if you agree to spend half an hour talking to your Grandpa Max while you have it. But" — he lowered his head while keeping his eyes on both the twins — "this is a one-off occasion, because it's your birthday, and as such does not represent a precedent."

Isabella had the sense that her grandfather had been enjoying the entire day for reasons that she could not work out. Less to do with what was being said, and more to do with some obscure and fragile agency between all the people in the room that he alone understood.

A few minutes later Masha left, taking with her the tea and her ferocious, convoluted demands on existence. Nicholas followed, bound for his study with his packet of cigarettes and a compact disk of harpsichord music that he had been carrying around with him all weekend, as if hoping someone somewhere would buy him a CD player. Max addressed Zhanna in Russian too fast for either twin to understand. She nodded and rose silently. Isabella watched her brother watching Zhanna as she walked. There was silence as the room realigned itself. The rest of the house retreated — their father's step on the creaking stairs, the kitchen door closing downstairs on their mother's incessant radio. And for a moment or two, now they were alone with him, Isabella experienced a strange feeling toward her grandfather: a feeling of closeness and yet a simultaneous feeling of the impossibility of closeness; calmness descending, decks clearing, silence, and yet still no clear sense of him as real, present; the calmness of a dense fog on a motionless sea. She wondered if her brother felt it too.

"Zhanna will bring us my very best cigarettes," Max said, and his eyes told them both to relax, as if he could stretch half an hour into years if he wished, or shrink a year into a minute and still have twenty-nine left over.

Gabriel stopped the last of his sulk and sat back in the chair across the fireplace previously occupied by Sam. Isabella kicked off her shoes, folded her legs, and perched on the sofa, her fingers kneading at the thick socks on her feet.

Like the bluish smoke from his Cohiba Especiales ("Fidel's favorite," as their mother had explained three dozen times), all the stuff they both knew and half knew continued to wreath about him — the myths, truths, legends, told to them mostly by Masha, of Max's life and work, of his membership in the Cambridge Apostles at university ("a serious secret society at a serious university, not this silly business you get now"). And all these stories that they knew and half knew, believed and half believed, mingled with all the other things that they had seen and half seen over their years: the endless winter-dark coldness between their father and their grandfather (Isabella had never once witnessed them alone together); the intense formality between Max and their mother (Gabriel could feel his mother recalibrating her tone even before she spoke to him, always of "the situation in Moscow," and never in Russian); the time, when they were very little, he had left the dinner table to take a telephone call and then run, physically run, straight out of the house with the keys to their father's car — Andropov dead, they learned the next day.

Isabella tried to copy her grandfather's trick of seeming not to be looking while she studied his face. He was watching the fire. She wondered if she could write an accurate report in ten minutes, as all good agents were trained so to do. Gabriel picked up a log and began to rebuild the fallen pyramid that Nicholas had constructed earlier in the day.

· · ·

Maximilian Glover was a thin and craggy old man—his sun-accus-
tomed skin lined deep, scored, crosshatched, but papery soft when
he kissed them, as he always did on leaving, on arrival. His hair,
which was white-brown-gray, he wore at an almost untidy length,
and it kinked and curled and everywhere stood up, so that his sil-
houette might look like a cockatoo's. His lower teeth were a little
crooked, like his occasional smile, but his back was as straight as a
cold steel sleeper, lending him the bearing of a taller man. Close up,
he could come across as either much older or much younger than he
looked from a distance—a question of emphasis, since his eyebrows
were wiry, white, and insane while his eyes danced a dark dance of
playfulness, wit, and collusion. Until they stopped. Then his gaze,
when it fell, felled everything. In these moments he gave the impression that if you engaged him in anything—argument, business, love,
chess, a wager, or a race—you would lose. And always in his bearing there was some quiet but indissoluble attitude that seemed to say,
Whatever you have thought and done with your life, I could have
thought and done with mine, easily, and I chose not to; but you
could not do or think what I have done and thought if I gave you ten
more centuries of trying. More and more, as they were becoming
adults, the twins felt this strength about him. They had begun to notice how other people, old and young, responded to him. They had
seen him, when he chose, be the magnetic north of a room—at parties in London and more recently on their permitted yearly visits to
Leningrad; and yet they were also beginning to notice (as remaining
at the family table became more interesting than running off) that he
could turn this force field up or down at will. As if his spirit had done
some secret trade and ceded all foreign policy decisions to his mind.
And this skill, though as yet only glimpsed intuitively, they found
glamorous and unconsciously copied when they were out with their
friends. He was also, plain and simple, their grandpa. Their only
grandparent. Grandpa Max. Kindly, wise, their greatest ally, their
greatest supporter; patron, correspondent, friend, and comrade.

Zhanna returned bearing a gold cigarette case and a small leather
bag.
     Max thanked her in Russian, said something else neither of the
twins understood, and then sat forward. He opened the case. Zhanna
left quietly. Isabella and then Gabriel came forward and picked out
their treats. The cigarettes were thinner than the standard English
ones they had started smoking, ivory-white with gold filters, as dec-

adent as the Winter Palace itself. Both had the same thought: that they wished they could take an extra one to bring out that evening at the club.

He spoke as they used his lighter. "Well, now, you two are a ferocious pair, aren't you?"

Isabella smiled.

Gabriel said, "You would be too, Grandpa, if you had to live in a fascist regime." He had heard the stand-up comics use the phrase on TV and enjoyed deploying it ambiguously whenever he could, to mean both home and the nation at large.

Max laughed silently. "Masha has been telling me that you are both obsessed with politics. She's worried that you will end up fighting each other to become prime minister."

"Gabs has no views of his own. He just hates Margaret Thatcher."

"So do you."

"That's not personal," Isabella said. "It's political."

Gabriel abandoned an attempt at a smoke ring a fraction too late. "The problem is that all the parties are a joke at the moment."

Max nodded. "Well, that is always true, I'm afraid. I shall be sure to let the prime minister know your feelings."

Isabella felt her head go light from the cigarette. She loved it that her grandfather was who he was. And wished that she could go and live with him in Leningrad and learn Russian properly and be his secretary and stop pissing about in London with all these trivial people.

"Let me tell you both something that I have learned since I was young and cross. A little secret, which very few people know, and which will help you both become prime minister." He held up his cigar hand to prevent them from jumping in, but perhaps also so that they could see him as he spoke. "All the conservatives that you will ever meet . . . Deep down, guess what? They all turn out to be secret liberals. That's their core." He inclined his head slightly. "And all the liberals — guess what? Deep down, they all turn out to be conservatives. Yes. It's true. And the more liberal they want you to think they are, the more conservative you can be certain they are inside." He smiled his crooked smile. "You might, for example, find yourself in the most anything-goes liberal-left house imaginable" — his cigar made a tight circle — "all art, all sexualities, all genders, races, and religions insistently equal, but look closely at the teacups and taste the cake. Or wait for the minute your liberal friends have children and just watch them scramble and scrape to get their little ones away from the rabble and into the very best schools they can find. Observe' how slyly sensitive they are to accent and background. And give them a homosexual son or an illegitimate child and, my God, the whole family will barely be able to breathe for shame and panic."

Isabella laughed as she blew out her smoke.

"The same is true the other way around." The cigar went counterclockwise this time. "All those conservatives you both complain of — the family-values task force — flog the criminals, stop immigration, go to church, know your place, the worshippers of the class system, the rules and traditions . . . Do you know what they want to do most of all in here?" He indicated his heart. "Cut loose. Be free. Escape the prisons of their own ridiculous rhetoric. More than anything else, deep down, they would like to *forget* their place, forget their wretched families, spend their Sundays in silk beds with beautiful Indian women, Ethiopian princes, Arabian concubines, high on Afghani opium, with a wasteful feast awaiting their merest whim."

"Have you ever taken opium?" This from Gabriel.

"The reason ninety percent of conservatives are conservative is not because they are conservative but because they cannot allow themselves to admit how much they want to be otherwise. They are afraid the world will end if they so much as loosen a finger's grip on their ideology. Meanwhile all your liberal-left ringleaders . . . well, secretly of course, they ache for the big house, the car, those sons who become good straight citizens and of whom they can be proud — they ache for the security of money and the security of property, security and status, status and security."

Max nodded slowly. "No. Very, very few people have their inner and their outer selves aligned in any kind of meaningful way. We are all self-deceivers. We have to be to survive. Not just in the Soviet Union but in America and Europe too. Hypocrisy, it turns out, is the defining human trait. A clever chimpanzee or dolphin might have a sense of humor, mischief, or maybe mourn his dead fellow, he might use tools, language, and even fall in love, but he will no more grasp the concept of hypocrisy than a stone will understand Schubert. So don't judge anyone, not even Maria and Nicholas, too harshly by what they say, because what they say — in fact what almost anybody says — is most often what they need to hear themselves say. *Not* what they really mean. We are all forever in the business of persuading ourselves. And if you want to make people love you or fear you or admire you, then the simplest trick is to let them know that you see their most private inner hypocrisy in all its contradictory tangle and guile and you do not think less of them for it. That's the secret, and that's what all great leaders do. They somehow let their people know that they understand the inner as well as the outer human life and that it's all right by them. And what power they have then, if they choose to use it . . . Lesson over. No." He held up both his hands to stop them from coming at him with a million questions and arguments. "I have something I want to give you both. Then you can ask me anything you like, even about opium, Gabriel."

He picked up the bag that Zhanna had brought down. Isabella leaned toward the table to tap her ash. Gabriel flicked his into the fire. Max took out three parcels neatly wrapped in brown paper and handed two to Isabella and the other to Gabriel.

"The big one is a VHS video of the Kirov Ballet from the sixties and seventies, which I wanted you both to have. Keep it, Isabella. You can remember our trip when you watch it. The others are rings — one for you, Isabella, Siberian gold, and one for you, Gabriel, which you must give to the woman you eventually choose to be your wife. Keep them safe."

"God. Thank you." Isabella held the little package in her hand.

"Thank you." Gabriel took his, a little confused and embarrassed but aware that he was probably taking charge of something very valuable and that the fact that Grandpa Max had given it to him was all that really mattered.

"And here" — Max opened up his jacket and took out a slim wallet — "is fifty pounds each for the nightclub tonight. Don't tell a soul."

28

Molly Weeks

N O, IT'S THE LEAST I can do. This is what being a friend is all about," Molly Weeks said, and meant it, shuffling another of Isabella's boxes into a tiny gap on the highest shelf in the crowded living room.

They were in Molly's apartment amid pretty much everything Isabella owned — her clothes, her music, her books, crockery, pictures, and papers. Viewed from one vantage, depressingly little; from another, far too much for one woman to expect a friend to store indefinitely.

"But thanks, though," Isabella said again.

Molly spoke without looking down from the chair on which she was standing. "When everything starts going dodgy — that's when friends should step up. So stop stressing. I'm fine with it. Things are bound to be crazy and fierce for you for a while." She passed down three of her own shoeboxes full of music. "Stick those on the floor and pass me up one more of yours. I mean, leaving Sasha out of it for a moment . . . well . . . you know — you lost your mother, and that changes everyone — at the fundamental level. It's bound to. Right now you have to deal with the underlying stuff, the real stuff."

Isabella offered her last box.

"You leave these bits and bobs here as long as you need to. You get on that plane and you stop worrying about the insignificant things." Molly began shoving and easing into the space created. "If you come back and live upstairs again, then easy. If you come back to live somewhere else, then we'll move all this to your new place to-gether. If you don't come back at all, then you just tell me where the hell you want them shipped and I'll ship them there."

"Of course I'll come back."

"You do what you have to do."

"Molly, I'm going to miss you like—"

"I have a big apartment is all." Molly twisted on the chair and looked behind. "Is that it, small box–wise?"

"Yes."

"Okay. Your books and kitchen stuff I will just mingle in with mine. So what have we got left?"

"Just those." Isabella indicated her clothes draped over the back of the sofa.

"We put that lot in my closet."

"But what about all your CDs?" They had pulled down about a dozen or so of Molly's neatly labeled shoeboxes to make room for Isabella's things.

Molly stepped carefully off the chair. "Well, I have got five thou-sands dollars' worth of stuff to go out before Christmas, so this will encourage me to get it done a bit faster. There'll be plenty of room. There's at least fifty orders that have to go to the U.K. by Fri-day."

On the spur of the moment, and because she felt uncomfortable whenever someone was being kind or genuine, Isabella said, "Well, listen, if you want to send all the British orders straightaway in bulk —in one go, I mean—then I'll give you the address of my mum and dad's old place in London. It's huge and more or less empty. You can store everything there for now. Then I can sort them and post them off individually from inside the U.K. next week."

"Thanks. But I should be fine." Molly had crossed to the table by the window. She walked back toward Isabella now, smiling mischie-vously. "I got you this—for the plane." She held up a CD.

"Molly."

"It just came in—it's nothing. Accept a little present with good grace, girl."

"What is it?"

"It's just alternative versions—outtakes—from the *Street Legal* sessions. You said it was your favorite album."

"It is." Isabella felt guilty and grateful and deeply touched all at the same time. "And my brother's. He'll be jealous."

Molly stood in front of her friend a moment. "I want to be hearing from you, though. I want news. And next time you can tell me the whole story top to bottom. Deal?"

"Deal."

"Okay, let's hang this lot up." She picked up an armful of Isabella's clothes from the back of the sofa. "Is this a *gold* miniskirt?"

29

The Fell Hand

THE NIGHT LAY HEAVY in its final hour. But his dreams were alive and restless, slipping back and forth across the borders of his consciousness, smuggling terror one to the other. One moment he was swimming against the Seine's current, desperate, lurching and gasping for breath, the side of his mouth somehow paralyzed, and the next he was beached in his bed, swaddled but immobile, head pulsing with a stretched and swollen pain that he could not relate back to his distress in the water. Then, suddenly, asleep and yet terrified of falling asleep. Then needing to drag himself up physically; the smell of Vaseline and excrement. Then back in the water, the numbness spreading, the whole right side of his body like the weight of some lifeless other, some dead thing. And then child-scared and thrashing . . . And suddenly he was lying wide awake on his back in the swarming darkness, kicking and convulsing with his left arm and leg, adult-terrified and dizzy and his breath coming short. Except it was not like any waking he had ever known, and his brain seemed as if it too were a separate being—seemed to swell and labor in a strange sort of stupefied horror even as he thought that the nightmare must surely pass. And yet now, as he opened his eyes, it went on—no nightmare but something else, something worse, something real. The shadows of the room shifted and blurred, and he could neither raise himself to sit up properly nor clear his eyesight so as to see anything save these dark, indistinct shapes. He was wet with fear. And the fear and shock were already giving way to panic—panic that he could not move his right side, panic that he could not see, panic that the pain in his head seemed to be billowing outward, shadowing even the retreating area of his mind that was able to panic. He was drooling onto his nightshirt, and he realized that his lip was sagging. And now he stopped thinking about anything but saving his own life. He began to call out for Alessandro, hoping that he was asleep in the guestroom but not knowing, not knowing, unable to remember anything. But trying to call out the boy's name over and over. (A stranger, a prayer, a piece of ass.) His own voice, though, sounded mad to him, sounded like the cry of a wild animal caught in some excruciating trap, dying in the night. He couldn't say the boy's name right. But he kept calling out. Any noise would do. As much noise as he could make. And if not . . . if not, if Alessandro was away somewhere else, then he had to reach the telephone. (The pain in his head everywhere now, so that he had to think like a man seizing acrid breaths in quick pockets of air amid the rolling smoke.) His cleaner had the keys. (Cleaners, pieces of ass, whores.) All his strength and all his monumental will to live focused on the single objective: to reach the cell phone by his bed and communicate that he needed immediate help. He called out again. But the sound was a hideous distortion—vowels only, yowled and croaked. He was Quasimodo reborn, howling out—Paris deaf. And if he could not speak, if spoken words were gone, then he would have to send a message, thumb it in. Send for help. Come on, move, you bastard. Move. Even his name did not matter. Move, you bastard. Move. The will to live.

Part III

DECEMBER

All that is solid melts into air, all that is holy is profaned, and man is at last compelled to face with sober senses his real condition of life, and his relations with his kind.

— KARL MARX, *Communist Manifesto*

CONSANGUINITY

30
Vsevolod Learichenko

C OLD WAS CRAWLING through the city like an invisible fog, crawling into every cranny, crawling into every cubbyhole, across the slums, up through the tower blocks, down along the Neva, elbowing aside all other concerns, crawling up the fat legs of its familiar winter throne. In three days the tyranny would be established anew. And those in the converted palaces and executive apartments would be forever on the threshold of their homes and offices and restaurants, forever putting on or taking off their heavy cloaks and furs and gloves and brightly colored department-store scarves; those on broken chairs watching TV in their subdivided rooms had already donned their redarned sweaters, their shawls, their ancient coats for the duration; and those lying in the lean-tos beneath the shadow of the power station now rose swaying to their feet and came out like thin sickened jackals scavenging for new cardboard, rags, rubbish to burn in their oil drums.

Henry lingered, shivering in the swelter of the superheated bank. He kept patting at himself — hand to knee, hand to cheekbone, one hand on the knuckles of the other. The first snow was falling on the Nevsky outside, and a filthy quagmire of evil gray was already caking the ground. He had mistimed it. In the past few days he had been forced to use only twice. The sickness was beginning, and he wasn't sure he could last. He wanted Arkady *gone*. Go, you bastard, go. He needed that passport bought and paid for. The train left at eight. He needed to be alone, back in his cell, the door barred against himself. Belly full of sleeping pills. He had absolutely no faith in his endurance, nor in his spirit, least of all in the veracity of his intention to actually stop. He had done this only once before, and had lasted less than twenty-four hours. And he was afraid, terrified.

He closed his eyes, seeking other thoughts, another Henry. But for a moment there was no other Henry to turn to. Addiction was his entirety. He was sweating—sweating, shivering, shaking. His last hit had been more than thirty-two hours ago. His nose was running. And the roots of his teeth felt like a jagged line of glass splinters in his gums. He bit his cheek. Maybe he should buy one last hit— Leary might even give him some. He wanted wanted wanted wanted. He could not trust himself with this money as far as the end of the Nevsky. Just get home for now. Then maybe buy some. No. No no no *no*. No, come on, Henry.

The worst of the nausea wave passed and he screwed himself up and stepped through the door. The road was striped from the center with gray sludge—plain gray, dark gray, darker gray, and black gray, churned and squashed and churned again by the endless traffic. The blackest gray at the edge where the exhausts of the filthy buses disgorged their worst. The snow not as a blanket, he thought, but as some kind of blotting paper instead, revealing at last the colors of the truth. He pulled his collar up and his woolen bobble hat down. Buried deep in the inside pocket of the huge greatcoat he wore was the very last of his money and his passport. He would not tell Arkady, but he had borrowed right to the limit of his meager overdraft.

Concentrating on his footsteps—his old black leather Sunday service shoes utterly inadequate, the hole ever-worsening—he walked right toward the river, moving slowly through the crowds on the treacherous surface. Though indistinguishable on the outside from most others passing by, likewise bound in coats and hats and scarves and blinking snow out of their eyes, Henry was thinner now than he had ever been. And beneath his hat he had shaved his head.

He kept his eyes down and stared at the ground. He prayed rosaries by way of trying to claw back some calmness, mumbling to himself, his hands struggling to pat even where he had jammed them into his armpits. The pavement had turned into a thickening medley of slush and mottled gray ice. Pedestrians were squelching, sliding, sloshing along. Hard to believe that from the moment the snow left heaven until the moment it touched the earth, it was virgin white.

Arkady's coat felt unendurably heavy, as though his skeleton might give way beneath its weight. And his bones ached as though they were being gnawed by emaciated rats from within. But the wind

—a capricious Beria to Stalin's steely cold—was coming down the river to tighten the regime (he could feel it now as he passed beneath the Admiralty), and to remove the coat was unthinkable. He had a sudden cramp in his gut and tightened his jaw's clench against it. He began to shuffle to avoid jogging his stomach more than necessary and to minimize the risk of slipping on his gripless soles. His toes were numb.

At the far side of the little park, he thought he heard someone behind him and turned . . . He stopped a moment, his jaw working, looking back, standing by the railings beneath the Bronze Horseman, Peter's mount rearing against the snake of treason. There was nobody. He peered back into the snow, seeking if not the who, then at least the why and the how. But his past was all confused, fretful, restless. He could no longer find the main vein.

But it was there—beneath, beside, between all the other damaged tributaries of the blood, twisting, twining—the thread of his life.

Old Henry, Henry Stuart Wheyland, was the only issue of a loveless marriage, brought up by a mother whose latent Catholic piety rapidly ossified following not a divorce but a parting-of-the-ways trauma into a great and rigid structure of brittle dicta, observances, rituals matched only by the adoration she gave to her one and only holy child. Henry rewarded her with endless exam successes—a flare for chess, for reading, for doggedly enjoying choral music in the face of the wholesale mockery and ridicule of his fellows. He was altar boy and sacristan, teacher's pet, assiduous student, and seminarian —all before he dared to look himself in the eye.

Then his mother died. Called to Jesus one evening crossing the road outside the junior school, where she had been putting up decorations in preparation for the school play. Called to Jesus by a minibus driver with a belly full of cheap beer, navigating with his knees, one hand pincering a cigarette, the other clamping to the side of his head a cell phone in which could be heard the recorded voice of a woman promising all callers that her pussy was getting wetter and wetter.

And that was it for Henry. The gates opened, and ready or not, real life came swarming through. Faith was quickly revealed as a farce, belief a beguilement, the whole religious enterprise simply a mighty and mesmerizing distraction from the heart of existence. A colossal and redundant folly. The crisis was not a crisis, it was the termination. He had an audience with his bishop and told him that he could not go on.

Continuing to live in his mother's house, he retrained as a teacher. He read and read and read. He traveled alone to London — to concerts, spending his tiny inheritance on tickets, modest meals out, solo gin and tonics. Two years later he was qualified and teaching at a comprehensive school. But he was nervous, awkward, jittery, and the children could smell his fear. They savaged him. He drank cheap wine in the evening. His classes were a joke — the only quiet pupils were those who were openly doing their homework for another subject. He considered it a success if he could get through the week without any physical violence in his class. He started to drink at lunchtime. His afternoon rages quietened the children for a while. And he resorted to forcing them to read aloud. But still they mocked him, by breaking off whenever they felt like it. Emily Brontë sucks fat donkey ass, they said, what was the point? And he could not remember what he was supposed to say in response. Perhaps they were right: perhaps she did suck fat donkey ass.

He sold his mother's little home in the real estate boom, he paid off her little mortgage. He added the sum to her little legacy and set off for Asia, relatively rich. Good for at least as many years as he could see ahead, assuming he wasn't profligate. And for a while it worked. He was born again. He was still young enough, and nobody suspected the failed teacher, the seminarian, the skinny priggish schoolboy.

Through Thailand, Cambodia, Vietnam, the Philippines, then by plane to Tunis, Tripoli, and Cairo, from Egypt to Jordan, Syria, Turkey, Greece, the Greek islands for a summer; then back east to India — India east, south, west, and north, an odyssey within an odyssey. He acquired the dusty disguise of the traveler. And for a time, at least, the chugging contentment of momentum was his. A quiet beer on the go from noon where possible, his sipping spirits where not.

And yet all the while a shadow of awkwardness continued to track him, forever at his back — however far he went, however fast he went there. Shy, clumsy, tongue-tied and graceless with the women, ignored by the men, he was forever ill at ease among his fellow travelers, save for a brief half-hour between inhibited sobriety and introverted drunkenness. Gradually, gradually, the truth that his youth had failed to grasp stole upon him: that no traveler alive yet escaped himself. And this realization caused his mind to falter and slump, and he began to see the world in its old familiar ways again. But worse: because now, he realized, he had replaced his former parochial hopelessness with the hopelessness of entire continents; the futility of addressing himself to schoolchildren had become the futility of addressing populations. Everywhere humanity seemed to seethe and shriek before him, redder yet in tooth and claw than nature ever dared to be. The Hindus hate the Muslims, it whispered, and the Muslims hate the Hindus; the Jews hate the Arabs and the Arabs hate the Jews; the Protestants hate the Catholics, the Catholics hate the Protestants; the Sunis hate the Shiites and the Shiites hate the Sunis; Animist versus Orthodox versus Islamic versus Hindu versus Buddhist versus Hindu versus Sikh versus Islamic versus Jew versus Christian versus Jew versus Islamic versus Orthodox versus Animist — caste, creed, and capital, the unholy trinity and the keenest blades of the cutting world. Too many fucking people fucking. And so, one multicolored afternoon, to a certain dragon's lair with Anthony, a fellow teacher of English as a foreign language.

The exact moment of his fall was never clear to Henry. Perhaps the first pipe. Perhaps the hundredth. Perhaps later. In any event, he stopped drinking altogether. If a balm for the eczema of his spirit was all this time what he had been seeking, then this was a better balm than his wildest imaginings. He never touched booze again. He went north with Anthony, where it was easier. They crossed into Pakistan — Lahore, Gujranwala, Islamabad. They fell in with others. They passed east into Kashmir. Anthony went to Thailand. But (cool now, relaxed) Henry made his home in a commune of sorts with Dutch, American, Scots, French, and various Scandinavians. Others passing through. Captain Charlie and his wife, Anjum, ran the place, had been there since 1965. There were other teachers, aid workers traveling, an English-language Web site designer, bad musicians, lapsed missionaries, students, wasters . . . Henry and his new friends sat high on escarpments and looked down the iridescent valleys while their pipes bubbled. He dreamed of paradises lost and found. He laughed and was at ease with the women and the men alike. Nine months passed. He worked a little at teaching again, happy to have rediscovered a vocation. One May day he was paid well to go to a young lawyer's home village, near the border with Jammu, to help two younger brothers with their English. The commission was for a month. But Henry became sick after four days and had to go back to the commune and return the money. He did not even realize that he had withdrawal symptoms. It was one of the Scots, Craig, who told him that he was hooked.

In the late summer there were new rumors of helicopters. People began to leave. The military was said to be arriving. Police. Some of the local boys stopped coming for the cricket at Captain Charlie's pitch; Charlie blamed the Americans "for ruddy well polarizing the ruddy world." One afternoon the little Internet place in town refused to let Henry use the computer. Meanwhile, Craig and Amy, a New Yorker pretending to be Canadian, were going north in three weeks. There was a road open. They could get forty-eight-hour transit visas.

Henry caught the bus with them. Overnight, in Kabul, Amy acquired a cache of unopened syringes — from the army, she said. You needed less, much less, this way. It was better than smoking and cheaper.

And so Henry moved on.

Dushanbe, Tashkent, Qaraghandy, Astana . . . and eventually to Russia. Omsk. Their chief difficulty not scoring but the supply of clean needles. Henry was lucky. He had good veins.

A week or so later, Amy went one stage further and got married for money. So Henry caught the train for Moscow with Craig.

The relationship was no longer casual. He had to take it seriously. Time to settle down. Become a creature of habit. He taught a little in Moscow, rented a place with Craig in a clean and decent flat near the Ismailova Park. He used twice a day. He still had plenty of money. New Henry was . . . cool.

By the time he made his first visit to Petersburg six months later, Henry was shooting up only to return himself to normal. The drug was having no other effect. He went back again and again (on what he called the Anna Karenina train), and each trip to Petersburg enchanted him further — the easier size of the city, the relative safety, and its beauty. The music. (So much music so close by.) At some point in the interim Craig started stealing from him. So before the winter came, he decided to move again, taking his two ballasts with him — the satchel and the scag bag — to keep him on an even keel. He found a generous and reliable dealer. He fell in love.

Henry came now to the wide-openness of the river, where the wind was driving the snow obliquely, closer in, so that the cars were forced to slow and loomed one after another out of a closing veil of yet more gray. Already there were swirls of thickened water in the Neva below, ice forming in darkening slabs, the remaining river running strange and contrariwise in channels in between. He went on, face turned away from the angle of the snow. Momentum.

On the far side of the bridge he slipped and fell awkwardly on his side, twisting his knee and scraping his hand despite the gloves. The accident ripped him from his silent rosary to the full consciousness of the present, and he was forced to take off his glove to suck at his hand, where he had somehow drawn blood. He swore, a litany of the worst words he knew. He had come far enough on foot. But he had no money, he had no money, *they* had no money. Actually, yes, he had money. He had all this money in his coat. No, he had no money. Yes. No. Yes. No. Just get home. And then. He turned left toward the warship, walking with some difficulty along the embankment. Now the snow was really sticking, each flake seeming to outlast the previous. He did not have the strength, he knew it. He did not have the strength for anything. But he struggled on, arguing with himself, praying, then cursing.

He was assailed by a sudden surge of panic: that his inner pocket had given way during the fall. He turned his back to the snow, bit off his glove, painfully undid two of the buttons, and reached inside with numb fingers to feel for passport and the plastic wallet they had given him at the bank. Both were still there.

He buttoned up and went on, shuffling forward, hands jammed under his arms. He had noticed that the urge toward self-sacrifice was growing more and more powerful the weaker he became — something to do with purgation, he thought, or with providing his life with meaning. And the fact of his own blood amazed him. Astonishing that it carried on circulating so devotedly when he had long ago ceased to care for its welfare. Yes, the harder things became, the more he wanted them to become even harder. Test me then, you dead, dumb, deaf little god. Test me. See if I care. See if I value this life you claim to have given me. Perhaps this state of mind was the secret of all holy men and women. The urge to make a life mean something. Yes, what the prophets really wanted — Christ, Muhammad, Moses, and the rest — was to give their lives *meaning*. And what a feat of persuasion, if you could pull it off: my words are God's words, my life redeems all humanity for all time, my life is the only guide, my life is the example for eternity. Selfish, histrionic little narcissists. He had no more money. Zero. He was going to kick his baby, his bitch, his beautiful angel, his boy. Arkady was going to get the passport he needed. And go. Don't let him down now. Don't you dare let him down, Henry Wheyland.

But he could walk no farther and he had come far enough and the point, if there was one, was that he should not injure himself or be late on account of sticking to a smaller vow when the larger sacrifice was what really mattered. A ride from here would make little or no difference; Arkady would have a few rubles, surely. What were a few rubles in so many thousands anyway? Yes, he had come far enough. He crossed the road and stuck out his arm. A brown Lada skidded to a halt almost immediately, bald tires gliding through slush. Henry climbed in, rubbing at his knee. Across the river, the buildings of the English Quay watched him through the snow.

By chance or design, Arkady was already waiting on the curb when the Lada drew up — boots on, mittens and some giant old and ugly striped sweater that Henry had never seen before. Christ, he's going to be cold, Henry thought; and then he remembered that he himself was wearing his friend's coat.

Arkady opened the far door and leaned in.

"Okay?"

"Yes. We'll be a few rubles short." Henry looked across. He felt the need to explain, to apologize. "Sorry — I meant to walk. I hurt my hand, I —"

"Doesn't matter." Arkady got into the car, his knees squashed against the front seat, and gave the address in Russian — up by the Black River.

The driver nodded, eyes briefly in the rearview, crunched the brittle engine into first gear, and began to turn around, yanking at the wheel as though it were the door to a breached compartment on a submarine.

"I will tell Leary," Arkady said. "The bastard will enjoy it anyway . . . Shows him how he has everything — every ruble. That we have nothing left. Not even to pay for a fucking ride back."

Henry's lips worked. He felt nauseous again, unable to acknowledge anything. Maybe it was the engine fumes being pumped in by the car's cheap little heater. He unfastened the coat, reached inside, and handed his friend the plastic wallet.

"This is everything."

"I can go alone," Arkady said.

"No."

They had stopped at the end of the street, the driver waiting for a gap in the careering traffic.

"You do not have to come."

They both knew that he was hoping for an extra hit.

"I am coming."

Arkady met his eye. "Okay."

Henry wound the window down — stiff and awkward on the ratchet — and turned his head to breathe the icy air. Under the cover of snow, the darkness was slipping in.

The driver was young and in a hurry to earn his money. The car slewed. The wipers squeaked and the heater scraped. Henry watched the lights of the other cars coloring the snow. Of course it had turned out that Kostya's contact was Grisha, which meant Leary. Bitter wasn't the word for it. (There were far better words in Russian.) And yet it was to Vsevolod Learichenko — Uncle Seva, as Grisha called him — that the two were now driving. Arkady knew of nobody else. Petersburg was not such a big city. Moscow, London, New York, Los Angeles, even Paris, there might have been alternatives. Fake-passport purchase was still easy enough with money and contacts, Henry understood, but not half as easy as the newspapers pretended. The biggest danger was of being scammed by amateurs. Paradoxically, you were safest going with the gangs. Or you risked being arrested at the airport, your money already spent, your forgers long disappeared. They could have gambled and gone to Moscow, but they were in a hurry, and there was something perversely persuasive, Arkady reasoned, in trusting Leary: since he had already reduced them to nothing, he would not therefore risk cheating them further. Leary would assume, rightly or wrongly, that Arkady (a native of the city, unlike Leary himself, and friends with fringe citizens enough) would seek some kind of violent recompense if further torture were inflicted. An unnecessary irritation that Leary would not wish for. Far better to have Arkady well served. Far better to have Henry on his staff. Far better to keep out of petty troubles. So Arkady had calculated Leary would calculate. And Henry had been in neither mood nor condition to argue.

The car slithered to a stop. Henry sucked at his injured hand, then clutched at his leg, which was twitching again, threatening cramp. The snow was thicker than ever as the two climbed out. Arkady went to the driver's window to hand over the rubles for the ride. Henry eased his way around the back of the car, little scoops of snow wedging themselves through the hole in his shoe. Arkady was pointing at a low covered passageway wide enough for a single cart.

The center of Leary's operation — or one center of it, at least — appeared to be a filthy, soot-blackened brick building six stories high, constructed in the middle of the nineteenth century on the outskirts but stranded now amid a squalid swath of scum and shortage that

stretched like a tide mark around the edges of the city. Henry shuffled over and stopped beneath the shelter. He had taken off his hat in
the car, and he looked like some bewildered creature of the gulag —
shaven-headed, gaunt jaw chewing on nothing, kneading at his hat
with both hands. Arkady came over at a run and ducked within.

The passageway was heaped with putrescent rubbish — cans, split
plastic bags, rancid food, old clothes — a rotten mouth that swallowed them whole. They groped their way forward until ahead of
them they saw a curtain of snow, pale strands of saffron lit by a
weak lamp beyond. They passed through, into yet another mini-
courtyard.

And this time hell wasn't down but up. They climbed the communal stairs in the darkness as far as an innocuous door on the second
floor. Here they stood still with their hands where they could be seen
through the spy hole and waited for the unlocking process to begin.
When the door finally opened, it was Grisha — face like a cheese
grater, fingers like bratwurst — who motioned them inside.

They were led to a large front room, which, save for an incongru-
ously yellow bicycle helmet hanging from a nail by the blinded window, was entirely bare.

"Wait there."

Grisha went back out into the corridor and began to relock the
main apartment door.

There was nowhere to sit, so they stood. Henry's nose was streaming, his body sodden with sweat inside the greatcoat, despite the
cold. He was praying that the cramps would not come back. Time
snagged like a forgotten rag flapping on a barbed-wire fence.

An hour later — or it might have been five minutes or three days —
Grisha reappeared.

"Let's go."

"Where?" Arkady asked. They were speaking in Russian.

"This way."

"How long is this going to take?"

"You have to go somewhere?"

"I have to take my dog to fuck your mother again. She already
paid for it."

Grisha turned and answered him with a grin like a scar.

Through his ache, Henry wondered vaguely what was going to
happen. But Grisha carried on walking. Henry thought that maybe
they were going out into the communal hall again, but instead they

continued down the corridor, past a series of shut doors on the right, and entered a room at the opposite end of the apartment, this one furnished haphazardly, as if uncertain whether a lounge, an office, or a doctor's waiting room.

"Wait here."

Grisha disappeared, and they heard a moment's conversation in Russian as he opened another door and then nothing again.

Arkady looked around with mixed scorn and tense wariness. "Now he has let you see this place, you know that he will kill you if he thinks you fuck with him." He addressed Henry directly in English. "I am serious. This is not a child's thing. People die in this world all the time. Nobody cares."

"I know people die. I am not going to fuck with him and I am not going to work for him."

Arkady fixed the Englishman with his candid, sunken eyes, his gaze seeming to come from a long way within. "I hope. But you are far from your place in the world now."

Henry could neither answer nor stand any longer, and so he lowered himself into the disheveled armchair against the far wall and closed his eyes. How in the name of God had he come to this? At least he had stopped caring about anything—even Arkady. All he wanted. The only thing in the world he wanted. And he wanted it with every cell of his body. Was his fix. Maybe this was the point where the virgin tapped the shoulder of her son, busy in the office of his heaven, and made her intercession on Henry's behalf? He hoped so. Do it, woman—do it now.

Arkady took the upright chair on the far side of the desk, which sat more or less in the middle of the room.

And then they waited some more.

Eventually Leary came through the door, quiet, almost stealthy, like a media mogul who enjoyed understating his power. He had an overbite, a receding lower jaw, and the beginnings of a double chin, so that his face appeared to slope away smoothly from the overhang of his front teeth. His hair was longish, curly, and black; he had protruding dark eyes, suntanned skin, and a slight but habitual hunch that created the impression that he was always addressing people from below, looking up with bulbous solicitation from between the curtains of his hair, though he was tall enough to meet most on the level. He was carrying a neat blue plastic wallet, and he sat down almost cheerily in his leather swivel seat behind the desk, opposite

Arkady. He might have been a helpful if unsavory high-street travel agent. Grisha followed a moment later, cigarette burning, and heavily stationed himself on the ragged sofa just behind.

Arkady continued to stare at the ceiling, his head back on the lip of his uncomfortable plastic chair, legs stretched out directly into Leary's foot space. In his deeper armchair behind, Henry was likewise ignoring the arrival, though for very different reasons: he was sitting back but gripping the frayed armrests, his knuckles all but popping from their sockets, his face as white as dough, a cold sweat shining on his forehead. His pupils seemed to be widening visibly, twin black holes gorging on nerve and cell. He was shivering spasmodically, and every few seconds he leaned forward, pressing his head toward his knees against the cramp. Then he'd straighten up, stretch his jaw, yawning, before clamping his mouth shut again, lips working.

Leary's eyes slid over Henry for a moment, and then he began carefully to take out the contents of the wallet and check them through. When this task was completed to his satisfaction, he glanced up with studied casualness.

"Grisha, get me something for this fuckup." His Russian was heavily accented but from where exactly was impossible to tell. "Before he shits himself on our lovely furniture."

Henry was rubbing his hands together as if to start a fire then and there between his palms.

"Leave him alone." Arkady leveled his gaze and faced Leary. His voice was the flatter Russian of a pure Petersburger. "He's coming off. Leave him."

Leary frowned and then smiled his selachian smile. "I am *giving* it to him. I am not asking for money."

Grisha remained unsure, an indeterminate menace, about to get up, about to continue sitting down.

"He's coming off," Arkady repeated. "Just leave him."

Leary sighed. "He won't get through it."

"He will."

"How long has it been?"

"A day and a half." Arkady eyed the passport and papers that Leary was returning to the file. "Is this everything I need?"

"Yes."

Arkady held out his hand.

"Of course." Leary handed the file across the desk. "Okay, yes. He might get through the withdrawal—most of them manage it once or twice. Even the scum. But he won't make it through the months afterward." Leary's expression was all amused weariness. "I am sure you know this. You must have seen it a hundred times. They can get off, but they can't stay off. It's not even the drug. It's the addiction itself—they can't replace the addiction. Addiction is . . . is part of them. It's the conversation they want to have with themselves. It's who they've learned to be. And when it goes, they do not know what to fill the emptiness with."

"Is this the visa?" Arkady indicated a page of the passport.

"That is your visa." Leary nodded.

Arkady examined it closely.

"Even when they quit five or ten times, they always come back. It's a cycle. And you know it. So don't be stupid and don't be cruel. Look at the poor guy. He might as well save himself the pain . . . because he will be back in three days, a week, a month, six months." Leary addressed Henry directly in English. "Henry? Henry? You want something?"

Henry was facedown again—head in hands, hands back and forth across shaven scalp. He nodded repeatedly. Then straightened abruptly. His face could not have spoken of need more eloquently. His lips peeled back from his yellow teeth. "Yes." He gave a series of shallow nods. "Yes. Fuck. Give it to me."

Arkady passed Henry's money across the table. "Here is the money," he said in Russian.

Leary was distracted. He began to count—climbed as far as ten thousand rubles and then stopped.

Henry was patting.

"Grisha, please." Leary had likewise returned to Russian. "Before he starts shitting himself. The best. And some to take away."

"I said leave him." Arkady eyes were as level as his voice.

Grisha stiffened. Leary looked up, his own eyes seeming to bulge and swim while Arkady's remained still, sunken. There was a moment when a different future might have begun. But perhaps Leary did not want any bodies in his office. More than this, perhaps there was something about Arkady that made Leary want to outwit him rather than injure him, as if physical pain were what the other expected and would not therefore hurt him.

"Arkasha," Leary said, in the manner of someone explaining the rules of the house, "I don't want to start some bullshit with you. I have nothing against you, and it is a waste of my time. What is the point? But Henry needs what I have."

Grisha sat down.

Leary's voice hardened. "And please remember, I don't make him take the shit. I don't make anyone take it. He takes it because he wants to take it. They all have a choice. And if it weren't me, it would be someone else giving it to him. And you know — you *know* — that it will never stop." Leary lowered his head but kept his eyes on Arkady. "If the governments were not such gutless suckers of rat cock, they would hand it out to these people. They would have their taxes. All that money they have been missing would suddenly appear. Chechnya, Afghanistan, Bolivia, Indonesia . . . all the shit holes fixed. The world's big problem — gone."

Leary licked finger and thumb and paused as if waiting for Arkady to speak.

But Arkady said nothing.

So Leary's eyes went over to Henry again (who had his head back now, mouth gaping) before swiveling once more onto Arkady. He continued his count, saying the numbers out loud. Then he softened his voice. "At least mine is pure and safe. He takes more of mine, he will be okay. He comes off now, he goes back on tomorrow or the next day or the day after that. When you have gone. His body is not used to it. It's fucking chaos for him. He buys some cheap shit from Kostya or worse. He overdoses. That's how it happens. We've both seen it a thousand times." He shrugged, his hands poised to finish their count. "Or . . . Or he works for me. He sells to the million young wankers who are coming . . . Prague, Riga, Tallinn, they're moving east. The Europeans are returning. They'll do away with the visa here soon enough and the place will be crawling with fresh young whores and used old bank notes." Leary indicated the Englishman with a small thumb. "And Henry will be fine. Safe — from the police, from me, from himself. He takes what he needs. I put him in a decent apartment. Buy him some clothes. Then, when the day comes, when he really wants to stop, he stops. Because that's the only way it ever happens. He stops because he wants to stop for real. Not because of some bullshit. Not because his boyfriend won't fill his dirty hole for him. You know that I am right." He counted the remaining stacks quickly. But laid the last note down slowly. "You're short. But I let you off."

Arkady stood up, holding the file. "I do not give a fuck what's right. Right means nothing to me."

Grisha was also back on his feet, cigarette burned down almost to his inner-tube lips.

Arkady crossed to Henry and began unclasping the Englishman's knuckles from the armrests of the seat. He bent down to face his flatmate, pausing for a moment to look into the vacancy of his pupils. Then he hooked the great magnitude of his hands under Henry's armpits and hoisted him forward to the edge of the chair.

"I need some fucking shit, Arkasha," Henry said, grimacing. Then again, half crying, half whispering: "I need some fucking boy."

Arkady put down the file a moment, turned his back and squatted, and reached behind himself for Henry's body. Then, grasping both legs, he dragged the Englishman from the chair and up onto his back. He bent awkwardly to gather the file and then stood up with the appearance of ease.

"Not this time," he said. "Not today. Not while I am here." He shifted his friend's body. "And you know, Seva, that if this passport does not work, I will kill you myself." He turned. "Grisha, open the door. We are going."

31

A Message Returned

S ATURDAY NIGHT. Second night back in London. And already
she felt different. The fury and the apprehension were still there,
but the long free fall was over. She had money for three months
—four, at a stretch. And she was determined. For far too long, far too
much crap had clogged her mind. (Her own, she readily admitted, as
well as everybody else's.) And it was true, crap had a way taking over
a person's days, little by little, until there was nothing *but* crap. Now,
instead, to face with sober senses the real conditions of her life and
her relations with those about her. No more false starts. No more my-
thology. She heard her friend's familiar voice calling up the stairs.

Five minutes later she stood in the large front room, two children at her knees, as Susan Thompson and her husband, Adam,
backed parentally out of the front door onto Torriano Avenue, Kentish Town, London.

Susan spoke as she searched the pockets of her red coat for the
house keys. "The terrible two will probably stay awake longer than
normal, just because you're here and they're excited, but Joe should
sleep straight. Fingers crossed. There are loads of books in their bedroom—you can refuse to read to them unless they get into bed.
That's what Adam does. They like anything with monsters and a
good story."

Adam shouted from halfway down the steps, "Monsters! Monsters do the trick. You'll have to read until they are both asleep,
though, or they won't let you go."

Susan, having found her keys, added softly, "Any problems, just
call the mobile."

"Same goes for you," Isabella said wryly.

Susan smiled and rolled her bright green eyes. She had shoulder-length midbrown hair and was pretty in a plain kind of way, or plain in a pretty kind of a way; medium height, medium build, and English all the way back to pre-Roman Gloucestershire. The two had known each other since they were three or four. They went their different ways for a while, during Isabella's turbulent college years, but they had also lived together for eighteen months before Isabella left for the States.

"Okay. So go. See you later on." Isabella put her hand on the head of the eldest, Mark.

"Be good for Auntie Isabella, both of you. If I hear of any trouble, then . . ."

"Bye, Suze. Go. Go on, go."

"See you later. Don't wait up if we're late."

"Oh, I'll be up. Jet lag."

"Bye-bye." Susan gave her children one more wave.

"Will you come *on?*" Adam shouted.

Susan widened her eyes as if to say "Poor man, he thinks he's in charge," and for a moment Isabella was aware of the curious effect of their shared surety of each other, something that seemed to affirm that long before Adam, the terrible two, or baby Joe, they were friends. A weird thing, Isabella thought as she shut the door, this sense of knowing someone of old. Seeing someone in the thick of her circumstances — woman, wife, mother — and yet being familiar with so much of what had led to these circumstances that the circumstances themselves seemed merely that: circumstantial.

Isabella followed the two children (already racing ahead) to their playroom upstairs, watched them go inside, and then entered Adam's tiny office. She turned the computer on and waited for it to come alive. She was grateful that she had not been enlisted in the evening herself. Adam had cheerfully invited her, and Susan had been required to slip her deftly from the noose. There were going to be ten or so other guests at the dinner party, "singles as well as couples," Adam had said encouragingly, so he thought. Increasingly, though, Isabella found the very idea of a couple annoying. Not because she herself was now "single" — another word she could hardly even think, let alone say, without retching — but because to her mind the whole (previously interesting) female dialectic between being part of a "couple" and being "single" seemed to have somehow metamorphosed into this sprawling, transatlantic, society-wide giant squid of a cliché that insisted on stinking and dripping all over more or less everything — most viscidly of all at dinner parties. It wasn't the blithely impoverished fiction or the dumb TV series that killed her the most (though these were surely written by the soulless undead) but the fact that so many women she met seemed to reach so quickly for the tentacles of this mighty cliché, the better, they believed, to swing into their conversations. Indeed, so tightly did they seem to cling to these tentacles that it was as if the very fact of their being alive at all had become secondary to their being "single" or "coupled up" or married.

She had no good mail. An invitation to buy more Viagra so that she could go harder for longer more often, and a chance to own a pair of little Suki's freshly worn knickers. She surfed some news sites awhile, then looked idly at one-bedroom flats to rent in North London, then went to Molly's home page, then typed Molly a simple "Hi there, it's me — made it so far" e-mail.

Feeling at a loose end and yet with too much energy, she got up, left the computer on, and went to check on the baby. He was safely asleep. She wondered for a moment why her own mother had not had any more children. Then she wondered who would be the father of hers. She bit her lip and half smiled. After all the remonstration and dissent, perhaps she would just offer herself to the most hand-some and intelligent doctor she could find. Get the good genes and the delivery care all done in one go.

She shut the door quietly and returned to the playroom, there to behold the baffling multilayered miracle of her oldest friend's son and daughter playing two characters in their computer game version of *The Lord of the Rings*.

She had a moment's misgiving, trying to remember if they were al-lowed to play on the console, and if so, which games. But both chil-dren seemed so adept at what they were doing — butchering orcs — that she could only assume this was normal.

"Okay. You two. You're allowed to play for another half an hour, then your mummy says you have to help me make hot chocolate and popcorn."

Girl hit pause. Boy sighed.

"We're not allowed." This from Louise.

"What?"

"Popcorn." This from Mark.

"Why not?"

"Mark made a right mess when we did it last time and spilled everything on the floor and nearly burned the whole kitchen down and the house."

Mark made a face of profound older-brotherly scorn. "No I didn't."

"You did. Mummy basically had to ring the firemen."

Mark: "No."

Louise: "Yes."

"You are such a liar. Mum did not have to ring the fire *brigade*."

He took a six-year-old's pleasure in knowing the right word. And Isabella observed his emphasis take the wind out of four-year-old Louise's tiny new sails.

"Well, your mum said it was okay to try again as long as I helped this time. So — you guys carry on for a bit. I'm going to be upstairs on the computer if you want me. And after the hot chocolate and the popcorn, we can decide what story you want."

"Hobbit," Mark said, turning back to the screen.

"It's the prequel," Louise added, nodding assuredly.

The slaughter of orcs began again with renewed vengeance.

She decided to compose a letter on the computer. She could write it out by hand tomorrow. Francis would have the address. If she could get something down, then she could post it straightaway. Two days maximum to Paris. No sense delaying. And e-mail clearly wasn't getting through. She sat down, refreshed the screen, and felt her entire body go tense.

My dear Isabella,

Thank you for your last three e-mails. And I am very sorry not to have replied until now. The reasons for my silence are both silly and rather more sobering. Simply, I did not have my computer for much of November and so missed your first and second of earlier that month; and then, unfortunately, I suffered a stroke, and so missed your third until yesterday. Fortunately, I am home from the hospital now, and the individual who had the loan of the laptop has returned. And so, what a welcome surprise to hear from you, the first name I saw on my first day back.

Of course there is so much that I wish to write — in response to your thoughts about your mother's death, your curiosity regarding her life, and in response to your oblique, but no less kind for that, inquiry about my circumstances. But forgive me if I plead a twofold pardon for the moment: though I am very lucky — the stroke was relatively minor, and recovery has been frustrating but steady — it is still rather difficult for me to concentrate (or type) for too long; and, second, well, there is so very much I would like to talk to you about that it seems altogether overwhelming to begin here on e-mail.

For now, then, let me say that I am well enough, the computer thief has become my carer by way of recompense, and so I am looked after. That I continue to live here in Paris. That I am awed by your being so long in New York and would love to hear more about this and the rest of your life. That, most of all, I am sorry we have been incommunicado for so long and hope this change is a permanent righting of that wrong. And, finally, that I think of you every day.

More very soon,
Nicholas

32

Crossing the Borders

I T SEEMED to Arkady Alexandrovitch as if the night itself had
grown hoarse. He lay sideways across the wear-smoothed wooden
seats and listened to the clank and thunder of the train heading
west, his bag a pillow, his coat a blanket. He had not been able to
sleep properly but wandered back and forth, sometimes wakeful,
sometimes in deep reverie, never quite gone from himself. There was
little purpose now — the border could not be far off.

He heard everything distinctly: the whir of the heater in his compartment, the chatter of the shutters where they refused to fasten
down, the low rumble of the wheels as they plundered the uneven
track and the creak of the carriages as they concertinaed through the
slow curves, the grate and scrape of every road crossing, the clink of
points, the jangled wail of station bells rushing by, the grunt and
snort of the engine itself, the sudden press and whoosh of the tunnels, the heavy breath of spur lines, and, beneath it all, the bass
croak of the sleepers. If there were such a thing as music's jealous rival, then this train, on this December night, was it.

There was nobody else in his compartment. He had extinguished
all the lights and pulled down all the screens so that he lay in darkness save for the passing of shadows. The heater was feeble — might
even have been blowing cold — and he kept himself still so as not to
disturb the pockets of warmth beneath his greatcoat.

The carriage jolted over some unknown junction and he pressed
his hands deeper into his armpits. He had never left Petersburg in
this direction before. He had never left Russia before. But he did not
feel afraid — there was nothing further that the world could really

do to him. All the same, though he did not recognize the feeling to give it a proper name, he was lonely.

The plan was to take the train through the Baltic states as far as Riga in Latvia. There he would transfer to a direct flight to London Stanstead on the new route operated by some bullshit British airline. It was the cheapest way, Henry said, and Stanstead was easiest. Henry had purchased his train ticket, Henry had paid for the flight, Henry had given him thirty pounds, but the two hundred and forty dollars that Arkady had in the money belt strapped to his chest were his own — secret money he had saved.

In reality, Arkady did not expect to make it as far as Riga. He expected the whole thing to go to shit as soon as he came to the Latvian border. His passport to be laughed at, confiscated, ridiculed as counterfeit. Or perhaps he might be able to bribe his way through. But that would be all his funds gone — then he'd be refused his place on the plane, and he'd have to walk or hitchhike all the way back, probably though Estonia, and hope to slip home into Russia cross-country through the forests, the only fool going the other way. He was glad of his boots and his coat.

He shut his eyes. The train hammered on. His mind wandered close by sleep again. His imagined hell was a quasi-religious one (the memory of the dormitory whisperings of the secret "our savior" cabals): a black and broiling landscape as far from the white of a Petersburg winter as possible; nameless long-necked creatures flying across a red moon that rode out as quickly as it disappeared; a discarded sickle by the banks of an oozing yellow lava stream; and a narrow path that climbed the caldera, snaking through the smoke and sulfur, one switchback after another, people lying by the side, people crawling, people pressing in beside him, all of them dressed in rags and dying of thirst, nothing but disappearances and desolation spoken. And whatever they hissed, it was his curse not only to expect three times worse on this journey but also to encourage it — as if to prove, again and again, that neither luck nor God existed. Though why he had to demonstrate this to himself when he knew it for a fact of experience — as surely as he knew that there was blood on some of the sheets at the orphanage and that it never quite washed out — he did not know. With the piano gone, perhaps the only thing that was saving him from vodka (as he became aware of the engine altering pitch) was the thought that he needed to stay alive to hunt down Leary if his bullshit papers failed.

The brake squeal when at last it came was deafening. He rolled

over, stood up, and put his coat on quickly before the warmth fled its
folds. It was becoming colder. He grimaced. There was a Petersburg
saying he had always liked: "Just when you think it can't get any
colder, it gets much fucking colder." He reached his hand up to the
heater. Broken. If he made it across the border, he would change
compartments, even if it meant sharing. He found the light, lifted
down his bag, and opened up the zip to pull out some music to read.
He and Henry had made up someone to be. They had made up
somewhere to be from. But he was a pianist still, and the same age.
Might as well look the part.

He wasn't anxious — rather, he just wanted his fate decided. So
that he could resign himself to it. But there was no way of knowing
whether the passport and visa would pass inspection. And neither
did he know what would happen to him if they did not. He had
looked through everything, of course, but he was no expert on such
documentation, so it was a pointless inspection. And Henry was use-
less.

He read the notes on the score — heard them within — and the
sound rinsed his imagination clean of the whining. He liked to read
the orchestral part to these concerti — he liked to understand what
the other instruments were doing. He liked to hear the companion
songs to his own.

Eventually the train shuddered to a stop. He let a moment pass.
Then, cautiously, he opened the door to his compartment. Nobody
around. He began to make his way toward one of the doors at the
end of the carriage. There were voices. A dozen or so people had
gathered. Men smoking, a woman with two children bundled in
hats and scarves, their noses streaming, their cheeks red. Somebody
said the border guards would start at the front and work their way
through. Another said that it could take two hours. Another ten
minutes. A fourth pushed open the main door and descended, cigarette angled, hands already cupping for the match's brief spark.
Arkady hesitated a moment, but he had no wish to talk and nothing
to say, so he followed this man down.

The cold was absolute and brutal. The snow crunched sharp and
the air smarted in his throat, crackled in his nostrils. The train had
stopped at some forgotten place. A long platform: a hut at the one
end; farther away, cracks of light; a tower at the other end, all dark.
What was to prevent a man from walking boldly to his freedom in
whichever direction he thought it lay? Nothing. But then, not so long
ago all of this was Russia — right, left, forward, back.

Though the snow was no longer actually falling, it lay heavy, and his boots left a deep trail. At first, as his eyes adjusted, the forest seemed to hem in on either side, but gradually Arkady thought that he could make out the deeper black of water through the narrow belt of trees across the opposite track. It was hard to be sure. A freezing fog beset the ground there, seeming to curl in and out of the trunks. Perhaps a lake mist. There was no sound. And the silence was blissful after the train.

He turned and stood another minute peering down the narrow cutting of the track due east, from whence he had come. The smoker climbed back up onto the train. Something stayed him awhile yet. For the first time in his life he was feeling the traveler's thrill: a mixture of apprehension and excitement.

"All of Mother Russia is old — old rock, old geology," his history teacher had said, "and there is nothing that she cannot provide. Why would any of us wish to leave her? The Soviet Union is the hope of all mankind!"

Someone was coming along the platform. He assumed it must be a border guard. But as the figure drew closer, he realized it was some madman of the night, carrying a samovar wrapped in heavy blankets.

"Get back on the train," the man said in heavily accented Russian, "or they will leave you here. They give no warning. They don't care. The real border is farther on." He inclined his head backward to point the direction he meant but did not pause, continuing on his way to the end and entering the last carriage.

Arkady's eyes followed where the man had indicated. Then he withdrew his hands from his armpits. They were going numb. He held them out in front, looking at them as he flexed the muscles. Then, slowly, carefully, he unwrapped the bandage on his index finger and let it drop to the ground. He kicked it across the snow until it fell onto the track, between the wheels of the train. Then he squeezed both hands hard into two big fists and shoved them deep into his pockets.

Fifteen minutes later, cradling his tea, the music still open on the seat beside him, Arkady Alexandrovitch Kolokov (as he now was) offered up his passport. The squat guard, whom no cap nor boot could elevate, barely looked at it, nodded, and left the compartment. Arkady sipped some more and felt the heat coursing inside him.

Five minutes later another official — this time a taller Latvian —

entered the carriage. He sat down on the bench opposite and took out his flashlight, though the light was working well enough. He examined the passport. He pointed the beam into Arkady's face. Arkady blinked. He examined the passport again. Then shone on the music.

He spoke in Russian. "Where are you going?"

"London."

"Good."

The Latvian stood. Passed back the passport. And then he was gone. That was it.

Arkady swore repeatedly under his breath. Stay here. Put some more clothes on. The cold wasn't so bad. Better than having to talk to people. In any case, he had another glass of tea lined up.

He sat alone, listening to the guard moving down the carriage. He wondered if the British authorities would be quite so easy.

Twenty minutes later the train hauled itself into the night, heading due west again.

33

Highgate Hill

THE NEXT DAY, Sunday, was wintry sharp but pleasingly so, the faintest frost still whispering white on the branches that the two women stooped beneath, the cold air thicker on the breath. Mornings like this reminded Isabella of Petersburg—the colors all reduced to their essences and only the bravest red flash of a robin's breast daring to challenge the cobalt of the sky. They were walking together up Swain's Lane, the steep road that divided the famous Highgate Cemetery into two plots—east, west—and took them up to village beyond. The pavement narrowed every few steps to accommodate the wayside trees, so they went along sometimes side by side, sometimes in single file. Roots had cracked and cleft the path, and they had to be careful not to stumble or slip.

At Isabella's suggestion, and then at Susan's urging, they were on their way to call on Francis, the keeper of the old Highgate house. As girls and then teenagers, they had done this walk many times before, though it was the first time Isabella had been back in nearly five years. She realized that this was her allotted session: Sunday morning—cordoned off from Adam and the children, negotiated, set aside; and ordinarily such a choreographed falsity would have irritated her. But there was something about old friends, something that exonerated Susan from the usual strictures of Isabella's unforgiving mind.

The two women passed the last tree in the immediate line and the pavement widened so that Isabella could step beside her friend again—Susan's sensible walking shoes click-clacking on the pavement while her own sneakers made no noise.

Susan looked across. "So you can store your stuff in the old house? If you decide to move back properly, I mean."

"If I'm coming back, I want my own flat." Isabella shook her head ruefully. "Just watch me — twenty-four hours in London and all the psycho crap will be forgotten and I'll be after all the usual: job, flat, man. Not necessarily in that order."

"I doubt it." Susan smiled and went ahead as they came to another tree. Over her shoulder she said, "And you know you are welcome to stay with us for Christmas."

"That's kind, Suze."

Susan stopped to retie her lace. "You didn't write back this morning?"

"No. Not yet. Which is pretty stupid, since I started it."

"Why not?"

"I don't know. Because . . ." Isabella stood watching her friend fashion a methodical double bow. "I suppose because I'm shocked to hear from him at all. Because it's been ten years. Because of his stroke. Because I don't know exactly what to say. And because I still really, *really* dislike him. Because everything."

"Do you feel sorry for him?"

"I feel sorry for anyone who has had a stroke . . . but. It's hard to explain, Suze . . . It doesn't change anything. It *shouldn't* change anything."

"But it does, it does." Susan rose and they went on. "You do want to stay in contact now, right?"

"Yeah. It's just the idea of actually doing it that makes me feel sick. It's almost worse, now that I know he is actually reading what I write. And I definitely can't face the thought of talking to him on the phone or — Christ — seeing him. Then there's the whole thing with Gabs."

"You mean you can't tell Gabriel if you are in touch with your dad?"

"No. No way. He would be really upset. He'd be crazy. He'd think that it was some kind of betrayal." She paused.

"Are you sure of that, Is?" Susan asked.

"Yep. It's probably the only thing I can't talk to him about."

"It's still that bad?"

"It's worse."

"Gabriel wasn't that keen on your dad when he was little." Susan clicked her tongue. "Well, either we have to think of a way of telling Gabriel or you have to stop bothering with your dad."

They were side by side now.

"Yeah. Except I feel like I owe Gabs. I want to help him despite himself, if you know what I mean. Apart from anything, he's been so good to me with all my fuckups. I don't want to give you the twins shtick, Suze, but there *is* something about being born on the same day or whatever — you know, a weird kind of extra loyalty. Maybe it would be different if we had more siblings, but . . . Well, seeing as it's just us two and we've always been that way and—"

"But come on . . ." Susan waited for the noise of a passing bus to die down. "Come on, Is, surely he's got to take care of himself?"

"Yeah. Yeah, of course, in some ways . . . But I worry that he can't see the problem. It's as if . . . as if Gabs carries this backpack of hatred or hurt with him everywhere these days. And he never takes it off or talks about it. But it stops him sitting still, and it gets in the way when he wants to move. Basically, it's hindering his whole life. And only I can see it. It's ridiculous. I was exactly the same. Until, for some reason, I think Mum's dying changed me." They were coming to the steepest part of the walk. "I left Petersburg two days after Gabriel, Suze, and I was on my own and I had to go back to her flat again and box some more of her papers and stuff up to be shipped here. And I was in the maddest state I have ever been in. It's hard to describe — it's like total obliterating-everything sadness and you feel so on your own with it, because she was no one else's mum, I suppose, and you *are* on your own with it. And I was walking along the canal where she used to live and I crossed the bridge outside — it's the Raskolnikov bridge, where he stops in the book — and I wasn't even crying. More like I had just been punched in the stomach or whatever and was completely winded, completely empty, everything gone inside, everything totally gone, like a child turning around from the fun at a playground and realizing that her mum has left not just for a minute but *forever* — feeling really, really desolate. But on that bridge it was as if I suddenly caught sight of my true reflection in the water — as if I suddenly saw myself with this huge lump of a backpack on my back. And even though it has taken me weeks to get the shit off, all that time in New York sitting at my stupid desk at work, I have definitely done it now — I've taken my backpack off and I've got it where I can see it. Unpack. Face. Sort."

"It's difficult for me to imagine. I've never lost anyone." Susan slowed. They were coming to the entrance to the cemetery. "But I sort of understand. You're stuck. You can't tell Gabriel if you speak to Dad, and you can't speak to your dad without telling Gabriel."

"And now I'm worried that I'm running out of time with Dad too."

They stopped. A crowd was gathering for the next tour of the morning.

"What on earth happened between those two, anyway?" Susan asked.

"Oh, about fifty million things. Apart from the general fact that he was the worst father of all time, Dad used to like to mock and humiliate Gabs in front of other people when he was young. Belittle him. Although it was only when Gabs was older that Dad got seriously nasty. He used to go around to Gabriel's girlfriends' parents' houses and tell them not to trust Gabriel." They set off again. "All kinds of shit went on between them. You remember when Gabs came home from college and put on his play at the Gatehouse? *As You Like It* — you remember?"

"Of course I remember. I went. It was fun."

"Yeah."

"Shame about that horrible review," Susan said. "He was so upset."

"Right." Isabella nodded. "It was a massive thing for him — you know, he had borrowed money from the bank to finance it, rehearsed all the actors, persuaded them not to go up to Edinburgh, directed the play, more or less designed the set, the lighting, everything . . . It was a huge risk, and it meant everything to him — you know what it's like when you're twenty-one. He really wanted to be a director badly. And he thought this was make or break." Isabella looked across. "Well, anyway, that review: Dad wrote it."

Susan stopped. "Oh shit — *no*." Her mouth fell open and she shook her head slowly, her even features aghast. "No . . . That's . . . that's *sick*. All that stuff about how students shouldn't be allowed near the stage?"

"Yep. All of it. Dad was mates with the theater critic and they swapped jobs that week for a joke."

"And Gabriel found out?"

"Wasn't difficult. Dad *told* him."

"You're kidding."

"No. Dad gave him this long horseshit lecture about how he had to understand the cut and thrust of the adult world, and how it was an honest review and it was better that Gabriel heard the truth from him rather than someone else. Let this be a lesson to him. That he should have got a proper summer job and learned how to support himself and stop hanging around. Earn his keep. And . . . and Gabs just lost it. He went crazy. I don't think they ever spoke again. Not alone."

Susan let out a low whistle. "I didn't know. I mean, I had absolutely no idea . . . That was your *dad*."

"Well, Gabriel didn't want anyone to know. So we kept it quiet. What else could we do? It's not exactly the sort of thing you can explain." Isabella shrugged. "And nobody came to the play then, of course, so he lost the money he had borrowed as well."

"My God."

Isabella began walking again. "That was just one thing, Suze. There was a lot of other stuff too. And physical violence between them. All the way through. Though I don't think Gabriel ever struck back. Even though he could have put Dad on the floor."

Susan's voice hardened. "Did your father hit you?"

"Yes, sometimes. When he was angry. Until I was about thirteen."

"Your mum?"

"Not sure. I don't think so. I reckon Dad has all the classic misogyny stuff going—women are to be worshipped or denigrated. Virgins, whores, princesses, dolls, waifs, angels. I think it would go against some twisted machismo of his to hit grown women. He prefers to use money to fuck with their minds."

"No wonder you both hate him."

"I don't hate him, Suze." Two gray squirrels shot out in front of them and raced across the road. "Maybe it's something to do with Mum dying. Or maybe I never absolutely hated him. Not like Gabriel hates him. I just think he's . . . I don't know—that he's emotionally selfish, that he's a bully, that he's congenitally manipulative, abusive . . ." Isabella made a face that acknowledged the ironic humor. "All the things Gabriel has in his magazine."

They were almost at the top of the hill.

Susan clicked her tongue. "You know, I completely missed all the stuff that must have been going on in your house. I mean . . . I suppose you don't see the whole story when you are little. You think someone's dad is strict or whatever, or their mum is a bit mad, but there's no reason that you'd get beyond that." They stood aside to let a family pass, and Susan turned to face Isabella. "Of course, I remember the stuff when we were older. All that palaver about your boyfriends. What was *that* about?"

"Don't ask."

"And those fights you used to have with him. You screaming. Bloody hell, Is, it makes me cringe just to think about them."

"Not as much as me."

They came to the edge of Pond Square.

"Now I think about it," Susan said, "the last time I saw him — God, it must have been before you went — the last time I saw him was in your kitchen. He started telling me all this rubbish about how hard it is out there and you've got to learn your lesson and pull your weight and pay your way and all of that. He was so snide. I didn't know what to say. I was furious."

"There's nothing *to* say. Dad just repeats himself to anyone who is around. Or he used to. It's a kind of self-validating mantra or something."

"And I thought, Hang on a minute — I work seventy hours a week and what the hell has he ever done, anyway? Six or seven jobs on local rags — part-time at best — while his wife has worked solidly for twenty-five years as a copy editor on a serious and stressful newspaper *in her second bloody language.*"

Isabella had to smile.

"Apart from anything else," Susan said, "it's very hard to understand why a man like your dad, who's basically had a pretty good life, should have such a sense of grievance."

"That's just it. That's exactly it." Isabella nodded and turned her head to meet her friend's eyes, appreciative of the accuracy of the observation. "He *does* have this overwhelming sense of grievance. And it sort of permeates everything he says and does and thinks. He can't get away from it. Every conversation, every action, everything has some reference to this grievance of his. Which we all have to acknowledge and dance around, even though none of us — including him — have any idea what specifically he is so aggrieved about."

"I guess it's also a way of building himself up," Susan suggested. They were walking along one side of the square, watching for a break in the traffic.

"If you're doing better, he wants to pull you down," Isabella said. "If you're doing worse, he wants to gloat. He's only got one mode of discourse. He can't converse — all he can do is goad."

"Maybe that's just how he is with people our age, Is, or his children or something." Susan shrugged. "Maybe he's completely different with other people when you're not around."

They crossed the main road and walked toward the Grove, the tall Georgian houses seeming all the finer in the sharp winter's sun.

Susan looked across. "Have you thought what you are going to ask Francis?"

"I'm going to ask him lots of questions about the house and I'm going to be very normal and then —"

"No. You need to actually ask him outright if he was your dad's lover, Is." Susan's expression was pure, wholehearted sincerity. "You need to do that. You have to be absolutely no shit now. And you've got to start today. If you don't, I will. I mean it. You cannot spend the rest of your life kowtowing to whatever messed-up version of reality your dad enjoys. We'll just have to think of a way of telling Gabs."

Two hours later, Susan caught the bus back down the hill and Isabella set out alone, wearing her friend's gloves for the return walk, the sky still a burnished December blue. She knew two more things for certain now: that she could enter her old home without weirdness after all, and that gentle old Francis had indeed been her father's lover. Most of all she felt relieved. But, curiously, she also felt (at last) that she was nearly as old as her father and mother — not in age, but in the sense that she was no less an adult than they, and not in the fake way she had pretended to be an adult in her twenties but for real: parity. Perhaps it had been Susan's influence.

The cemetery tours were thriving. Old ladies bossily shepherding groups this way and that.

Karl fucking Marx.

Fierce histrionics or fierce history (there was, as ever, no way of telling), she had once seen her mother cry real tears at that grave. Tears for the parlous state of her marriage, tears for her fate, tears for the fate of nations. Or tears for Karl himself and all the murder done in his name. Impossible to know. Impossible even to guess. But she could remember the afternoon clearly — could see the fresh flowers, bright yellow and crimson, lying scattered on the hard cut stone, could the hear the hushed voices of the visitors (as if the dead might be further offended — beyond the final insult of mortality), could feel her mother, not much older than she was now, letting go of her arm to press the heel of a hand into the corner of one eye, then the other.

And even as an eight-year-old girl, Isabella was conscious that she was supposed to see her mother's tears. And conscious that she was absolutely *not* supposed to see them. That was the whole reason she had been brought along: to see tears and not to see tears.

34

For His Due

THE SICKNESS was on him. The sleeping pills were wearing off. He hadn't got any. All he had to do was get up, somehow. Go. Find some. (Call Grisha.) Then this would be over. He hadn't got any. (Club Voltage — go there.) The stink was unbearable — acrid. Each cramp a fresh agony. Make it quicker, God, make it quicker. You bastard. Make it quicker. The smell was the worst thing. And this was him: this body, in these moments. He was this man. Cramp. Shudder. Flesh like a gray plucked goose. (All he had to do was get up.) His stomach squirting. So onto his side, braced against it. His eyes squeezed shut and watering. His nose streaming. Then eyes open again — used syringes. Onto his back. The sallow ceiling. So ill. He was sweating the mattress sodden. Then eyes shut — a blackness made of headache reds and flashing yellow shapes. He wanted to die. All he had to do was get some. (Get up and go. Find. Easy. Half an hour?) He was hot. His armpits wet. He wanted it over. (No. Stay — take the rest of the pills.) He could not keep his legs still. Twitching, shifting, jittery. Worms burrowing through his stomach. So back onto the other side. The pain in his bones, an aching that seemed to dwell in his marrow's marrow. Oh God. All he had to do was get some, end it. Then it would be over. (Don't take the pills. Get up and go.) Lizards' feet on his skin. A nip. A tremor. Take the rest of the pills. Use them all up now. Adrenaline. Oh God, he hadn't got any. All he had to do was get some. Roll over. The sear of a sudden spasm. Oh. God. There was liquid shit in the bed now. He could not do this. He could not believe this. He could not believe that this was he, living and conscious through these moments. This was his life. And he had made it so. (All he had to do was get up. If he got up, he could stop the pain. Go out. Get some.) He gulped at the water. He swallowed the sleeping pills, all six. Make it quick. Take this from me, God, you bastard. I owe nothing. (All he had to do.) I have nothing. I know nothing. I am nothing.

35

The Sir Richard Steele

GABRIEL DOUBLED BACK on the Northern Line, a trip no Northern Liner truly enjoyed: down to Camden, then across the platforms, and then up again to Chalk Farm. Felt like treachery, somehow, going up the other branch. He broke ground, the swarming city there to greet him, walked left around the sharp corner, and so set off up Haverstock Hill. He was looking forward to drinking, Sunday or not. He bent forward as the incline bit. The morning's frostiness had been replaced by an unusually strong wind; it was one of those dark and low-skied cloud-scudding London nights when the windows rattle in their casements and the tarpaulin that hangs on the scaffolding flaps and slaps as if it might fly away at any second. Sudden gusts snatch at scarves, toss careful hair awry, or chivvy at the cracked chimneypots and threaten to tear the roof tiles loose, and the forgotten trees sway and creak, heavy branches bending hard upon their natural snap.

He was late. He reached the cheerfully ever-empty Chinese restaurant and the off-license, passed the tall, amber-lighted, stained glass windows, walked beneath the old-fashioned lamps that hung from the side of the building, under the old sign (swinging heavily) on which Sir Richard Steele himself (a little drunk in the wind) continued to watch the footsore folk of London making their way up the endless hill away from the cramp and toil of their city, and so he entered the pub, tousled and ruffled, through one half of the oddly narrow double wooden door.

The noise rose to greet him like a friendly dog as he stepped into the fug. Just inside, to the left, a two-piece band was playing — or rather had that very second finished a song, which Gabriel recognized as "It's Alright, Ma." He excused his way through their audience (all standing and trying to clap with their drinks in their hands) and made for the bar. He took stock a moment and then eased his way along, checking the huddles and clusters sitting cozily in the deep red seats at the tables on his right.

He had the impression that he was moving amid an old, old scene. The pub, proudly named after a fourth-rate playwright, had stood in much the same aspect as he saw it now for some three centuries, a wayside host to countless conversations, fights, kisses, partings, declarations, collapses, dances, intrigues, songs, jokes, and tears — everything but work in fact, and therefore everything important in the lives of its denizens. He loved the place — as did his sister. The Steele's great secret being that it never allowed any one deputation of humanity to get the upper hand. Indeed, he sometimes thought that it was as if the very wood of the long crook-shaped bar held it a truth that any section of society quickly becomes unbearable if left to congregate and fester unchallenged among its own.

There was no sign of Isabella. He had the feeling that she would be in the back room, so he edged around the narrow end of the bar, past the turtle-backed stool-sitters (whose drinks arrived without their seeming to make the slightest movement by way of an order), and then ducked left again, around by the big old table that was really the heart of the place, and so came through the low doorway to the semisecret snug at the rear of the building. In here were four or five homely wooden tables, an aged iron brazier in which a fire glowed, a tall mantelpiece on which several candles burned in empty gin bottles, a high mirror above these, and rows of unread books on either side of the chimney breast. For reasons nobody could quite remember or guess, there was also a life-sized mural of a seminaked and rather camp-looking Christ on the interior wall — he was standing entwined in what appeared to be vines, an expression neither particularly ecstatic nor redolent of recent crucifixion on his face. Isabella was sitting at Christ's feet, poring over a printout of some description.

"What you reading?"

She looked up and raised her eyebrows in greeting. "Dylan interview off the Internet."

"Anything interesting?"

"Not really — more or less says that he can't understand why anyone would want to bother interviewing him when everything that is important is right there, clear as day, in his songs."

"I could have told you that." He smiled and came around to her side of the table to put his arm around her for a moment.

"You have. Many times," she said with mock-weariness. "And you will again."

"They were playing 'It's —"

"I know."

He eyed her glass. "You want another drink?"

"Six vodka and cranberries — easy on the cranberry and as much vodka as they can spare."

"You as well?" Gabriel smile became a grin.

"I blame the parents," she said.

He set off back to the bar to find himself a Guinness to go with his sister's request. It was always good to see her. He had missed her when she left. And he missed her still. She looked as sharp as ever. Though he was not sure quite what he was expecting — her jet-black hair suddenly gray, her brown eyes red with sleeplessness and grief? It had been nearly seven weeks. Was it just his imagination, though, or was she looking thinner since the funeral? Hard to tell. The minute he saw her, he felt that it was his responsibility to ask, his responsibility to look after her. More so now than ever. A strange feeling, because of course she could look after herself in all the obvious ways . . . But still, he had always felt as if it were his duty to keep watch on those deeper parts that she herself did not even acknowledge or recognize.

"So you're at Susan's?" He dropped into the chair she had been saving for him.

"Yeah. Just for a while. I was wondering if I could come to you for a few days, actually. Next week."

"Yeah. Of course." He sipped his Guinness. "You on holiday? What's going on with work?"

"Actually, I have taken a bit of a sabbatical . . . Well, they have let me have a sabbatical."

Gabriel observed his sister closely. Yet another contradiction that Isabella had inherited was that though she was almost clinically obsessed with knowing the whole truth about everything, she herself was one of the world's foremost tellers of halves.

"You mean you sacked it? Or they sacked you?"

"No." Isabella's eyes met his, absorbing his sarcasm. "No, really, I am on a sabbatical. I told them about Mum and that I had stuff to sort out and that I was leaving and that they could either take it as a resignation or whatever but that if they didn't mind, I'd look in on them again when I got back."

He considered. "Sounds like you just walked out and they've no obligation to you—"

"Forgot you were an expert on corporate obligations," she said.

He made a have-it-your-own-way face. But it was principally a way of avoiding taking her on. He considered the wall and Christ's ever-increasing gayness thereupon, then asked, "Are you all right for money?"

"Yeah, for a while. A month or so. I've got a few thousand in the bank, but obviously I'm going to have to sort something out."

"So . . . what are you planning? Coming back to London?" He looked at her. "Or staying in New York?"

"I don't know." She met his eyes.

"Jesus."

"I left Sasha and moved out."

"Jesus."

"Had to."

"Jesus."

Not for the first time, Gabriel found himself stunned by his sister's self-assurance.

"It . . . it's over," she continued, mashing the ice in her drink with her straw. "He is a nice guy, but really he's a child. You know—all kind of secretly competitive and point-scorey, silly subterranean ego games. Can't see the good in good people because he's in the way of himself. And you know—it has to end, or it has to become something new."

"Right." Gabriel understood that these reasons, though quite possibly true, were but the tips of whatever icebergs Isabella had been towing across the Atlantic. But he also knew her well enough to guess the mighty and jagged shape of what moved beneath. And again he could only admire her certainty. "I'm glad for you, Is. If you are sure."

"I'm sure."

He sipped his drink. "Must have been difficult," he said. "Especially since you didn't even hate him."

"It was. It *is*. And no, I don't hate him." She sipped hers.

They fell silent for a moment. He wanted to let her say more of her own volition rather than press her. But the silence continued, and he recognized that she did not wish to do so. There was no demand or strain or artifice between them. He knew she understood that there was a bottomless well on which she might draw at any time. So instead he looked around and asked, "Where are you with not smoking at the moment?"

"I've got this new thing."

"Go on."

"I'm not smoking. But I am smoking. It's like . . . I don't, but I do."

"Oh, right. How does it work?"

"Easy," she said. "I don't smoke. But if I want to, I smoke."

"Uncanny. That's exactly where I am."

"Shall I go and get some, then?" she asked.

"And some more drinks, seeing as you're up."

"Jesus, Gabs, we've just started these."

"I know. But what if there's a terrorist attack and everyone panics and we can't get to the bar?"

She returned seven minutes later carrying glasses in both hands and the cigarettes under her chin.

"You know," Gabriel said, "I wish someone would give *me* a sabbatical."

"*Self-Help!* still shit?" Isabella offered him her match.

"Shittier than ever." He inhaled and felt almost immediately sick. "I'd like a sabbatical from myself too, while they're at it. A year off. A year out. Whatever they call it." He noticed that the two men who had sat down at the other table had started looking at Isabella. "Want to come and work for Randy?"

"No," she said flatly.

"Great benefits — enough homoeopathic water to drown your sorrows, tankloads of Rescue Remedy if that doesn't work, and herbal teas to revive you at the end of your long hard day of fooling yourself. You'll love it. Hmmm . . . these cigarettes taste lovely. Tar, nicotine, ash. Gives me that special inner glow everyone talks about."

Isabella smiled. "Why do you need another bad writer on the staff?"

Gabriel took a deep drink of the fresh pint to cleanse his mouth. "I need anyone who is prepared to do any work of any description without crying, walking off, sulking, bitching, pretending to do it and then not doing it, phoning their union representative, or calling me names. I may well be an utter penis. I accept this charge. But we still need to do the bloody work." He paused. "Christ, Is, even to see a member of staff coming back from lunch would make me uncontrollably happy."

"Maybe you should get a motivational speaker in." Isabella leaned her head to one side. "I hear that they are very . . . motivational."

"Oh, they are. I've heard a few. They're highly effective. They motivate everyone to become motivational speakers as fast as possible. Lots of money for the same old shit over and over again. Easy hours. Everyone loves you. And nobody can hold you to account or remember what you said. Perfect way to earn a living." Gabriel smiled, then suddenly remembered a work conversation from a few days previously. "Hey — actually a friend of mine, Becky, told me about an assistant producer job on this new *Culture Show*. I'll get in touch with her if you'd like to meet up. Might even be good. You never know."

"Thanks, Gabs. Why not? No sense ruling anything out." Isabella squinted against her shortening cigarette's acridity. "Well, that's our careers dealt with. And I've done my relationship news. Over to you. What's the Lina situation?"

Gabriel considered his drink. He had three quarters of pint to finish before he could legitimately lobby for the next.

"I don't know," he said.

"You don't know? Or you do know? But you don't know how to end it?"

"Both. Neither. All three."

"What's the core of it?"

"I can't live without Lina. I can't live without Connie."

"You can." Isabella stubbed out her cigarette.

"Which?"

"Both."

"Easy to say. Not easy to do."

"For your own good."

"My own good is entirely lost to me. I know you're clear about everything, Is. And I'm pleased for you that you are. Really. But for me — I don't know — everything is complicated and shaded and there's no clarity."

"Not true."

"What do you mean?"

"You know what you hate."

"Do I? Sometimes I think I just invent that as well."

Isabella bent to drink from her straw, looking up at him as she did so. "Are you having a breakdown?"

"No." Gabriel sat up straight. "I am the one still at my job and still with my girlfriend. Still living in the same place. Are you?"

"Still with two girlfriends. Still hating your job. Still pretending."

"Don't knock denial. Sometimes it's the healthiest place to be." He tapped his remaining cigarette. "Humanity has achieved all of its greatest successes in denial. I'm a big supporter of denial. If you could march under denial's banner without denying it, then I'd be at the front of the parade."

Isabella looked back at him and said, half seriously, "I think you should talk to someone."

"That's because you've been living in America."

"No it's not."

"I don't want to investigate myself, Is. I don't want to hold up any more mirrors to myself. I'm sick of myself. I'm the most tiresome person I know."

"I feel insulted."

"Okay, the most tiresome person I know apart from you." He passed the halfway point of his Guinness. "Christ, Is, I'd *love* to talk to someone, but I haven't got five years and the thousands of pounds needed to wade through all the idiotic so-called therapists, shrinks, and other secret lovers-of-the-self to get to the someone who actually knows anything useful or pertinent. Take it from me, psychology is just the same as every other subject in the world — there are five people who know what they're talking about. And they're not talking. The rest are just rehearsing various forms of ninth-hand crap. Anyway, you're the one who has left everything — boyfriend, work, continent. You're the one on the run here. I'm all sorted. Look at me. Happy. Happy as an organic pig in fair-trade shit."

"Not the same as a breakdown. I am running *toward* the issue. I am truly sorting things out. Taking things on. Not hiding." She stopped to drink through the straw again. "It's bad, isn't it?"

"What?"

"Going around with your brain in flames all the time."

"You do that too?" He poked his cigarette violently into the ashtray.

"More or less every second of the day. I wake up and I can't stand the news — the radio and the TV — not just the crap that's on but the *way* that it's on, and the way that the people behind it try to make it seem. I hate the whole thing. I hate that the newsreaders stand up because their stupid producers told them that standing up is cool. And I hate it when they sit down because some idiot told them to sit down again."

Gabriel picked up. "Oh, I am way past that. I have started actually hating individual words. I hate the word 'mayo.' I hate . . . I hate 'latte.' I hate people who say 'win-win' or 'going forward.' I hate sports writers who cite that fucking Kipling poem."

"That's nothing. I have even started to hate the *font*—that fucking font they use on those women-and-shopping books. I mean, how can a *typeface* become so insidious?"

"No. Don't." Gabriel shook his head. "Do not start me on typefaces. That stuff gets me really angry."

She narrowed her eyes. "I hate every billboard I ever see. Like, I am *not* in conversation with your fucking stupid brand. There is no relationship. I don't know you. I don't like you. I don't want to know you or to learn like you or feel part of your phony cl—"

"Okay. Okay, okay." Gabriel interrupted, holding up both hands. The two men at the adjacent table were listening in, he could tell, watching his sister's animation with ever more frequent glances. "Feel better?"

"Yes. Thank you." She finished her drink. "You?"

"Remember, you are a nut case, Isabella. The rest of the world is just going to work, the supermarket, on holiday. We are the ones with the problems."

"Speak for yourself."

"I do. That doesn't help either."

Chumps, the pub cat, an intelligent-looking ginger with bright eyes and a languid manner that spoke of a happy, untroubled life full of food and the loving whispers of some latter-day Aphrodite in both his ears, blocked Gabriel's route to his chair on his return. Man and cat exchanged glances a moment; cat accused man of crimes innumerable, man pled guilty and enduring disgrace; then cat set off at a contemptuously slow pace toward the kitchen, allowing Gabriel to put down the drinks at last.

"Did you get any letters?" Isabella asked.

"No. Only one or two ages ago. Like I said, I used to get phone calls. More or less every night . . ."

"I don't know if that is more or less weird."

"It was pretty harrowing . . . she wouldn't let me go. She kept me on the phone for hours."

Last orders had been called. The men at the other table had left and they were alone in the room. One of the candles was guttering on the mantelpiece. Jesus seemed to be slouching a little above them. And the alcohol was deep and warm in their veins. Their conversation had ranged and wandered, but now there seemed to be nothing else worth talking about.

"What did she say in her letters?" Gabriel asked. "I'd love to read them. I get scared I am forgetting her."

"You won't. You never will."

"I wish I'd recorded her voice or something."

"Don't you hear her all the time in your head?"

"I used to—a lot," he said. "But now . . . now it's changing. Now I talk to her, but she doesn't talk to me so much. You?"

"I catch myself all the time—thinking with her mind, almost. Thinking her thoughts. But no, you're right—I suppose I don't hear her voice specifically."

Gabriel picked at the dried wax on the neck of their candlestick-bottle. "What did the letters say?"

"Nothing, really . . . Well, that's not true." Isabella sipped her pepper vodka. "Just all mixed up, you know—about the Russian government and Chechnya and all of that . . . America going backward too, the stuff I told you about—Jefferson—that the Founding Fathers were great men who believed in all the right things and how disgusted they would be if they could see what was happening. And you—she talked about you a lot . . . About your work and what you were going to do and how you had to be shocked into something radical."

"I wish."

"And other stuff. About how . . ." Isabella's latest cigarette seemed to make her cough. "About how she loved Dad. And how I was supposed to go and see him."

Gabriel looked up, his eyes liquid black and shimmering in the candlelight. "What for?"

Isabella frowned, lowering her brows as if to duck the direct question that she feared he might ask. "She said . . . She said that he would . . . She said that he was a little schemer or something and that he would be sure to distort everything."

He kept his gaze on his sister, compelling her to continue.

"She said that he would want to be certain —"

"About what?"

"Certain that I . . . that I loved him, Gabs, especially now that he was getting older."

"He made her life a wasteland of misery and suffering *for over thirty years*. Every good thing she offered him, he sneered at, he scorned, and he trampled upon. He can be certain that —"

"But distort *what*, Gabs?"

"Who gives a fuck?"

"I need to speak to him to find out."

"No. No, you don't." Gabriel took half his Talisker at one sip. "You need to speak to him for oth —"

"Gabs, Dad has had a stroke." She lowered her eyes. "I went home to talk to Francis about storing some stuff there this morning. He told me. Dad has had a stroke. I thought you should know."

36

Pat's Place

H E WALKED WITHIN HIMSELF. And there was nothing about him to suggest that he was Russian and only six hours in the country — none of the usual giveaways, at least: not the luminous tracksuits of the poor, nor the leather jackets of the racketeers, nor the overdone designer suits and jewelry of the moneyed; nothing to suggest he was a foreigner at all save a barely detectable apprehension in the movement of his head, which turned too quickly this way and that, seeking to absorb as much of the vast, strange, teeming city as he could. He feared police, spot checks, authority. He was in his boots, his jeans, and an anonymous sweater — no coat, despite the gusting wind. Beneath, he felt as tense as a submariner under the ice. But his aim was invisibility.

After the Internet café — his first job to make contact — he had decided to attempt the exploratory journey from his hostel on foot, surreptitiously following the map he had printed out — eight cheap pages that did not quite meet at any of the borders. He did not expect anything back today, but he hoped that tomorrow, by noon, this Gabriel would reply.

Presently he stopped again, turned his back on the traffic, and leaned into an alleyway, trying to read the smudgy print. He had been sick on the plane — a terrifying experience that had left him knotted and shaking — and even now the queasiness lingered and he hunched rather than stood at his full height.

He reemerged and met the suspicious eyes of a man setting up a newspaper stand. He went quickly on. A muscle worked in the hollow of his cheek. The map appeared to indicate that the Harrow

Road flowed easily onto the Marylebone Road or crossed the thick-drawn Edgware Road at an obvious right angle, but there was no clear way through the giant intersections he had come upon, and the foot tunnels confused him further. So for half an hour he wandered around the Paddington basin, crossing and recrossing the pretty canal, which reminded him of home, except for the great glassy office developments and thunderous overpasses, which reminded him of Moscow. Eventually he saw a sign pointing to Paddington station. He followed its direction. At least the station would be a way of placing himself on the map again. From Paddington to Marble Arch looked easy enough.

Gone the tenebrous gray of the Russia he knew best — the suburbs, the orphanage, Vasilevsky's dilapidation. Gone the ruin and collapse. And gone the somber monotone of Russia itself. Instead, as he came to Oxford Street, his ears were full of the strange singsong beauty of the English spoken all around, and the air seemed to resonate with the chimes of a hundred different registers, voices, music. He could scarcely believe it. I am in London, he whispered to himself. *Ya v Londone.*

The dusk swept in. He could not think what else to do, and the warmth and hum of the Soho bum-boy bars made him feel his foreignness and poverty too hard. So he stood in the doorway of a sex shop and read his map by the intermittent light of a flashing plastic cock. Then, resolved on his new direction, he set off to look at the South Bank.

Gone too the heavy brown assumption that had long smothered his life and that he had not known the shape or meaning of until now: gone the assumption that change was impossible. And nobody — no police, no militia — asking for his papers.

He crossed the river by Waterloo Bridge and stood for five minutes, staring in disbelief at the Queen Elizabeth Hall, where so many of his heroes had played. He had imagined some great theater — something like the Mariinsky perhaps — not a concrete Soviet-style shit hole.

After a while he turned to face the blustery Thames and take in the abundance of lighted buildings on the opposite bank — old, new, grand, plain, stately, and grotesque — seemingly built without care or reason, to his Petersburg eye, as if a drunk had long been in charge of planning, only sober once every fifth day.

He walked upriver. The water relieved his apprehension a little. Faintly he felt the stirrings of new desires, appetites he had not known before. In the underpass he shook his head at a homeless young guy begging, who asked him, "What's so funny?" Then, all of a sudden, he came upon the exact picture he remembered from the history textbooks of his childhood. The bullshit Houses of bullshit Parliament. The light from the windows shimmering in the water.

Halfway across Westminster Bridge, he slowed and then stopped. The passersby were in hats and coats. He realized they must think it cold. He leaned on the rail. And he wondered if he had the nerve to stay—regardless. The water was black, but not as black as the Neva. The wind blew his hair this way and that.

Pat's Place was grotty even by Russian standards. And his morale had fallen on the long walk back, the elation vanished, the map driving him mad and the night wind bringing with it a return of his sense of foreboding and vulnerability. His moods were like the weather. He lived within them. And he no more thought of asking why he experienced one feeling rather than another than he would have thought of interrogating the snow.

A collapse of drunks shouted something to him as he crossed to the door beside the minicab office. The two sitting on the stairs outside were users. Inside, another—Turkish by the look of him—was lying on the floor of the landing, pretending to have lost his key, but Arkady doubted that he had ever had one. Scum—everywhere, scum. Bosnian bullshit. Albanian sewage.

If he did not eat, go anywhere, or do anything, then he had enough money for ten nights. His flight back to Riga was booked for the Sunday fourteen days hence. So somehow he was going to have to find somewhere even cheaper, or join the Turkish bear-fuckers on the landing. Unless tomorrow's reply contained the offer of an immediate meeting and plenty of money up front. Not fucking likely. Probably just a bullshit coffee and a bullshit conversation. In fact, the sooner this whole bullshit was over, the better . . . Why was he even here? What a joke. What an embarrassment.

He walked softly up the narrow stairs to the second floor and stood framed on the threshold for a moment. He stepped within and moved slightly to one side so that the dim light of the corridor behind could better illuminate the small dormitory room. There were

four bunks—two on either side, with the narrowest of aisles between them. The one above his was empty. But he saw that those
opposite were now taken. The window beyond was open. Hence the
noise. Two tattered backpacks were propped up beneath the sill, a
towel draped over one, a baseball cap on the other.

He checked under the bed. His greatcoat was still there. And his
pack had not been touched. He was angry with himself. He would
take no further risks.

He took off his sweater and his shirt and unbuckled his money
belt. There were no covers, no blankets, not even a second sheet.
Pat's Place provided beds, and beds only. And he had not brought
anything to sleep under. He stood for a moment, considering. People
were shouting in the street below. He pulled off the sheet, and the
streetlight shone dully on the surface of the rubber pad beneath. At
least here in London they tried to save the mattresses from the worst
of the alcoholics. He put down the money belt where his head would
lie and drew the sheet back over it. Then he turned to the window
and fastened it shut.

He listened for a moment before stepping carefully out of his
jeans and rolling them up. He removed a plastic bag of clean laundry
from his pack, took out a T-shirt and pulled it on, then flattened the
rest of the bag out to fashion a pillow. He laid his jeans across the
top and the shirt he had been wearing over them. The room was too
close. He needed cold air to sleep. He opened the window again, fastened the latch against the wrench of the wind. Then he placed his
pack against the wall, picked up his greatcoat from under the bed,
and laid himself down beneath it.

Yes, the sooner this bullshit was over, the better. All he had to do
was survive two weeks. He wondered what he would do back in Petersburg. The thought of playing in the bars made him so angry that
saliva poured into his mouth and he wanted to spit. Work for Leary.
Make a fortune. That stupid bitch. He closed his eyes and turned to
face the wall.

But he neither slept nor rested. Long after the other two returned
(talking at normal volume in Moldavian accents before belatedly
whispering when they became aware of him), and long after they
had fallen asleep, he lay uneasily alert, watching the lights and the
shadows on the wall sweeping, merging, steadying—swelling circles, diagonal lines, penumbras and silhouettes—the headlamps of
the cars as they turned, the streetlights, the glow from the shop op-

posite, the fizz and flicker of the neon sign that advertised cosmetics. Apart from anything else, he wished that he were here as himself. There would be some comfort in that.

Mice moved in the wall. The elder of the two Moldavians began to snore on the lower bunk, less than four feet away. He set himself to listen to the city instead. But all the usual sounds — car doors closing, breaking glass, motorbikes, cans being kicked, drunken shouts, the muffled thump of angry music, the hiss and squeal of bus brakes, unnatural birdsong, a dog barking crazily somewhere on the edge of his hearing — all the city sounds seemed now to threaten and loom, alien and strange, as if each were just another moment in a gathering drama, the aural narrative of developing violence that would soon involve him and that would surely culminate in a vicious raid — gangs or, worse, the police bursting through the door. The blaze and stab of flashlights. Guns, snarled orders. The Moldavians panicking.

All the while the wind was growing stronger, banging and slapping, rattling at the window. He turned and turned again back to the wall. He told himself that London was nothing compared to Moscow or Petersburg. In the long years he had waited for his place at the conservatory, though only on the fringes, he had seen more death than those of his fellow orphans who had joined the army. But the difference was that in Russia, he knew the face and weight of every danger; in Russia, he knew what they wanted, why, and how they planned to take it. Here, now, he had no idea. He was blind.

A woman screamed.

She sounded as though she were directly beneath the window. A car pulled away, engine straining. Doors slammed. He lay rigid. Voices. Men. Swearing.

He had heard the stories and believed them well enough — London, the European capital of organized crime: the Albanians, the Turks, the Croats and the Serbs, the Jamaicans, the triads, the Irish, the Islamic cells, other Russians, the Nigerians, the Colombians, the plain old-fashioned mafia; people smugglers, drug smugglers, weapon smugglers; prostitutes, heroin, explosives. The whole world liked to squat right down and do its nastiest possible shit in London. He was not afraid for his well-being or even his life (if only they would take it quickly, get the fucking thing out of the way), but he feared the police, he feared robbery, and most of all he feared violence.

Blue lights came swirling across the ceiling, sweeping from one side of the room to the other, then stopping directly above him, as if spotlighting him for some provincial nightclub's amateur dance competition. The Moldavians were awake now. They would all be arrested as part of the raid or fight or whatever it was that was happening out there. He would be sent back. Before he had his chance. All three floors of the hostel, he knew, were heaving with people that even a blind Gypsy cocksucker would recognize as illegal — construction workers, cooks, waitresses, cleaners. He could not understand why the police did not raid it every night.

There was the sound of heavy footsteps on the stairs, but going down, not coming up. He did not know whether to rise and dress or lie still. Where would he go? More voices outside — a man and a woman's, raised. Another, quieter voice answering. The older Moldavian got up from the bottom bunk. The sirens had stopped, but the blue continued to swirl.

Now there were footsteps coming up. If the money went, he would have to steal. If his passport went, he would never be able to prove he was the man he was pretending to be. But even that he could survive. It was physical violence that scared him to a tight and silent shiver. Not because he was physically afraid — he had faced a gun, *preferred* a gun — but because of his lifelong curse: he had to protect his hands. Simply, he could not fight back. He could not lift a single finger to defend himself. He could not risk anything. As long as he held to the identity of musician, he was as vulnerable as a limbless cripple. Oftentimes in his dreams he had hoped for some knife slash to sever the tendons, some hammer to crush his fingers, some axe to separate a joint, so that it would be over, the stupid hope, so that he could ball his fist just once.

The Moldavian spoke in his heavy accent, the sound of Russian comforting all the same. "The police are taking the woman away. It's okay, Mikhail, lie down. Just filthy British motherfuckers again. Cannot take their drink."

37

The Subtle Logic of Desire

MONDAY. WORST DAY of the week the wage-slavery world over. But at least the wind had dropped. And at least the next magazine—"You Meets You"—was a good while away yet. He looked idly through some of the putative cover questions:

"If you met yourself, would you like yourself?"

No.

"If you met yourself, what would you say?"

Fuck off, asshole, and sort your life out while you're about it.

"If you met yourself, where would you go for a romantic mini-break?"

Palestine. Rwanda. Or maybe East Timor.

"Why?"

Teach myself a lesson.

Aside from the worst piece he had ever read—"How to Be Single and Satisfied"—this was the entirety of the "You Meets You" issue thus far.

He did have an idea that he would like to commission: "How to Laugh about Everything in Your Life When It's Not Funny at All." But for this to work, it would have to be a spread, a good read, and that would require him to find a knowledgeable writer capable of an engaging style and a sophisticated grasp of tone and register. Fat chance. Anyway, bollocks to it—the deadline wasn't for two weeks and he was ahead of himself: he'd got the issue title, which was more than he usually had at this stage. He clicked on one of the news pages he kept as a favorite . . . Another day here on Earth. Another

day of attrition, murder, beauty, and birth. Another day of six billion
soloists at full lung, all hoping for some miracle of harmony.

And for him, sitting there, drifting through all this on screen after
screen . . . For him, another day of thinking in ever tighter circles.
And no doubt about it, he was as implicated as anyone else. His
world, his time, his life. Agreed, nobody expects meaningful every
day or even every week, but intermittently worthwhile must surely
be possible, right? How to make something of his life while he still
had a chance, though? How to weigh in on the right side, whichever
side that was? Before it all tapered down to feed, clothe, pay for,
look after the children, hang on to the wife, get *through* it. Hey, Ma,
you'll be proud: I got through it! I worked. I had some kids. Made
some money! Yep, I really followed my own path out there. I'm a
granddad! Anyway, it's over. Coming, ready or not. And how had he
arrived in this position? (His hypocrisy he imagined like a mucous
membrane around everything — everything he thought, said, did.)
How had he become so very faithless and unfaithful? Hey, Ma, help
me: what what what *what* do I really believe?

Phew, lunchtime.

He called Connie.

One good thing: eagerly, before he left, he replied to the e-mail from
his mother's Russian friend suggesting that if this suited, Arkady
Alexandrovitch should come around to his home this Sunday, for
lunch — Gabriel's sister would be around then, and she would love
to say hello too. He wanted a proper afternoon with the guy. Not
some quick after-work thing. He wanted to hear stories of his mother.

The six o'clock call to Stockholm revealed all to be well, but on
nights like these, when he wasn't supposed to be here, there, or anywhere, the corners of his eyes swarmed with dangerous people: unexpected encounters with long-lost friends ("It *is* you. I thought
so. How are you? I must give Lina a buzz . . ."); chance escalator
passings-by of her colleagues (puzzled faces, recognition, belated
wave); yet another of her half-brothers covertly spotting him on the
platform at Swiss Cottage. It was a slim chance that he'd run into
anyone while out with Connie, but then, slim chances were the entire
story thus far — *Homo sapiens,* evolution, gravity, the universe itself,
one overwhelmingly slim chance after another.

· · ·

Eight, and they were locked into yet one more urgent conversation in the bar at the end of her street in West Hampstead: lovers trying to be friends trying to be sensible trying to be good trying to be anything but lovers trying to be friends.

Midnight. And oh, but how the subtle logic of desire mocks the plodding reason of the mind.

Tuesday morning. He awoke beside her. Instantly he knew he wasn't going in to work.

They drank tea and talked and ate sweet pears with broken pieces of chocolate. And he watched her kneeling on the floor in her white sweater and nothing else as she watered her plants — all brought inside to protect them from the frost and placed on the money pages of the weekend papers, side by side, in their little pots beneath her bedroom windowsill.

"I still don't agree," she said. "When lies are thought to be okay — more interesting than being honest. And when what is true carries no weight — in the family, or in the country, or in the press, whatever; it's the same principle — when what is true carries no weight, then everything becomes equal and alike and there's no firm ground. Everything is everything. Everything is nothing. We can't find our way."

He sipped his tea. "And so what happens then?"

She turned to look at him and smiled. "If we are clever, we glamorize amorality as our defense. And we burnish this defense until it shines brighter than any other. We strip the truth of its privileges. And we become powerful. Because we can destroy anything we wish." She pointed the old kitchen spray bottle that she was using as a watering can at him. "As in the family, so in politics, so in the press."

He wanted to pick her up, carry her the three steps back to bed, kiss her pretty knees.

"You're right. In one way. Maybe it is a defense. But not against others."

"Against who, then?"

He reached out to touch her, but she kept her distance, weapon at the ready. "I think that when everything is everything, as you put it, then the result is not really power — no, it's more like obsessive doubt. A distrust of all sides of the argument. Or a belief in all sides of the argument. It amounts to the same thing. Belief and doubt become identical twins."

"You're too clever and too stupid to deal with," she said.

"When everything is discredited—when everything is discreditable—then we are able to believe only to the extent that we can doubt. Neither one outbraves the other."

"But I like you." She met his eyes and held them. "This is the last time, Gabriel."

The first snow started that afternoon as they climbed Parliament Hill. Though they had left her bed only an hour earlier, it was past four and the light was fading. They walked side by side. There was almost nobody else abroad, and even the path ahead was vanishing as they went on. Despite the cold, his hands felt warm and his blood was easy. They reached the top and halted, standing together. London lay before them, but disappearing now, house by house, quarter by quarter, as the city wrapped itself deeper in its shroud. A fresh flurry bent in from the north, heavier still, and she let go of his hand to pull up her hood so that all he could see as he turned to her was her face framed, and the snow alighting in the escaping wisps of her fair hair, half melting, running clear down her cheek to her lips, which beckoned as though the very pair to his own. And gradually it seemed to Gabriel that once again the world itself was fading—that time and space themselves were in retreat, and that there was only he and she standing there alone in the holiness of the snowfall.

Later, when they came to a place where the path was muddy and there was no way around, even though she insisted that there was no need, he bent and lifted her onto his back because he wanted to carry her across. He held her legs in his arms and he felt her warm breathing by his ear, her body against his; and if he could have halted everything, if he could have commanded the world to cease its turning and all creation to end, he would not have hesitated. Without a moment's pause, he would have stopped the beating of every other creature's heart—all in the name of his selfish certainty that he would never again know a moment as pure and replete with happiness and love as that instant.

38

A Proposal

My dear Isabella,

I write with a proposal. Why don't you come here for Christmas? You don't have to answer straightaway. But do have a think about it. I need hardly sell you Paris as a "destination." (Aren't they awful, these words the journalists come up with? I assume it's they. It usually is.) Do you remember the Île St. Louis — the place where we used to have those ice creams? It's just upstream from Notre Dame. I can't remember the last time we were all here together. I think it must have been when you and G were much younger. Twelve, ten? I daresay you've been here many times since then, though — probably know the city inside out. In any case, everywhere is nearby, and you must feel free to bring whomsoever you choose so that you can do as you please. There's plenty of room. And I'm very lucky: it's a beautiful apartment — the original buildings date from the 1400s, though there have been one or two rebuilds since then. You should see the place for yourself: the front windows face the Seine, and the guest bedroom (yours whenever) looks out over the courtyard. It's really no great leap of the imagination to see the horses drawing in and the servants bustling about and all of that. Perhaps I am spending too much time indoors — I cannot get out without help at the moment — but you know what I mean, I think.

No word from you for a while . . . Perhaps you are away or busy at your job. I confess, ever since your last, I have been looking forward to hearing from you. How is New York? I find it hard even to imagine your life there. I've started to think I might never see the place . . . I'd love to have your impressions—though I suppose they are more than that now. How long have you been there—four years, five? America needs a fundamental rethinking, I would say. They all seemed so much happier over there in the sixties and seventies. Maybe it's just the folk that make the news bulletins these days, but suddenly the country seems so terribly adolescent again. It's as if they're going backward. (This was a favorite idea of YKW, of course . . .) The new Americans all seem so embattled and apprehensive and overwrought all the time. Whatever it is that they feel they have to assert, defend, uphold, it doesn't appear to be doing them any good. I'm going on, I know.

Frustratingly, my recovery is much slower than I had first hoped. It seems to go in stages. Quick spurts and then nothing tangible for a week or two. I still can't really walk properly, though my speech is almost fully recovered, thank god. I can't describe the sheer *irritation* that comes with not being able to do at all that which only a few weeks back one could do without thinking.

Anyway, I don't know what your plans are, and you may well have something lined up for Christmas by this stage. If so, New Year's? It would be lovely to see you. I know you will be cross, but my circumstances are different now, and I feel that I can claim the invalid's privilege of directness. I am happy to pay for your flights (and those of your friend), and if you really do not wish to stay here (and I would quite understand), there is a fine hotel just around the corner; I'm sure I could arrange for you to stay there.

As you see, I have managed to write a fair amount without addressing a single one of your questions about Masha, our lives together, or anything else! I'm sorry, but I don't think I yet have the energy to write all that down in an e-mail. It seems so cold, apart from anything else. But I would dearly like to talk to you again—about that, about everything. So do please have a think about my offer, and maybe I will see you for Christmas!

Yours with love,
Nicholas

39

Gabriel Decides

THE FOLLOWING SATURDAY, the sky was like the underbelly of a sick gray seal. They were out searching for he did not know what — a desk, new covers for the futon that matched the old, stripy tea towels, a fashionable garlic press? He could not remember. Camden Market was as thoroughly wet and cold as he had ever known it. Damp saturated the bones and the winter rain fell — unremitting, unenthusiastic, unwholesome. The old brickwork of the arches above the bigger stores seemed to be cold-sweating out two hundred years' worth of fever and toxins; the awnings of the smaller stores sagged and threatened calamity; the hot-food booths were lost in steam, and it was impossible to see any of their offerings through the glass counters for all the pinguid condensation.

Somehow time had managed to crawl as far as three-twenty, and Gabriel was now crammed up at one end of a damp bench, thigh to thigh with a family of tourists from Salford. Doggedly, he was forking his way through a medley of multicolored Chinese food, all the favorites thrown in together — sweet and sour, black bean, oyster mushrooms, nonprawn prawn, reconstituted chicken, debeefed beef. Imagining that he was an astronaut helped: then it tasted kind of interesting, and he felt oddly grateful, appreciative of human science.

It seemed as if it had been three-twenty for ages; as if the whole day had subsided at three-twenty and now lay in a slag heap of wet dust, rubble, and contorted masonry. It felt as if old Father Time himself — exhausted, depressed, sick to the back teeth of the endless tick-follows-tock of it all — had simply downed tools (at long last) and strode offsite, bound for the recruitment agent's office — I want to switch dimensions, chief, I'm through with the fourth; it's not a job, it's bloody slavery, that's what it is. It's about time I traded up. Something out of the range of these ignorant bastards, please. I hear the ninth is cushdie.

The last other time Gabriel could remember was seven-seventeen, when he had been woken by Lina's alarm clock. She liked to set it three minutes before she wanted to get up. And about three hours before he did.

The outer edge of the nearest plastic awning did not quite cover his table, and an uneven veil of runoff water was dripping onto the heads of the poor tourist children opposite as they waited for their oblivious parents to finish ramming spring rolls into themselves. Lina had disappeared.

He returned his attention to his own carton. He wondered how far from an actual chicken a piece of chicken in a Chinese chicken dish could go and still get away with being called a piece of chicken. Of course, these nameless cubes (tasting of chalk and chamois leather) had nothing to do with young hens roaming around the farmyard; nothing to do with the main bits of even a battery bird, not leg nor breast; and nothing to do with the secondaries either — the wings or the feet; nothing to do with livers, gizzards, or neck; nothing to do with bones or beaks or feathers. No — at best, it was just about possible that these bits he was now eating had once been on the same factory floor as other meats that had known a few chicken pieces in their youth. And that was probably all the acquaintance with chicken they had ever garnered. So you had to credit them for their audacity — they were quite prepared to go out into the world armed with nothing by way of a briefing save these old-timers' stories of what chicken used to be and just . . . just fake it, just belligerently pretend. Come on, then, you fuckers, if we're not chicken, then what are we? Huh? If we're not chicken, then don't eat us. Ha . . . see . . . you are doing it! You're eating us! Fucking A.

They had been attempting to have their lunch together amid the busy food booths in Camden Market because it was here that Lina had arrived at the end of her endurance. Having wandered from place to place all the way up Camden High Street, turning down each with some (admittedly accurate) remark on the decor or menu or staff or seating plan, she had become so hungry that she could barely speak. And for some reason her hunger increased at the same rate as her annoyance, so that by the time they arrived at the Old Stables booths at

the Chalk Farm end, she was furious. She could go no farther; she
had to eat. Like Joan of Arc sacrificing herself (for God, for France),
she had thrown herself into the midst of the antiprawn prawns in
sauces unnamed and unnamable. Do unto me what you will; I care
no longer.

Mercifully (or even more destructively), Lina's rages were always
speechless and internal. And though Gabriel genuinely felt for her —
was he not a fellow soldier in the silent wars of the subconscious? —
he had learned to say nothing when she got this way, as she did three
of four times a year. No species of humor, no mode of cordiality,
no method of clowning or conversation could draw her out of the
tight angry spiral into which her spirit plunged. His every gambit
only made it worse. A few days later, when she was herself again,
she would calmly explain that a whole host of troubles contributed
— her parents' divorce, things not exactly perfect, local rudenesses
suffered (perceived or actual), the cold, the wet, the passages of the
moon — but no, he was not to worry, it certainly wasn't anything to
do with him. More and more, though, he had started to doubt her.
No, that too was disingenuous. Actually, he had long been utterly
convinced that he was the root cause — the dark energy that caused
her universe to continue falling apart when it should by now have
stabilized. And if she was not lying to avoid some deeper conflict or
issue (and he could think of one or two), then her endlessly generous
subconscious was protecting them both from the same by citing the
moon. She was displacing. Yes, it was all him.

And so there they were, an hour later, with plastic chopsticks, car-
tons, and sodden napkins. Desperate. The rain and the cold did not
help. Nor that she had not found whatever it was that they were supposed to be looking for. Nor that the whole expedition had been her
idea because she wanted to "do something" with her Saturdays. Nor
that he was, if anything, in far greater disarray than she. Nor, indeed,
that he still loved her with a confusing conviction.

He had watched supportively as she had bought herself her carton's worth. He had watched tenderly as she carefully spread three
purpose-recruited plastic bags across her side of the bench to ensure
no possibility of dampness. He had watched gingerly as she had put
a chopstick's worth into her pretty mouth. He had watched forlornly
as she promptly spat it out into her napkin in disgust.

"I can't eat that," she had said, a look of horror on her face — as
if they two were alone in some forgotten Vietcong camp facing roach
fried rice forever. "I can taste the dye."

"Get something else, then." He was deep into his own carton already.

"How can you eat it?"

"It's not too bad."

She had looked at him as if he were a man capable of surprising her only in his ability to conjure up new lows from human existence. And of course he felt there was nothing else to do but go for another mouthful.

He had meant to antagonize her, perhaps. But he had also actually meant it: there were a million worse meals being served up on the planet every second, and a whole lot of meals not being served up at all. It *wasn't* too bad. He had watched her fold the napkin neatly (almost madly, he thought), lean over, and place it in the nearby bin, following it quickly with the rest of her food. Then she rose silently — incandescent — and set off to get something else to disgust her.

Now she had disappeared.

He wondered how much time he had.

Preoccupied wasn't really the word for it.

He was disintegrating.

And even this he wasn't doing properly, because every time one part of his mind began to address the questions, every time he felt the emotional panic rising as he tried once again to confront himself, another part of his mind would remind him of something horrific happening elsewhere on the planet and in so doing render his own problems and predicament infinitely unimportant, unworthy of thought or time or even feeling. And in this way he continually hijacked himself. But this too he only managed to do unsatisfactorily. (Mania, definitely a mania of some sort.) Because of course he continued to live and think within himself, and within himself the questions remained, returning every few hours, cycling back up to the forefront of his mind regardless of the rest of the world and all its undeniably greater misery. Despite these hijacks, despite everything, he was still himself; still young enough, not subjugated, not tortured, not diseased, not dying, but still living where he lived, a healthy representative of the first adult generation of the new century. The very latest wave of humanity. And he was still required to make an intelligent fair-hearted go of it, just as all the parallel Gabriels he imagined among the Victorians or the Renaissance courtiers or the flappers or the Athenian senators or the Minoans or the Aborigines or the Jutes or the twelve tribes of Israel or the Mongols had been required to make a go of it before him. (Curiously, the beef tasted of . . . of real chicken.) And yet it seemed to him that he was uniquely required to live and act against a social background of near-total doubt. Any other Gabriel from any other time and place would at least have been able to believe in *something*. Sure, these other Gabriels might have had a lot of shit on their plates — war, disease, violent death, and so on. (And better chicken.) But not this . . . not this complete and utter evaporation of all possible belief, or consistency, or any good way for the intelligent man to live. (Might this pale and watery sphere once have been a proud water chestnut?) These other Gabriels had not had to face the fact that God was now well and truly dead, over, a calamitous joke. They had not had to face the fact that the medieval religions had grown senile, demented, and crazed, unable to contend with or relate to the present world in all its instant and tentacled reality (the flavor was inconclusive — might just as well have been a lychee); that, devoid of any great countervailing idea or ideal, capitalism was sweeping all before it (definite oyster mushroom); that conventional politics had been reduced to little more than a fretful soap ("crab" "stick"); that art was now measured not by any external litmus of quality or skill or even endeavor, and that so many seeming acts of creation turned out to be mere gesture and these were celebrated out of all proportion (prawns again, or maybe . . . goat); that all ideas had become small or embarrassing or superficial, languishing in the lowercase (bean sprout — GM, definitely GM); that the strength of an argument was now gauged only by the emotional temperature at which it was delivered; that science had become too fast for the executive or legislative to understand; that the media had grown mad with chasing what they thought the public wanted and the public mad with what the media fed it; that personal experience had become the tyrant of truth (rind? squid? pig's ear?); and that right and wrong were now as lost to the world as a pair of penguins in an underground car park long ago sealed off by an earthquake and flooded over by a tsunami.

All that was left was hedonism and acquisitiveness; all that was left was the self. For the first time in history, it seemed to him (watching the rain drop as the family departed) that for the thinking man, absolutely nothing credible existed; or rather, as he had said to Connie, nothing that could not be readily discredited. And he just wasn't sure the self was up to it. The self much preferred to be selfish.

Worst of all, though, with a third part of himself, he suspected that he was thinking about all this as a deliberate distraction — a means whereby he might cloak his inability to sort anything out in the secular-holy robes of some spurious and self-deceiving faux humanitarianism. Unbelievable: *yet more horseshit*. Which in turn made him feel guilty. To add to the plain and simple guilt that he already felt—and here the cycle began again—about how he was treating the women in his life whom he sincerely loved . . . *Both* of them. Yes, both, Ma: two at the same time. Which was the immediate point. And *stop* dodging it, Gabriel . . .

The veil of rain thickened.

He put down his chopsticks.

Oh Ma, I am the torturer in chief. I am the double traitor with two lives hollow. I am the counterfeiter. I am the simulacrum. I am the one with a shard of ice in his heart. They throw open the secret chapels of their hearts, I walk in, plant my monitoring devices, and leave; they come to me with open eyes, I tweak out their tears. Or else I am hidden, Ma, I am closed off and locked away. Where am I, Ma, where am I, your son? In what lead-lined bunker did you leave me? For what reason? And who . . . who am I? This director of propaganda. This creature never present. This looking-glass man.

But for something like seven seconds a month, the power failed, the burning spotlights were all extinguished at the same time, the noise was roundly silenced, his heart slowed its battering, his breathing deepened, and he glimpsed the naked truth stealing across the darkened stage of his mind between costume changes.

And now at last the decision came, not like a butterfly or a ray of celestial light but in the shape of a fat pigeon beaking its way through the daily jamboree of the fallen Chinese.

Leave her. Leave everyone. Do it now. Start it now. Give yourself no choice.

And he set off at a run through the rain like a man chasing a thief that only he could see.

40
A Raw Day

W HEN THE CALL CAME, she did not recognize his voice. She stood in Susan's hall with the children running this way and that and tried to make sense of what Gabriel was telling her. But she could not process the words — she felt instead as though listening to a stranger describing the actions of a supposedly mutual friend that she wasn't actually sure she knew.

"I've left Lina."

"What?"

"I've taken a room. In Chalk Farm."

"What?"

"I'm there now."

"Gabs?"

"In a shared house. There's a guy from work — they were looking for someone. I've given them a deposit. I had to do it straightaway, Is. I've been . . ."

She clutched the receiver closer, hoping that might help her understand. "Gabs — what — what are you talking about? What have you done?"

"I keep on feeling it all from —" He interrupted himself. "It makes me so angry for every . . . About me, I mean. And sad."

"What — what have you done?"

"Sorry. I have made a decision, Is. No idea if it is the right one. But I couldn't carry on. The whole thing was killing me. Trying to think my way through it all. Seeing it from all the different angles. I just got sick of thinking. It's like the way Mum used to say that Kasparov would beat his opponents: he would complicate it and complicate it until they just got sick of thinking about the problem. Then, eventually, their stamina went. Well, I'm beaten. That's it. I'm moving out."

"Jesus, Gabriel, you're moving out of your flat? You're splitting up with Lina? Are you . . . Where are you?"

"And—and I need you to help me. I have to go back and talk to her now—she'll be worried about me, she keeps calling my mo-bile—but I . . . I need you to help me move my stuff out. I've hired a van. I'm picking it up in King's Cross at eight. I'll do the first run tonight—as soon as—or it will be too late. Sort the rest to-morrow."

"Gabriel, where the hell are you?"

"Grafton Terrace."

"Where's that?"

"Chalk Farm."

"That's just around the corner."

"I know."

"I'm coming . . . I'm coming now. I'll be there in fifteen minutes. Tell me where exactly."

When she arrived, his behavior was the most unnerving she had ever known, odder even than when she had discovered him earnestly playing charades with total strangers on the heath during one of his boyhood disappearances. He was being grotesquely normal. And yet only she seemed to be able to see through the threadbare ordinari-ness of his manner. His dark eyes danced with his intelligence and yet they were ringed with tiredness as if with tar; his hair was straggled dry from the rain and smelled of smoke; his jeans were still soaking at the bottom where he'd obviously drenched himself in puddles. And he would not shut up.

Just like that, he introduced her to all his new flatmates, all five of them in their late twenties and early thirties, as if this were just an-other routine and reasonably considered move in a life of steady progress. There was talk of handy shops. Talk of the local. Talk of a dinner party so that he could get to know their various "other halves." Talk of bills and a few house rules. Talk of a cleaning rota. Talk of the garden's being lovely in the summer. Excited talk of a New Year's party they were planning. He was all agreement, regular-ity, and straight, easy charm. She couldn't believe he was fooling them. A good actor—she had forgotten that—a very good actor. Because he meant it. While he was saying it, he meant it. And he made *her* feel discomfited and deceitful for not going along with it. As though she would be letting down not only him but these great new flatmates too: Claire, Chris, Sean, Louis, and Taz. So she just had to stand there and nod and smile and listen.

Stunned, anxious, panicked, she climbed into the moving van at eight the next morning, the Sunday sky raw as pale flesh before the flogging starts. He had not answered his phone all night. She had left three or four messages. And a part of her was plain relieved that he was here, alive, staring dead ahead from behind the blue plastic wheel, dressed in paint-stained green overalls that she could not imagine her brother wearing, let alone owning, in a million years of trying. She took one look at his face and knew that he had not slept for a moment, nor bothered to try. She said nothing. He would speak or not, as he wished. The radio told of yet another leadership crisis. They set off, brother and sister.

After a while he began to talk — brusque and broken sentences, which she did not question. She understood that Lina had last night cried such terrible silent tears that in the end Gabriel had carried her across the threshold in his arms and driven her, wrapped in a blanket, to her mother's in the van. The bitter opposite of marriage, he muttered. Then he himself had gone to his friend Larry's, at one or two. Beyond that, more or less all he would say was that it was not as bad as Mum, not as bad as Mum, not as bad as Mum, over and over again.

He was no longer pretending to be normal, at least. Instead, for the rest of the morning he was mostly silent or blank. She had not known a more suffocating day — the very air seemed to be shrinking and shriveling from the evolving pain.

And the day did not relent. At one, still feeling helpless, anxious, and now hungry, Isabella stood alone in the cream-colored bedroom that her brother had shared with Lina for the past four years, packing a torn English translation of *War and Peace* into the final box of this trip and wondering if she would make it down to the car with all the remaining plastic bags and the holdall in one go. She did not want to come back up. Gabriel had set off again in the van. Adam was in the car waiting for her. He had been roped in (by Susan) to help. Poor, poor Lina was at her mother's.

Staring at the book, she allowed herself to access the secret cargo of guilt she had been carrying since Gabriel's call for help: perhaps

. . . perhaps indirectly she had been the cause. Had she not in some way prompted him to this decision in the pub? Had she been too forthright about leaving Sasha? By showing off about her decisiveness (and that, she knew, was what she had been doing), had she not thrown his indecision into relief, made him feel his inaction as a fault? And now he had gone and done this. Taken a cheap room in a shared house in Chalk Farm on what looked like the rashest impulse of his life.

She opened the book, knowing well that the inscription would be in her mother's hand.

> Dear Gabriel, I hope one day you will read this book and find in it all the life that I do! Life is all there is — it seems obvious enough, but you will be amazed at how many people forget. And for Tolstoy, as for his Pierre Bezukhov, the only duty is to life itself: "Life is everything. Life is God." Even in the fever of our wars and the squandering of our peace. Happy Birthday! Again!
>
> > Love,
> > Mum

Isabella had the same edition herself, also a birthday present from her mother. Though, as she recalled, her inscription was to do with Tolstoy saying that "the one thing necessary, in life as in art, is to tell the truth."

Oh Mum, Mum, Mum.

The doorbell rang, startling her. Or rather, the doorbell chimed. She put the book in the holdall with the rest, swung it over her shoulder, and then bent to pick up the box and various plastic bags. She remembered (with a bite of her lip) that it had once been one of those nerve-shredding London buzzers, before Lina took action. Now it was a Serenity Chime.

And Isabella had to let it chime serenely all the way to the final chord as she struggled into the hall, the holdall creeping forward and refusing to stay properly over her shoulder, the plastic bags straining at her fingers, the box weighing her down.

Jesus. I'm coming. Persistent bastard. Surely not Gabriel? No, he would come straight up. For a horrible moment she thought that maybe it was Lina, returning impromptu from her mother's, and that there would now be more tears and that terrible slow-motion anguish. And what in Christ's name was she, Isabella, going to say? But then she realized with relief that Lina, of course, had keys to her own flat. And Lina would not come back now the decision had been made, however unconvincingly, however madly. Because in her own way, Lina was far stronger than Gabriel knew. And though he was the emotional vandal now, in the long run it would be her brother whose suffering was greater. Dear God. Ten percent more or less of a bastard and Gabs would have been fine.

The chime built toward its final chord again. She managed to put down the box on Lina's little telephone table without everything underneath sliding to the floor. It must be Adam. He had been waiting with his car and partially blocking the narrow road — maybe there was a warden. Desperate to prevent the whole cycle from beginning again, Isabella grabbed the entryphone, one hand still balancing the box, fingers now white and taut from the heavy handles of the bags.

"Hello. I'm just coming down."

But it wasn't Adam. The accent was East European. "Hello — this is Gabriel Glover?"

"Nope."

"This is Gabriel Glover's house?"

"Yes . . . No. Yes. For about another two minutes, anyway."

"I am sorry. May I speak with Gabriel Glover, please?"

"I'm afraid he's not here at the moment." Some strange friend of her brother's, she guessed. "But I'm coming out. Hang on a second."

For heaven's *sake*. She hung the thing back on the wall, placed the key in her teeth, hoisted box, bags, and holdall, pulled the door shut behind her with her trailing foot. Probably some Sunday thing her brother had forgotten about. Not surprisingly. She put everything down on the stairs, locked the door, jiggling the key against the stiffness, picked everything up again, cursed her brother, and set off for the front door.

She did not regret offering to help Gabriel move, of course — she would gladly have offered to fetch his things from hell itself — but she was conscious that innocent Adam had been volunteered as a supplementary driver without being present at the discussion. And having carried out the best part of a trunk's worth himself, he was no doubt anxious to return to his own (much better) life. She reached the front door in a hurry, therefore, as well as a fluster.

A tall, gaunt-looking man in a dreadful dark brown suit was waiting just outside as she stepped into the colorless light with the box underneath her chin, threatening to spill. She was aware of Adam double-parked and leaning across so he could see out of the passenger window. And the books were heavy.

Before she could say anything, though, and just as the main door swung shut behind her, the man spoke.

"Hello. I am here to see Gabriel Glover, please. He said to me to meet him here at one. Is he inside this house?"

She tried to nod over the box as she paused in her stride. She recognized the accent now — Russian. Of course. But it was hard to tell if the formality of his manner was a function of his speaking English or the purpose of his visit. Obviously her brother had some strange friends — either that or gambling debts.

"I'm afraid he's not here at the moment. Now is not a good time. What is it about? I'll tell him that you ca — oh, shitting hell." The holdall had swung around again, off her shoulder, and she was in danger of losing some books from beneath her chin.

The man stepped forward, and before she had time to wonder what he was going to do, or for that matter to be afraid, he had taken the box.

"Thanks. Thanks . . ." He remained motionless while she sorted out all the bags. She looked up and met his eyes — sunken, turquoise, arresting. "Thank you."

"Are you Isabella?"

The question took her completely aback. They stood on the doorstep facing each other for a second.

"Yeah — yes. I'm Gabriel's sister." The books clearly weren't half so heavy for him, though he held the box oddly, she noticed, resting it on his arms, which he stretched out in front of him as if he were a forklift, hands free at the end. The guy must know her brother quite well after all. She relaxed a few fractions.

"Sorry." She indicated the car. "We're in a rush. You're lucky you came today. Gabriel is moving out. This is all his stuff. Or unlucky, I suppose. There's been a bit of an upheaval. You're —"

"My name is Arkady Artamenkov. I am here from St. Petersburg. Your brother told me to come to this house to talk to him . . . to talk to both of you. This is how I know your name."

And only now it occurred to her that it was something to do with her mother. Her curiosity sparked. The bags were murdering her fingers again.

"Hang on." She started toward the car. Adam reached over his shoulder and opened the back door, and she placed the bags and holdall on the floor.

"Sorry," she said to Adam, "just one sec."

The man was now standing behind her, holding the box. She turned, took it from him, and dumped it flat on the back seat.

"Thank God for that." She stood up straight as he took a step back. "Is it something to do with the flat?"

"No, no." The other's face changed, as if he realized that she was mistaking him completely. "No, I am sorry. I am a friend of your mother from Petersburg. I know your mother very well. Today I was going to speak with your brother about this, about her. He said you would both be here."

"Oh. Oh God, sorry." She wanted to send Adam home alone. She considered a second. No, it simply wasn't fair. Her curiosity was burning her up now, though, and she felt her neck going red. She must get his number and organize another time. Gabriel should be there too. The guy's English was better than she had first thought. She softened her tone. "Oh, I *see* . . . Sorry. What a balls-up." She put her hand through her hair. "It's just a very bad day today. My brother is — *Gabriel* is — moving out because he and his girlfriend, Lina, are splitting up. For a while."

"I used to practice on your mother's piano at her apartment on the Griboedova in St. Petersburg."

"You are a musician?" Why hadn't Gabriel told her anything about this?

"Yes. I play the piano. She . . . she said to me many things about you. We were supposed to talk together today."

"Right, right, right. Oh, well, we have to arrange another time." She glanced at the car. A scaffolding truck was turning into the road. It would not be able to get past. "I — we — would love to meet up. We really would. Is there a number I can call you on? I'm so sorry about this."

"No. I — I — I do not have a phone."

"Okay. Is there a way of getting in touch with you?"

His head fell and he seemed to be looking at his feet.

"How about . . . how about this Friday?" Give Gabriel some time, she thought; yes, he would want to be there. "Erm . . . whereabouts are you based?"

"I do not understand." He looked up again.

"Where are you staying?"

"Oh, near Harrow Road."

"Well, to be honest, the simplest thing to do is say . . . seven-thirty on Friday evening . . . at Kentish Town tube. I will *definitely* be there.

Hang on a sec." She opened the passenger door, reached pen and paper out of her bag, apologized to Adam again, and scribbled down her cell phone number on a piece of paper. The scaffolding truck pulled up behind the car. "This is my number. Call me anytime to confirm. I promise I will be there. Friday, Kentish Town at seven-thirty. What's your e-mail?"

He told her an address.

"Write it down." She handed him the pen.

The driver leaned out of the window of the truck. "Oy, love, how long you gonna be? We've got houses to rob."

"Okay. See you . . . on Friday." She met the Russian's eyes a second time, hoping to convey her sincerity. A car was coming in behind the truck.

"Yes, okay." He seemed to be about to say something but then stopped.

"Friday at Kentish Town. I promise. I am so sorry about this."

"I will call you."

"Yes, call me whenever. I'd love to talk. I'll send you an e-mail to confirm." She turned to open the door and climb into the car. When, three seconds later, she looked back through the window to wave, he was already walking away.

41

That Most Blissful Zero

HE SICKNESS PASSED toward the end of day four. He washed himself over and over in cold water on day five. Shaved. Face and head. Bin-bagged his bedclothes and as much of his filthy room as he could. Carried the bags out into the narrow hall. Left them by the hole. He ate a tin of beans, a biscuit, and some dried figs. As much as he could stomach. Then he took the last of the sleeping pills and moved into Arkady's room. He slept for ten hours in the cleanliness of his friend's bed.

On the sixth day, he thought he could appear almost normal again, though his knees ached and his stomach was still uneasy. He dressed in Arkady's oldest clothes — sweater sleeves and trouser legs rolled, the same gulag prisoner but liberated this very morning, emaciated and all but drowning in borrowed civvies. He lugged out the black sacks. Hauled out his mattress, kicked it down the stairs one flight at a time. Burned everything on the fires outside.

There was never any real daylight in the winter. A light snow began to fall.

He climbed the stairs one flight at a time, amazed at the simple functioning of his lungs. He found another sweater, put some socks on his hands, squeezed into his old raincoat, and walked slowly all the way to Sennayska market. He went straight to Tsoikin, the CD seller from whom he had bought so much of his beloved library. The darkness returned. He walked back. He sat waiting. (Had he known all along that he would sell the music? It now seemed so.) Tsoikin arrived at seven and offered him a derisory sum for everything. He accepted immediately and took the cash. He apologized for the hole in the wall and the dust on all the cases. He explained that he was leaving. He asked to keep a single disk — Vivaldi's holy music. He left Tsoikin boxing up and went straight out to call Grisha from a pay phone.

He hung around Primorskaya station, scared that he would miss him, nursing tea that was forever cooling. Three hours later, at eleven, Grisha arrived in his car. They went for a ride. Henry agreed to meet with Leary the following day. He gave Grisha his money. And Grisha, all grins and goodwill, gave him a little extra in return.

He climbed out by the bank of the Neva. He waited while Grisha pulled cautiously away — mirror signal maneuver, fog lights on, a scrupulous and law-abiding driver. The wind had dropped, but snow was falling thickly again, flakes like crumbled Eucharist, sticking to everything. The river was frozen. He stuck his hand out and took the first car that came skidding in to the curb. At the lights the man offered him half a bottle of vodka — very special, he said. He gave the man the rest of his money. Just what he needed to make sure.

Tsoikin was gone. The room was empty now save for the dust, the stereo, and the tattered sofa. He found an unused syringe in his desk. (Had he been saving it there for this? It now seemed so.) He put on the only CD he had kept, seeking *Beatus vir, in memoria aeterna*. He knew his tolerance level would have dropped. But he prepared a bigger hit than his usual. He drank some of the vodka as he did so, wincing against the sting. Vivaldi's voices sang. He thanked God for his good veins, thanked God that he had taken care to rotate. He swigged another slug of vodka. He thought, I do not want to be here. He thought, This is my friend. He thought, This is coming home. He thought, Don't push it all in at once. Push and stop. Push and stop. Push and stop.

And when it came, it was like the pure-purer-purest relief and the tranquil-happy surge of every good thing in the world, every sweet taste, every scent, every sound, and then an ever-flooding and perfect absence; and the music played and he didn't care, and his breathing slowed, and he really didn't care, and he lay back, and he felt himself going going going and he didn't care. And his breathing slowed a little more. And he knew he was going over. He knew he was going over. But he didn't care. His soul at last was circling that most blissful zero, angels falling, ragged wings ripped and broken, circling that very center of nothingness.

And on the seventh day he was dead.

42

Blood Fever

LONDON WAS IN A DAMP and rheumy mood when he awoke at six; his windowsill wet with the night-long tears of some passing ghost or other. A hundred generations of Londoners seemed to have been weeping in the streets when he set off half an hour later. The parked taxi opposite, the red pillar box on the corner, the trees and the lampposts—all seemed to loom at him out of the murk as if to signify a cold aggression on the part of his new surroundings. So suddenly did the first figure he encountered appear that he almost fell into the dead pools of the other's eyes before he had time to stand aside. They stopped a moment before passing each other, and the stranger muttered something unintelligible, which Gabriel's imagination took to be more of the same: "What are *you* doing here? Get out of the way. Yes, you, asshole."

Perversely, he was relieved that he wasn't sleeping. Now that he had been off work for a week, he would have resented waking up in the cold darkness and setting out for this breakfast meeting if it meant missing out on lying warm in his bed. But for the first time in his entire adult life, his bed was womanless and had become little more than a cradle for nightmares, waking or otherwise.

He emerged onto the main road at the bottom of Haverstock Hill, walked past the Salvation Army, and crossed for the tube station. There was no real reason for him to be going. Though that did not bother him: there was no real reason for doing anything. Actually, there was a reason: perhaps he half wanted to find out a little something about the job himself. Or was this too an effort on behalf of his subconscious to pretend? In fact, he didn't give a fuck about TV.

Why lie to himself? He would rather edit the new bottled-water magazine in the Roland Sheekey basement than waste his life's dwindling energy making yet more crap for Channel Eight and its ten million catatonic viewers. Hard these days to convey how little he cared for what people did, said they did, wanted to do. His life henceforward, he feared, would be all about disguising himself, concealing his natural reaction, burying it deep. Oh Christ . . . Not yet six days and he missed Lina like his own limbs. And Connie, whom he must not call again. Never again — unless and until he was clear. His head ached, physically ached, so that he thought maybe he really did have the flu. He went underground.

Thirty-seven minutes later he surfaced at Westminster and was surprised to see the day no better established in the presence of the mother of all parliaments. Opposite, even Big Ben seemed a little less sure of itself, its assertion of height — bigness generally — less convincing than ever, its Gothic angles all shapeless and shrouded in the still clammy air. The time was only seven-thirty. He was hopelessly early. He decided to walk out onto Westminster Bridge. He could easily make his way back to the café in good time — have something hot and warm and wait for Becky and Isabella to arrive.

The sleepless Thames rolled on beneath. The top of the Eye was blurry in the mist, the great wedge of the South Bank barely distinguishable from the gray of the sky, air, and river. Embankment Place seemed less a building than the carapace disguise of some mighty insect — sleeping, awaiting the allotted hour. And the air was so dense with the hoary damp that it felt as though his jump would have been no great fall but slowed, bit by bit, by thicker and thicker vapors until the water swallowed him with barely a splash.

He stood awhile in his coat, hands warming in the pockets, gazing downriver. London was awakening. He had the impression that the entire city was working to keep the city going so that the entire city could work there. He would have liked a job on the river. That would be good: to see the living Thames every day. To work the water. Some sort of pollution-monitoring patrol. Or something to do with boat registration, perhaps. Rescue the odd whale. Something that started early. Something real. What river jobs were there?

He turned and began to walk slowly back, looking up again at two of the four faces of that ever-ticking clock. And suddenly he felt the stabbing hurt of memory again — his mother's only half-joking belief that he would one day be prime minister. (Madly, he encouraged her voice every time it came now, preferring this pain of bereavement to the possibility of her vanishing.) That she had believed this of him, her confidence in him, her *certainty,* her ready support for any step he might take on this chosen path, her thermonuclear opposition to anything that might dare to stand in his way — these things pierced him to the heart. And here he was, all alone with the utterly insane fact that he could not pass the Palace of Westminster without feeling it to be some kind of challenge (there was plenty of time yet), the utterly insane fact that she had somehow made even the great British parliament her mouthpiece — had somehow enlisted it as surely as if all within and even the chambers themselves were merely vassals of her greater spirit. The sheer power of this: to make all things pertain to her will.

He was still early. Becky and Isabella were due at eight-fifteen. He decided to wait inside — a choice he immediately realized was a mistake, given his unhealthy state of mind. La Cantina was one of those phony places he found spiritually weakening, the whole "concept" more than likely conceived by some pathologically mediocre little masturbator of a city boy with individual interior decor supplied by the inevitably "artistic" girlfriend. Oh Christ. He looked around, wondering whether he was ill or not: polished light wood and chrome everywhere, the newspapers in racks, eggs Benedict for an outrageous sum of money, and a bad wine list presented on a blackboard as if (just this minute) written out in the hand of a motivated and cheeky member of staff. Dotted about, a clientele that deserved nothing less. He went for the sofa in the window and ordered himself a tomato juice and some coffee. He simply couldn't read the newspapers anymore, and he had forgotten his book, so he just sat there, wishing they would turn the awful pretend jazz off, glancing around, trying not to hear the conversation coming from a nearby table.

One mind tried to remind another mind that the choice of venue was not Becky's fault. Just near Channel Eight and convenient. So stop. Stop this. What was happening to him? (He *was* ill. Definitely. Fever.) And what the hell was happening out there? Beyond the window, the whole of London seemed to be engaged in an embarrassingly transparent struggle for some kind of authenticity. And yet the more they asserted their passion for this or their great love for that, the more he saw the neediness, the emptiness, the desperation. Their only authentic endeavor was their endeavor to appear authentic. Help me, Ma.

Becky was exactly on time. And for a while she rescued him. He was amazed by how good it was to see her. She was an old friend from when they were both working on the local papers, and he had forgotten how genuine her good nature was. She had tales of ex-colleagues. She had industry news. She had personal news. TV journalism was a piece of piss compared to print. There was none of the bother. The story only had to stand up for the three minutes you were telling it. And everything was forgotten immediately afterward. Oh, yes, my God: she was engaged. She was getting married to Barney. Remember Barney? (No.) How was Gabriel?

He glossed his mother's death as "really sad, but it was a beautiful funeral," his job as "not a bad holding station for now," and his relationship as "a trial separation." This last a phrase he particularly loathed. And it occurred to him while saying these things that it was he who was the fake. Of course.

Unbelievably, Isabella was nearly half an hour late, arriving barely ten minutes before Becky indicated that she needed to go. But there was no point, Becky said, in their getting together unless she gave Isabella the whole picture. So she, Becky, would hang on for another twenty. No problem. (Gabriel was touched by her kindness and her loyalty to him; he knew that she was seriously inconveniencing herself.) It was a low-paid job as a production assistant on a new magazine-style culture show. Isabella should emphasize this, leave out that. It was a long shot, admittedly, but the program was also going to cover the media, and Isabella probably knew as much about this as anyone — the U.S. connection might be useful too. The best bet was just to be honest.

"That was a waste of time," Isabella said.

"No, you made it a waste of time."

"Did I?"

"Yes."

"Are you okay, Gabs?" Isabella put down the menu and looked up at him.

"Becky isn't stupid."

Isabella frowned. "I didn't say she was."

"No, but you treated her as if she was — and as if everything she was saying went further and further toward confirming it."

"That's not true."

"It is," Gabriel pressed. "It's just that you can't see it."

Isabella looked at her brother with rare crossness. "What's the issue here, Gabs? I've said I'm sorry that I was late. I'm sorry."

"The issue — the *issue* — is that Becky got up at dawn to come here and meet you. And the only reason she did so is because she is a friend of mine, someone who might be able to help you. And so what do you do? You turn up half an hour late and immediately start in at her about her work and her life. That's the issue." He scowled. "Oh yeah, and the fact that you've left yet another job without the slightest idea what you are going to do. Which I wouldn't ordinarily mind, because I'm used to it — you've never managed to do anything for more than a few hours since you were five — except . . . except that this time you're bullshitting *me* about it. Sabbatical, my arse. Three issues."

"Jesus Christ, Gabs." Isabella put her coffee down to one side as if clearing the space between them. "Where did all that come from?"

"You don't know what you're doing here. You don't know what you were doing there. You walked out. You gave them the usual Isabella treatment. You fucked everything and you —"

"So what if I did?" Now she sat forward to return the attack with interest. "I didn't ask you to find me a job here. Yeah, you're right — you organized this for me. I didn't really get much say in it, did I? It was more or less an order. Come down to Westminster at eight-fifteen, Is, I'm sorting you out." She paused a moment and narrowed her eyes. "Oh, I get it. Now that Mum is dead, you've decided that you are in charge of my life. Is that it? You're obviously an expert at running lives."

"Leave Mum out of this."

She looked around for a waiter. "I don't have to listen to you."

They had not fought in twenty years. And even now they could have stopped, left the café, and perhaps survived without serious wounds. But some furious force was impelling them both.

"No. You don't. You don't have to listen to anything, Is. You never have before. Why start now?"

She turned back to him, her eyes suddenly ferocious. "Oh . . . oh, you have a *lesson* for me. That's what this morning is all about."

He met and held the violence in her gaze. "One day you are finally going to see that other people can be clever too. One day you are going to get it into your tiny stubborn mind that, yes, other people can be intelligent as well — *in different ways*. And sometimes a whole lot more intelligent than you. One day you will understand that not everyone thinks and feels the same as you — not everyone has the same prejudices. Not everyone has reached the same conclusions. There are lots of different kinds of intelligence. Besides yours."

Her voice was heavy with scorn. "Say whatever it is you're trying to say."

"I'm not *trying* to say anything. I *am* saying it. You think you are this . . . this genius at seeing inside everything, at understanding what's really going on. You think you have some kind of social x-ray facility. But you're going to have to wake up and realize that you've no such thing. Because the truth is . . . the truth, Isabella, is that you never — you *never* see anything from the other person's point of view. You never even come close." He leaned toward her, and his words were measured to deliver their payload. "Just now, your body language, your manner, everything about you contrived to make the whole thing a waste of time. You weren't listening at all. Not really. Every gesture and every remark, you made only to demonstrate your worldview to Becky. That's all you cared about. Getting across what sort of a person you are. Whatever the conversation was ostensibly about, all you wanted to do was make her understand your way of seeing things, and not only that, but . . . but that your way of seeing things is . . . is in some way the *coolest*. Except she wasn't really going along with your jocular little tone — about how it's all shit and a bit of a game and anyone could do it with their eyes closed. Because she *works* in television, for Christ's sake, Is. That's her job. She doesn't share your opinions. Of course she doesn't — she can't. She's got a job and she is doing it. Sticking to it. Doing it. Going the distance. Actually committing to —"

"I didn't realize you thought Channel Eight was so great."

"That's not the point and you know it. I don't give a fuck about Channel Eight." He had cowed her for the moment. "What I'm trying to get through to you is that whether or not you are ultimately existentially right about Channel fucking Eight, other people have different opinions, and they might, just might, turn out to be as clever and as insightful as yours. And you have to start understanding that. Because otherwise you can't learn anything. Because otherwise all your insight and x-ray vision will amount to nothing more than the worst kind of pathetically disguised egotistical evangelism.

Because otherwise these other people will get up and leave, like Becky did just now, thinking you are an arrogant, naive, conceited little bitch."

"Whereas you — you are all heart, right, Gabs?" Her throat was reddening but she was leaning forward to meet him now, the space between them narrowing. "You think and feel on their behalf, on everyone's behalf . . . and then — and *then* — you go right ahead and do it anyway. Straight to the torture: fuck with everybody around you, but it's all okay, because you're doing all the feeling and thinking on their behalf." She jeered at him. "Very kind. Thank you on behalf of all the women you are so graciously caring for."

His voice was flat and cold. "All your life you have just come in and taken my friends and used them, transparently, when you thought they could help you, and then ignored them the minute you thought they could not. You even bullshit one lot of my friends about how close you are to another lot if you think the second lot can get you something. But you never understood that the reason they're my friends in the first place is because I give back, I put in, I keep the fucking friendships going. I don't just turn up and ask, 'What can you do for me? I'm waiting.' I write the letters. I make the visits. I listen to their stories. I try to help them in return."

"I don't want your help."

"But you've always taken it anyway."

"Because . . . because you know what? Your help — which is a joke anyway — your help comes with way too much baggage. Your help comes with too much moralizing and too many conditions. And you know the sickest part? The sickest part is that you're not even sure what your fucking morals are. Or you're too much of a coward to act on them. So in the end your help just comes with one big fat stamp on the side that says *control*. Isn't that right, Gabs? And you know who that reminds me of? Speaking of cowards and controlling bastards. No, no, of course you don't want to hear it."

He recoiled. "Fuck you."

"Why don't you come out and face it?" She was sneering. "Deal with it. Deal with the fact that you lie to yourself. Get past —"

"Oh, fuck *off* with your therapy bullshit."

"Sorry — that's your area, isn't it? What are you afraid of, Gabriel? You're —"

"I am not afraid of anything."

"What are you afraid of?"

They faced each other.

His scornful features mirrored hers exactly. "We'd all love to quit our jobs, Isabella, and sit around crying or screaming or smashing our heads against the wall. Or however the fuck it is you like to spend your time. But you're going to have to grow up now, Is. Life is about ignoring the fact that life isn't about anything. That's it. Get used to it. And stop looking for excuses."

"You are afraid of being yourself. You are afraid of facing up to what and who you are. Now you sit here trying to control *me*. You do, you do, you remind me of—"

"You never faced one single thing."

"I face the fact that my father is my father."

"I have lived every day—every day since I left college—in the real world. Facing it. Doing it. Doing it despite. *Despite* the fact that I know it's senseless."

"Well, then you *are* an idiot."

There was raw rage in their voices now, bloodiness in their eyes.

He pointed his finger. "You're the one who can't face anything. Can't do it. Keeps on avoiding, hiding. Cowering away from real life. You know why? You know why you don't have the nerve to try anything for long enough? Because you're afraid that after all, you might not be very good at anything. You might just be a talentless piece of shit. The same as the people you think you are so much better than."

"Whereas you seem delighted with your mediocrity."

"You . . . you sit here bullshitting *me*. Lying to *me*. When I know . . . And I've known it ever since you came back. I *know* that you are in touch with Dad. Why lie to me? Why lie, Little Miss Facing Up? When it's so fucking obvious that you've been calling, writing, probably planning a cute little family Christmas get-together. So obvious. And yet you haven't got the guts to tell me to my face. Who's the coward? Who's controlling you now, Is? Today? Right now? Doesn't feel like you're in control to me. You contact Dad behind my back and expect me not to realize. Then you bullshit me, hide it. Feels like Dad is in control to me. Feels like Dad is stopping you from having some kind of a conversation with your brother. Feels likes he's totally in control."

"I can't believe how fucked up you really are. It's actually a surprise."

"Is he giving you money as well? Is that how come you're so relaxed about not finding work that you can tell Becky her life is a bag of shit? Fine, take his money. Enjoy it." He got up. "This is crap. Use some of his money to pay the bill. I don't want to talk to you any- more. I'm going to work."

"That's a lie too," she said to his back. "You haven't been in all week."

But he was gone.

43

A Numbness

ALL THROUGH THE CITY, her brother's words stalked her. Sinister clowns or blithe assassins — she could not tell. A few steps behind, peeping after her around the corners she had just turned, pretending other business if ever she swung around to confront their whispering.

By eleven a vicious staccato wind that came in from the east had begun to whip at the last of the morning's mist. By noon it was utterly impossible to imagine such a silent foggy stillness as had delivered the day, and by two she was being lashed by the belts of freezing sleet that the easterly carried in its chattering train. From Hackney to Acton and from Finchley to Balham and at all the bitter points between, the weather nagged and thrashed at the city, and nowhere was there enough shelter or relief. The doorways were all too shallow, the roofs of the buildings never quite overhung the pavements, the shops had insufficient frontages, the streets were all too wide. There was nowhere to get out of it, no Renaissance-built arcades, no Mall of America, nowhere to hide, nowhere to escape. On days such as these, she realized, the people of London felt it hard in their bones that their city was fashioned for neither one thing nor the other: not for sun or shade, rain or snow.

All day long she struggled through this weather, looking at one flat after another: a crepuscular Vauxhall basement ("excellent access"), a converted half-floor on the Maida Vale border ("vibrant community"), a "reclaimed" council flat in Bethnal Green ("superb views — up to your ears in real London here, love"), an attic in Balham ("good new bars"). Had she actually been seriously looking for somewhere to live, she might have said something. But she wasn't. Or not anymore. Indeed, she did not know what she was doing. All she was sure of was that she was grateful for two things: that the day was full of appointments to mark out the hours so she was continually moving, and that the moving itself was done on the blessed tube — dry, sheltered, out of it. If anything, she wished that she had been even more haphazard in selecting possible flats — the more time traveling, the better.

It was four now and she was back on the Northern Line, on her way to see a cluster of places near Susan's in Kentish Town, the last of the day. The rest of the passengers looked nervous, overvigilant, tensed and ready, their heads jerking involuntarily to the maddened old tune of the centenarian track, but the racket and clatter were to her a lifelong balm. When she and her brother were young, they used to joke that happiness was a sign that read HIGH BARNET 1 MIN. The Northern Line was theirs. And the High Barnet branch was as good as home.

She wasn't upset, or unduly depressed, or indeed angry about what had happened that morning — or not near the surface. Rather she felt as if she were on some kind of clumsy emotional painkiller, the sort of thing they handed out to people who could not take too much reality; she felt vaguely irritated, but she also felt cosseted from the rampage of what she knew must be the truth of her feelings. Yes, they stalked her. And she knew they would catch up with her. But not here and not yet. Not yet.

This weird fuzzy numbness had begun almost immediately after her brother had left the café. She had not been that worried. Instead she simply assumed — her spirit simply assumed, regardless of her mind — that somehow — and she had absolutely no idea how — they would find a way back. She really could not imagine what this way would be. For they had said far too much, they had said the unsayable, and she knew that she and her brother were fearsomely (and disastrously) equal in the ferocity with which neither would now yield an emotional millimeter without evidence first of a capitulation on the part of the other. Of all the people she had ever met, with the sole exception of her mother, only her brother had a focused will that equaled her own.

Everything was fucked, of course. That much was obvious. She couldn't go on staying with Susan, though Susan had made it very clear that she was to remain as long as she liked. On the other hand, she was now no longer sure she wanted to remain in London at all.

Hence the half-assed way in which she had been seeing the flats. She realized that she'd been banking on staying with Gabriel and Lina until . . . until she'd sorted herself out. But that too was out of the question.

At Warren Street, she experienced her first real pang for Sasha, for New York, for the East Village, for her life before. At least the old mess was properly understood: Mum—Russia; Dad—who cares?; Gabs—London; Sasha—annoying but good-hearted and actually a nice guy to hang out with. Oh God. She forced herself back into the present.

At the opposite pole from her fuzziness regarding her brother was her lucidity regarding her father. The dilemma was over. Gabriel knew. Fine. Now the way was open for her to have a clear run at Nicholas. All roads led back to him. She had enough money to see her through Christmas and a little beyond, after which she would absolutely have to work. So she *must* use the time between then and now to deal with the things that had brought her back to London in the first place. She had to talk to her father about her mother. And yet the thought of actually going to see him still repulsed her.

She fished her printed copy of his last e-mail out of her bag as the tube came to a standstill outside Camden.

Insidious. That was the only word for it.

> My dear Isabella, I write with a proposal. Why don't you come here for Christmas? You don't have to answer straight-away. But do have a think about it.

His charm, as ever, was so false and so real at the same time . . . It crawled under her skin, squirmed, hatched there. And all that stuff about ice creams and when they were all a little family. Yuck. Drawing on her sense of him as a father, of course, niftily leading her back into the role of little one, daughter, dependant. Then all that assumed mutuality—"you know what I mean, I think," "yours whenever"—as if they had been the closest of families through every hour of her childhood and the very best of friends every day since. As if they had spent the past ten years popping around to borrow jam from each other. Next the rant about America, disguised in that faux-humble outside-observer tone ("I'd love to have your impressions") but really yet another covert attack: an attack on her for going there and, by implication, on her judgment, on her taste, on her very personality, her life. The disguise reinstated at the end: "I am going on." And so back to him again. (Nothing new there—

always back to him.) Followed by the offer of payment, the closing terms, the arrangements — ostensibly offering her choices but actually choices that were all alike under his control. Thus, finally, to the blackmail: I'm not going to play your e-mail game; come and see me or you learn nothing.

Part of her felt cruel. Her father had suffered a stroke, and a stranger unaware of his menace would, she knew, have been appalled at her interpretation of the poor man's kindly invitation and evident generosity. And yet that was precisely the point with her father. Both things were simultaneously true: he was a selfish cowardly bullying bastard and a charming intelligent thoughtful man at the same time. The one did not cancel out the other. Besides, there was much new in this e-mail. There was loquacity, there was sentimentality, there was even, lurking back there, fear, panic, and loneliness . . .

She had forgotten about the weather. When she surfaced at Kentish Town it came at her again, as if she had returned to the deck of some desperate storm-pitched boat in the North Atlantic instead of stepping up onto the high street. The rain was almost evil, bending down in the wind to come up and under umbrellas, hoods. The cell phone she had borrowed from Susan beeped. There was a message. She stepped back inside the station's shelter and huddled with all the other refugees. It was the guy from Petersburg, confirming their arrangement for that evening.

She had forgotten. And of course she hadn't reminded Gabriel. *Shit*. Now her brother would not hear whatever the Russian had to say. She bit her lip hard. Well, fuck him.

She had already spoken to Arkady Artamenkov earlier in the week — this was how she knew Gabriel had not been at work, because the Russian had told her so. Anxious, Arkady had explained that he had been calling Gabriel, leaving messages, increasingly apprehensive as they were ignored, until eventually one of her brother's colleagues had picked up the phone and explained that Gabriel was ill and not expected in before the weekend. Given the fiascos thus far, the Russian was clearly very worried about the reliability of Glovers in general. And so during that call she had reassured him and promised to confirm again on Friday. Yet again, therefore, she had failed to keep her word.

She listened to the Russian's voice a second time. The message was short. She guessed that he was on a pay phone. "Hello, this is

Arkady again. We are meeting tonight at Kentish Town tube station. Please call me on . . ." He read out the number slowly, and then again. And suddenly she was looking forward to talking with this man more than any other thing in her life that she could remember. What did he know of her mother? Please God he was still going to come.

"Hello, Pat's Place." A hard voice, of Northern Irish extraction.

"Hi. Can I leave a message for someone?"

"You can try."

She was caught out a moment. "Oh. Can I—"

"There's seventy people in and out of here every day, and half of them don't speak a word of English, and none of them give their right and proper names. But go on—your fellow just might be the one exception. Who's it for?"

"Arkady Artamenkov."

"You'll have to spell that."

Isabella did so.

A weary breath and then: "Go on then, now. Your message."

"Just that—just that I will be at Kentish Town tube at seven-thirty tonight as planned."

"Your name?"

"Isabella Glover." She hesitated. "Will you be able to give it to him? I'm pretty sure that's his name."

"No—no, we won't, I'm afraid. We'll put it on the notice board. That's where we put all the messages. You'll have to hope he can read."

"Thanks."

There was nothing else she could do. She pulled up the hood of her borrowed anorak and stepped into the sleet.

44

Mi Vse Soshli S Uma, Mama

AFTER HE LEFT La Cantina, there was nowhere else to go, so he started for home—or rather the new place. He got off a stop early to go to the supermarket in Camden; he needed to eat, something wholesome.

The weather was worsening when he came out—the wind was rising, and the pavements were no longer misty but ravaged and gnashed. He decided to walk back—up Camden High Street. Rain was coming.

It was not yet eleven. But the legion of drunks swerved and swayed and sloshed around the Camden Town station entrance, cans still cocked despite the wind, rictus grins, top of the morning to you, but even they knew that the veil was too far torn and hell was leering boldly through. The dealers and the pushers talked among themselves. The junkies lined the high street to beg his approach and plead at his heels as he passed by. He crossed the old canal, shaking his head and muttering "No, thanks" over and over. Somehow, somewhere, all that would-be counterglamour of punk, hippie, goth, and skin had drained away, vanished with last night's disappearing tides of money and youth, and those people who remained—running the PVC and piercing stores, rolling tobacco on the street corners—now seemed far too old for their bolted brows, their blue-green hair, their black facepaint, and their careful beads. Gabriel saw through the respect-expected manner of their bearing, saw instead the undefended lines of past decades scored deep in the battlefields of their faces, the thin glaze of self-confidence like joke-shop contact lenses disguising the color of their frightened eyes.

He hurried on as the first rain came, past the petrol pumps, past the brothel, past the school. He turned onto Prince of Wales Road. Another drunk pawed at him as he came to the Maitland Park monument. This time he paused, capitulated, gave what he had, and waved away the abject thanks. There is nothing sadder than a drunk in the rain wishing you well. He reached the new and unfamiliar house, climbed the street stairs, and let himself in after struggling with the sticky lock. The others, his new flatmates, were out. Regular people. Regular jobs. Regular lives. He stowed the milk in the choking fridge and put the rest of his provisions in their places, then made straight for his bedroom at the very top.

It was a mess.

It took him a moment to understand.

He had been burgled. His laptop was gone. His portable stereo. His printer. His scanner. The floor was covered with his clothes, his compact disks, books, papers, everything.

He turned on his heel and went across the tiny attic landing to check Sean's room. It was the same. Some part of him felt an odd comfort. They weren't just after him.

Probably he should go down. Probably he should find out where the burglars came in. Probably he should call the police.

He looked out of his attic window for a while: defunct chimney-pots and hooligan seagulls. Then, slowly, grimly, he turned. He bent under the bed. He dislodged the baseboard. He wriggled his fingers into the gap. Thank Christ. He pulled out the little box. He opened it up. The ring that his grandfather had given him was still there. Like everyone else, the burglar wasn't very good at his chosen occupation. The mess, as ever, was just a way of diverting people from this fact.

He locked his door. He took off his coat. He prized off his shoes. He selected "Señor" on his MP3 player and threw himself down on his bed with the ring. There was no place a man could go, no matter how high or how low, that Dylan had not been before. You lay down your head in the strangest of rooms and the guestbook by the bed always said that he had passed through this way at least once before — sometimes last week, sometimes a lifetime ago.

He half woke. The weather was raging. Sleet scratching at the windowpane. A million invisible claws.

He half slept. He wanted a woman so badly that he felt he could barely breathe. Yes, this room, this mess, all of this would not matter if only there were some woman with whom he could now lie down and open up the constricted passageways of his heart. He turned away from what light was left in the day. From the age of fifteen, he had never gone more than a fortnight without someone to share his thoughts, to touch, to listen to, to laugh with — some he had admired, some he had simply desired, and those very few whom he had loved. And, oh Christ, they were haunting him now, slipping away just beyond the edges of his vision, their laughter vanishing just as his ear seemed to catch the happy chime. He drew the blanket over him. A woman's kiss. The whole sorry, shitty, solitary slog of a man's life could still be redeemed by a woman's single kiss.

He was going to have to go back. He thought he was strong, but he was not. He was going to have to call her. Get up, man, get up. Rest awhile first.

He slept and dreamed that he awoke. Spiritual asthma — the whole world is suffering from spiritual asthma. In his dream he could not fall asleep.

Seemingly there was no end. He felt as though he were falling, falling, falling into ever colder and darker space, the wind rushing faster and faster, snatching at his face. He felt expelled, as though he had been thrown summarily out of heaven and the shock of it was continually ripping through him as he plunged away. He felt abandoned and lonely beyond all loneliness he had ever known or thought or imagined: abandoned even by his own better self, as if he were a lost cause to his own intelligence; and lonely to his core, terrifyingly certain that no other person would or could ever know where he was or what he was feeling — not only that no companionship was available, but that no companionship with him was *possible*. And there were no voices as he fell, none of the old voices of hope, argument, or reflection remained — all silent, gone, deserted — only the flat whisper sounding somewhere behind the deafening scream of the panic as it tore merciless through his flailing body. *I told you so, I told you so.*

He opened his eyes for just a moment. The light was strange — not quite dark, not yet; the sleet running like shivers in the jaundiced glow of the streetlamps.

· · ·

And it's like you always said: in the heart of power sits fear enthroned; and it's as obvious as banknotes.

Mama, mi vse soshli s uma. We are all sick, Mama. We are all sick. In friends, I find evasion; in children, tautology; and love itself, an election more of blindness than of hope. I am sick. I cannot stop my mind. I cannot rest. Cut my chest, look inside, you'll see it's all burning.

The night came on. There were sounds in the house, a rude banging at his door. Others were home. He turned deeper into the bed.

The price of courage is loneliness. Is this the price you paid, Ma? An awful feeling — something hollow but tight that lurks in no definite place deep inside, something impossible to banish, like days and days of accumulated cold that has crawled into the secret fissures of the bones and won't be chased out. A wretched feeling, a feeling to really drive and determine a person's life — actions, decisions, plans — more so than love or hate or any of the other supposedly powerful emotions, hey, Ma? Loneliness, and the fear of loneliness — it could make a person do, say, think almost anything. Yes, Ma, I am beginning to understand why people settle for the most appalling circumstances, the most appalling *people*. The inexplicability of wives, husbands, partners, lives — I see it now, Ma. It's all becoming a little more comprehensible. And I realize what that indefinable thickening is that I notice in the faces of the bride and the groom: it's *relief* — relief from the loneliness. Yes, that halo of happiness comprises three parts relief to one part love. Look Mother, look Father, look friends, I have someone; someone I can settle for has settled for me! I'm settled. We're settled. It's settled.

But what if it's not settled after all? Or what if (as we suspect) settled is merely death's best-decorated antechamber? What if we *refuse* to settle, Ma? What if we refuse to settle for this life as we find it, these rites and rituals, this government, these gods, this ever-growing herd of golden calves? What if we will not settle for the derisory covenants of this disreputable age?

I'm with you, Ma. I refuse.

I have no great plan, I cannot even summon a coherent point of view, but I will not back down. I will stand here and I will say, I see through you, I see through you, and what you believe in is a lie, and what you have become is a falsehood.

Yes, it's true, Ma: your great indignity is now mine. That last time we spoke, you were passing it on to me, weren't you, Ma? One more time, just for good measure. As if it weren't already thrice inscribed in the double helix of my every single cell.

I refuse.

Give us the counterpoint and you can keep the tune. Isn't that right, Ma? Give us the contrapposto and you can keep the straight and narrow. Give us the counterintelligence and you can keep your presentations and your pulpiteers. Give us the counterlife. Every time.

But where does my refusal lead me, Ma? And where did it leave you?

I see it now: your courage and your loneliness and your despair. And I feel it: they do not ebb and flow, but they remain constant, like radiation, gravity, and death.

You were lonely and powerless in that old house, stranded in a foreign country with so faithless and selfish a man while your pride and your dreams were year by year mocked and belittled.

I refuse.

Count me for the living, not the dead.

45

The Gift

OR ARKADY ALEXANDROVITCH, the moment had arrived. He did not care to question or to understand. The truths within lies, the lies within truths, thoughts within feelings, feelings within thoughts — they were all so many beguiling matryoshka dolls to him. And now that it came right down to it, he was revealed at the last to be his mother's son. This discovery he did not recognize or consciously acknowledge. Rather he felt it, he experienced its expression, and its expression was stamina. His entire being was certain that whatever fate had in store, he could endure. His mother's most eloquent and effective gift was passed on silently, secretly, inarticulately, and without her agency. Yes, now that it came right down to it, life turned out to be mostly about not flinching. Keeping going. And he knew that it *had* come right down to it. He could feel it, tingling in his fingers and hanging out there in the cowardly weather that would neither rain nor snow but hovered between the two.

He had not been idle. He had printed a map that showed everything, however generally, on one page. He had talked to everyone he could — fellow Russians, fellow East Europeans, fellow men and women. It started at the hostel. One contact led to another and to another. He had borrowed a cheap anorak (against the endless rain) from one of the Moldavians, and with them he had visited building sites in Harlesden. From there to Hammersmith to meet an electrician. From there back up to King's Cross to a go-cart track, looking for a mechanic. From there, three cafés in Fitzrovia; they'd need a short-order chef before too long, they always did. And thus he had spent the week walking, his boots forever devouring the pavement.

He moved by general direction, learning his way as he went. He stayed clear of drugs, but everything else he investigated. Nightclubs, escort agencies, hotels, minicabs, restaurants, pubs, shoe booths, florists, hairdressers, Finsbury Park, Neasden, Golders Green, Stockwell, Vauxhall, Ealing, and Bow. District by district, he must have covered more than fifteen miles a day. He listened and he learned. He was on a dozen job waiting lists. Turn up here at six-thirty, whatever day you want, they said, and there will be labor. He stopped worrying about the police altogether, his identity, or his papers. He drank water from the tap. He stole fruit from the outside racks whenever he passed a fruit shop. He had one hot meal — a baked potato with tuna and sweet corn — every night in the café that the junkies used farther up on the Harrow Road. Besides that, he spent no money at all.

Even so, thanks to the cost of his bed alone, he was now down to his last one hundred and twenty dollars. And he owed four more nights — the maximum debt they would allow, even with his passport. So already there was a shortfall. Time to be moving on.

He placed the borrowed anorak on one of the Moldavians' backpacks with a half-full carton of cigarettes he had stolen. He picked up his own pack and went quietly into the narrow corridor. Carrying his boots, he walked down the stairs as far as the second floor. Luck was with him: the woman on the desk downstairs was having a cigarette and her back was turned as he crossed the landing behind her. He squeezed into the tiny, filthy shower room, which stank of mildew. The sleet was thrashing and the wind was blowing as he loosened the catch. He dropped his pack out the window into the alley below. He threw his coat out after it, stuffed inside two plastic bags.

He put on his boots. But came out of the shower room quietly, only beginning to make a noise as he stepped down the flight of stairs to the desk. He took the cigarette from behind his ear, stuck it in his mouth, and asked the witch for a light in his friendliest English.

"I owe you for four nights," he said. "And I want to stay two more, please. I am going off to the bank now — I need my passport for identity. Is it okay?"

She looked at him suspiciously. "You'll get soaked to the skin in your shirt. It's raining like the end of the world out there."

He blew smoke toward the nicotine-stained ceiling. "I will run."

She tutted. "Where's your coat?"

"I left it upstairs. Locked in the room. It's not good for the rain."

"What's your name?" She bent down, disappearing from view, and he heard her opening up the safe.

He leaned over the counter. "Arkady Kolokov."

She reappeared. "Okay. I need your room key until you come back."

He handed her the key.

She handed him his passport.

Once outside, he walked right, out of sight of the desk, and then slipped down the alley. He ground the unwanted cigarette beneath his boot and unpacked his coat, leaning against the side of the building. The sleet hacked down relentlessly.

He carried his pack in his hands in case he was challenged as he came out. But the weather had emptied the street. So he walked swiftly away from the hostel without looking back. Right, then left. He walked fifty yards farther with his pack still in front until he reached the twenty-four-hour shop, where he ducked beneath the awning. Ignoring the supplications of yet more bullshit homeless people, he fished out a black garbage bag that he had stolen from the cupboard by the toilet. Then he retrieved his cap from one of the side pockets and slung the pack onto his shoulders, loosening the straps to accommodate the bulk of his coat. He made a hole in the bag, took off his cap a moment, and pulled the thing over his head. Then he put his cap back on and set off, his feet warm in his boots.

It was only just four. Partly because of the necessity of pretending that he was going to the bank, he had given himself three and a half hours, plenty of time. His idea was to walk along the canal, which he had come to know quite well since that first night, when he had lost himself in the Paddington basin. The route would be quieter and it was direct to Camden. He could stop along the way without needing to spend any money. From Camden, it looked straightforward to Kentish Town.

At first it was easy, but soon the water disappeared into a tunnel where there was no path, and for a while he wandered around trying to find where the canal reemerged. He asked a passerby, but she knew nothing. (Nobody in London seemed to know where they were, or where anything was, or where anything might be.) When finally he saw the water again, brown and turbid in the rain, he could not get down to the bank, so he was forced to walk on the road above until the fence was low enough to vault.

The towpath was deserted and he slowed a little, more confident.

He listened to the sounds of his boots and his breathing. His previous anxiety — that he had not actually stolen anything that night when Oleg had left the hole in her window — had ceased to bother him entirely; it seemed irrelevant now that he was actually here in London and so close. His plan was to be sure to find out where the brother was. Find out if Gabriel Glover was ignoring his e-mails and calls or if his silence was something to do with all the bullshit that had been going on last Sunday. Either way, he wanted to see Gabriel too. Make sure that there was no chance at all of anything from brother as well as from sister. Make sure there was nothing offered, nothing to hope for. Nothing.

Once he knew how to get hold of the brother, then . . . then he would simply tell the sister the truth. There was no longer any reason to piss around with the strategies that he and Henry had talked about — ways of getting to know them while making up further bullshit about Maria Glover and her fucking piano. There was no time and no point. If the sister did not want to know, if she was hostile, then fuck it. He would go and find the brother. And if he did not want to know either, then fine. His choice would be made. His new life would start. Good. Fuck the piano. Fuck the conservatory. Fuck Mother Russia. He was staying here and he was going to make money like everybody else. It would be bullshit at first, but he would get through that phase quick enough. Hundreds of Russians were doing the same. Brothers, sisters. Yes, he was down to it.

He passed a mooring. There were no lights on any of the boats. His cap was sodden but his feet were still dry. He passed some fine buildings, pale-colored and elegant, and he was reminded of Petersburg. He saw pretty gardens on the opposite bank. He passed beneath a bridge that dripped and echoed away into the narrowing darkness wherein he could not see. He passed what seemed to him to be giant nets that loomed crazily against the wet heavens. All the while the sleet continued to come down, bending this way and that in the wind, slapping against the plastic of his makeshift cloak. The path ahead was slick and shiny. He kept on, breathing steadily, the water streaming down his face.

46

Between Its Disguises

SIX FORTY-FIVE and the Internet café on Kentish Town High Street was half empty. She seemed to be spending her life at these places, but she did not want to go back and disturb Susan and her family. She had said that she would be out until late. And she wanted to let them have their dinner uninterrupted. The last two flats she had seen had been a total waste of time. She'd canceled the third, and now she had three quarters of an hour.

There were a few tourists tapping vigorously at the cheap keyboards, Australians mostly, and a circle of Lebanese huddled around a screen in the corner, but most of the seats were unoccupied. She was facing the wall near the entrance, one empty booth in from the front window. A cheap neon sign advertised unspecific "exchange" to the world beyond, and the back of the flashing light caused the frame of her screen to glow red-gray thirty times a minute.

Outside, the lashing continued, but more sporadically now. If she looked up and turned her head to the left, she could see directly onto the high street. Minicabs, vans, and rented limousines arguing one inch at a time up and down, up and down, up and down. The sleet like thin liquid wires in the headlights.

She must have been sitting in something like a trance, staring at the screen, when she first became aware of someone behind her. A steady, unmoving presence. Not someone hovering, as if hoping to interrupt with a quick question, but someone in the business of waiting, steadily—waiting for her to look up, look around, turn her attention toward him. Which she purposely did not do for a minute or two, having learned a long time ago that the best way to handle unwanted men in public is to ignore them completely. She deleted part of the question she had typed: "Did you ever meet her mother, Russian granny?" And then deleted the whole paragraph.

Her second thought was one of irritation. She wanted to reread what she had written alone. But the presence was still there, refusing to go away, a force field behind her chair. Her irritation began to escalate . . . She didn't want some bloody random bloke . . . For Christ's sake. With anger jackknifing her brow, she swung away from her screen to meet the face, a curse on her lips.

The man standing a just-polite distant behind her was tall, thin, and trying to smile. He had messy, longish blond-brown hair swept to one side off his forehead, and he was wearing an ill-fitting older man's suit jacket with faded blue jeans and what looked like hiking boots. But it was neither frame nor clothes nor boots that stopped her mouth: it was his face. Hollow cheeks, head raised a fraction in defiance despite the effort at a smile; close-shaved; nose, lips, and brow as even as an icon's, and a sunken pair of deepest turquoise eyes. It struck her for a second as the face of some ancient human tribe from an unknown pinnacle of civilization long ago. Not handsome — indeed, the sort of face that made "handsome" sound silly — but striking, enduring, prototypical in the way of those faces on ancient vases or the ones cut in stone. And the eyes . . . the eyes stopped her dead. All of this before she recognized him — then a flood of confusion as she realized who he was, bafflement that she had not seen these features for what they were on the street when loading Adam's car. Followed, just as suddenly (as he held out his massive hand), by the thought that he looked nervous and tense.

"Hello. I saw you in the window. I was going to the station where we arrange to meet. I am sorry for the surprise."

She recovered herself. Evidently it was just writing to her father that was heightening everything. She noticed now that the jacket he was wearing was the upper half of the suit he had been sporting on Gabriel's doorstep.

"Hi. No, not at all. I just didn't recognize . . . How are you? What time is it?"

"I am early. It will not be half past seven for forty minutes."

"Sorry. No, I didn't mean that." She didn't. She realized that it was quite normal for a Russian to stop in if he saw an acquaintance; only Londoners crossed the street and pretended not to have seen each other so as to arrive at an appointment separately.

"Hang on, I've just got to save this and shut down and then we are gone."

"Of course. But please, there is no problem if you need to finish. I can wait."

"I'm finished." She turned back to her screen, saved her mail as a draft, and began to log out.

"How much is this café?" he asked.

"How much to use the Internet?"

"Yes."

"It's four pounds for the first hour and then one pound for every half-hour after that."

"It's expensive."

"Yes."

"People must be millionaires in London."

"I know." The computer dropped offline. She swiveled in her chair and stood up. Now she noticed his coat and his backpack on the floor behind him.

He said, "How much is the subway to here?"

"The tube? It depends where you are traveling from."

"Harrow Road."

"There's no station there—you have to use Warwick Avenue, or Westbourne Grove is better. Three quid, something like that. Too much." They stood in line to pay. "How did you get here?"

"I walked."

She had forgotten how seriously poor the vast majority of Russians were. Even those on student visas were way below Western student poor. But the real Russians, the sixty-dollars-a-month Russians, simply couldn't survive a single day in London without immediate work. And thereafter they continued to be staggered by how much Londoners casually spent and the stuff they chose to spend it on. Isabella retuned her sensitivity. She realized too that she had suddenly developed butterflies. Too many reasons to be anxious, perhaps.

It was becoming colder—the sleet thickening, the ragged wind snatching at the door. She had not been to the Petrel for five, maybe six years, since before she moved to New York. As she remembered, the pub used to have a full-sized old-fashioned pool table and regulars talking football and what-happened-to-Frank. It had been an unpretentious, unpremeditated pub: dog, London Pride, and piano. So she was surprised, and then not surprised, as she went in, to see that it had used the intervening years to convert itself into a faux-authentic, faux-gourmet place. She realized she was torturing herself again. Or maybe it was simply because she was seeing the place through his eyes. She turned. He was standing just inside the door, tall in his coat, carrying his backpack in front of him a little awkwardly, taking the measure of the place. She felt a prickle of shame, shame that she had bought him here; and embarrassment too, that he might think she liked this sort of phoniness. As ever, she overcompensated and went back toward him too quickly, eager to cut down the distance between them.

"Christ, it's busy," she said. "They've changed everything since I was here last. Do you want to stick that over there? We can grab that little table by the window." It occurred to her that he must be about her own age. "I'll get them. What do you want to drink?"

He didn't smile or soften. "Just water."

She absorbed her first real impression of his personality — cold, distant, unyielding. She nearly asked him still or sparkling, but checked herself in time.

"Water — are you sure? Not a glass of wine or something?"

"Or tea. Tea. If there is tea here."

"There will be . . . I'll ask."

She set off to the bar determined to procure tea, telling herself to relax. She could feel curiosity writhing in her blood alongside the overexcitement. (How did this man know her mother? What when how why who?) What was the matter with her? She told herself to calm down. Half of her childhood friends had been Russian. Even now there were twenty people she would love to see the next time she was there . . . An awful thought occurred to her as she eased her way past a group of men arguing about ski resorts: maybe now that her mother was dead, she wouldn't be going back to St. Petersburg anymore; maybe there was no reason to; maybe now that her mother was dead, her connection with Russia itself was dead, severed. She had not considered this until now. She pushed forward and reached the counter. Tea. She wondered whether he was a teetotaler or merely too proud to ask for a drink when he knew he could not buy her one in return. Tea — tea would do it. How did this man know her mother? What when how why who? Something that mattered. Something that counted. In all of this.

"So how long are you in London?"

"I do not know. It depends."

"Are you working here?"

"No."

"Is this your first visit?" She knew already that it was.

"Yes," he said. "Do you have your brother's new address? I must write it down."

"Yes, of course."

He pulled a small exercise book from his jacket pocket. She told him the number on Grafton Terrace and watched him write it down in English. She was used to this curtness. Not with the boys in the trendy Petersburg bars, but with the men she had met with Yana in the crumbling table-football-one-beer-and-one-vodka bars away from the center, away from the tourists. Their definitiveness wasn't rudeness; rather, they simply didn't do small talk. There was talent, there was beauty, and there was power; either you had one of the three or you talked about one of the three or, by and large, you shut up.

She tried another line. "Where are you staying?"

He replaced his book. "I was staying at this place near Harrow Road."

"And where now?"

"It was full of scum."

She registered this but did not know where to take it, so she said, "Your English is way better than my Russian." She intended genuinely to compliment him, but it sounded patronizing.

He didn't notice, or he didn't care. "I have a very good teacher. An Englishman. I have his letter."

The waitress arrived with the tea and they broke off. She had ordered some bread and olives because she felt awkward ordering nothing but tea. Now she felt awkward that she had ordered something besides the tea. The carefully careless patterns of the balsamic vinegar in the olive oil were somehow ingratiating, insulting, inappropriate. Then she noticed that the waitress caught Arkady's eye as she set the pot down. And that he met it steadily, without looking away. It was a shock to see the waitress blush.

Too hastily, she asked, "Whereabouts do you live — in Petersburg?"

"Yes." He misunderstood.

The waitress left.

"I meant where in the city — which part?"

"I live on Vasilevsky."

She waited for the usual "Do you know St. Petersburg, have you been there a lot?" But it didn't come. "And do you work there?"

"I have worked. But now I am a student."

"At the university?"

"No."

"Oh."

He looked at her directly. "At the conservatory."

Finally he was volunteering something.

"Oh, yes, you said. Of course. You are a musician. You're studying music?"

"Yes." And then he added, "All my life."

Simply, fatuously, disarmed by his avowal, she said, "I love music."

"Do you play an instrument?" he asked.

"I used to play the violin. But only as an amateur."

"Can you play . . . can you play a Mozart violin sonata?"

Straight to it again. "No. Yes — I used to. But I am really bad."

"If you play a Mozart violin sonata, you are not so bad."

"I haven't played for years."

His face almost softened. "There is no bad. We are all students. We find the pulse. We make the first note. We start the journey."

She could feel the thawing that the subject had brought them. And maybe it was the tea, but her tiredness finally left her and with it the troubles of this most awful day. The rest of the pub faded away and her naturalness returned and she was concentrating again, meeting his eyes with her own.

This time it was Isabella who came straight to it. "How did you know my mother?"

"I met her."

"You met her."

He sat forward. His voice dropped. "Yes. We met. A woman introduced us."

"Who — I mean, what was her name? Was she one of my mother's friends?"

"I don't remember her name. Zoya, I think. She was a detective."

"A detective?"

"Yes."

"Why? I mean — why did a detective introduce you?" She searched his impassive face. "Was my mother in some kind of trouble? Was my mother involved in something?"

"I don't know. Your mother — she hired a detective to find me."

"To find you?"

"Yes."

This time she was prepared to outwait him. She noticed his hands on his cup — big hands, nails pared right back. Even the cuffs of his sleeves were frayed.

He set his mug down by their untouched milk. "Your mother — did she ever say anything to you about her family?"

"What do you mean?"

Now he waited for her.

So she continued. "You mean, did my mother talk about her mother or her sisters? Her extended family? No, she didn't say much about them. Why? I never met them."

"I do not mean this. No."

"Do you know something about my mother's family?"

"Did she ever say to you anything about her life before she left Russia?"

"Yes. Sometimes she did."

"About . . . about having a son?"

"No." And now it gripped her, shook her, plunged her — that strange and sudden emotional vertigo of physically knowing what someone was going to say without her mind's acknowledging that she knew.

"Did my mother have a son?" She was leaning forward, her voice as quiet as snow.

"Yes."

"How do you know? I mean, do you know him? When did she tell you this? When was —"

"I am her son."

She could not speak. She could only stare. She believed him utterly. Her mother's eyes.

A moment of absence. From all that had gone before and all that was to come.

He spoke again. "I am her son. I am your mother's only son."

And then the world, her contexts, everything rushing back into the edges of the vacuum. "No . . . God, no. I mean, I . . . What you saying cannot be true, Arkady. My *God*. It's just that my mother . . . it's just that I have . . ." She could not say "another brother." "It's just that my mother has another son — my brother, Gabriel. Of course you know that, you were there at his —"

"No."

"Yes."

"No."

"I don't understand."

"Gabriel is not her blood son. And you, you are not her daughter." His face was as full of meaning as any she had ever seen. "She is your mother, of course. That is true. I do not change this. Nothing changes this. But she is not your mother from your birth. This is also true. I am her son by blood."

She was shaking her head, but no words were coming out.

"Here. I have a letter. You must read." He began to unstrap his pack.

Everything around her seemed to warp and swarm — the last of the vacuum vanishing too quickly, the wide world's daily normality layering itself upon her senses at the speed of light. People eating and drinking on a regular Friday night. Kentish Town, London. Date. Time. Place. Life itself unfolding, happening, every second, all around. And yes, just like when she had learned of her mother's death: the strange inconsequentiality of the general moment when for the individual the moment's consequence is everything, her whole life. And this is how news comes. A before, when you don't know. An after, when you do. A moment's glimpse of real life naked between its disguises. And stupid stupid stupid to look for it on the tops of yogic mountains or on your knees in the church or mosque or temple or staring at the setting sun, feet in the sand. When here it is all around you — in every view, in every instant.

He handed her the letter and said, "Maybe your father knows some of this."

47

A Letter from the Dead

Dear Mr. Gabriel Glover, Ms. Isabella Glover,

If you are reading this letter, then my friend Arkady Alexandrovitch has given it to you. So I'm glad that he found you and I'm glad that he's made it this far. It's been quite a struggle! My name is Henry Wheyland. I live here in St. Petersburg. I am Arkady's flatmate.

Before I go any further, I wish to convey my condolences. I lost my own mother some years ago, and I know that there is nothing anybody can say that makes the sorrow any less. You have my deepest sympathies.

I hope I can persuade you to believe that what follows is the truth as far as we know! What you choose to do or not do is, of course, up to you. I know Arkady well enough to be sure that he is too proud to ask for or expect anything that you aren't willing to give. I'm pretty sure he won't even read this. He wanted to make contact — just to meet you. The rest is mine. Anything you find presumptuous or thoughtless, therefore, please blame me, not him.

You'll also have to forgive the fact that we don't know how much of this you know! If you are already aware of everything that follows, then you might have decided that this is a part of your mother's life you want to have nothing to do with. In which case, I am genuinely sorry for having brought up what may well be painful. If, on the other hand, you are unaware, then all of this is going to be an awful lot to take in, and I'm sorry that it's through me this information arrives! My defense

is that at least Arkady himself is there and will vouch for my
best intentions.

This, then, is what I know about Arkady. He was born here
in Petersburg. He grew up in the Veteranov orphanage, where
he excelled at the piano. In 1985 he was chosen to play for
Gorbachev. He was supposed to go to the Petersburg Conservatory sometime around 1988 or '89, but when the country
collapsed his scholarship went the same way. I think he waited
for a few more years in the hope that he would still get his
place. He then spent five more unsuccessfully trying to raise the
money himself by playing in bars and so on.

Sadly, Arkady met his mother, your mother, only once. And
I'm afraid he reacted angrily to their meeting. She would have
liked them to become friends but had no desire to force herself into his life. Instead she offered him any kind of help he
wanted. He refused this. I don't think the meeting between
them went well, to be honest. He has never talked to me about
it beyond the barest outlines.

I met your mother twice. (I knew her as Mrs. Maria Glover.)
The first time, some days after she had found Arkady. And
then again, a few weeks after he started his course at the conservatory, when she approached me to ask if it was possible to
listen to her son play. On this second occasion I spent two or
three hours with her at her flat on the Griboedova Canal. This
was when she told me the story of her defection, her new family, as she called it — her marriage to your father and her adop-
tion of both of you. I understood that she had lived in London
for more or less all her life since leaving Russia and that she
and your father had no other, natural children. This life, she
said, became her whole life.

So in fact it was my idea to ask your mother to pay for the
course to get Arkady back on the right track with his music.
It's a strange thing to understand at first, especially of an out-
sider like Arkady, but an integral part of Arkady's ambition is
graduating from the conservatory. I didn't appreciate this for a
while, but it's to do with his institutionalism. As a Soviet or-
phan, he has total devotion to the institution, which, I suppose,
has always been his home, his surrogate parents, if you like. In
some way, he doesn't feel real unless he has passed through
the system fully, passed the exams and been sent out officially
stamped into the world!

Your mother kindly agreed and paid a sum before each term to the conservatory. (In my opinion, she rescued him.) I think the total was something like £8000 a term. He is now midway through his second year of three.

As well as for his own reasons already mentioned, there is a real practical career need for Arkady to finish the course: the whole system here still favors those who come up through the conservatories. It's virtually a requirement. This is how a pianist is first booked on the concert circuit. This *is* the system. This is how they get entered for the big competitions. And so on.

Personally, I'm not sure that he needs any more lessons, and I'd prefer to see him at the Moscow Conservatory anyway. But, well, after this term, which she also paid for in advance, there are three more terms to go. (Two a year here.) You would have thought there would be some provision for the likes of him, but I'm afraid the conservatory is a pretty ruthless (and corrupt!) place and he's too old now, I think, to qualify for the few established scholarships.

In short, Arkady is completely stymied without your mother's help. It's a sad and desperate situation.

Money being what it is, the remaining fees represent a huge sum if you do not have any, and nothing at all if you have lots! I would have liked to pay toward his lessons myself, but, well, that is no longer possible . . .

The fact is this: if you or the wider family can contribute, then you'll be giving the world a really great artist. And I always think we need them! And I'm afraid it does feel a bit now or never. Arkady has an all-or-nothing approach to his music (the Russian mentality!), and I have a real worry that if he does not finish the course, he will see it in some way as proof that he was never meant to do so, and consequently take another path out of something like spite. You will appreciate that because of his age, this is absolutely his last chance. There are already ten years' worth of talented young Russians elbowing him out of the way. But I honestly believe he's better than any of them. I am a great follower of music, and I say here without any shadow of a doubt that he is the best pianist I have ever heard. In any case, you can also be absolutely sure that your mother wanted him to finish the course.

In one way, I am afraid corroboration for all this is a bit thin on the ground. Below is the number of Zoya Sviridova, the woman your mother hired to trace Arkady. She is an independent private detective and will, I am sure, confirm your mother's instructions and corroborate much of what your mother told me. On the piano side of things, Arkady is registered at the conservatory and of course there is no better proof than listening to him yourselves . . . As for myself, if it makes any difference, I trained to be a Catholic priest at St. Steven's Seminary in Birkenhead, was then a teacher at St. David's College in Reading — by all means check the records! My e-mail is below, as well as my postal address. And of course I am happy to arrange to speak on the phone (we don't have one at the flat, I'm afraid, and I'm between mobiles!) or best of all in person if you are planning to come to Russia.

Once again, I am sorry so boldly to intrude on your grief like this and bitterly regret now that I did not establish better communication with your mother, whom I found to be a highly intelligent, warm, and charismatic human being. But I hope you will understand that I write with honest intentions. I wish Arkady only the very best of luck and the opportunity that he has so far not seen too much of. One feels a duty to do one's best by one's friends. And I am very fond of him.

Sincerely,
Henry Wheyland

48

The Snow Begins to Fall

T HERE WAS A TREMENDOUS BANGING. Some stupid bastard trying to break into or out of hell, he wasn't sure which and he didn't care. He wanted to shout and tell them that either way there was no *point*. But there was no point, so he didn't. And so the hammering continued. Which was annoying and distracting. Because he was alone in his cell — deliciously warm, sitting at his desk, trying to study for an exam, which he had in fact already passed the year previously but which for some reason he was now required to take a second time, tomorrow. He was going through past papers. Question number one: "By which great philosopher's light are we now living?" Now *there's* a question. Not Aristotle or Augustine, not Kant or Hulme or Bentham or Nietzsche, not Hobbes, not Marx (that cunning old mule), not Sartre nor Descartes nor good old Machiavelli, not even Christ (not if we're now going to be honest), nor Moses, nor Muhammad, nor Brahma, nor the Buddha for that matter, not even . . .

Shit! The door was opening. He sprang upright, yelling, awoken, hoarse.

"Jesus, Is. Fucking hell. What are you *doing?*"

"Ssshh. Ssshh. It's okay." She was standing just inside the room, the light from the hall behind her shadowing her face.

"It's not fucking okay. Jesus *Christ*." He stared at his sister.

"Ssssh. There are police downstairs. They don't know you are here. You were dreaming, Gabs. You were asleep. That's all. Ssssh." She closed the door behind her, but then it was completely dark again.

"Dear God, woman."

"Gabs, where is the light?"

"No! Don't you dare turn it on." He held up his hand in anticipation of the glare. "Use the side lamp."

"Okay." Leaving a crack of light from the door, she crossed the room and got to the desk.

"You scared the living shit out of me, Isabella." He was shivering from a cold sweat, and his heart would not go back to normal.

She found the switch and twisted the Anglepoise so the bulb lit the sloping attic wall behind, stretching the shadows.

"Get dressed." She was looking at him with the widest smile he had ever seen her manage. "You have to come. You have to come now. With me. Get dressed."

"Where?"

"Now, come *on*. Get dressed."

"Isabella, *what?*" He was recovering.

"You have to come with me." She beckoned. "I'll tell you everything in the cab."

"What in the name of fuck is this about? What are you *doing?*"

"Will you please just get dressed? Please, Gabs. Please. I can't explain everything here now. You are wasting time." Her face implored him. "There's a cab waiting. The driver has already tried to rip me off."

"Is, you can't just —"

"Gabs, please, I am. Come on." She was picking his clothes up off the floor.

"If this is about —"

"It's nothing to do with Dad." She paused. "Or this morning. Just please, please, *please* come on. Hurry."

He looked at her directly for a moment, holding out his jeans in the strange light thrown by the lamp, her eyes dark like his own; hurt contending with forgiveness, injury with loyalty, hostility with the closest lifelong kinship — kinship all the way back, and further. Further. Maybe *that* was the point. Something altered in the chemistry of his body. Almost against his will, aggression and anxiety deserted him; it was one of only two or three times in his life that he had felt the reality of his and Isabella's being twins — the actuality of it — in his twinned blood running, in his twinned heart beating.

"How did you get in here?"

She gave him a rueful smile. "If you come with me and it's anything, anything at all, that you think is me being a stupid cow or wasting time, then I promise, I absolutely promise, you don't have to speak to me ever again."

"Is, for Christ's sake. I'm never not going to speak to you."

"You would. You'd never say another word to me again if you thought it was a matter of principle."

"Same goes for you," he returned.

She threw his pullover at him. "But then, this isn't a matter of principle or whatever," she said. "It's get-your-fucking-clothes-on time."

He shook his head. "I thought I was way ahead in the race for insanity, but you've come right back into the frame tonight, I don't mind telling you. It's neck-and-neck again." He cast back the duvet. "I'm sorry for being such a total arsehole this morning. Where are we going?"

"Don't worry — that was another lifetime ago."

"Feels like it."

"We are both complete arseholes — no getting away from it." She picked up his coat, which was draped over the desk chair. "But I suppose one of us has always been hanging on to the safety rope to haul the other back before. I think we both leaped over the edge together this morning, that's all. We're just going over to Kentish Town. Now get *dressed*."

"Okay, okay, okay." He put on the pullover over the T-shirt he was wearing. "But seriously, Is. I am going mad. I'm really worried . . . I mean it. I'm not just saying . . . I've been in bed all day. It's been terrible. And now, just now — I had this dream."

"You're not going mad. You're seriously bereaved. You've left two girlfriends, whom you probably love, for no reason other than that there are two of them. You hate your job. You hate you father. Both with very good reason. You think that ninety percent of everything is total shit. And you're right. You've fallen out with me, the only family you have left. You haven't got any real money. You don't own anything. And you have no idea what to do with the rest of your life. You're pissed off. Seriously pissed off. Who wouldn't be? Even I would be pretty pissed off if I were you."

"Thanks." He stood and slithered into his jeans. "You missed one thing."

"What?"

"I've also just been burgled."

"I know." She started to laugh out loud.

He sat back down to drag on his socks. "Welcome to my life. Please, go ahead, laugh." He nodded sarcastically, but there was humor in his voice now. "This is one of the best bits. In a minute I am going to get into a very expensive cab with a total head case, also for no reason, and we are both going to speed as fast as we can to fuck knows where."

"I'm sorry, Gabs." She looked around her for the first time. The room was a mess: everything on the floor. "Laptop?"

"Gone."

"Scanner? Printer?"

"Gone. Everything gone."

"Fucking hell."

"But at least my sister is soothing to be around." He bent to tie the laces of his boots. "Anyway, what do you mean you know? How do you know?"

"The police are downstairs interviewing your flatmates. They're all in a state. One of them is shitting it because he's got drugs stashed in his room. One of the others is crying about his computer. That girl, what's-her-name, is saying that she feels like she's been violated."

"So much fun in one day."

"They thought you were out."

"Why?"

"Because your door was locked and you didn't answer when they banged."

"The door *was* locked. And no, I didn't answer. Why did they let you up?"

"I said I had a spare key."

"You are such a liar." He looked around for his wallet. "How did you get in?"

"You left the key in the door," she said.

"I left the key in the door in case anyone *did* have a spare key." He put on his coat.

"So I poked the key out onto a piece of paper on the floor and then dragged it under the door."

He shook his head in genuine consternation. "What are we going to tell the police?"

"They're all in the kitchen in the basement. If we leg it, we'll be fine."

"Seems a bit suspicious, given the general state of things."

Isabella said, "Okay. You go, and I'll tell them you aren't here."

"Jesus. Why am I never allowed to be where I actually *am* in my life?"

Outside, the sleet had finally made up its mind and a thin, ethereal snow was falling, though with no chance of sticking to the streets, which were running wet. The driver had turned and was idling on the other side of the road. Gabriel crossed and stood waiting behind the cab in case someone other than his sister came out. He was struck by the thought that Grafton Terrace looked oddly beautiful now—the street, unusually wide for London, stately even, broad enough for the cars to park diagonally to the curb, and the tall white terraces, London brick, London stucco, with the people warm and snug in so many rooms, and the streetlamps with their halos of light and flurry. Isabella appeared in the doorway, ran down the steps, and motioned to him to get in. He was no great lover of the word, but, well, it looked . . . on the way to Christmasy. Numinous. Maybe the snow would stick overnight.

The meter had already climbed past thirty pounds. The cabbie did not turn to look at them but spoke into his driver-to-passenger microphone. "Back to the pub then, is it?"

Isabella answered, "Yes. Back to the pub."

"No problem, love."

They braced themselves for the speed bumps.

Gabriel's curiosity was a starving crocodile. "Okay. Tell me."

"No. I . . . I can't tell you in the cab."

"Isabella, you *said* you'd tell me."

"Another lie."

"Tell me."

"Gabs, I honestly can't. I need you to understand all this for yourself. The same way I have."

"Understand *what*? This better be—"

"You won't guess." She looked at him, her eyes glassy and bright.

"I don't want to guess."

"Well, don't, then."

"I can't think of anything that you would come and get me for like this."

"Please, honestly, we'll be there in five minutes and then you'll understand. Everything will be clear. Everything in your whole life."

He looked across.

There was so much excitement in the air, raw and crackling, that he could almost taste it, like the near singe of lightning. He realized that the two of them were probably very close to hysteria, but he didn't care.

She paid the cabdriver his filthy millions, but she was first in through the door just the same. And for an awful, stalling second she thought she'd made the biggest mistake of her life. She had not even brought the letter. Gabriel would think that she was . . .

No. There he was.

Thank God.

He had just moved seats for some reason. She hurried over. She'd been gone, what? Half an hour, maybe more. She was aware — madly, peripherally — of two men talking about her as she passed their table. He was now sitting at a place for four, by the wall, underneath some fake-old advertisement for laundry detergent.

"Hi, Arkady, hi . . . Sorry, sorry it took longer than I thought. My brother was asleep and everything. Are you okay?" She bit her tongue. She was treating him like a child.

"Yes. I am okay."

"You moved tables."

"Yes, I moved the table — because now there is three of us and it seems a good idea."

She looked over her shoulder. Gabriel was inside the door, looking around. She felt a sudden surge of loyalty as she motioned toward him.

He came over.

"Lovely place," Gabriel said.

"Gabriel, this is Arkady. We met last week when I was helping you move."

"Hi." Gabriel offered his hand.

"Hello." The Russian stood. And she watched the two very different men greet each other the way men do — serious, eye to eye, shaking as if to affirm some ancient rite that women could know nothing about.

"Oh Christ," Gabriel said, sudden understanding declaring itself in his face. "Sorry. Your e-mail, last weekend — oh, sorry. I am so sorry. I wasn't there. I completely forgot. I was . . . I was moving."

"It is nothing." The Russian seemed oddly cheered.

"But you ran into Is?" Gabriel asked.

She smiled.

Arkady appeared puzzled.

"You met Isabella — last weekend," Gabriel said.

"Yes."

"Thank God for that. I am so sorry." Gabriel shook his head. "Various problems."

"I understand."

Gabriel asked, "Who wants a drink?"

"Arkady, do you want some more tea?" This from Isabella.

"You're drinking tea?" This from Gabriel.

"Yes, we are. Arkady doesn't drink."

Arkady himself spoke. "Maybe once a year. Maybe tonight I drink."

"You ever had a Guinness?" Gabriel asked.

"No."

Gabriel grinned. "Well, this is a good time to start. Made for weather like this. When it's not cold enough for vodka and too cold for normal beer. I'll get you one. Is?"

"Vodka lime."

He nodded.

"For Christ's sake, hurry up, Gabs. Arkady has some important information."

"And you are such a freak. Okay. I'm hurrying."

She sat down with the Russian. She felt that she might chew through her own cheeks. She felt nervous and insane and serene all at the same time. Part of her was staggered afresh by how quickly Gabriel could interpret a situation. (Even though he had no idea what was to come, already he had gleaned that this was Arkady's first time in London. He was putting the man at his ease as she never could.) And another part of her was attempting to be as normal as possible with Arkady and stop treating him like an endangered species from the most precious part of Russia.

Gabriel stood at the bar, conscious that Isabella was looking up at him and then back at Arkady, as if either one were about to die or give birth. He turned away to place his order.

The thought occurred that she was about to announce she was getting married — some hungry-looking Russian she had met two hours ago, and bang, they'd hurried straight to the nearest gastro-pub to seal the bond. He's the one. Hates all forms of convention. Loves music and doing what he damn well pleases in any kind of company. After all these years, it had taken her only two hours to *know* . . . True love—despite everything that happened in the desperate burning world, you still had to factor it in.

He himself was recovering now. Glad to be out of that accursed room. Most of all, he was eager—desperate—to discover how well the man had known his mother. He must have spent a fair amount of time with her, for Isabella to come in person to his own pit of despair. He hoped that they would become friends. Arkady was roughly his own age.

He turned, carrying the drinks. And he felt that sudden warm feeling suffuse him—the feeling of being sheltered inside on a winter's night, of cheer and good company. Yes, he was looking forward to a long evening, listening to Arkady's stories from Petersburg, eating together, talking, real things. The snow too made him ache for Russia. He could see it falling now through the plain glass of the upper windows, still thin and wispy, but falling nonetheless.

He placed the drinks carefully on their table and sat down.

"Here you go."

"Thank you," Arkady said.

"Is."

"Thanks." His sister looked as though she were about to collapse from some kind of overwhelming excitement or pain or something.

"Is, are you all right? Do you need to take your medicine or go to the loo or something?"

Isabella could stand it no longer.

"Arkady. Do you have the letter? I would like my brother to read it."

"Yes," Arkady said.

He took out the letter from the inside pocket of his old jacket and gave it to Gabriel.

"This is true," he said.

49

After Shock

SATURDAY, FIVE DAYS before Christmas, minus three outside, the coldest December on record, and they were running out of places to be. So they were now sitting in the kitchen of Susan's house, back on Torriano Avenue. Arkady was at Gabriel's new place on Grafton Terrace. Gabriel had moved into Larry's spare room. Isabella was still the guest of Susan and Adam. And Susan and Adam had taken the children out to visit Santa Claus, who had set up unlikely shop on the Finchley Road.

The heating, presumably on some kind of a timer, had switched itself off, and Isabella didn't know where the control was and didn't dare fiddle with it in any case. It was absolutely freezing. They were hunched over on either side of the kitchen table, which was covered with coloring books, crayons, and children's activity centers. Indeed, the whole room — with snow sitting on every cross-pane of the window frame, with the bright red plastic fire engine in the corner, the huge yellow rag doll, the piles of Lego on the high chair — the whole place had a faintly surreal, grottolike atmosphere.

Isabella was speaking animatedly: "Christ, yes, of course I'm angry. I'm probably in shock. I'm probably in worse than that."

"Yeah, me too." In contrast, Gabriel's face wore a lugubrious expression. "Me too."

"We have been lied to," Isabella added.

"What's worse than shock — what's the next grade up, medically I mean? Trauma? Is it trauma?" Gabriel narrowed his eyes. "It is, isn't it?" He nodded to himself. "I'm in trauma. That's what I'm in.

Make a note. I am definitely in trauma. Or is it disbelief? Or terror? What's next? What comes after shock? What's top of the scale?"

"All our lives." Isabella shook her head with mild impatience. "All our lives, we have been lied to."

"We don't know that."

"Okay, maybe not. No. But that's why we have no choice but to go."

Gabriel held up his palms. "I've said I'm not arguing with you."

"So . . . right, then. Let's go upstairs to the computer and I'll book you a ticket for later this afternoon."

"Was there anything back from this Henry?"

Isabella frowned at the diversion. "No. But I only e-mailed him this morning, and Arkady said he has to go to the café to check e-mail. He may not get it for days."

"Okay." Gabriel eyed the olive-green Martians in the comic that was open by his elbow.

"And yes," Isabella continued, "we *can* ask him to play the piano, but don't you think that's going to be just a bit awkward? 'Excuse me, Arkady, thanks for coming all the way from Russia with no money and living in a shit hole for two weeks while we ignored you but could you just please play us the Goldberg Variations while we, experts that we are, check out your talent to our satisfaction?'"

"I'm not saying—"

"And what if he is brilliant? Does it change anything as far as we are concerned—as far as *our* lives go? No." She shrugged excitedly. "It may or may not mean we feel duty-bound to raise the money for him to finish his course. But it makes no difference to who our real mother is—or isn't. And if he's dog shit, the same. We still have to go. We have to know everything. We need the answers to some pretty fundamental questions here. And the only—"

"Arkady said he's not going to play anyway," Gabriel cut in. "Not until he knows about the conservatory one way or the other."

"He *what?*" Isabella's flow stopped abruptly.

"That's what the guy said when I tucked him in last night."

"Jesus."

Gabriel blew into his cupped hands awhile and then said, "Even if it's all true, it doesn't change much—Mum is still Mum."

"Of course, Gabs, of course." Isabella knitted her brow. "Come on, I'm not—"

"We've been adopted, that's all. Happens all the time. But she was our mother all our lives. From the first moments of consciousness until . . . until she died."

"Of course. *I'm* not arguing with *you* about that. I feel the same." Isabella softened, hooked her hair behind her ear. "I feel exactly the same. In one way, it changes nothing." She paused a moment. "But in another . . . Anyway, Christ, come on — we don't even know if Dad is actually our dad. I mean, it's that basic, Gabs. We don't know the first thing about who *we* are. We might not —"

"Okay. Okay, I agree. You're right, we do have to know. But regardless of whether we have been lied to or not, the truth, as far as I'm concerned, is that Dad is Dad and Mum is Mum." There was another pause. Gabriel put his hands in his armpits. "Why don't *you* go?" he said. "Go now. You'll be at Waterloo in forty minutes."

"I'm not going. I can't. I . . ." Isabella tailed off and dipped her head to bury the lower half of her face in the scarf she was wearing. "Dad . . . Dad makes me feel so . . . so nauseous." The scarf dropped from her chin as her head came up again. "And anyway, look at the state of me. I can't be calm. I can't even pretend to be calm. I will row with him. I will. I'll start a terrible argument. I'll be absolutely furious from the minute I see him. I will be storming out before I've even stormed in. I can't hide it like you can. I haven't got your ability to . . . I can't . . . I can't make myself unreadable like you can. I'm polished glass to Dad."

Gabriel said nothing.

Isabella pulled her sleeves down over her hands. "And you know, the thing is that Arkady is . . . He is kind of like a solution. Not a problem."

"I'm not saying the guy *is* a problem." Gabriel grimaced. "Jesus, can't you do something about this intense cold?"

"Sorry, no." Isabella bit her lip. "I know you're not saying he is a problem, Gabs. But he's more than not a problem. Think about it. He's the answer. He's kind of brought us back from the brink — well, he's brought me back to my senses, anyway. You may well be past help." She smiled. "I mean, the guy has got nothing at all. He's totally fucked. He has absolutely nowhere to stay. He's got no money. He was actually saying that he needed to start *walking* to the airport for his flight tomorrow because the trains are too expensive."

"They *are* too expensive." Gabriel's eyes ran around the room and back to meet his sister's. "How long is his visa?"

"Six months. But that's not the point. He can't afford another ticket if he misses the flight. That's it. He's stuck."

"We'll buy him one if he wants to stay."

"More than that, he's given us the excuse we need, Gabs. He's the reason. Now you *have* to go."

"Now I have to go? Why me?"

"And . . ." Isabella dipped her head into the scarf again. "And he does look like her."

"Does he?"

"More than we do. Come on. He's got Mum's eyes."

"What do you mean, *I* have to go? If I am going, you are going."

She hesitated. "I don't know if I can stand it — even being in the same room. Seriously. We need to make him talk. Not fight."

"Is, if I am going, then you are going. At least to Paris."

"What about Arkady?"

"We give him some money, obviously. He can stay at Grafton Terrace if he wants. Or he can fly back tomorrow as he planned."

"But what do we tell him about the course? The conservatory."

"That depends." Gabriel stood up. "Can we make some tea, at least? We need *something* that's warm in here to focus on. I've got a bitch of a hangover, and I've been at the police station since eight trying to convince them that I haven't been robbing myself."

"Yes. Make tea. Why do they think that?"

"Divert attention from my robbing everyone else, apparently."

"Makes sense." Isabella smiled again. "Depends on what? What does what we say to Arkady depend on?"

"On whether it's all true. If Arkady is Mum's son for real, then Dad is going to pay for him to finish his course and a whole lot more. Whether the bastard fucking well wants to or not. Even if I have to walk out with an armful of his precious paintings to raise the money."

50

The Fates

THIS, THEN, IS WHAT it came down to: a dribbling and diminished old man sitting in silence beneath a blanket beside an easel on which there was a portrait he could not paint while a dirty winter's rain fell into the raddled old Seine outside.

Waiting.

Waiting for the light to thicken. Waiting for the day to end. Waiting for the week to pass. Waiting for a son who was not his son, a daughter who was not his daughter. Waiting, in essence, for the second stroke of death that surely must be coming — any night soon.

And suddenly now so fearful. Fearful of everything, even as it existed in his own imagination. Fearful of stagnation, fearful of travel; fearful of speed, fearful of stairs, fearful of the sea; fearful of other races, of the street-corner young, of every neighbor's real intentions. And every stranger suddenly an attacker, terrorist, swindler, or thief; every pavement a desperate, seething deathtrap of violence and crime; every ache or sneeze the herald of plague. Fearful of his own bones grown too brittle, his body too slow to heal, his mind too narrow, obsessive, or stale. Fearful of too much company, fearful of none. Fearful of conversation.

Fitting, though. Well shaped. He would give the Fates that. Those three squint-eyed goddesses, spinning their threads, black shawls about their heads, reckoning and rectitude in their every callused fingertip. Clotho: that he who had so traduced the family now had none. Lachesis: that he who scorned convention should feel convention's scorn. Atropos: that he who would so rudely take life's secret temperature in the bodies of a thousand lovers should now be left so cold and unconnected.

And yet. He felt no remorse. There were things he owed to Gabriel and Isabella. There were the duties of the truth. And he would pay these now — for in his own way he loved them both. He was the only father they had known. If they came, he would tell them everything. He would give them all the explanations they required. But no . . . no excuses.

For still he felt it — the old defiance, the lifelong *no*. Sluggish, furred, but undiluted and stirring in his blood still. That great and resolute *no*, swimming the wrong way around his heart. Perhaps this was what had caused the clot in his brain. One day this *no* of his had simply grown too gnarled and swollen to pass along the channels of his lifeblood. The same *no* that had kept him alive all these years was now trying to kill him. His eyes swept the sodden ashes of the winter's sky.

51

Paris

THE TRAIN ROLLED through those somber fields of northern France, the rain hanging in the air, the sky all bruised, low, lowering, washed-out purple giving way to gunmetal gray, the farms here and there, the narrow roads riding the slight rise and fall of the ground, and he sat by the drizzle-straggled window, bad coffee cooling, and thought the same thoughts he thought every time he passed this way: about the two generations of soldiers, unimaginably heroic, those who dug themselves into this mud and those who, twenty-odd years later, hurried back and forth across it, pursued or pursuing. Men dying for a cause, right or wrong. And this imagining kept his thoughts from anything else. Kept him silent and still, imagining most of all the sadness of all the million unwitnessed moments, the horror and the terror and the pain that a certain man might see or find himself amid, for just a second, utterly alone, with no other to corroborate the experience, testify. The loneliness of that second. Then, immediately, more fighting, or death. What generations they must have been.

And this led him to thinking of his own grandfather, Max, and how little he had talked to him — twenty-six-year-old Max, already working for the British with the Russians against Hitler. Or so the story went. But perhaps none of it was true. All that could be certain was that his grandfather lived in Russia, in Moscow and then in Petersburg, doing who knows what for most of his life. Weighing in on one side or the other, or both, and thereby canceling himself out. He wondered what his grandmother had made of it all. Dead thirty years now. Perhaps the real difficulty was that life was far too short.

Just as one generation learned their lessons, they died; and the next had to step forward and start again from scratch, with nothing to work from but those anonymous deep-coded atavistic imperatives, the secret commands of the genes, and whatever few cogent guidelines they had managed to rescue from the minute-by-minute demonstration of human contradiction, confusion, and hypocrisy that was their parents. Or guardians. Childhood: it was like trying to chart an entire continent by the brief flare of a firework. Except that you had no idea that this was your only chance to explore for free, and instead you spent the five seconds of precious light gawping at the sky, stuffing treacle into your mouth. And then it went dark again.

He could not love Paris. Because his father lived there and the whole place seemed to exude his father's manner. This was ridiculous, of course, and he knew it; but then, underneath he had started thinking that everything was ridiculous, so why discard one notion and hang on to others? Nonetheless, he decided to walk to his father's flat and see if the Christmas streets would make him happy, sad, angry, or full of goodwill to all men. He had the notion that he should start treating himself as a human experiment, an ongoing private investigation into the effect of environment on the emotions. Maybe even take some notes. A purpose, at least.

After arriving late yesterday afternoon, he had gone straight to the place he was staying, at the top of the Rue de la Chine, up in the twentieth. His friend Syrie, Anglo-French aspiring actress turned massage therapist, had given him her spare room; they had done a play together years and years ago.

Syrie had gone out early that morning with her boyfriend, Jean-the-physiotherapist. She had left him a map, but he knew the way, more or less — down to Gambetta, past Père Lachaise, and then in along the Chemin Vert. He had set off at twelve, in plenty of time.

Now he stopped at a café and ate a light lunch — mussels in white wine — preferring not to risk the tiredness that heavy food might bring on. He needed to be alert. He tried to read *Le Figaro* and regretted his bad French. He drank a delicious coffee, smoked a perfect cigarette, and watched the passersby. He was beginning to feel more and more disengaged — freewheeling, almost — as he set off again. Perhaps it was Paris after all, his London self hushed, the personality appeasement of a foreign city.

At length, after the Place de la Bastille and the canal, he came to the river and began walking north along the embankment in the direction of the Hôtel de Ville and the Pont Marie. The weather was cold, but at least it wasn't snowing or raining. He was glad of his gloves. Maybe, he thought, if it were not for Isabella, then he wouldn't have bothered. Sure, he would have believed Arkady. He would have uncovered Nicholas's whereabouts. He would have written Arkady a second letter addressed to his father, bought the Russian a Eurostar ticket, and sent him on his way. Sorry, but I can't help. These people, whoever they are — these *relations* — they're an accident. Please, take what you need, do what you can, and good luck. Shout if you are ever in London again.

He came to the bridge and turned left, over the river, a slight wind cold on his right cheek. Or maybe Isabella was right: maybe you simply needed to know. Maybe you could not go anywhere, in any direction, unless you knew where you had started. As a human being, perhaps you had a deep and inescapable requirement to understand your history, your genesis, as clearly and as fully as possible, however painful, however unpleasant. And those who did not, or could not, come to this knowledge walked the earth as if inwardly crippled, forever compensating, forever uneasy, forever secretive. (Jesus, just look at it: Notre Dame like some mighty queen termite, belly-stranded in the middle of the river by the sheer volume of her pregnancy.) But strange that being human was never enough on its own. That the need went further. The need to belong. To belong to one tribe or the other. This is my land, these are my people, this is what we believe — which is where the trouble began. Why could we not be content with species-pride, the staggering good fortune of belonging to humanity itself? Mankind, the mother of all miracles. Wasn't that enough?

And here he was: the Café Charlotte. So this . . . this must be the quay. He seemed to remember this street vaguely from a childhood trip. Ice cream. He turned left, looking up at the numbers as he went along. He had the odd sense of the day as intensely normal and abnormal at the same time — something like watching the closed-circuit footage on the news a week later: this is the station five minutes before the bomb. The sky was as many shades of gray as black and white could fashion. A little windier now, and a bite in that. Curiously, he had remembered the Seine as wider. But of course this was only half of it. This was an island.

Here.

He went under the arch and into the courtyard.

And now, now that he was actually at his father's address, his heart, his spirit, his mind, everything suddenly felt like a million maggots writhing. And he was astonished to find that there was no anger either — or no anger anywhere near the surface, no hostility, no upset, no sadness or seething. Instead there was only this overwhelming, excruciating sense of embarrassment.

He stopped at the bottom of the century-worn stairs. He felt painfully, agonizingly nervous, shy. He felt ashamed of himself. And it was beyond anything he had ever experienced before — terrible nerve-squirming embarrassment. Worse, he was not just embarrassed for himself but also, unbelievably, embarrassed for his father. Dear God. Despite everything, here he was, stuck still, empathizing with the old goat for having to enact *his* part in this ghastly meeting with so ridiculous a son.

He leaned against the wall in the semidarkness. He felt physically sick with it. Of all the reactions, he had least expected this one.

Time stalled. He could neither go up nor turn around. He became apprehensive that at any minute someone might come out of one of the other doors on the staircase and wonder what the hell he was doing. So, madly, he took his telephone from his pocket and began thumbing through the names in his address book for no reason. He had the idea that he might call someone. Might, in fact, call Isabella.

Christ, today was the wrong day. Maybe it was the train ride. But there was nothing there. No fury and no flame. No injury, no hurt. He was terrified that he wouldn't be able to remember what it was all about ever again, that he might go in there, go through with it all, and at no point do justice to whatever it was he had previously thought had been so traduced all his life. This was a new malaise altogether: standing in the shadows of his father's stairway, scared to move in case anyone heard him.

The door opened.

"Okay . . . I have to go," he said to nobody, into the receiver of his telephone, before making a show of pressing a button to end the call.

"Gabriel. I thought it must be you."

The figure in the doorway looked nothing like his father. He was an old man, completely white-haired, with rheumy eyes, and thin, very thin; and now, as the door was pulled back, Gabriel could see that this old man moved with great difficulty and with a cane.

"Gabriel."

The shock. "Hello, Dad."

Nicholas smiled, a little lopsidedly, but abruptly Gabriel saw that it was there—the light, the old familiar animus. It was as if the stroke had left his father with a death mask as his default face; as if eerie blankness was where he must begin and must quickly subside; and it was only when he physically, consciously willed himself to move his muscles that expression returned, flooding into his features.

"Sorry." Gabriel was conscious that he was already apologizing. "I just had to finish a call."

"Come in. Come in." Nicholas beckoned, his arm extended. "It's freezing out there."

Conscious too that he was apologizing for something that he hadn't actually been doing at all, something that was not in fact true. So it began.

"It's not too bad. I walked here."

"From London?"

"From the twentieth."

"Ah, shame—thought you might be able to teach me how to walk on water so that I can annoy my doctor. He's a very difficult man to impress. Danish. But walking-on-water-and-bugger-the-cane would do it, I imagine." Nicholas closed the door and turned. "It's very good to see you, Gabriel."

The charm was there yet. But for these two men, for whom physical contact and human touch meant so very much, there was no embrace. Instead Gabriel merely stood looking around at all the wood, the paintings on the walls, the elegance.

"How are you, Dad?"

"I'm fine. It's taking me longer to recover than I had hoped, of course—it sort of goes in fits and starts. I was quick at first, but not so now. Still"—he dragged his lips into a smile—"I'm able to get out of the apartment as of this week, and my walking *is* improving. I'm aiming to go all the way to Notre Dame and back by the end of the month. A pilgrimage. I count myself lucky. Very lucky. My speech wasn't really affected. The Dane says I'll be passing myself off as normal soon enough."

His face fell to nothing again and he shifted his weight onto his cane.

Gabriel remembered what his mother had once said about his father, about him being a man of so much energy, about that being what had attracted her to him. And now, a man of so much energy so reduced. He spoke to stop himself from sympathizing any further.

"These are beautiful rooms." They were in a paneled antechamber with three double doors leading off, ahead and to either side. Everything smelled of rosewood and furniture wax. The walls were hung with paintings by artists Gabriel assumed to be famous but whom he had no hope of recognizing. He looked about self-consciously. He focused on the fabric of the building instead: the slight bulge between the wooden beams of the ceiling, the slight slope of the parquet floor.

"When was this place built?"

"Bourbons." His father's eyes actually twinkled. "As haute bourgeois as I could manage. Here, give me your coat and gloves. And you go on through." He gestured to the door on the right. "We will sit in there — you can see the river. Though it's miserable on a day like this, I like to keep an eye on it just the same."

Gabriel took off his coat and handed it to his father and watched him turn slowly and half shuffle, half walk toward the stand. He didn't know whether to wait or go, so he waited. Nicholas hung his coat on a wooden hanger, but it was awkward for him using only one hand, the other on his cane.

As if reading Gabriel's mind, Nicholas spoke over his shoulder. "I have someone here to help every day." He raised his voice. "Alessandro?"

Then, his cane like the center point of a mathematical compass, he turned, one quarter at a time. "He comes by twice every day, which is useful. I told him to wait for you, so he could make us some tea or something. Do you want tea? Or would you rather —"

"Tea is fine." Though he said it lightly, Gabriel suddenly felt severe, like a puritan or an overearnest college sportsman. And he had forgotten his father's extraordinary ability to make every gesture count, every word weigh, as if there were always some underlying contest to each encounter, an underlying score to be kept, advantages gained, points lost, positions suspected, held, or revealed as false — the results of which somehow showed exactly what sort of person you *really* were. He felt compelled to add, "Tea is fine. I had a heavy night last night."

"Good French wine, I hope."

"Couscous, mainly."

"This is the age of the tureen."

"I am staying with people obsessed with couscous."

"These are the creatures of the twentieth?"

"Friends, Dad."

A man about his own age but pretending to be younger appeared from the opposite door.

"Alessandro, we're going to have tea. Could you bring it through and . . . and a jug of milk?"

The reminder of his father's many pathological subversions allowed Gabriel to recover himself, fortify himself. Though he disliked the trait, he was, he knew, fearsomely equipped with a similar arsenal. Updated, though. The next generation.

"Of course, Nick. Hi." The man waved as if to suggest that he was too busy or too discreet to come over. "I'm Alessandro. You must be Gabriel. I have heard so much about you."

Lies, Gabriel thought as he said a polite hello.

Five minutes later Gabriel stood by the high river window of the drawing room, waiting for his father to make the unbearably incremental journey from the door. In his mind's most secret eye (wherein he had foreseen that this time would eventually come), he had long imagined that they would sit down face to face, that he would mentally shuffle his papers, and that he would then begin — solemnly — to ask a series of questions, which Nicholas would — candidly — answer: the penitent former foreign secretary finally facing the nation's great journalist; why did you really invade, you oleaginous bastard, and what in the name of the living fuck did you think was going to happen once you were in there? But he had no chance to marshal his teeming thoughts — half hostile, half appalled; half compassionate, half desperate; halving and halving again every time he managed to fix on any single one in particular — no time to recover from the simple shock of the past three months, of everything, no time before Nicholas preempted him.

"What was the funeral like?"

"Surreal."

"On Vasilevsky?" Nicholas stopped two steps in, steadied himself, and looked up.

"Yes. The Smolensky."

"Surreal. Hmmm."

"I mean . . . it happened so fast . . . everything. Five days, I think. Isabella stayed longer, but I couldn't — I . . . I had to get back."

"It is a shame Isabella could not be with us today."

"The consulate was helpful. More than that."

"Of course." Nicholas moved forward. Cane. Pivot. Plant one leg. Shuffle the other. "You know that Masha always wanted to be buried there? In Petersburg."

"I didn't know that."

"No reason why you would." He stopped again. A crooked effort at a smile. "Yes, she was most enthusiastic about it. Very macabre woman when she wanted to be." Forward. "Well, I'm glad that there was a proper burial and that she was where she wanted to be, even if we did have to pay the bloody church for the privilege of using her own soil. I'm glad it went to plan." Nicholas bowed his head and concentrated on his walking.

Gabriel did not know whether he was supposed to apologize for not inviting his father to the funeral or thank him for taking care of the expenses, chivvying the consul, paying the hotel, all of it. So he stood and watched his father's labored progress and said nothing. Christ, why did he feel as though everything was always, *always,* a chess game with his father? And why did all available moves somehow always look disadvantageous? Zugswanged — that was the word. (Cane forward. Plant. Pivot. And shuffle.) Even in the most innocuous of conversations, it was impossible to escape the impression that his father had some great elliptical plan — had somehow foreseen this moment and made his moves in Petersburg the better to pin son and daughter when this precise and well-foreseen configuration arrived. Check . . . I think you will find that the only place you can go is there. But I'd like to think about it, Dad. Fine, but only one move is available, I promise you. Fine, but I'd still like to think about it. Perhaps that was one way to beat him: to refuse to move. Play for a time victory. His clock had a three-decade advantage. At least, he thought (as his father stopped again), at least it made him angry that it was always chess. At least *this* experience was customary. Even if all the rest — stroke, Paris, this apartment — was not. This anger he recognized. And he welcomed its return like that of a long-lost brother. Again, though, before he could harness his thoughts to speech, Nicholas surprised him.

"I was there. The week before she died. She was very ill. Cancer."

"I know she was ill. I guessed it was cancer. I didn't know you visited."

"We spent three days together." Nicholas raised his face once more, and this time Gabriel saw an unfamiliar expression — but whether it was the effect of the stroke or some twisted contour of grief, he could not tell. "We even managed to go to the Hermitage

for a few hours. I knew she was in agony, but I didn't really appreciate the sheer . . . the sheer *incapacity* of serious illness — not until
this." Nicholas gestured with his cane. "The damage it does to your
sense of self, your mind. The courage you need."

At last he collapsed heavily into his leather chair. "I couldn't go
back. Not after that. And — selfish, perhaps — but I have better mem-
ories this way. Masha lecturing me on painting techniques — those
eyes of hers, shining."

Gabriel took the chair opposite. There was a side table between
them. And the radiator beneath the window caused the hot air to
quaver as it reached the draft. He let his eyes go to the river, hoping
to bathe his mind clean. Then he reached across to stop his father's
cane from falling and prop it against the chair.

"Thank you. She forgot the pain, I think, for a few minutes each
day. I sourced some excellent pills for her — they don't sell them
here. Cox-2 inhibitors, they're called. I tried to persuade her to come
back. I was prepared to return to London and see her properly cared
for. We could live together in the old house. But she said, of course,
that she was *already* back. Typical. Headstrong. I don't think she really had a chance. In any case, I can't take bloody funerals. Make
sure they burn me, won't you, Gabriel?"

Gabriel flinched inwardly.

The door opened and Alessandro appeared, carrying a pot of tea
on a tray with two mugs. He had the manner of a bit-part actor who
wished the audience to know that they were witnessing not so much
a play (by whoever, about whatever) as one of the great injustices of
modern casting. Nonetheless, Gabriel found himself grateful for the
simple speed with which the guy moved.

"Thank you, Alessandro. Thank you for waiting in," Nicholas
said.

Alessandro seemed to make a point of ignoring his father and in-
stead addressed Gabriel. "I wasn't sure whether to go for Russian
Caravan or Lady Grey or Higgins Afternoon. In the end I thought
Russian Caravan."

Nicholas said nothing.

Gabriel said thank you.

Alessandro said, *"De rien."* And began to faff with the table and
then with the tea.

Gabriel's eyes returned to the river. The problem, as ever, was
that both things were simultaneously true. His father was struggling
more than necessary, Gabriel was sure, but the stroke, the indignity,

the difficulty, were genuine. His father was playing out his charm, but Gabriel sensed there had also been real relief and pleasure in his greeting. His father knew that he would not have been welcome at the funeral, but he also genuinely had not wished to be there. And now, most duplicitous of all, Gabriel could not escape the feeling that his father's revelation of a reconciliation with his mother was calculated to hurt as much as to heal. Sly, always sly; but steadfast too — never gave in. You think you're dealing with slime, you shut your eyes, you hold your nose, and just where you plunge in your hands, you hit granite. Perhaps after all his father had loved his mother, but he had also treated her like . . . like shit. For *decades*.

Alessandro was about to leave. This was it. Speak now; use the fact that the Italian was still in the room and his father's manners would require him to wait until they were alone. Speak. First. Speak now. No more of your theater, Father. No more. Now.

"Who is Arkady Alexandrovitch?"

His father's pupils contracted. "Arkady is probably your mother's son. Has he turned up? I thought he might."

"Don't speak in riddles, Dad." Nastier for the casualness, Gabriel thought. "Just tell me the truth. Who is he?"

"I am doing so. Masha had a son. Before I met her."

"And so you think Arkady . . . Why *probably?*"

"She was unmarried, of course. She was attacked. Or close enough to make no difference. She never discussed it with me."

That expression again on his father's face: the pain of memory, of movement?

"Why probably?"

"She never spoke of the matter at all. It was her secret. The father was somebody high up in the Party, I think. I really don't know. Assuming that this person, Arkady, is not lying, then it's probably him. That's why *probably*. I can't be sure."

There could be nobody else in the world who understood how to make a general nonchalance hurt so precisely.

"How do you know any of this?" Gabriel deliberately withheld what he knew of Arkady's story. He wanted to know if his mother had told his father that she had met her son again in Petersburg.

"Grandpa Max."

No, she hadn't.

"Grandpa Max," Nicholas continued, "took great care to tell me all about it when he knew I had fallen in love with her. He was that kind of a man. I'm afraid you didn't . . . But he miscalculated. If anything, it caused me to love Masha more. She was working for the Party then. She probably had to go and see the bloody brute who got her pregnant every day. Some fat fake Communist in a uniform. They were all such fakes. Except good old Joe. Oh, *he* meant it. Every minute. You want to know what I think?"

Gabriel said nothing.

"I think she tried to have the child aborted and there was some horrific botch job and —"

Gabriel's eyes reached for the river.

"That's why she couldn't have children."

He forced them back, dark as ink but incandescent, as if they might set fire to whatever they beheld, and he fixed them directly on his father. "Who am I, then? Who is my sister?"

"Don't worry. You are twins."

"Don't speak to me facetiously."

"Don't ask me these questions as if I am some kind of Old Testament mystic, then."

"I'm asking you as your son. You are my father. Answer me as a father."

"No. That's just it." Nicholas was unflinching. "I am not your father."

"We were adopted." Neither did Gabriel's face change. "I accept that. But you are still my father."

"And yet I can't speak to you as if you are my son. I have never been able to. That is our problem. That is what lies at the root . . . the root of all these twisted branches between us."

"Who am I?" Still Gabriel held his father's hollowing gray eyes.

"As a brother, though, maybe as a brother . . ."

"For Christ's sake, please, just tell me the truth. For once. As a fellow human being."

"Your real father is my father. Your real father is Max."

Only now did Gabriel let himself look away a moment. Then back. "And my mother?"

"Your real mother's name is Anastasiya. She was one of . . . one of our father's lovers. There were many."

Gabriel felt his blood prickle, as if her very name were causing it to seek the surface.

Nicholas said, "I have a single letter she wrote. It was in his papers. It's in Russian, of course. She refers to you as Maxim and Anna. Masha changed your names. She wanted to invent you all over again. As hers."

"How old were —"

"Not yet a year old."

"What —"

"I never met your real mother. I was at Cambridge when they began their affair, and she was not at any of the parties when I went back — or not that I knew. I don't have any photographs — I am sorry. You might want to look at some of the pictures of the Kirov from that time. She was in the chorus for a while, I think. A bad dancer."

"Is she alive?"

"No. She died. Our father ruined her life. He gave her money. And of course she was reported. Not very intelligent."

"How do you know?"

"I know that she is dead. I do not know how she died. In Max's will there is a provision for a certain sum of money to be paid annually for flowers. I went through everything when I went out there after he died. It was not an insubstantial amount. The solicitors gave me the name of the recipient of the money. It was a family of florists at Troitsky. It turned out that Max had arranged for them to put flowers on a woman's grave once a week. I called them pretending to know all about it. They were happy to tell me where it was — I went to see for myself. The grave is there. The flowers too. The name on the headstone is the same as that on the letter. She never married. I am sure she is your mother."

"Thank you." Gabriel dropped his eyes a moment. His face was expressionless. But inside he felt as though his lifeblood were reversing direction. He was empty. He was full. He wanted to suck air into his lungs. He wanted to be sick.

Nicholas put down his cup. "The funny thing is that I never thought I would have this conversation with you. I never thought I would be saying any of this, Gabriel, I really didn't. It was the one principle, the one silence I set myself to honor. For your sake. For Izzy's sake. For Masha . . . And yet now, all of a sudden — now I find that it's the only conversation I have ever wanted to have. Indeed, I realize I have been thinking about it all my life. Ever since the day I first saw you — here in this city, not two miles away. You and Is, side by side, crammed together in a single pram on the corner of the Rue des Islettes."

Gabriel, his eyes back on the river, gave no sign that he was still listening, but above the din of the revolution burning through his body, he was hearing something in Nicholas — his father, his brother

—that he had never heard before, and he was stuck fast to his seat, pulled equally between his ferocious desire to leave forever and his need to stay close to the sound of something true, to hear every last word.

"You were less than a year old, and . . . and you were helpless, Gabriel, totally helpless." Nicholas let out a tightened breath. "I had been with your mother some time then—let's call Masha your mother, because that is what she is. There were difficulties. She could not have the children she wanted. I had my own troubles. We were also very poor. Excruciatingly so. We were enjoying our lives in Paris, but we needed to find work. I had not heard from my father since I left Russia with your mother. Then, out of the blue, he sent a message—we did not even have a phone—he sent a message, with a messenger—can you imagine that?—sent a message that he was in Paris. He had come for a visit, he said. And just like that he arrived at our tiny apartment on Goutte d'Or."

Gabriel's face was still turned slightly toward the window. He was rigid against the waves of sickness within. He realized what it was: it was fear stalking his father. His father was afraid. As simple as that.

"But actually Maximilian had come to strike a deal with me. Do you want a real drink?"

"No thanks."

"Look, Gabriel." Nicholas grasped his cane. "I know you cannot forgive me, and really I don't ask you to—I am not interested in for-giveness—but I would like now to tell you at least some part of what my life has been. No excuses and no self-exoneration—I am not a fool. I know . . . I know that we are all of us able to choose, and my choices have been, with no exception I can think of, selfish. I do realize all of that—and such as they are, I stand by my choices. I and no other am responsible for my actions."

He sought Gabriel's eyes again, as if to fix them with an intensity that he could not evade.

But Gabriel, aware perhaps of their keenness, continued to look steadily away, his gaze on one particular turbulent spot in the moving water.

Nicholas, exasperated, sat back, his knuckles white around his cane. "In essence, the old bastard offered me the house in Highgate and an annual sum for maintenance—I'm giving you all the details —to adopt you two as my own. Your mother was desperate to have children anyway. I saw no grave harm in the idea. You were my brother and sister, after a fashion. I bore you no ill will. I never have. Our father would pay for your education and upkeep. For the rest of my life, I would be free to pursue what I was interested in rather than forced to work for work's sake. I said yes. And I — we, all of us — have been living with the consequences of this deal, for good, for bad, ever since." Now Nicholas also looked out. "That was the choice I made. I could have said no, of course. But I did not. I was offered a life of relative ease. I took it."

Gabriel felt his breathing becoming shallow. There was acid in his throat. He had faced all he had come to face. He was exhausted.

"I also rescued you. And I never once went back on . . . I never went back on my bond to you. However bad a would-be father I have been, I never once — though sometimes circumstances screamed at me to do so — I never once broke the spell. Not even when I was drunk and furious with you, with Isabella, your mother, myself." The cane fell with a clatter. "I kept to it. I kept you believing that she — that fine, fine woman — was your mother, and that I — I was your father. I have always wanted you to believe Masha was your mother." He held his shaking hands out in front of him over the table, staring, as if appalled that they belonged to him. "I did it . . . I kept the necessary secrets . . . I did it as much for your mother's sake as for any other. I knew she was capable of loving you as her own. And I wanted . . . I wanted her always to have you two — you two pretty, clever, troublesome children — to love and to care for. In her exile. And you both to love her in return, as if she were your own flesh and blood. To love her without distance, bridle, or complaint. Unequivocally. Since . . . since I have always known that I would be a failure in this. I did it for my wife."

Gabriel looked down at his father's trembling hands for a second, then abruptly stood. His vision was suddenly blurred. And his heart was traveling too fast, ricocheting from fury to confusion to numbness to exhilaration and back again. He could not trust himself anymore. He had to leave. And no, he was not ready to agree to this last devious bargain: to accept his father as a brother was to absolve him as a father, and this he could not do. When in fact nothing was changed. Not a single cruelty was excused. Not to him, his sister, or his mother. No, there could be no understanding, and certainly no forgiveness.

"I am sorry, Dad. I do not know you as my brother. Only as a father. Only as *my* father. This is all I know." The taste of bile was in his mouth. "It may not be true, it may be founded on this lifelong lie, but that lie became my life. And for now, what is true is of no consequence. I have to go."

"The letter?"

"Isabella will take it. Don't — I can see myself out."

"Are you going to come back tomorrow?"

"Goodbye, Dad."

He leaned over the water and heaved his stomach inside out. The convulsions ripped through him, sudden paroxysms that gripped his body and emptied his mind. The river carried the sickness slowly away.

52

On the Waterfront

THE NEXT DAY, Sunday, the fifty filthy shades of gray were all gone, unimaginable, and instead the sky was uniformly blue. A sharp winter's cold was on the lips, a soft winter's light on the cheek; the river walks were busy again beneath the embankments with people in striped scarves and coats and gloves; the drunks were out beneath the bridges, their stocks of brittle bonhomie briefly replenished; children were running ahead of chatty mothers, fathers in responsible colloquy two steps back, joggers; a blue-fingered juggler, a dozen walkers of a dozen different dogs, an elderly couple renewing their lifelong domestic hostilities, a slouch of teenagers (stereo thumping), tourists taking and retaking the same shot with a digital camera, and a man with white hair having considerable difficulty walking beside a young woman in an elegant pale coat.

And there ahead Notre Dame, a great leviathan, she thought, turned to stone by some gorgon of even greater dominion.

"Who is Alessandro?" she asked as her father drew up alongside. The Italian had just left them on the riverside walk and was climbing back up the stone stairs to the quay.

"He is a friend, Isabella, whom I pay handsomely."

"Strange friend."

"The most reliable sort."

They walked on. And she fell into something of a pattern: she would wait patiently for Nicholas until she sensed that his effort to make progress was crossing from authentic to performance. Then she would take two or three steps of her own, ignoring him awhile, before turning back to address him once more.

"Besides everything else, why didn't you tell us you were gay?"

Nicholas did not pause or look up but continued to concentrate on walking.

"I strongly dislike that ridiculous little word. Do you really want to talk about my private life? Is that why you came?"

"No . . . no. I suppose I just want to . . . to understand." She felt herself weakening and so repeated her pattern of going ahead for a while. "I want to understand why you treated Mum so badly."

He stopped, looked up, and raised his voice, as if the distance were at least double the three strides. "You think, at this late stage, that if I declare that I am conveniently homosexual, this will be a satisfactory excuse."

"No," she said. He genuinely did not care what other people thought of him; she would give him that.

"Well, then." Her father shook his head.

She did not know what else to say on this matter—suddenly there seemed to be nothing *to* say. Perhaps that was his skill. In any case, she had vowed to Gabriel, to herself, not to argue. So she fell silent, watched her father, waited, walked on, waited.

She had spent yesterday morning with Arkady. She had given him money for the train to the airport. And then she had caught a late-afternoon Eurostar. Gabriel had met her at the Gare du Nord, fresh from his ordeal. Blankets stolen off the beds and thus wrapped against the cold, they had stayed up most of the night, sitting on the tiny balcony of their small hotel room, looking down through iron railings on the Rue des Grands-Degrés, drinking red wine, water, hot tea. Talking.

"As far as the third bench up there." Nicholas brandished his cane.

"Okay."

They were side by side for a moment.

Softly he said, "I am very fond of you, Isabella. I admire your intelligence. And your pride."

She resisted the urge to take his arm.

"The pills, Zeloxitav, that you gave Mum—I looked them up. They have been withdrawn in this country—I mean in England—because they are thought to have side effects."

"Where? Where did you look them up?"

"On the Internet."

"I see." Nicholas dragged up his eyebrows in an expression of disdain.

She went ahead and turned her back on her father to look at the cathedral again. Gabriel had been right: every second was agony.

"It's astonishing how sharp the flying buttresses look in this light, isn't it?" he said from behind her. "So exactly defined against the sky."

"Yes." How did he know what she was thinking?

Another family was coming toward them. The parents, not much older than she, smiled as they passed, telling their children to take care, take care. Nicholas stood still until they had all gone by. Then on again he went, head down. There was something heroic in his effort, something almost ferocious. It occurred to her that he had taken on a similar air to the one she remembered Max having — that air of irreducibility. Although it was different, of course, with Nicholas, tinged with bitterness and anger — an irreducibility despite everything he was rather than because of everything. But the spirit had traveled — in the blood, in the manner. The genes passed on their codes, like it or not.

They walked on together for another ten minutes, stopping and starting in their odd fashion. They had covered less than fifty yards.

"Here, I have a handkerchief. You can wipe it dry."

Isabella attended to the bench. She wished she had brought a hat. Her ears were cold.

Nicholas sat down.

She sat beside him, facing the river, her hands curling and uncurling in the slim pockets of her coat. Then, without turning her head, she said, "You probably killed her, you know. The pills were withdrawn because they caused strokes."

"I loved your mother all my life."

"You may even have done it deliberately."

He looked across.

And now she turned in time to see his face attempt to express irritation and then fall blank again, though whether because the effort was too much or because he thought better of signaling enmity, she could not tell.

"But you can also be very foolish sometimes, Isabella. For all your intelligence, you continue to act on your emotions. Whenever the wind is full in your sails and you are careering forward, it's your feelings powering you. You are wholly at their mercy. Until they subside, you have no choice but to race on. And if the wind changes direction, then you do too. You should learn to tack."

"I didn't come all this way to hear you talk rubbish, Dad."

"Yes you did, I'm afraid." He managed a smile and turned back to face the river, holding his cane in front of him, his sheepskin gloves perched together on top.

A pleasure boat was passing by.

"She was dying, Izzy, she was dying. And do you want to know something?"

"What?" Isabella raised her chin a fraction, watching the tourists sitting with their faces pressed up against the windows of the boat.

"By the end she was begging me to kill her. Day and night, she implored me to help her die."

Isabella stiffened.

"That's what we really talked about for those long three days — death," Nicholas continued. "Death. That's *all* we talked about. It was bloody terrible. The one thing she wanted most in the world was to die while I was still there. 'To oversee it,' she said. Everything, Izzy, everything — a game of chess, our trip to the Hermitage, each cup of coffee — everything was to be 'for the last time.' She would not do anything — she would not even lie down — unless we pronounced that it was 'for the last time.' And I had to go along with it. I thought . . . I thought if I played along, then I could take her to the Hermitage 'for the last time,' and that way I could get her out so that she would see life again, life outside, her favorite paintings, at least, and then maybe she would stop, come to her senses. No more death. But I was wrong. She did not stop; she carried on. 'If you love me,' she kept saying, 'help me.' She was scared. So scared. 'If you ever really loved me, help me.' She begged me when she was angry. She begged me when she was crying. She did not believe . . . She did not believe there was any point. It was beneath her dignity." Nicholas raised his cane a millimeter or two and tapped it down after each phrase to lend his words emphasis. "But still I refused. I refused to allow her not to fight on. I arranged for her to see a specialist. I booked myself a flight back to Russia. I was determined that she should live."

"I do not understand you," Isabella said quietly.

"And those pills — those pills eased her pain tremendously. Those pills blocked out the suffering of her body. They allowed her to think and to talk again. When you are in serious pain, Isabella, you cannot do either. Those pills gave her back the privilege of her mind. The human privilege. No, Isabella — you do not consciously kill the ones you love. And I was then, I have always been, and I am still very much in love with Masha. She is the other half of what I am."

"I do not understand you at all."

"I do not ask you to."

She turned to him and searched his face. This was it — at last, this was it: the real questions behind all the other questions.

"Why — in God's name, why did you cheat on her so . . . so openly, for so long, and with such *contempt?* Why torture her? How do you think that made her feel?"

"I tried not —"

"And why cheat on us? We could never trust you. Do you have any idea how it feels for a child to know that her father is fucking every man and woman who comes through the front door?"

"Yes, I have a very good idea of how that feels."

"Then all the more so — why? I knew. Gabriel knew. Dad, you had people — you had lovers *to the house.* You rubbed our noses in your . . . your . . . your —"

"I could not leave. I had made a deal. I had made a commitment to your father, to Ma —"

"Rubbish. You could've left. You could have worked it out with Grandpa — with Max. Left for good. Properly. Split up. Gone. We could have visited you at weekends or whatever. You could've spared Mum — you could've spared us all — the torture of having to know you and . . . and *witness.* You *wanted* an audience."

His eyes held hers.

She did not look away.

"Isabella, I cannot explain any of this, least of all to you."

"Why not? I would say that it is specifically to me that you owe an explanation."

"Because the answer is not rational."

"But only a moment ago you said that I was the queen of the emotional high seas, that —"

"Because —" His voice raised, he cut her short. "Because you are who you are — my daughter, in every important way." He looked away, then softened, speaking again to the river. "And if I even begin to attempt to explain myself to you, it will only make you . . . only make you dislike me all the more. No child likes to hear of her parents' true lives."

But she was mesmerized by the moment. And involuntarily, her hand reached sharply for his sleeve, as if to grasp hold of something within her father that she had not seen or touched before.

"For Christ's sake, Dad, please stop. Stop shielding me. Stop acting for me. Stop trying to control everything. Let me decide. Let me know. Let me deal with whatever I have to deal with. It is not for you to worry about me — if that is what this is."

"You sound like Gabriel's bloody magazine."

"Forget that I am who I am. Forget that we are who we are. Forget everything. Just try to tell me the truth, as one person to another. A stranger, if it helps."

"Clever of you to understand that strangers help. Your mother saw that too." Nicholas sucked his crooked teeth, then turned to face her again. "Very well." He drew his cane toward him so that his chin was almost resting on his hands and half turned, speaking into the space between them. "All my life, for reasons that I do not know, Isabella, I have wanted — no, I have *needed* — the intimate company of other human beings. Dear God, believe me, I have thought that it was psychosis, I have thought that it was insecurity, I have thought it was loneliness, madness, vanity, selfishness, lust, anger, depression . . . And it's all of these things, I admit it. I admit it to you — as surely as those idiots on that boat would admit that they wished they had paid the extra for the headphones instead of pretending to themselves that they can speak French. But more than any of these, much more, it's actually to do with feeling alive. And I can say that now and really mean what I am saying." He inhaled heavily through his nose, as if to emphasize how much he had come to value every breath. "This fact your mother understood. Intuitively. Yes, it is to do with feeling life's only meaning close up. You know — the chaff and chatter all stripped away, the naked beauty of creation right there and present and real. Action and reaction, the body and the mind, offer and response. Where words end and even freedom itself flags, that's where the act of love begins. And I know, of course I know, that for some people — for most people — a single other is enough, is all they want, is satisfaction. But for me — for me, not so. Again, your mother understood this. And there was shelter in her understanding. And I loved her for it. I never wanted ease or comfort or familiarity or affirmation or the certainty that bills would be paid and children fed. I did not want any of life's kindly smothering disguises. I could not be contented like that." His voice strengthened, and he raised his head as if to address the river itself. "No, I wanted life naked and truthful, and I wanted to gaze upon its revealed face over and over again by the changing light of a hundred different souls. I wanted to feel its brutality, its gentleness, its recklessness, its caution, its power and its weakness, its give and its take. I wanted to fix it in my arms and see it shining in every pair of eyes I lay with.

I can't play the violin or — Christ knows — paint, I really *cannot* paint, Isabella; I can't write; and I have neither the hands to work the land with nor the obsequiousness required for any kind of office. I can't teach or heal or make." He seemed to wince against some new pain. "Forgive me, Isabella, but the act of love was — is — as close as I could get to life's disappearing quiddity. I was born that way. Or I became that way. Born or made — who knows? You can answer that question better than I. But every nerve of mine asks me to it again and again. Even now, it is what forces me to take each one of these tortured steps. For me, it *is* life."

Isabella was silent awhile. The river ran on.

"And yet, Dad, there are some lies still, even in what you've just said. Because you *did* have the bills paid, you *did* have security. Okay, we never had much money, I know that, but —"

"Some lies too." Nicholas interrupted her quietly. "Always some lies. The salt."

"But in fact," Isabella continued, ignoring him, "you never had to worry about feeding or clothing your children. Our true father saw to that. If we'd only known the real reason he was giving you money. We both thought he was just being a nice grandpa! Christ, did you ever have any of your own, Dad? Was it all his? I bet Mum paid for our summer holidays with the money she *earned*. But how did you fund all those trips abroad that none of us went on?"

Nicholas said nothing. And suddenly she was empty and tired and she wanted desperately to leave him. To go, swiftly, directly. To Russia. She turned away. "Do you have anyone? Apart from Alessandro."

"I have lots of friends here."

"You know what I mean."

"There is a woman — Chloe — whom I would like you to meet . . ." He hesitated. "If we are to become friends again."

"Is that what you want?" she asked. She felt his eyes on the side of her face.

"I would like it if we could see each other from time to time. Continue this conversation."

"I don't know if I can ever have this conversation with you again. I'm sorry, Dad." She looked at him again but could not meet his eyes anymore. "You're right. I *am* your daughter. Maybe not born but made so. And I can't suddenly be your friend and . . . and everything. Not just like that."

"I do not expect anything to be quick. But let's at least admit that we find each other interesting company, if nothing more." He tapped his cane. "Where are you staying?"

"No. I am not staying. I'm going home this evening. Back to London with Gabriel."

"What about Christmas?"

"We are ignoring Christmas. We are going to Petersburg. We'll have Russian Christmas in January."

She stood.

Nicholas nodded slowly. "Your mother's flat is paid for and empty until the summer, if you wish to stay there."

"I'm not sure."

"And what about you, Isabella, what do you want?"

"I want what Mum wanted. I want you to pay for the course for Arkady. I want you to write me a check for the full amount now. You can give it to me with the letter when we go back. Then I want you to set up a fund so that he gets enough to live on for the next ten years. If you don't have enough, then you must sell the Highgate house and do it with that money."

"Is he any good, this Arkady?"

"I don't know."

Nicholas held up his arms, asking to be pulled up. "You don't know?"

She had no choice but to help him to his feet. "I haven't heard him play."

53

The Smolensky

I AM GOING." Arkady spoke suddenly from behind them.

They had left him only five minutes. They themselves were still looking, scraping off the snow and trying to read the names.

Gabriel turned.

The Russian stayed back on the shoveled path. "Thank you," he said. "For showing me the place. It is a coincidence—I came through here many times."

Isabella straightened and tried to smile, but it felt like her skin was frozen and cracking, even deep inside her rabbit-fur hat.

"So. It's cold, no?" There was a trace of humor in Arkady's voice.

"Yes," Isabella said. "Properly cold."

"How long will you be?" He indicated their work.

They had uncovered a dozen names between them. There was only four hours of light per day. Barely that. An hour or so left. And though Isabella had brought a flashlight, neither wanted to spend any time out here in the darkness.

"Not too long." Gabriel stopped and stamped his feet. The snow fell in wedges from his soles. "We know it is one of these. We will do a few more. Come back tomorrow if we don't find it."

Arkady nodded in the manner of someone trying to be polite while urgently required elsewhere.

Gabriel squeezed his nose, which was starting to freeze. "Then Yana is going to take us straight to Cosmonaut, if you want to come."

They had all driven out to the Smolensky together in Yana's wreck.

"Some people we know will be there," Isabella added. "It will be fun. Bring your friends. Bring Henry."

"No. I . . ."

"Or come down later." Gabriel grinned. "I promise I won't buy you a drink."

"No. Thank you." Arkady looked up. A flock of black birds was flying across the white page of the sky like an ever-changing bar of music. "I need to practice. I need very much to practice."

Isabella spoke from deep within her hat. "You are going back to play Mum's piano?"

"Yes. I am going to play this piano."

"That's great." Isabella spoke excitedly.

"The spare keys are stiff, but they do work," Gabriel said. "You remember the combination to the main gate?"

"Yes." Arkady nodded. Then, his voice matter-of-fact, he added, "You should know—Henry is dead."

"What? Henry is dead?" This from Gabriel.

"Yes."

Isabella took a step forward. "That's terrible," she said. "That's really terrible. We were going to . . . God. I'm so sorry."

"It's okay." Arkady's face was blank.

"Was he ill? Was it an accident or something?" Gabriel asked.

"No. But I think he did not want to live." Arkady shrugged. "Some people do not think life is so great."

"Jesus. Well, I'm very sorry to hear about that." Gabriel shook his head in a gesture that expressed sympathy as best he could from beneath two wool hats.

"He sounded like a nice guy," Isabella said, raising a mitten to her head. "In his letter, I mean."

"He was. But that makes no difference."

The three stood in silence a moment. There did not seem to be anything more to say. But it was too cold not to be moving.

"Okay. So. I will see you later, maybe. My friends will help me move the piano tomorrow. We will wait until after lunchtime in case you sleep."

"Oh . . . Okay." Isabella looked at her brother. Then said quietly, "Well, neither of us can play it."

Gabriel was silent.

Arkady nodded slowly for a moment, seeming to assess them both anew. "Good luck," he said.

Then he turned, murmuring to himself in Russian. He looked like a soldier in his greatcoat and his bearskin. They watched him go, walking oddly, his hands deep in his coat pockets, hurrying through the snow.

They were nearing the end of their endurance. Isabella was using her flashlight recklessly as a scraping device.

"Give it another five and then we're off," Gabriel said. "Yana will be waiting."

"Hang on. I think I've found it."

Gabriel came over as fast as he could through the drifts.

"Yes, this is it." Isabella rubbed the rest away with her elbow. Frozen flowers.

He was beside her. "Let me see."

Isabella turned on the light. Nothing. She shook it. The sudden il-lumination made the surrounding snow glimmer, almost blue. They stood back. In Cyrillic letters, the name spelled out was Anastasiya Andreev.

"That's her," Gabriel said.

"Yes." Isabella played the beam back and forth across the name.

After a while the bulb cut out completely. But even then it seemed a shame to stop looking while there was still a little light lingering in the sky.

She spoke softly. "What now?"

"Start again," he said. "Every day, start again."

ACKNOWLEDGMENTS

My thanks go to my friend and agent, Michael Carlisle, for providing that rare blend of brilliance and sound advice. I am also very much indebted to Webster Younce for his insight, for his wise literary counsel, and for being such a fine editor to work alongside. Likewise, Sasheem Silkiss-Hero, Andy Heidel, Martha Kennedy, Liz Duvall, and Carla Gray have all worked hard on this novel, and I am greatly appreciative of their help, their care, and their dedication.

Next a thank-you to my friends in Russia. In particular Angelina, for her indefatigable spirit, for taking me with her to all those parties, and for reading the draft. Also to Lena for a very informative Uzbek lunch and for teaching me "I love you." I am grateful to Sean McColm, formerly of the British Consulate in St. Petersburg, for a beer, his time, and his refreshingly detailed knowledge of the facts. Thanks to Yana for pointing out the best graveyards. Thanks to Sergei for the most dangerous car rides of my life and coming with me on the dodgy stuff; I'll buy you some new tires one day, I promise. Thanks to comrade Paul for his company and conversation through the long nights of whatever it was we were doing and for catching the "Anna Karenin" train with me, just for the ride.

In London I owe a great deal to everyone at the Westminster Drugs Project; they work tirelessly to make troubled lives a little less troubled regardless of the endless farrago of misinformation and misunderstanding "that will carry on for as long as there is fear and loathing." My appreciation especially to "Jacqueline" for her generosity in sharing her experiences with me, most of which were harrowing and painful. Thanks also to "Mark" for holding my hand, for the turkey sessions, and coming off all over again — keep on running. On this subject, I want most especially to express my gratitude to Dr. Tom Carnwath, long-time friend of my family and one of the country's leading psychiatrists on addiction. Thanks for the hospitality, the patience, and the benefit of three decades of your daily experience. Those who wish to know more should read Dr. Carnwath's book, *Heroin Century,* without doubt the most even-tempered, informed, and informative appraisal of this subject.

I want to acknowledge the support of some kind people who let me hang around their houses while apparently doing nothing. Bob and Elisabeth Boas for their generosity regarding Rome and for providing me with the happiest editing environment to date. And Stuart and Kate, for the use of their apartment on Lake Orta where there really is nothing to do but write the goddamn book; thank you.

I am grateful to Simon Mulligan for an enlightening half-hour on the phone. To my brother-in-law, Dr. Vincent Khoo, consultant at The Royal Marsden, for ensuring medical accuracy where required and pointing me to the right pills. And to Ian Leslie, an early reader, who took me to Veselka when I was starting and El Bulli when I had finished.

Here, too, the fondest of tributes to my brothers and sisters, who always get it, even when no one else does. Especially this time to Adelaide, who has the finest literary taste in the English-speaking world — always quick with that roll of tens; thanks, JP; nothing is revealed.

Last and most important, a great deal more than thanks to Emma — there's nothing I can say that would cover it; you are the beauty and the light and the better part of what I am.

And after it's finished, and before it all begins again, a thank-you to BD: still the greatest living artist, the only soul to whom I listen every day, and one of the few who know what it can cost a man to really get something done around here.